ROMANTIC TIMES PRAISES
NEW YORK TIMES BESTSELLING
AUTHOR MADELINE BAKER!

UNFORGETTABLE

"Madeline Baker continues to delight fans with her passionate Western adventures that thrill and captivate."

SPIRIT'S SONG

"Madeline Baker consistently delivers winning, heart-wrenching, passionate romances and *Spirit's Song* is no exception."

UNDER A PRAIRIE MOON

"Madeline Baker writes of a ghost, a curse, and a second chance with such power and passion readers cannot help but be mesmerized."

CHASE THE WIND

"This sequel to *Apache Runaway* is pure magic and packed with action, adventure, and passion. Madeline Baker fans, get ready to laugh and cry from beginning to the surprising ending."

LIGHTNING STRIKES

"Amanda."

She took a deep breath, but before she could speak, he was kissing her, his arms strong and sure around her. There was no doubt, no hesitation. He knew what she wanted better than she knew herself.

The rain, the room, everything seemed to fade away as Trey's mouth moved over hers, never rough, never demanding, ever gentle.

She surrendered to him with a sigh, every fiber of her being caught up in the sweet fire of Trey's lips on hers. Impossible. Magical. Heat flowed through her.

His hand slid under her sweater, encountering warm flesh, making her quiver with desire as he cupped her breast. An image of the bed only a few feet away flashed across her mind.

He murmured her name, his voice sandpaper rough with desire as he kissed her again, his tongue sliding over her lower lip in silent entreaty. Like a flower opening to the sun, she opened for him, aching, yearning. . . .

Chase the Lightning

MADELINE BAKER

LEISURE BOOKS NEW YORK CITY

A LEISURE BOOK®

October 2001

Published by

Dorchester Publishing Co., Inc.
276 Fifth Avenue
New York, NY 10001

ISBN 0-8439-4917-1

Visit us on the web at www.dorchesterpub.com.

To author GAIL LINK
for a particular phrase. She knows which one.

To DAVID VALLA
at Penske Motor Sales, Inc., West Covina, CA, who made
me fall in love with the Jag my heroine is driving.

To SPIRITWALKER
for sharing his knowledge of Indians
and the Old West with me.

To GLENN H. WELKER
for allowing me to use The Origin of Animals story.

And, last but not least,
to WILLIAM R. BURKETT,
who gave me the idea in the first place
and made it come alive.

Thanks, all.

Prologue

The Apache warrior faced his enemies defiantly. Surrounded by the bodies of his slain comrades, he lifted his war lance high overhead, his death cry riding on the wings of the wind.

His enemies laughed and made rude gestures at him. The warrior would die this day. And tonight they would sing of the Apache's death while they danced, his scalp and that of the other Apaches dangling from their scalp poles.

The Apache warrior watched them impassively as he chanted softly, his prayer for deliverance wending its way to the Great Spirit even as he set his face toward death. "Hear me, *Usen*, grant me courage that I may die well."

A sudden stillness fell over the land.

The wind moaned through the tall prairie grass.

11

Curling fingers of thick gray mist rose up from the ground.

The Apache warrior fell silent. Glancing over his shoulder, he narrowed his eyes as he saw a horse emerge from the gathering mist. The stallion's hooves echoed like thunder, striking lightning from the earth as he galloped toward him. Sunlight danced over the stallion's dazzling white coat, glinting like liquid silver in his flowing mane and tail. A thin black scar, shaped like a bolt of lightning, adorned his right flank.

The warrior's enemies fell back in superstitious awe as the ghost horse approached. The Apache warrior stood his ground, the eagle feathers in his hair fluttering in the rising wind.

The stallion slowed as he drew near, stopped to paw the ground.

Grasping the stallion's mane, the warrior swung onto his back, and with a wild cry, he rode through the midst of his enemies, toward freedom, toward home.

Chapter One

Arizona Territory, 1869

"Come on, gents, it's time to go." Trey Long Walker watched the frightened bank clerk as he shoved a handful of currency into a sack. Trey hated bankers, with their mortgages and interest. Their big words and small, unforgiving minds. His old man had lost their ranch when he couldn't pay the mortgage. The owner of the bank, J. S. Hollinger, had refused to give Trey's father an extension, saying it was beyond his control, but at the age of fifteen, Trey had been old enough to know the truth. Their ranch had been located on a prime piece of grassland, one that J. S. Hollinger had coveted for as long as Trey could remember. The bitter memory of his family's eviction and all that had happened afterward was forever etched in his mind. He had ridden across their old homestead before coming

13

into town today. If he had needed fresh fuel for his smoldering anger, he had found it. The house where he had grown up had been torn down, replaced by a new one with leaded glass windows and lots of fancy trim. The outbuildings around the original barn were all new, freshly painted. The whole place reeked of prosperity and complacency.

Sight unseen, Trey had hated the new owners. But today he would have his revenge.

He waved the long barrel of his Colt under the prominent nose of the man responsible for all he had lost, smiled behind the kerchief that covered the lower half of his face as J. S. Hollinger's eyes widened in fear. Revenge, though it had been a long time coming, was sweet indeed.

Trey backed the portly banker into a corner, confident his men would keep Hollinger's nervous employees under control. Turning his back to the rest of the room, Trey slowly lowered his kerchief so Hollinger could see just who was going to kill him.

The banker's face paled in recognition. "No." He dropped heavily to his knees. "Please, I have a wife . . . a family."

"So did my old man." Trey thumbed back the hammer of his Colt. It was time to make Hollinger pay.

"Please," Hollinger whimpered. He covered his face with his hands, as if that would somehow protect him. "Please, no. Don't . . ." Tears ran down his cheeks, dripped down his neck, wetting his starched white collar.

Another minute, and the man would be wailing like a baby.

Feeling nothing but contempt for the man groveling at his feet, Trey rested the muzzle of his revolver against Hollinger's forehead, his finger curling around the trigger.

Time seemed to stop. But he couldn't do it, couldn't pull the trigger.

Grunting an oath of self-disgust, Trey tugged the bandanna into place and backed toward the door.

Ben Needham and his brother, Chris, each grabbed a bag bulging with greenbacks and followed him toward the entrance, where Ed Strouse waited, covering the door.

Strouse opened the door, and Trey glanced quickly up and down the street. All was quiet.

Pulling the kerchief from his face, Trey stepped outside, his gun hand down at his side. Stores on both sides of the street were just opening for business. An old woman across the way was sweeping the area in front of her shop. He could hear the ring of the blacksmith's hammer from down the street, the chime of a distant clock.

Moving slowly so as not to attract any attention, he dropped the loot into his saddlebag and took his horse's reins from Sonny Clark, who had stayed outside to keep watch and hold their horses.

He had just swung into the saddle when a pair of gunshots cut across the still morning air. A moment later, Strouse ran out of the bank, blood dripping from his left shoulder.

"Dammit," Trey exclaimed, "there wasn't supposed to be any shooting!" He had warned his men about that time and again on the way to Wickenburg. Only one man was supposed to die, and that man was probably still shitting his drawers.

"You should have mentioned it to that stupid clerk," Strouse retorted. "He pulled a derringer from under the counter. Let's get the hell out of here!"

Trey touched his left heel to his mount's flank. The white stallion reared, turned, and took off at a dead run.

A sporadic hail of gunfire followed them down the dusty street. Trey risked a quick glance over his shoulder. Ben and Chris were close on his heels; Strouse followed a few yards behind. Sonny was sprawled face down in the street in front of the bank.

Trey swore under his breath. Dammit, there wasn't supposed to be any shooting!

Trey didn't slow down until they were well away from the town. Angling the stallion away from the escarpment that stood above the desert floor to the south, he didn't stop riding until they had put a good thirty miles behind them. It was near dark by then. The other horses were covered with lather and blowing hard. Only Trey's stallion seemed unaffected by the long run. Trey remained mounted, brooding silently, while his men climbed down and loosened the girths of their saddles.

Chris was the first to speak. "Too bad about Sonny. Do ya think he's dead?"

Ben nodded. "Can't get no deader. He took a bullet clean through the heart."

Trey glared at Strouse. "There wasn't supposed to be any gunplay."

16

"The clerk pulled a gun," Strouse replied belligerently. "What was I supposed to do? Let him plug me?"

"I reckon not." Trey leaned forward to stroke the stallion's neck. He had big plans for the stud; foolish plans, perhaps, for a man with a price on his head.

"We oughta be thinking about a place to bed down," Strouse remarked. "Our horses are about played out, and my shoulder hurts like hell."

Trey grunted softly as he swung out of the saddle. "This looks like as good a place as any." There was water and graze for the horses, a large outcropping of rock to block the rising wind, a patch of flat ground where they could spread their blankets. "I'll look after the horses. Ben, see what you can do for Strouse. Chris, why don't you rustle up some grub?"

Trey waited for his men to finish off-saddling their mounts, then took up the reins and led the horses down to the stream. Standing at his horse's head, he scratched between the stallion's ears. "We're getting shut of this bunch right quick, 'Pago," he muttered, "before Strouse gets us all killed."

Chapter Two

Canyon Creek, Arizona

Amanda Burkett looked out her bedroom window, rubbed her eyes, and looked again. "A horse," she murmured. "There's a horse in the corral."

A horse that, even to her untrained eye, looked like it had been ridden hard and put away wet. A big white horse, with a black scar on its rump.

She slipped on her robe, stepped into her slippers, and went out the back door. Where on earth had it come from? And what was she going to do with it?

She glanced at the old barn, with its red paint faded almost pink, and wondered how long it had been since it had been used. The paint was peeling, the roof was sagging, one door was off its hinges, but, if she remembered correctly, there had been some lead ropes and halters hanging along one wall.

The door creaked like something out of an old horror movie when she opened it. Grimacing, she stepped inside. The place was probably crawling with spiders and mice. Shafts of sunlight danced across the floor; huge lacy cobwebs hung from the corners. Lifting the hem of her robe, she picked her way across the floor. A bunch of old gardening tools were piled in one of the stalls. There was a wheelbarrow, a post hole digger, a couple of old milk cans.

She found an old halter and lead rope hanging from a nail on the back wall. The halter, made of leather, was stiff and cracked with age; the rope was frayed at the end, but it was the best of the bunch. She found a small wooden box filled with an assortment of brushes, curry combs, and hoof picks on a shelf. Dropping the halter and lead rope into the box, she tucked it under one arm and left the barn.

The horse whinnied softly when she appeared, shook his head as if to ask what had taken her so long.

She hesitated a moment when she reached the corral. She hadn't been around horses since she was nine or ten. And this one was a lot bigger than any she had ever ridden on her grandmother's farm in Cucamonga. Still, he looked tame enough.

Taking a deep breath, she ducked between the rails. After setting the box on the ground, she approached the stallion cautiously, one hand extended, palm up. "Hey, boy, how'd you get in here?"

The stallion made a soft snuffling sound as it sniffed her palm, and obligingly lowered his head so she could slip the halter in place. She attached the lead rope, tethered the stallion to the fence rail, patted the

19

horse on the neck, then rummaged through the box. She found a dandy brush that was in fairly good shape and spent the next half hour brushing dirt and grime from the stallion's snowy coat. She had forgotten how much she had always enjoyed grooming horses. It was soothing somehow. She remembered something her grandfather had always said, something about the outside of a horse being good for the inside of a man.

When she was finished, she stood back to admire her handiwork. The stallion's coat gleamed like white gold, its mane and tail looked like strands of white silk. The scar on its right flank was shaped like a bolt of lightning.

"You look just like the horse Hopalong Cassidy rode in all those old Westerns," she mused, grinning. "I suppose I could call you Topper, but somehow it just doesn't seem to fit a handsome stud like yourself. Or I could call you Silver, after the Lone Ranger's horse. . . . No, I don't like that, either."

She ran her fingertips over the scar on the horse's flank. The stallion's muscles quivered at her touch. "How about Lightning?" She nodded. "That seems to fit."

Rummaging in the box again, she found a hoof pick and scraped the mud caked in the horse's hooves.

When she finished, she took up the horse's lead rope and led it out of the corral toward a patch of grass, then sat down in the early morning sun, her robe tucked under her legs, while the horse grazed.

She had a new house. She was starting a new job next month. Of course, it wasn't really a job. She no longer had to work. And, best of all, she was engaged.

She lifted her left hand, watched the sunlight sparkle on the diamond ring on her third finger. She was going to be married. The thought scared her half to death. Her parents were divorced. Most of her girlfriends had been divorced, at least once. Her cousin had been divorced four times. When she had introduced Rob to her best friend, Mary, Mary had leaned over and whispered, "He'll make a good first husband."

Amanda sighed. Didn't anyone stay married anymore? If it wasn't going to last, why bother to get married at all? Was she making a mistake? She loved Rob, she really did, but she felt something was missing in their relationship. With a sigh of exasperation, she thrust the thought from her mind. She wouldn't worry about it now. After all, the wedding was still almost a year off.

She studied the house. She had bought it with money left to her by her Uncle Joe. She had always been his favorite niece, the only one who had kept in touch with him after Aunt Susie ran off with another man. It had been Amanda who had moved in with him when he got sick, who quit her job to stay with him because he didn't want to die in a hospital.

It was a small two-story, three-bedroom house, with a wraparound porch. Downstairs, there was a fair-sized living room with a brick fireplace, a sunny kitchen, small dining room, remodeled bathroom, and a small guest bedroom. There were two large bedrooms and a bathroom upstairs. She had fallen in love with the place at first sight. Best of all, the house itself didn't need any work. Someone with a love for old buildings had restored it to what it must have looked like back in the 1870s. Of course, they had added some modern touches, too, like a dishwasher, but it still held its Old West charm. The exterior of the house was painted white, with dark green trim. The chimney was red brick. Red bricks formed the walkway up to the house. The only thing she planned to change was the interior paint. At the moment, all the rooms were Navajo white. It was a color she could live with, but not for long. She had planned to tear down the old barn and corral, but that hadn't been high on her list of priorities, and now . . . she glanced at the horse. If no one came to claim the stallion, she would keep him. She glanced around. She had fallen in love with the surrounding countryside as well as the house. The distant mountains. The huge saguaro cacti with their waxy white flowers, the paloverde with its pretty yellow blooms. There were no other houses nearby save for an old adobe shack about five miles away and a few scattered ruins here and there.

She stood up as a car pulled into the driveway. She waved at the slim, fair-haired man who emerged. No one, looking at Robert Langley, would ever guess he was a bounty hunter. She'd had no idea such men still existed in this day and age. Dressed in a dark brown shirt and cream-colored trousers, he looked more like a Hollywood movie star than a man who made his living hunting other men.

"Hi, Mandy." Rob looked at the horse and shook his head. "Where'd that come from?"

"I have no idea. He was in the corral this morning when I got up."

Rob stroked the stallion's neck. "What are you going to do with him?"

She shrugged. "Keep him until the owner comes looking for him, I guess. If no one shows up in a day or two, I'll have to buy some hay. So, do you know anything about horses?"

Rob chuckled. "Only the ones I bet on at the track."

"A lot of help you are," she muttered.

"I thought we were going to breakfast?"

"We are." She thrust the lead rope into Rob's hand. "Turn him loose in the corral for me, will you? And see if you can find a bucket or a barrel for some water. I'll go get dressed."

Rob glanced down at his cream-colored slacks and beige loafers. "I guess I should have worn jeans and boots."

Amanda made a face at him, then ran up the narrow brick path to the house. She took a quick shower, ran a brush through her hair, then slipped into a pair of navy blue slacks, a short-sleeved white sweater, and a pair of sandals.

She brushed her teeth, dabbed on some cologne, grabbed her purse, took a last look in the mirror in the entryway before leaving the house.

Rob was waiting for her on the porch. He whistled softly. "Nice."

"Thank you, kind sir. Ready?"

"Well, since we're playing cowboy today, maybe I should quote the Duke," Rob drawled. He rolled his shoulders in a passable John Wayne imitation. "Little lady, I was born ready."

Laughing softly, Amanda slipped her arm through his. "Let's go, big boy."

Rob was leaving on an assignment that evening, so they had planned to spend the day together. They ate a late breakfast, took in an early movie, did a little window shopping, and then went to lunch at her favorite restaurant where Amanda indulged her passion for chocolate fudge cake.

Rob looked at her and shook his head. "Are you going to eat all that?" he asked dubiously.

Amanda stuck her tongue out at him. "Eventually." The slice of cake on her plate was four layers of chocolate, with fudge frosting between each layer. She sighed as she took a bite. "Heaven," she murmured, closing her eyes. "Pure heaven."

Rob chuckled. "You look like you're having a religious experience."

"Almost," she said. "Want a bite?"

"No, thanks. I wouldn't want to deprive you of a single mouthful."

They lingered over coffee until Rob declared it was time to go. "I hate to leave," he said, "but I've got to take you home and get back in time to catch my plane."

"All right."

"You want to take a piece of that heavenly cake for later?"

"No," Amanda said, laughing. "I don't think so."

Rob paid the check and they left the restaurant.

It was after four when they pulled into the driveway. Rob switched off the engine and slid his arm around

Amanda's shoulders. "I wish I didn't have to go."

"Me, too. How long will you be gone this time?"

"As long as it takes. I'll call you when I get there."

"You love it, don't you?"

"Yeah."

"I'll bet you'd have been a bounty hunter in the Old West, too." She grinned at him. "Or maybe Wyatt Earp."

Rob laughed. "You'd win that bet, missy. Bounty hunting runs in the family, you know. I was named after my great-great-grandfather. He did some bounty hunting in his time. What are you doing tomorrow?"

"I don't know. Probably finish unpacking."

"You're still unpacking?"

"I have a ton of books to put away." She grinned at him. "And I have to get busy and write up my ideas for Mr. Hennessy. Our first meeting is only two weeks away. I should probably buy a new suit. What do you think?"

"I think you should stop worrying."

"This is important to me, Rob. I want to make a good impression."

"I know, but, honey, you'll do fine. I know Earl Hennessy, and he's not going to be looking at your clothes, believe me."

Amanda made a face at him.

"It's true," Rob said. "The man may be a brilliant lawyer, but he's the biggest womanizer I've ever known."

"Bigger than you?" she teased.

"I told you we went to school together. Who do you think taught me?"

She punched him on the arm. "You just behave yourself, mister," she warned with mock ferocity. "Don't make *me* come looking for *you!*"

"Tough chick," he muttered, drawing her into his arms.

"Darn right."

"I don't know why you want to work. Especially for what he's paying you."

It was true. Her uncle's will had left her independently wealthy. She had spent the last two years taking care of Uncle Joe because he was afraid of doctors and hospitals. She had known her uncle had some money, but she'd had no idea just how much until the lawyers had settled his estate.

"I've got to do something with my time," she said. "Anyway, it's only a couple days a week." And it wasn't really a job. Earl Hennessy was thinking of opening a halfway house for abused women who had no place else to go, and Amanda had volunteered to help him set it up.

"Well, whatever you decide to wear, you'll be a knockout." Lowering his head, he kissed her. "I'll miss you."

"I'll miss you, too."

He glanced at his watch. "I've got to go."

Exiting the car, he walked around and opened her door for her. She took his hand, and he helped her out, then drew her into his arms. He kissed her again, deeper, longer.

"Hurry back. And be careful."

"I'll do my best." He glanced up at the house, which sat on a small rise. "I still don't know why you wanted to move clear out here. It's a long drive into town."

"I just wanted to get away from everything."

He lifted an eyebrow at her. "Including me?"

"Of course not. I was just tired of the noise and the traffic, you know? I'll only have to go into the office a couple times a week, so the drive's not that big a deal."

"Well, you can always stay at my place, if you need to."

"I know."

"Okay, hon, I've gotta go."

One last kiss, and he was on his way.

Amanda watched his car until it was out of sight; then, with a sigh, she went into the house and changed into a pair of jeans and a shirt. She couldn't sit around moping over Rob. She had a horse to take care of.

The stallion whinnied softly when she approached the corral. Sliding between the rails, she attached the lead rope to the halter and led the horse to a patch of grass near the one where it had grazed earlier that day.

"Looks like it's you and me," she muttered as she sat down on a fallen log. And then she smiled. "Guess I'll get to spend the evening with a good-looking stud after all."

Chapter Three

Trey woke with the dawn, eager to be on his way. As always, his first thought was for his horse. Stretching the kinks out of his back, he settled his hat on his head and walked over to where the stallion stood, grazing on a patch of short grass.

Frowning, Trey ran his hands over the stallion's neck and back. The horse's coat felt smooth beneath his hand. If he hadn't known otherwise, he would have sworn someone had come along during the night and given the stud a good brushing, but that was impossible. And yet, there was no denying the proof of his own eyes. Someone had groomed the stallion.

He glanced over his shoulder as Ben Needham approached him.

"Hey, Ben," Trey said, "you didn't happen to groom the horses last night, did you?"

Needham shook his head. "Why would I do that?

Hell, I been too tired to groom my own self."

Trey laughed as he continued to stroke the stallion's neck. He'd never heard of horses grooming themselves, like a cat. But 'Pago was one-of-a-kind, and Trey wouldn't put it past him. He looked over at Ben, aware that the man had asked him something.

"What'd you say?"

"I was wondering where we go from here," Needham said.

Trey shrugged. "I'm headin' north," he said casually. But it was a lie.

"Alone?"

Trey nodded.

"What are you gonna do?"

"Find me a little spot where nobody knows who I am and settle down. I've had enough." He had already found it, a nice patch of ground near Canyon Creek, but he saw no need to tell Ben that. The last thing he wanted was for Needham and the others to know where he was headed.

An hour later, after a hurried breakfast of bacon, beans, and campfire coffee, Trey was on his way, alone. They had split the take four ways; Trey had wished the others luck, stuffed his share in his saddlebags, and ridden away, just like that. It felt good to be on his own again.

He found himself thinking of Sonny Clark. No doubt the kid's body was on display in a rough pine coffin in front of the undertaker's parlor down the street from the bank. They'd let him sit there a day or two, a grisly warning to other outlaws, before they planted him in boot hill. Trey hadn't intended for anyone to die but the banker, and he'd failed at that, too. Guilt gnawed at his innards. He had led them into the bank; like it or not, he had to accept some of the blame for Sonny's death, but not all. Sonny had been riding the owlhoot trail long before he threw in with Trey, as had the others. During the division of the loot, Strouse and the others had made jokes about how they'd be sure to tip a few for Sonny as they spent the larger share his death had brought them. Trey hadn't been able to laugh. He had found himself wanting to say some words for Sonny, something to commemorate the kid's courage, but he'd let it pass. From now on, he was going to play a lone hand, and not lead others into danger.

Before the day was half done, his circuitous route had led him back to the escarpment above the desert floor, and to a trail known to but few. Lost in thought, Trey let the stallion set his own pace. Losing the ranch had been a bitter blow to his old man. Louis D'Arcy had worked hard to earn the money to buy the land, had worked hard all his life, and then he'd had a run of bad luck that had forced him to borrow money from the bank. But the bad luck continued, and he'd fallen behind on the payments.

Louis had gone to the bank and asked for an extension, but it had been refused. Trey could still remember the day the bank had foreclosed on the ranch. If he lived to be a hundred, he would never forget the look of defeat on his old man's face as they loaded their personal belongings into the back of the ranch wagon and rode out of the yard for the last time while

J. S. Hollinger stood with the sheriff on the front porch, looking smug and self-righteous.

Louis had never regained his self-respect. Lost in self-pity, he had turned his back on his wife and son and started in on booze, looking for solace in a bottle. Trey had been sympathetic, certain that, sooner or later, the father he had loved and respected would shake off his defeat and regain his self-esteem. But it hadn't happened. D'Arcy had become a familiar sight in the saloons, working odd jobs for liquor money, cadging drinks when he could. Trey couldn't remember seeing his father sober after the first year. Trey's mother, White Antelope Woman, had done the best she could. She built a snug lodge and planted a garden. Trey hunted game.

It hadn't been a bad life, until that day his father went into town liquored up and spoiling for a fight. Louis had gone to the bank, confronted Hollinger, and accused him of stealing their land. According to witnesses, Hollinger had taken refuge in his office and Louis had followed him inside and slammed the door behind him. The people in the bank lobby claimed to have heard him yelling, followed by three quick shots. When the head teller had tried to open the door, it was locked. When Hollinger emerged from his office, Louis D'Arcy was sprawled on his back, his shirt soaked with blood, an old rusty Colt Navy, unfired, on the floor beside him. Hollinger claimed Louis had gone for the gun, and he had fired in self-defense.

Trey had known that was a lie. His father had long since pawned his six-shooter to buy whiskey. Trey had had to hide the Winchester he used for hunting to keep his father from trading that for liquor, too. His father hadn't been armed when he rode into town. He'd had no money to buy a gun, and even if he had, no one would have sold him a gun in his drunken condition. No one admitted to selling D'Arcy the old black-powder pistol. But the fact remained, it was there, near the body, and the coroner's inquest had returned a verdict of self-defense.

Trey had wanted to go after Hollinger, but his mother had begged him to take her home to her people. There had been enough trouble, she had said, and with tears in her eyes, she had asked him for his promise that he would not go after Hollinger so long as she lived. And because he loved her, because he could not refuse her, he had given his word. They had buried his father, packed up their meager belongings, and then burned their lodge and everything that had belonged to his old man. The next day, he had taken his mother back to her own people.

Trey had loved living with the Apache in the years that followed. The time spent with his mother's people had been the best time of his life. His grandparents had welcomed them home. His grandmother, Yellow Calf Woman, had comforted his mother; his grandfather, Walker on the Wind, had taken him in hand and instructed him in the ways of the People, instilled in him a sense of who he was, made him proud of his Indian heritage.

The Apache were a close-knit people, loyal to their own. All other people were looked upon as the enemy. Trey soon discovered that the one and only ambition of every male was to become a warrior. To that end, he'd had much to learn. Walker on the Wind had taught him to hunt and track in the way of the People, to live off the land. His grandfather knew every inch of the land he called home. Every canyon, every creek, every rock and tree and water hole.

Trey learned that a true Apache warrior could travel for days, carrying what little food he needed, finding edible plants along the way. He could cover more than fifty miles a day on foot. The land shared her secrets with the Apache. A stone that had been overturned, a branch that had been broken, horse manure found along the trail, all carried a message for those who knew how to read it. Warriors were able to cover themselves with dirt and plants so skillfully that unwary enemies would come upon them unaware of their presence until it was too late.

He learned how to read smoke signals, and send them. A sudden puff of smoke that came and went quickly signaled that strangers were in the area; if the smoke was repeated over and over, it signified that the strangers were numerous and well armed. It was an education in warfare and survival that had served Trey well even after he had left the tribe.

The Apache warrior held truth in high esteem. He did not steal from his own. He shared what he had with others, paid his debts, loved his children, supported those who depended on him.

The People did not eat bear meat, or pork, or turkey, nor did they eat fish or any other creature that lived in water. But almost every other animal was considered a source of food: deer, buffalo, prairie hens, squirrels, and horses. Mule meat was considered the best of all.

Bears were to be avoided, as were their trails and droppings, as the People believed that bears were the reincarnated ghosts of people who had been evil in life and were made to live as bears in punishment for their misdeeds.

They hunted the turkey and the hawk and the eagle for their feathers; they hunted mink and muskrat and beaver for their skins.

Trey had learned that colors played an important part in the daily life of the People. Black was the color for the east, yellow for the west, blue for the south, white for the north. East was the holiest direction, and the People believed that things were best begun in the east. Four was a sacred number, as there were four directions, four seasons.

The Apache were a sociable people, and feasts and dances were held often. Gambling was indulged in not only by women and men, but children as well.

Wood from a tree struck by lightning was considered to be powerful medicine. Trey had a piece he had taken from a tree he'd seen split in half during a storm. He had worn it on a string around his neck while he lived with the Apache. Now, it adorned the stallion's bridle.

He had learned to make arrows from mountain mahogany or mulberry wood. He had used the feathers from a hawk for fletching. His most prized possession had been a bow his grandfather made for him. It had been a powerful weapon, strengthened with layers of sinew on the back. An Apache warrior could shoot an arrow five hundred feet with fatal effect.

Trey had practiced with the bow every day, and every target had been J. S. Hollinger. And every day, he had vowed to avenge his father's death.

He had stayed with his mother until she died of a fever eight years later.

He had bade his grandparents good-bye, had promised Walker on the Wind that he would return when he had avenged his father's death.

His last good-bye had been to Red Shawl, an Apache woman who had flirted with him on more than one occasion and who had let Trey know that if he asked for her hand in marriage, she would not refuse even though she was several years older than he.

But he'd had no time for a woman, no thought of settling down. Vengeance rode him with whip and spurs, filling his every thought, guiding his every action.

It had taken time, but Trey had formed a gang. His men were hard-edged, willing to do anything he asked of them. They had held up one bank after another until they reached Wickenburg. He'd had every intention of gunning down J. S. Hollinger, but when the time came, he couldn't do it. There was no honor in killing a coward. The need for vengeance that had driven him so mercilessly for so long had faded like smoke in the wind as his old enemy cowered before him, sobbing and begging for mercy. All that was left now was an aching void.

Trey rode until nightfall, then made camp in a dry

wash. Dinner was beans and hardtack for himself, a patch of dry yellow grass for his horse.

Sitting there, he promised both of them a bath and a good rubdown at the first town they came to.

Amanda woke with a smile. Any other time, she would have been a little blue at Rob's absence, but not today. She dressed quickly and hurried outside, eager to check on her new horse. But the stallion was gone.

Frowning, she checked the empty corral. The gate was shut, all the rails in place. But the stallion was gone. Had she dreamed the whole thing? She picked up the brush she had left on top of one of the fence posts, ran her fingertips over the long white hairs caught in the bristles—solid proof that the horse had been there. She glanced inside the corral, reassured by the faint hoofprints discernible in the dirt. The horse had been there—of course he had. After all, Rob had seen him, too. Perhaps the stallion had jumped the fence. Or been stolen. Or, most likely, the real owners had come along and taken him back. But if that was the case, there should be tracks of some kind.

With that thought in mind, she circled the corral. But there were no fresh tracks to be found. No sign that the stallion had been led out of the corral, no tire tracks, no footprints except her own and Rob's. And over there, the stallion's hoofprints where she had led him out to graze. If only Rob were here. He was always bragging about his ability to hunt things down. Maybe he would have been able to find her phantom stallion.

*   *   *

A vibration in the earth roused Trey from a deep sleep. In his experience, only two things made a rumble like that: a stampede, or a posse hard on the trail of its quarry. Caught between shit and sweat, he didn't stop to wonder how they had managed to trail him this far so fast.

Gaining his feet, he saddled the stallion, rolled his blankets into a tight cylinder and lashed them behind the cantle. There was no time for anything else. Swinging into the saddle, he urged the stallion into a gallop.

He rode the stud hard and long. A lesser horse would have been winded and covered with lather by the time Trey drew rein in a copse of trees that marked a desert water hole. Relámpago mouthed the bit impatiently, still fresh, still ready to run, but Trey needed a break.

Dismounting, he loosened the saddle cinch and let the stallion blow while he stretched his back and legs. He drank from the water hole, filled his canteen, and then let the stud drink before tightening the cinch and swinging back into the saddle. And then they were riding again, heading east, setting a more sedate pace. There were no sounds of pursuit. They'd left the hard-riding posse, if that was what it had been, far behind on lathered and worn-out horses.

He rode until sunup, backtracking, covering his trail the way his Chiricahua grandfather had taught him. He let the stud drink from another desert water hole that was concealed by a tangled thicket of mesquite trees, then dismounted with a weary sigh. The mesquite was dense enough to hide them from any observation. He stripped the rigging from the stallion, spread his bedroll on a relatively flat patch of ground, then gathered armfuls of dry mesquite needles and spread them in a wide circle on the outskirts of his camp, making it nearly impossible for anyone to sneak up on him. If by some chance he didn't hear them, the stud would.

Bone weary, he sank down on his blankets, too tired to eat. He stared at the stallion. Relámpago had been a gift from his Apache grandfather, Walker on the Wind. Walker was a medicine man blessed with many powers, among them the gift of sight. He had given Relámpago to Trey the day before Trey's mother died.

"You will be leaving us soon," Walker on the Wind had said. "The path you take when you leave here will be long and filled with danger."

"A white horse?" Trey had said, taking the reins. Few warriors rode white horses. They were far too easy to spot from a distance.

"This is a spirit horse," Walker on the Wind had said. "He is as swift as lightning, as surefooted as a mountain goat, as reliable as old Father Sun. Treat him well, and he will always carry you away from danger."

Trey grinned into the gathering darkness. Walker on the Wind had been right about that, he mused. Relámpago had carried him away from danger on more than one occasion.

Thoughts of danger brought the posse to mind, making him wonder anew who it was that had been chasing him, and where the hell they had come from. And when they would give up and go home.

"One of these days this will all be behind us," Trey told the stallion. "I'll build me a house on that land I found, put up a barn for you, and we'll settle down. We'll find a couple of good mares for you," he said, yawning. "And maybe a pretty redheaded woman for me."

Saturday morning. Amanda slept late, then lingered in bed, thinking about Rob, and wondering where her phantom horse had gone. It was so strange that the animal had appeared and then disappeared as if by magic.

Finally, hunger drove her to her feet and into the kitchen. Feeling lazy, she settled for a bowl of cereal, a glass of orange juice, and a cup of coffee. After putting her dishes in the dishwasher, she took a quick shower, then dressed in a pair of jeans and a bulky green sweater. Sitting on the edge of the bed, she pulled on a pair of green socks and laced up a pair of old tennis shoes. Having a horse, even for a day, had reminded her of how much she had once enjoyed riding. Maybe, instead of tearing down the barn and corral, she would get someone to come out and repair them, and then get herself a horse. Rob was frequently out of town on business. Having a horse would give her something to do when he was away.

Rising, she glanced out the window, blinked, and blinked again.

The stallion was back in the corral.

Hurrying down the stairs, she went into the kitchen, grabbed a couple of carrots from the fridge, and ran outside.

The stallion whinnied softly and tossed his head.

"Hey, fella." She ran her hand along the horse's neck. "How did you get back in here?"

She fed the horse the carrots, one by one, then walked around the corral. The stallion followed her, prancing back and forth, blowing softly.

Amanda examined the ground around the corral. There were no fresh hoofprints outside the corral, no sign that anyone had opened the gate to let him in. He could have jumped in on his own, but there were no hoofprints leading up to the corral, no indentation or torn-up earth to show where he would have landed.

"Curiouser and curiouser," she muttered.

She laughed as the stallion nudged her shoulder. "I see you're in need of a good brushing again. What do you do when you're not here? Roll around in the mud?"

She ducked inside the corral and plucked the halter and rope from the box she had left near the gate the day before. Again, the stallion obligingly lowered its head so she could slip the halter in place.

"You certainly are well trained," she said as she looped the lead rope over the top rail, then picked up the brush. "Where do you go, anyway?" She ran the brush down the stallion's neck, over his back and rump. He was a beautiful animal with near perfect conformation and wide, intelligent eyes that seemed almost human at times.

She hummed softly as she worked, everything else forgotten. One thing was for certain. If she didn't get to keep this horse, she was definitely going to get one of her own.

Pausing, she glanced around the yard. She had several acres here. Maybe she would buy a couple of horses. Maybe raise them. . . . She shook her head. She didn't know enough about horses to do that. But she could learn. She could start small, with a good stallion and one or two mares.

She smiled as she patted the stallion on the shoulder. She wouldn't have to look far for a good stallion. She had one right here.

"There you go," she said, giving him one last swipe of the brush. "All done." She turned the stallion loose, dropped the lead rope over the top rail of the corral, and then filled the water bucket. "I'm going to order some hay and have a cup of coffee," she said, giving the stallion a pat on the shoulder. "I'll bring you an apple when I'm done."

The stallion nuzzled her arm, snuffling softly.

Amanda smiled. "Yes," she said, "I like you, too. Don't go away now, hear?"

Macklin's Hay and Feed Store delivered a ton of alfalfa later that morning. Amanda dropped a flake in the corral, then went into the barn. Throwing the doors open wide, she grabbed a rake and went into the first stall. She had always enjoyed the work associated with horses. She didn't mind shoveling manure, didn't mind the smell. She raked out the old hay and straw, then got a bucket of hot water and washed the walls of the stall. She put a flake of hay in the feeder, filled the bucket with water from the hose.

She spent the rest of the morning cleaning out the barn, sorting through all the old junk she found in bins and boxes. She held up an old pistol and cartridge belt which looked good despite their age. She was about to toss them in the trash, but something stayed her hand and she hung the belt on a nail instead.

She paused for lunch, spent a few minutes scratching the stud's ears, then went back to work. By dusk, she had finished cleaning out the stalls and had hauled all the junk she didn't want outside.

Snapping the lead rope to the stallion's halter, she led him into the barn. "Well, what do you think?" she asked. "Not bad for a day's work."

The stallion tossed his head as if to agree.

She led the horse into the stall and closed the double doors behind him. "See you in the morning." Removing the halter, she gave the horse a last pat on the neck, then left the barn, closing the door behind her.

The phone was ringing when she got back to the house. "Hello?"

"Hello yourself. I was about to hang up."

"Hi, Rob. I was outside, cleaning the barn."

"Oh, right. The horse. How's he doing? Guess no one showed up to claim him."

"No, but the strangest thing happened. He was gone the morning after you left, and then this morning he was back again."

"That is weird."

"Yeah. When will you be home?"

"I'm not sure. I tracked Bolander to his last known address, but he's gone. It might take me a few days to find him again."

"Be careful."

"Always. Listen, hon, I've got to go. I'll call you tomorrow night."

"All right."

"Love you."

"Love you, too. 'Bye."

" 'Bye."

Smiling, she went into the kitchen to fix dinner.

When she went out to check on the stallion before going to bed that night, the stall was empty.

Chapter Four

Trey swore. Dammit, he must be losing his mind. Rolling out of his blankets, he walked over to the stallion and ran his hand down the stud's neck and along his back. Clean as a whistle. He lifted the stallion's foreleg. Someone had even cleaned the stud's hooves.

He froze as a sudden stillness seemed to settle over the land. Head cocked to one side, he listened, but heard nothing. No cactus wren called. No whitewing dove warbled. Something had frightened them, but what? Then he heard it, a rustle in the dry mesquite he had spread around his campsite the night before.

Hunters. And he was the quarry. He jammed his hat on his head and quickly saddled the stallion, glad that he had packed everything but his bedroll the night before. He quickly secured his saddlebags and bedroll behind the cantle, took up the stud's reins, and swung into the saddle.

Something hummed past his ear and smashed into a nearby cactus. The flat report of a rifle stung his ears. Without hesitation, he bent low over the stallion's neck and drummed his heels against the stud's flanks.

The stallion responded instantly, lining out in a dead run. More shots sounded; Trey heard a hoarse shout for him to stop.

Trey risked a look behind him as Relámpago broke from the cover of the trees. Half a dozen men rode out of the timber to his left. Sunlight glinted along their rifle barrels.

Ahead of him, the desert unfolded, bereft of cover. No place to hide. The stallion thundered over the ground, the quick tattoo of his hooves drowning out any other sound. Trey knew the big horse could outrun their pursuers if a bullet didn't bring him down, but he yearned to put something more than distance between himself and the guns behind.

Trey searched the surrounding area, but there was only flat ground, no place to hide, no place to take cover. Looking further ahead, he saw a hill and he reined the horse toward it.

He glanced over his shoulder again. The posse was stretched out in a line behind him, riding hard. A rider mounted on a long-legged gray pulled ahead of the others. Trey frowned. The gray might just give his horse a run. Something about the gray and the way the rider sat him niggled at the back of his mind, and then he swore aloud.

Of all the miserable luck! Bob "Wolf" Langley had a reputation as the best tracker and man hunter in the whole Southwest. It was said he had some Yaqui blood in his background, that he had brought in every man he had ever gone after. Some of them alive. Damn! With a touch of his heels, Trey asked the stallion for more speed.

For a moment, it looked like he was putting some distance between himself and the posse, but then the stallion stumbled and went to his knees. Trey gave a sharp tug on the reins and the stallion regained his feet.

Trey swore as a hail of gunfire exploded around him. A bullet struck his hat and sent it flying. Dammit, that was too close! Other bullets plowed into the ground. One caught him in the back, knocking him out of the saddle. The stallion shied away but didn't bolt.

Trey groaned as he hit the ground, hard. The right side of his back and shoulder felt numb. Scrambling to his feet, he made a grab for the reins, cursed when the stallion backed away from him, spooked by the scent of blood.

"Relámpago, stand!"

Ears twitching, nostrils flaring, the stallion came to a halt. Taking hold of the reins in one hand, Trey grabbed the saddle horn and hauled himself onto the horse's back.

The posse was almost upon him.

Trey slammed his heels into the stud's flanks and raced up the slope of the hill that loomed ahead. If he could just get to the top, maybe he could find a place to make a stand. At any rate, higher ground would give him an advantage, however slight it might be.

He clung to the saddle horn as the stallion climbed

upward. The initial shock of the wound was wearing off. Pain jarred through his back with every impact of his mount's hooves. He was aware of a sticky warmth running down his back, of a growing sense of weakness.

Trey glanced over his shoulder once again. The posse had gained too much ground when he went down. The riders were close now, so close he could see the look of triumph on Wolf Langley's face.

Even knowing it was useless, he couldn't give up. There was a scraggly patch of ocotillo and saguaro on the crest of the ridge. Not much, but the best cover around.

"Come on, 'Pago," he urged. "Don't fail me now."

Trey blinked the perspiration from his eyes as the world around him seemed to grow hazy. The upraised arms of the giant saguaro swam closer. A swirling gray mist rose up from the ground, obscuring his vision. A soft buzzing filled his head. And then everything went black.

Amanda poured herself a cup of coffee and carried it into the living room. She'd slept late again, spent an hour reading the Sunday paper, eaten a leisurely lunch. Picking up the TV remote, she flipped through the channels, then clicked it off. More stations than ever, and nothing worth watching.

She wandered through the house for twenty minutes, thinking she would be glad to go back to work. She had way too much time on her hands. Too bad the horse had disappeared again. It was a lovely day for a ride. She had gone out to the barn several times last night and again first thing this morning, but the stall remained empty. She shook her head. It was a mystery beyond solving, she mused, how that horse came and went, and she wasn't in the mood for a mystery.

Deciding she had been cooped up in the house long enough, she grabbed her purse and keys. Since she couldn't go horseback riding, she'd drive into town, maybe take in an early movie.

She came to an abrupt halt when she stepped out onto the porch.

The stallion had returned. And there was a man slumped in the saddle.

Chapter Five

Amanda dropped her handbag and keys on the porch, hardly aware she had done so as she stared at the stranger. Straight black hair fell just past his shoulders. His long-sleeved brown plaid shirt and black pants were covered with alkali dust, as were his boots. He wore a bandanna around his neck; there was a black leather gun belt and holster strapped around his waist. The worn wooden grips of a revolver jutted from the holster.

The stallion whinnied softly, and she noticed that the horse, too, was covered with a fine layer of dust, as if it had made a long, hard journey.

She went down the steps slowly, warily.

The stallion pushed his nose against her shoulder, and she stroked his neck absently while she studied the man. He was dressed like an old-time cowboy. She wondered if he was a movie star or an extra, though

49

she hadn't heard of any movie companies on location in the area. His face, neck, and hands were very brown; his features were strong and well defined. Bent low over his mount's withers, he seemed to be unconscious.

Lifting one hand, she placed it on his brow. He was burning up. It was then that she noticed the dark stain that spread down the back of his shirt and down his pant leg.

Blood.

She touched his leg gingerly. The material was still damp, the dust clotted into maroon mud where the blood had flowed.

Where on earth had he come from? If he was with a movie company, where was the rest of the crew? And what was she going to do with him?

A low groan escaped his lips, and then, without warning, he started to topple sideways. She threw her arms around him to keep him from falling, grunted softly as she supported his weight.

His eyelids fluttered open and he stared at her from beneath straight black brows. His eyes were a deep, dark brown, glazed with pain.

"What . . . the . . . hell?" he muttered.

"I'm surprised to see you, too. Here, let me help you down."

He lifted his left leg over the saddle horn and slid to the ground. She staggered back under his weight. His shirt was damp beneath his arm. Lord, he was a big man! She had to get him into the house.

"Can you walk?"

He sagged against her, his head resting on her shoulder. "Sure, sweetheart," he replied, his voice thick.

"Good, 'cause I need to get you to a doctor, and I can't carry you to the car."

He shook his head vigorously. "No! No doctor."

"But you're bleeding."

He shook his head again. "Don't need . . . doctor. Not hurt . . . that bad."

She looked at him, at the almost desperate look of pleading in his eyes. "Well, I don't know about that. But I'm taking you to the hospital."

He pushed away from her, staggered backward, and bumped up against his horse.

"What are you doing?" she asked.

"Going."

Chewing on her lower lip, she stared at the blood on his shirt. She couldn't just let him ride away, not when he was bleeding. The most important thing now was to see how badly he was hurt.

"All right," she agreed reluctantly. "No doctor."

He looked at her suspiciously. "Your word?"

"I promise," she said.

With him leaning heavily on her, she managed to get him up the porch stairs and into the house. She paused a moment to catch her breath, then guided him down the hallway to the guest bedroom. She propped him against the wall, held him there with one hand while she pulled the covers down, and then slipped her arm around his waist, holding him upright while he staggered toward the bed, where he fell face down onto the mattress.

He was unconscious again. She stared at him a moment, at the ugly wet stain slowly spreading across the back of his shirt. Swallowing hard, she reached down and pulled his shirttail out of his trousers. Lifting it, she felt her nausea rise. Blood leaked from a neat, round hole in his back. Had he been shot? She'd heard about realism in moviemaking, but surely this was carrying things too far!

She thought of all the old cowboy movies she had seen, the Westerns she had read. There was no exit hole in front, which meant the bullet was still in there somewhere.

What to do, what to do? She cursed softly. Why had she made such a ridiculous promise before she saw how badly he was hurt? She blew out a sigh of exasperation. She couldn't just let him lie there and bleed all over her clean sheets! Thank goodness she had taken a first aid class not long ago. At least she had some idea of what to do, and how to do it.

Going into the bathroom, she found her first aid kit and a pair of sharp scissors. Shoving a washcloth into her pocket, she carried the kit and the scissors into the kitchen. After placing them on the table, she filled a pan with water and put it on the stove to heat, then went back into the guest room.

He was still unconscious. She rolled him onto his side as gently as possible, unbuckled his gun belt and hung it over the back of a chair. In addition to the holster, she noticed there was a very large knife in a beaded sheath.

She removed his shirt as carefully as she could and dropped it on the floor, removed the kerchief from his neck, then pulled off his boots, which were badly scuffed and worn at the heels. And a very tight fit: she was panting with exertion when she finally got them off. She peeled off his stockings, wrinkling her nose at the smell. Dropping his socks on top of his shirt, she wondered when he had bathed last. She unfastened his belt, unbuttoned his pants, and tugged them down his long, long legs.

"What the heck?" she muttered as she dropped his trousers on the floor. He was wearing what looked like the bottom half of a pair of old-fashioned long johns. Whoever this guy was, he had really immersed himself in the part. With a shake of her head, she rolled him onto his stomach again.

She folded the washcloth into a neat square and pressed it over the bruised-looking hole in his back, which was still leaking a thin trail of blood. At least it wasn't pumping strongly, which she thought meant the bullet had missed any major arteries.

As she applied pressure to the compress, she studied his profile. He had high cheekbones, a square jaw roughened by a dark beard, a nose that had never been broken, a nice mouth with a full lower lip. And dark skin—uniformly dark from his face to his waist. Either he spent a lot of time outside without a shirt, or he was just naturally dark. From the strength of his features, she thought he probably had some Indian blood in his background.

Going back into the kitchen, she slipped an old apron on over her clothes, boiled a slender-bladed knife and the scissors while she rummaged through a drawer for some soft, clean dishrags. She filled a bowl with hot water and placed it on a tray, along with the dishrags, the sterilized knife, the scissors, and the first aid kit, and then, saying a silent prayer that she wouldn't faint, she went back into the guest room.

He hadn't moved. His breathing was steady, but labored and shallow. She put the tray on the table beside the bed, stood there a moment gathering her courage, and then began to wash the area around the wound. The muscles in his back twitched and he moaned softly; then he was still once again.

She wiped the area dry, then picked up the knife. "You can do this." She stared at the blade, at the way it shook in her hand. "Sure you can," she muttered, "and when you kill him, you can just bury him out in the backyard."

Taking a deep breath, she began to probe the wound, surprised and grateful when the tip of the blade hit the slug on the first try. Maybe he was right. Maybe he wasn't hurt all that bad. The bullet hadn't penetrated very far or hit anything vital. Bright red blood oozed from the wound. She wiped it away with a dry cloth, wiped the perspiration from her brow, and probed a little deeper into the wound until she got the tip of the knife under the slug. When she thought she had it just right, she gave a little flick of her wrist and the slug popped out, an ugly, misshapen lump of lead covered with blood.

Dropping it on the tray, she quickly washed the wound and the area around it and drenched it with disinfectant. After patting his skin dry with a clean cloth, she covered the wound with a pad made of gauze, and taped it in place.

She'd done it! She stared at the bloody knife on the tray, felt her knees go weak. Sinking down on the edge of the bed, she closed her eyes, unable to believe she had actually dug a bullet out of a man's back.

Taking a deep breath, she opened her eyes and stared at him. Who was he? Rising, she took the bowl into the bathroom. After washing her hands, she dumped the bloody water into the sink, rinsed the bowl, and refilled it with hot water from the tap. Grabbing a bar of soap and a bath towel, she went back into the bedroom and washed the man's face, neck, arms, chest, and feet. The more private parts of him would just have to wait until he could do it himself.

When she was finished, she pulled the covers over him, gathered up his clothing, and went into the laundry room. She filled the washer with cold water and tossed his bloody clothes in to soak. Removing her apron, she tossed it inside, too, along with some color-fast bleach, and then she went outside.

The stallion stood near the foot of the stairs where she had left him. The horse whinnied softly as she approached, rubbed his cheek against her shoulder.

She scratched the stallion between the ears. "So, I guess he belongs to you?"

The stallion tossed his head.

"Well, come on." Taking up the reins, she led the horse across the yard and into the barn.

After loosening the cinch, she lifted the heavy saddle from the stallion's back—her muscles were really getting a workout today, she mused—and then spread the damp saddle blanket over a bale of hay to dry. Leading the horse into the stall, she slipped the bridle off its head, and then dropped a flake of hay into the feeder.

She ran her hand along the stallion's neck, then shook her head. "Doesn't that man ever brush you?"

The stallion made a noise that sounded suspiciously like a horselaugh.

Grinning, Amanda patted the stud's shoulder. "I'll be back later to clean you up. Enjoy your lunch."

Back at the house, she picked up her handbag and keys from the porch and tossed them on a chair in the living room, and then went to look in on her patient. He was still unconscious. What would she do if he didn't wake up? Oh, Lord, what would she do if he died?

She laid her hand across his brow. His skin felt as if it were on fire. Picking up the bowl she had left on the table, she went into the bathroom. She filled the bowl with cool water, took a washcloth from the drawer, and went back into the bedroom.

Sitting on the edge of the mattress, she pulled the covers down, then dipped the washcloth in the bowl. Wringing it out, she ran it over his broad back and shoulders.

"You're a lot of trouble, you know that?" she muttered as she gently wiped his face and neck, his arms, and then his back again. "Kind of handsome, though, in a rugged sort of way."

She sat there for close to an hour, dragging the cool cloth over his face and neck and body, admiring the deep bronze of his skin, the feel of his hair against her hand. Once, yielding to some urge she couldn't refuse, she ran her fingertips over his lower lip.

"Who are you?" she wondered aloud. "Where did you come from?"

He looked like a cowboy. If he wasn't missing from a movie company, he could be a genuine cowboy. There were ranches in the area. Had he come from one of those? Did cowboys in this day and age wear guns? She supposed they might. There were wild animals in the hills. Snakes. Even supposing working cowboys wore guns, she was pretty sure they didn't go around shooting each other, although, being men, it was not out of the realm of possibility. The nightly news was full of stories of men, old and young, who seemed to think guns and violence were the answer to everything.

She thought for a moment. Perhaps he was one of those reenactors, the ones who had made a hobby of dressing up in Old West duds and firing old-fashioned weapons at targets. Maybe someone had fired wildly, and this had been an accident. He was just as wounded as if it had been intentional, though. And how had he shown up here? Her mind raced with questions.

But she wasn't likely to find the answers to any of them today.

She sponged him off several times during the day and into the night, even managed to get him to drink a little water. He was incoherent the few minutes when he was conscious, but for the most part, he slept.

It was after midnight when she went to bed, only to awake at every sound, always aware that there was a stranger in the house. The last thing she had done before she went to bed was put his gun belt on the floor in the back of her closet. She felt safer, somehow, knowing it was in her room, and out of his reach.

*　　*　　*

She woke early after a restless night. She started to go downstairs in her gown and robe; then, remembering the stranger, she decided against it. She dressed quickly in a long-sleeved tee shirt and jeans, turned up the heat, and went downstairs to check on her patient.

He was lying on his stomach, his long legs curled up under the covers, his head turned toward the door. She thought he was asleep, but his eyes opened the moment she stepped into the room.

He stared at her through narrowed, pain-glazed eyes. "Who are you? Where am I?"

"Who are *you?*"

He rolled onto his side, groaning softly. "What happened?"

"Well, I'm not sure what happened, or how it happened, but you've been shot."

He grunted softly, his gaze moving around the room. "How'd I get here?" He had a voice like aged whiskey, she thought, warm and smooth. And sexy.

Amanda shrugged. "You tell me. And while you're at it, you can tell me who shot you, and who you want me to notify."

"You can't tell anybody about this."

"Surely you want your family to know you're all right."

He shook his head, then licked his lips.

"Are you thirsty?" she asked.

He nodded.

"I'll get you a glass of water."

Trey watched her leave the room, his mind filling

58

with questions. How had he gotten here? Where the hell was he? And who the hell was she?

He glanced around the room again. White walls. Blue curtains. A blue rug that covered the whole floor. A three-drawer chest. A table beside the bed. A lamp on the table, but a lamp like none he had ever seen. It had a flowered shade, no oil, no wick. Where the hell was his gun?

He started to sit up, swore as pain lanced through his back. Easing back down on the bed, he closed his eyes. How had he got here, wherever here was?

He opened his eyes at the sound of footsteps. The woman offered him a drink of water and he drank it greedily, then sank back on the pillow. She was a pretty woman, tall and slender, with a wealth of wavy red hair, dark green eyes, and a mouth that begged to be kissed. Long, slender legs encased in a man's jeans. He hadn't known many women who wore pants, surely none as lovely and curvy as this one, and he averted his eyes, afraid he had stared at her legs too long.

She gazed down at him, a worried look in her eyes. "Are you hungry?"

He shook his head.

"Who shot you?"

"What difference does it make?"

"Well, you should probably report it to the police."

Report it? He wondered if she was out of her mind, then realized she had no way of knowing he was on the dodge. "I'm obliged to you for taking me in, but I'd best be moving on."

"Don't you think you should rest a day or two? You've got a fever."

It was tempting, but he couldn't stay here, not with Wolf Langley hot on his trail. Damn! "Thanks, but I'd better get going."

"And I think you'd better stay right where you are, at least until tomorrow. Anyway, your clothes are soaking in the washer."

He frowned. "Washer?"

"You know, washing machine?"

He stared at her, wondering what the devil she was talking about. "Where's my horse?"

"In the barn. You really should keep an eye on him, you know. He's been here several times in the last couple of days."

She was crazy, he thought. There was no doubt about it. "And my gun?"

"Safe enough. You need to rest," she said, "and I've got some work to do. Why don't you go back to sleep, and I'll bring you something to eat later?"

He nodded, closed his eyes, and was asleep.

Amanda stared at him for several minutes, her mind churning with unanswered questions. She didn't know who he was or where he'd come from, but she intended to find out.

It was dark when he woke again. The bedroom door was open, and he could see a glimmer of light in the hallway. Bright white light that burned steadily. Too bright for a coal-oil lamp. He could hear someone moving around in the next room. The crazy woman? He wondered if she was married, or if she lived alone.

He frowned as a strange ringing noise broke the stillness. It was an odd noise, one he had never heard before. With an effort, he sat up. Dizziness swamped him. When it passed, he stood and made his way to the door. He stood there a moment, one hand braced on the frame, and then walked slowly down the hallway, his bare feet making no sound on the carpet.

He could hear her talking now. From what he could hear of the conversation, it sounded like she was talking to someone else, but hers was the only voice he heard.

Peering around the corner, he saw her standing with her back to him. Her hair fell halfway down her back in a mass of waves. She was wearing the long-sleeved shirt and those jeans that clung to her like a second skin, outlining the shape of her long legs and well-rounded buttocks. He had seen working ranch women in trousers from time to time, but nothing like these. She was holding something to her ear.

"All right, Rob. I've got to go. Be careful, okay?"

Silence. Was she talking to herself? Crazy, no doubt about it.

Then, "I know. I love you, too. 'Bye."

She put whatever she had been holding to her ear down on the table. His gaze followed the sway of her hips as she left the room.

Curious, he padded across the floor, picked up the thing she had been holding, and put it to his ear. What the hell! He jerked his head back when he heard a strange buzzing noise. Putting the thing down, he glanced around the room. It looked like any other house. And yet, it didn't. There was a red brick fireplace with a raised hearth. Some pictures on the wall. A sofa and two chairs, and a couple of low tables. A pair of those strange lamps with their eerily silent bright light. Some new kind of gaslight? A large square box that had a window you couldn't see through on the front. Some doodads and knickknacks women were fond of.

At the sound of footsteps, he glanced at the doorway. It was the woman.

"What are you doing out of bed?" she exclaimed. She made a shooing motion with one hand. "Go on, get back into bed. You look like you're about to pass out again."

He glowered at her, then turned and retraced his steps to the bedroom. Every movement sent slivers of pain shooting through his back. He sat down gingerly, took a deep breath, then stretched out on his side and closed his eyes. Dammit, he felt as weak as a newborn colt.

Moments later, he sensed the woman's presence in the room. "You must be hungry."

"Yeah."

"What would you like to eat? I've got some chicken noodle soup."

"Soup!" He opened his eyes and glanced at her over his shoulder.

"Well, what do you want? Steak?"

"Rare."

"All right. What do you want with your steak?"

"Anything you've got is fine."

"All right." If he was hungry enough to eat a steak, he couldn't be too bad off. She moved around to stand in front of him. "Here." She handed him a glass of water and held out her hand. "Take these."

He stared at the two small white things in her hand. "What're those?"

"Aspirin."

He frowned up at her. "Aspirin?"

"For your fever." She shook her head. "For heaven's sake, you'd think you'd never seen aspirin before."

Well, she was right about that. He took them from her hand and popped them in his mouth, grimaced at the horrible taste.

The woman sighed. "You're supposed to wash them down with water."

He drained the glass, rinsing the bad taste from his mouth, then handed it to her.

"Where are you from, anyway?" she asked.

"From here."

"Arizona?"

He nodded.

She looked at him oddly for a moment. "Have you got a name?"

"Trey."

"Just Trey?"

He nodded, unwilling to share his last name. "And yours would be?"

"Amanda."

"Just Amanda?" he asked with a wry smile.

"Just Amanda. Are you sure there isn't someone you want me to notify that you're here?

"I'm sure."

"Well, I'll go fix that steak," she said, heading for the door. "Rare."

He stared after her. There was something strange going on here, something not quite right. He couldn't put his finger on it, but something was definitely wrong.

Chapter Six

Amanda stood in the kitchen, staring out the window while she waited for the potatoes to boil. She didn't know what it was, but there was something definitely wrong here. Something out of sync about . . . what was his name? Trey. Just Trey.

He was a handsome man, not pretty-boy handsome the way Rob was, but handsome in a rugged, masculine way. She smiled at her reflection in the window. Sort of the way Tommy Lee Jones was sexy, with that gravelly voice and killer smile. Why hadn't he known what aspirin looked like? Why was he wearing a gun? And clothes that looked sort of . . . outdated? If he really were an actor, or one of those guys who liked to play cowboy, perhaps the trauma of getting shot for real had blurred his memory.

She had washed and dried his shirt and pants. His trousers were folded over the back of a kitchen chair;

his shirt was draped over the trousers. She ran her hand over the shirt. Long-sleeved, and made of rough flannel. With a neat, round hole in the back where the bullet had gone in.

Just who was that man in her guest room? And why was she so attracted to him?

She checked on the potatoes, opened a can of white corn, put the steak under the broiler. Opening the fridge, she reached for a carton of milk, then shook her head and grabbed a can of the beer she kept on hand for Rob. She couldn't imagine the man in the guest room drinking milk.

She turned the steak, mashed the potatoes, turned the fire off under the corn. She put his dinner on a plate, put the plate on a tray, added some silverware, and the beer, and carried the tray down the hall to the bedroom.

Her patient was sitting up in bed, the sheet draped over his hips. She felt a flutter of appreciation in the pit of her stomach as her gaze moved over him. Long black hair fell past his broad shoulders. His stomach was flat, ridged with muscle. And his arms . . . she had always had a weakness for men with well-muscled arms, and Trey's were right up there with the best she had ever seen.

She felt a wave of heat wash into her cheeks when he looked up at her, one dark brow raised inquisitively.

"Here's your dinner." Embarrassed at having been caught staring at him, she deposited the tray, none too gently, on his lap.

"What the hell!" he exclaimed.

"Sorry," she muttered. "Can I get you anything else?"

He glanced at the tray. "How about something to drink? Beer, if you've got it."

She tapped a finger on the top of the can. "What do you think that is?"

Frowning, Trey picked up the gray container, which was similar to a tin can but lighter somehow, with a fragile feel to it. When he gripped it, his fingers sank into the metal. It was cold, almost icy to the touch. The words "Natural Light" were printed in blue and red letters, and below that, in very small print, the words "Beer . . . brewed for a naturally smooth taste."

"Don't tell me you've never seen a can of beer before?"

"Can't say as I have." Trey studied the woman, Amanda, for a moment. He had never seen a woman who looked quite like her, either. Her lips were too pink to be natural. The long-sleeved shirt she wore looked like something a man would wear, but there was nothing masculine about the way it hugged her body, outlining the curves of her breasts. And those trousers . . . He swallowed hard. Had she been wearing a short red dress and black stockings, he would have said she was a tart, but she didn't act like one, or talk like one. If she had been for sale, he would have paid for her time in a heartbeat. Just thinking about it aroused him, making him grateful for the tray across his lap.

He met her gaze, felt the unmistakable sizzle of attraction that passed between them.

Her gaze slid away from his. "You'd better eat it

while it's hot," she suggested. "I'll be back later for the tray."

Damn, but she looked good walking away. He spent a pleasurable moment watching her leave the room, then looked down at the can in his hand. How the devil did she expect him to open it?

He ran his finger over the top of the can, grunted softly when his fingernail caught in a small metal ring. He gave a tug, and, to his surprise, there was a small hiss and an opening appeared, leaking a small dribble of foam. He could smell the hops. He lifted the can to his lips, took a drink, and almost spit it out. There was a weak beer taste, but the stuff was watery, thin. He sure as hell wouldn't dignify it by calling it beer!

Setting the can aside, he cut into the steak and took a bite. Damn. The beer in this place was undoubtedly the worst he had ever tasted, but the woman knew how to cook a steak.

It had been a long while since he'd had a decent meal, and he savored this one. He'd never had beef this good in his life.

With a sigh, he put the knife and fork down and set the tray on the bedside table. Leaning back, he closed his eyes.

He woke to the sound of rain on the roof. He figured the woman had looked in on him while he slept, since the curtains were closed. That strange bright white light from the hallway spilled into the room. She had removed the dirty dishes from the tray on the bedside table and left a bowl with an apple and an orange, a glass of water, and a small knife with a blade that might cut through butter but not much else.

Feeling a whisper of warm air, he frowned. He didn't recall there being a fireplace in the room. And there wasn't. Turning over, he searched for the source of warm air. It seemed to be coming from some sort of vent in the wall up near the ceiling.

He heard angry voices coming from the other room. A man and a woman, arguing. The sound of a woman's scream, a gunshot. He bolted from the bed. Damn, where was his gun when he needed it? He glanced at the knife disdainfully. It wasn't much, but it was the only thing that resembled a weapon in the room. Grabbing it from the tray, he moved as quickly as he could into the parlor. He glanced around the room, looking for the shooter, but there was no one in the room save for the woman. She was seated on the sofa, looking at him over her shoulder.

"What are you doing?" the woman exclaimed. She stood up, frowning when she saw the knife in his hand.

"Where is he?"

"Where's . . ." She glanced at the knife again. "Where's who?" she asked tremulously.

"The man who . . ." He broke off, started again. "I heard gunshots . . ."

She stared at him and then, to his utter surprise, she burst out laughing.

A sudden noise filled the room. Trey looked toward the sound, blinked, and blinked again, unable to believe his eyes as he stared at the large box. There was music coming out of it, and voices. But that wasn't nearly as shocking as the colorful moving images.

He lowered his arm, the knife in his hand forgotten as he moved toward the box. With some trepidation, he bent down to stare at the window. It looked like glass. Reaching out, he touched it with his fingers, jerked backward when the glass crackled with a sound like lightning.

Straightening, he turned and looked at the woman. "What kind of chicanery is this?"

"Chicanery?"

"This!" He gestured at the box with the knife, chagrined to see his hand was shaking.

The woman shook her head. "What? The TV?"

"TV?"

"They're coming to take you away, aren't they?" she muttered, remembering the words to an old song.

His eyes narrowed. "How do you know that?"

"Know what?"

"That they're after me?"

The woman folded her arms across her chest. "One of us is talking crazy," she said, "and it's not me." She smiled at him. "Why don't you just put that knife down," she said, her voice softly coaxing, as though she were speaking to a not-too-bright child, "and go back to bed?"

He glanced at the moving pictures in the box again. A burly black man was talking to another man, but the words made no sense. A hundred questions pounded in his head, demanding answers, but he was in no condition to pursue them now. Feeling like a damn fool, he dropped his hand to his side.

The woman hurried toward him, her brow furrowed. "Come on," she said. "You look like you're about to faint."

He felt that way, too, though he wouldn't have admitted it. He leaned heavily on her as she helped him back to the bedroom. She was, he thought, the cleanest, prettiest-smelling woman he had ever met.

"You're bleeding again," she said.

He grunted as he fell face down on the mattress, only half aware as she took the knife from him and tossed it on the tray. Sitting on the edge of the bed, she removed the bandage from his back. Her hands were soft, gentle, as she swabbed the wound with some sort of strong-smelling ointment, and replaced the bandage.

He heard her mutter, "men," as she gathered up the soiled dressing and carried it out of the room.

In the brief time before sleep claimed him, he wondered just what it was he had seen inside that strange-looking box.

Amanda tossed the soiled gauze and adhesive tape in the trash, then poured herself a cup of coffee. Carrying the mug into the living room, she sat down on the sofa. She had a sneaky suspicion that her patient was a brick short of a load. Anyone who didn't recognize a can of beer and didn't know what a TV was had to be crazy. But, oh my, the man was gorgeous. And gallant, she thought, remembering how he had burst into the room, ready to defend her with nothing more than a paring knife.

Setting the mug aside, she went to look out the window. The rain had let up for the moment. Grabbing her jacket and a flashlight from the closet, she went out the back door, picking her way through the mud to the barn.

The horse whinnied when she opened the door. If she decided to keep the barn, she was going to have to get some electricity in there. She dropped a flake of hay in the feeder, made sure there was water in the barrel, then spent a few minutes petting the stallion while he ate. There was something soothing about being around horses. A flash of lightning illuminated the darkness, followed by a drumroll of thunder.

Amanda gave the stallion a last pat on the shoulder. "See ya later, boy."

On her way out of the barn, she paused by the saddle and removed the saddlebags tied behind the cantle, thinking there might be something inside that her guest would need, or want.

It was raining again when she dashed across the yard toward the back door.

Inside, she took off her jacket, shook the rain out of her hair, dropped the saddlebags on the kitchen table. Head cocked to one side, she stared at the twin pouches a moment while she had a silent argument with her conscience. She had no right to pry into his belongings. Still, there might be something inside to tell her who he was, or where he belonged.

Feeling a little guilty, she opened the bag nearest to her, reached inside, and pulled out a dark red wool shirt, a pair of jeans, three heavy boxes of ammunition, a frying pan, a blue and white speckled coffee pot and a coffee cup, a spoon and fork, a sack of what looked like beef jerky, a box of wooden matches wrapped in what she thought might be oilskin, a short length of rope, and a pair of leather gloves. No ID of any kind.

She put everything back inside, opened the other pouch, and reached inside, only to stare, mouth open, at the sack she withdrew. It was a money bag. The words "Property of First National Bank, Wickenburg, Arizona" were stamped on the front in black block letters.

Dropping the sack on the table, she untied the string that held it shut, then looked inside, her eyes widening. It was stuffed with greenbacks. She pulled out a couple, and frowned. There was something odd about the bills. They seemed larger than they should have been. Counterfeit?

She glanced over her shoulder to make sure she was still alone, then spread the bills out on the table. She stared at them a moment, then picked one up. It was a ten-dollar bill. "This note is legal tender for ten dollars" was written across the top. "Will pay the bearer ten dollars" was printed across the middle; the words "Treasury Note" were written across the bottom. There was a picture of a man in the lower left-hand corner, and some sort of historical scene in the lower right. The back was a rather bright green with "Ten" written on the left side and "10" on the right. There was some small print in a circle in the middle that she couldn't quite make out.

The next bill was, without doubt, a twenty. There was also a two-dollar bill, and a five, each unique in its own way. They were certainly more colorful and more interesting than the money in use today. There were some gold coins in the bottom of the bag. She picked one up, surprised at how heavy it was.

Where had her patient gotten hold of such old money? And what was he doing with a money bag obviously taken from a bank? Was he a collector? Good Lord, what if he was a bank robber? She shook the thought aside. Banks probably didn't keep money this old. Had he robbed a museum, then?

She glanced over her shoulder again before scooping up the bills. She put them all back in the sack, dropped the gold coin on top, and closed the bag.

It occurred to her that she should call the police, that she should have called them when that man first showed up in her yard with a bullet in his back.

"Better late than never," she decided. But when she picked up the phone, the line was dead.

She frowned at the receiver a minute, and then grinned. Wasn't the phone always dead when the movie heroine went to call for help? With a shake of her head, she dropped the receiver back into the cradle. No doubt the recent rains had damaged the line. It had happened before.

Going down the hall, she peeked into the guest room. Her patient was lying on his stomach, snoring softly.

Returning to the living room, she grabbed the book she had been reading for the past week and carried it upstairs. She paused outside the bathroom. She usually read while soaking in a hot bubble bath before going to bed. But not tonight. With the phone out and the mysterious stranger downstairs—and that unexplained stash of old money to trouble her—she knew that sitting naked in the tub would leave her feeling far too vulnerable.

Going on down the hall to her bedroom, she tossed her book on the bed and locked the door. She reached for her nightgown, and then decided to sleep in her clothes—just in case. Mindful of the stories Rob had told her, she took the ladder-back chair from her desk and placed it under the doorknob. And then, still not feeling safe, she pulled Trey's gun belt out of the closet and put it on the floor beside the bed.

She stared at his gun a moment, and then, overcome by curiosity, she reached for it. The big six-shooter came out of the holster easily enough, but it was much heavier than she had expected. She glanced at the front of the cylinder. She didn't know much about guns, but those heavy leaden noses showing in the chambers didn't look like her idea of blank cartridges.

She lifted the gun with both hands and aimed it at the door. Would she even know how to shoot it, if it came to that? Would she, if she could? A line from an old John Ford Western floated through her mind, something to the effect that even an empty six-gun commanded respect.

She shoved the heavy old gun under her pillow, then sat in bed, her back propped against the headboard, trying to read.

But the plot of the story was not nearly as intriguing as the white stallion, his good-looking rider, or the ancient loot.

Chapter Seven

It rained on and off for the next two days. Trey spent most of his time catching up on lost sleep, giving his body a chance to heal. The wound in his back wasn't serious, but it was sore as a boil. He wasn't usually one to laze around in bed, but he needed the rest, and he had to admit he enjoyed having the woman look after him.

Now it was morning again. Dark gray clouds hovered low in the sky. A fierce wind blew across the face of the land. Trey stood at the window, looking out. He had always loved desert storms—the violence, the beauty, the unbridled strength. His Apache grandfather had told him there was power in the wind and the rain and had admonished him to call upon that power in times of trouble.

Trey grunted softly. He was sure as hell in trouble now. And where the devil was his gun?

He glanced over his shoulder as the door opened. The woman stood there, a plate in one hand, a cup in the other, a newspaper tucked under her arm. He was struck again by her quiet beauty.

"I thought you might like something to eat," she said, moving into the room. "I brought the paper, too." She shrugged. "In case you want something to read."

"Thanks." He sat down on the bed, his legs stretched out, the pillows between his back and the headboard.

She handed him the plate, put the paper and the cup on the bedside table. "How are you feeling this morning?"

"Better. How's my horse?"

"Your horse is just fine, don't worry. We've become good friends."

"Is that right? He doesn't usually take to strangers."

"Well, he seems to like me." She laid her hand across his forehead. "Your fever seems to have gone down some." She backed away from the bed. "I hope you enjoy your breakfast."

"Smells good." It looked good, too, he thought. Eggs and bacon and fried potatoes. And a cup of black coffee.

With a nod, she left the room.

He ate quickly. Life on the run didn't give a man much chance to enjoy a good meal. With a sigh of contentment, he put the plate aside and unfolded the newspaper, which had a lot more pages than any he had ever seen before.

He frowned as he read the headlines. "Mideast Peace Talks Called Promising," "Dow Down 70, Nasdaq Gains 27," "California Nears Plan for Energy Cri-

77

sis," "Bush Reaffirms Missile Defense," "India Quake Recovery Under Way."

He shook his head. He read the words, but they made no sense. Peace talks in the Mideast? Hell, the war had been over for years. And what the hell was Dow? And Nasdaq?

He turned the pages, words and phrases he had never heard of swimming before his eyes: ReelTime Reviews, Cyber-squatter, Toshiba, Internet Banking Is Here Now, Shop the Web.

He glanced at the top of the front page again. It was then that he noticed the date. January 26, 2001. He read it again. Wiped his eyes. And read it again. January 26, 2001. Two thousand and one! What the hell?

He looked up as the woman entered the room. "What is this?" he asked, rattling the paper.

"A newspaper?"

"It doesn't make any sense. And what about the date? January twenty-sixth, *two thousand and one?* Is this some kind of joke?"

She frowned at him. "A joke? What joke? What are you talking about?"

"The date. Dammit, the last time I looked, it was eighteen sixty-nine."

A rolling crash of thunder punctuated the sudden silence in the room.

Amanda stared at him. "Eighteen . . . sixty . . . nine?" Well, that would explain a lot of things, she supposed. His clothes, the money in the sack, the reason he didn't know what a can of beer looked like . . . Oh, but it was impossible. Crazy. And she was crazy for considering it, even for a minute. "Where did you get all that money?"

His eyes narrowed. "How do you know about the money?"

"I found it in your saddlebags while I was looking for some ID. Identification." She blew out a sigh of exasperation. "You know, something to tell me who you are."

He glanced at the chair across the room. "Where's my gun?"

"I have it. The money? Where did it come from?"

He shrugged. "A bank."

"You robbed a bank?"

He didn't answer. Swinging his legs over the side of the bed, he stood up. He didn't like being unarmed in a strange place. And though the woman looked harmless enough, and seemed to be alone, he couldn't forget that he was a wanted man.

Amanda backed toward the door, her mind reeling. He couldn't be from the past. It just wasn't possible. He was just some nut. . . . She took a deep, steadying breath. He looked suddenly ominous standing there, even though he was clad in nothing but the lower half of a pair of long underwear.

"Just give me my gun and my clothes, and my money, and I'll be on my way."

"You can't go, not now." She gestured toward the window. "It's raining cats and dogs out there. And you've still got a bit of a fever." *And it's probably not safe for you to be running around without a keeper*, she added to herself.

He looked at her speculatively. "You wouldn't be

trying to keep me here until the law arrives, would you?"

She shook her head, trying not to notice how dark his skin looked in contrast with his long johns, or the breadth of his shoulders, or the way he stood there, tall and lean and dangerous looking, with his eyes glinting at her and every muscle taut. He was trembling, his face gray looking despite the natural bronze of his skin.

"Why don't you sit down?" she suggested. "I'll get your shirt."

She didn't wait for an answer, but turned and left the room. She didn't want him to leave, not yet, though she shied away from the reason she wanted him to stay.

She turned up the heat on her way to the laundry room, where she'd hung his clothes. She took his shirt from the hanger, thinking she could use a cup of coffee.

He was in the kitchen when she got there. Sitting at the table, he was staring out the window, his expression troubled. He must move as quiet as a cat, she thought. He had obviously followed her out of the guest room, and she had never heard a sound.

"Here."

She handed him his shirt. It had been washed and ironed, the bullet hole neatly mended.

"I was going to have some coffee," she said. "Would you like a cup?"

"Yeah, thanks." He shrugged into his shirt and buttoned it halfway up. "Did you tell the law about me?"

"When would I have had time to do that? The

phone's out, and I couldn't very well leave you alone to go into town."

"Phone?"

"Never mind." She moved to the counter, pulled two mugs from the cupboard, and poured a cup for him and one for herself. Carrying them to the table, she handed him one of the mugs, then sat down across from him.

He folded his hands around the cup. "Where am I?"

"What do you mean?"

She watched him glance around the kitchen, frowning as his gaze rested briefly on the stove, the refrigerator, the microwave on the counter, the hanging light over the table, the sink.

He made a broad, sweeping gesture with his hand. "Where the hell am I? What are all these . . . these . . ." He broke off, having no words to describe what he saw.

"Don't tell me," she said. "You've never seen a stove or a refrigerator before, either."

"Of course I've seen a stove." But nothing like this one. Stoves were made of heavy dull black cast iron, they weren't gleaming white with glass in the doors.

"Well, then?"

He shook his head. "I must be outta my mind."

"That's what I think, too," she muttered.

He slammed the palm of his hand on the table. "I'm not crazy!"

"All right, all right, calm down."

"None of this makes any sense."

"You're telling me." She took a deep breath. "All

right, if you're from eighteen sixty-nine, how did you get here?"

"I don't know." He rubbed a hand over his jaw, remembering the day he'd been shot, the strange buzzing sound in his head, the thick gray mist that had enveloped him, the way the world had seemed to blur before his eyes.

"You can't have come from very far," she said, thinking aloud. "Your horse has been here before several times. He's quite a jumper, isn't he?"

"My horse?"

She nodded. "He showed up in my corral one day. I thought he must have strayed from one of the ranches in the area. He was gone the next day, and then he was back again."

Trey stared at her. "My horse," he murmured. "You brushed him, didn't you?"

"Someone had to," she retorted. "You certainly don't."

"My horse." *Treat him well.* Walker on the Wind's voice echoed in the back of his mind. *And he will always carry you away from danger.* Relámpago had sure as hell carried him away from danger this time, Trey mused. Damn, if what the woman said was true, Relámpago had carried him over a hundred years into the future.

He shook his head. "No, it can't be."

"I don't believe it, either," Amanda said. "But here you are."

Trey sipped his coffee; then, putting the mug aside, he stood up and moved toward the refrigerator.

Amanda watched him run his hands over the outside, slide his fingers over the handle, and give a tug. His eyes widened as cool air moved over him. He stared at the bottles and jars and containers on the shelves inside, then put his hand on the top shelf. It was cold to the touch.

"That's a refrigerator," Amanda said. "It keeps food cold so it stays fresh longer." Rising, she opened the freezer door. "This keeps food frozen until you want to use it. Have you ever had ice cream?"

He shook his head. "What is it?"

"You'll see. You look like a chocolate kind of guy to me," she decided. Taking a carton from the fridge, she scooped a generous amount into a bowl, then handed it to him, along with a spoon. "Go on, try it."

He looked at it a moment. Took a small bite, and then a bigger one. It was so cold it felt as if it burned his tongue. But the taste was delicious. He swallowed too fast, and the cold burned a trail down his gullet. He coughed, washed the sting away with a swallow of coffee, and smiled.

"It's good, isn't it?" she said.

"Yeah." He stood there, eating, while she showed him how the appliances worked. Natural gas, electricity—she might as well have been speaking some foreign language. When she turned on one of the burners on the stove, he jerked backward, then moved closer, fascinated by the fact that she could produce a small blue flame at the turn of a knob.

He finished the ice cream, licked the spoon, and handed her the empty dish. She rinsed it off and opened a shiny door under the kitchen counter. He saw a rack, with other dishes in it. A cupboard? She put the plate and spoon in the rack and closed the door with a soft thunk.

Trey glanced at the sink. "You don't wash your dishes?"

"Of course I do. This is a dishwasher. It washes them for me."

He shook his head. "More elec-tricity?"

She smiled. "Yes."

She pulled a chicken leg out of the cold storage cupboard she called a "fridge" and placed it on a napkin. He watched as she opened a small door on the counter. A light came on inside the box and she placed the chicken inside, closed the door, and punched some numbers on the front panel. The light came on again and he peered inside, watching the chicken leg go round and round on a glass plate.

"What are you doing?" he asked. "Why'd you put it in there?"

"That's a microwave oven. It heats things up in a few minutes."

In a few moments there was a sharp "ding" and she popped the door open and handed him the chicken. It was warm, but not too hot. He munched on it while she showed him how the garbage disposal and the electric can opener worked, how to switch the lights on and off. She turned on the faucet, let him feel the hot water. Next, she dropped a slice of bread in another gadget called a toaster. The bread came out warm and crusty. He ate that, too.

She grinned, thinking how amazing it must all seem to him. Truth be told, it was amazing to her, as well, now that she thought about it. Even though she took such modern conveniences for granted, it was none-theless miraculous that she had heat and light and power all at the flip of a switch. And her computer . . . of all the wonders of modern technology, it was the one that amazed her the most. To think she could send words and pictures across the world with the touch of a mouse . . . well, it was just mind-boggling. She decided to save a journey into cyberspace for another time.

She showed him the stereo, sat him down on the sofa and turned on the TV. He watched in wide-eyed fascination as she picked up the remote and flipped through the channels—news, commercials, the latest Brad Pitt movie, a rerun of *M*A*S*H*, an old episode of *The Lone Ranger*.

He pointed at the screen and laughed. "I've never seen a cowboy that clean in my whole life," he remarked. "Or heard an Indian talk like that. What tribe is he supposed to be from?"

"Well, the Lone Ranger isn't exactly a cowboy," she said. "Anyway, it's all just make-believe."

"How does it work, this tele-vision?"

She tried to explain it to him; no easy task, since she wasn't really sure how it worked, either. In the end, she admitted she just didn't know.

"How can you not know? How do you make the pictures move and talk?"

"I just turn it on. I'm not an electronics wizard. I have no idea how or why it works. It just does."

She felt a familiar thrill when she heard the theme music for *Star Wars*, stopped switching channels as the opening scene of *The Empire Strikes Back* unfolded on the screen.

Trey leaned forward, completely caught up in the magic of the story he was seeing. She couldn't blame him. It was one of her favorites, one she had watched numerous times.

"This is all just . . . just make-believe?" he asked incredulously.

"Yes. Amazing, isn't it?"

"That man, he's not really dead, then?"

"No. They're just actors, you know, like on stage?"

He nodded, his gaze riveted on the screen. He stayed that way until the movie was over, then leaned back on the sofa, looking slightly stunned.

Amanda smiled. She had been stunned at the end of the movie, too, though probably not for the same reason he was.

She tapped her fingers on the arm of the sofa. What now? Impossible as it seemed, she actually believed he had somehow come here from the past. Thank goodness the phone lines had been down. She hated to think what would have happened to him if she had called the police. No doubt he would either be in jail for a crime he'd committed over a hundred years ago, or in a rubber room wearing a straitjacket.

"How on earth did you get here?" she asked.

"I don't know. One minute Relámpago and I were ridin' hard, and the next I was here."

"Relámpago?"

"My horse."

"So that's his name. I've been calling him Lightning,

you know, because of that scar on his rump. What does Relámpago mean?"

Trey stared at her, his eyes narrowed. "Lightning."

She stared back at him as an icy shiver ran down her spine. "Imagine that," she said.

He nodded.

Amanda shook her head. There was no reason to feel eerie just because she had called the horse Lightning, not when it had that zigzag scar on its flank. It was nothing more than a coincidence.

"So," she said brightly, "you expect me to believe you and your horse were just zapped here?"

"Zapped?"

"You know, just showed up here from out of the blue."

He shrugged, grimacing as the movement pulled on the wound in his back.

"Are you all right?" she asked. Leaning forward, she placed her hand on his brow. "You still have a bit of a fever. I think maybe you should go lie down for a while. You look like you could use a nap."

He nodded. He needed some time alone, he thought, time to mull over everything he had seen and heard.

"I'll be in later to check on your wound."

"I reckon you saved my life. I'm obliged."

"You're welcome."

His eyes were dark, dark brown, intense as they gazed into hers. She felt a pleasurable shiver steal down her spine, a curling heat in the pit of her stomach as sexual awareness sprang to life between them. He was tall and dark and sexy as hell with his tousled hair falling over his broad shoulders and the beginnings of a beard shadowing his jaw. He looked rough and dangerous and far too appealing for her peace of mind.

Finding it suddenly difficult to breathe, she inhaled deeply, let her breath out in a long, shuddering sigh.

A slow smile spread over his face. He was all too aware of his effect on her, she thought irritably, but she couldn't deny it. She tried to tell herself it was nothing. Just a simple case of lust. After all, he was a ruggedly handsome man, and she was a healthy female. It didn't mean a thing. Besides, she was engaged to Rob. She tried to summon Rob's image, but all she could see were Trey's eyes, suddenly heavy-lidded as he watched her.

She felt warm all over, knew her cheeks were flushed. "Well," she said briskly. "I think I'll go and—"

"Running away?" he drawled.

She stood abruptly, angry that he saw through her so easily. "Of course not. But, I'm . . . I'm hungry. I think I'll go make a sandwich. Do you want one before you go to bed—" She bit down on her lower lip, chiding herself for her choice of words. "Before you take a nap?"

He nodded, his expression telling her she hadn't fooled him for a minute.

She didn't care. She practically ran out of the room.

In the kitchen, she stood with her hands braced on the counter. She had to get him out of here. Now!

She gasped as a pair of well-muscled arms slid around her waist and drew her up against a masculine body that was, without doubt, aroused.

"What are you doing?" she exclaimed.

"What we both want." He turned her slowly to face him, his hands lingering at her waist.

And then he kissed her.

It never occurred to her to push him away.

She closed her eyes, leaning into him as awareness spiraled through her. His body was hard and unyielding, cushioning the softness of her own. He tasted like chocolate ice cream and smoldering desire. Heat exploded through every nerve and cell of her body and she sagged against him, her heart pounding wildly.

He drew back, his gaze burning into hers. And then he kissed her again.

She had been kissed before, many times, but never like this, never with such intensity, such soul-shattering passion. Heat flowed through her, touching places long cold, leaving her feeling weak and slightly dazed.

When he drew back this time, his breathing was as erratic as her own.

She looked up into his eyes, her pulse racing, her whole body on fire, and knew, in that single moment of time, what was missing in her relationship with Rob.

Chapter Eight

Trey paced the floor in the bedroom, his bare feet sinking into the thick rug. He had never been in a home where the floors were completely covered by anything like this. Expensive hotel lobbies, yes. Houses, no. But he had never walked through a hotel lobby barefoot. He liked the feel of the carpet beneath his feet.

The woman, Amanda, had fled the kitchen when he let her go. He had scared the hell out of her, he thought. Hell, he was feeling a mite shaky himself. Women had never been a problem for him. Young, old, married, single, respectable or otherwise, he'd pretty much had his pick, but there was something about this one. Pain and fever notwithstanding, he had wanted her from the moment he had first set eyes on her. And he wanted her now.

He stopped at the window and stared out at the rain, the ache of wanting her momentarily stronger than the ache of his wound. He had kissed women before, a lot of women, but none of them had ever affected him like this. He had kissed them and forgotten them. Made love to them and forgotten them. But Amanda . . . he closed his eyes, the taste of her still fresh on his lips, his arms anxious to hold her again.

He stared out the window. He didn't belong here. As soon as the rain let up, he would saddle Relámpago and find his way back home. . . . He grunted softly. He had no home, but he didn't belong here, that was for damn sure.

She avoided him the rest of the day, coming to his room only twice, once to bring his dinner and again to check on his wound and collect his dirty dishes.

He sat on the bed after she left, the long night stretching ahead of him. He wasn't used to so much inactivity. He could hear her moving around upstairs, the sound of water running. Did she have a bathtub upstairs, too? His mouth went suddenly dry at the thought of her sitting amid frothy bubbles, her luxurious red hair pinned up, her skin flushed from the hot water, covered with lather. . . .

Damn!

Lightning flashed across the sky, followed by the footsteps of the thunder people. The fury of the storm seemed to intensify his restlessness and he prowled through the house, too edgy to sit still. He switched on a light, switched it off, then on again, marveling that such a thing was possible. Marveling that he was here, more than a hundred years in the future. How the hell was he going to get back where he belonged?

Amanda sat back in the tub and closed her eyes. She could still feel Trey's mouth on hers, feel his body pressed intimately against her own. Lord, but that man could kiss! She had always been afraid there was something wrong with her because, although she enjoyed kissing, it had never set her on fire. Even with Rob, it had been pleasurable, but never more than that. Perhaps that was why her sexual encounters had been so few when she was younger. The boys she had dated in high school had called her cold, a tease, when the truth was, none of them had made her want more. But this man, this stranger from the past . . . one kiss, and she was on fire and aching for more.

Dear Lord, what was she going to do? She had a horrible feeling that he knew exactly how his kisses had affected her. How was she ever going to face him again?

She hid out in the bathtub until her fingers and toes were pruney and the water was cold. She imagined him prowling, cat-like, downstairs, peeking into the fridge, playing with the lights. She could hear him running water in the sink. She smiled at his wonder at all things modern. How strange her world must seem to a man who had lived in a time when women cooked on wood-burning stoves and did their laundry by hand and hung their wash on clotheslines. Washers and dryers were relatively new inventions. She could still remember her grandmother hanging her laundry on a line in the backyard. And electricity—in Trey's time, light had been provided by candles or lanterns or maybe gaslights. People had traveled by horse or carriage, or on trains pulled by steam-driven locomotives.

She grinned as she stepped out of the tub, wondering what he would think if she took him for a drive in her car. She dried off vigorously, slipped on her nightgown and a robe, stepped into a pair of slippers, and then stood there, wondering if she should go downstairs and check on him, or just go to bed.

She was still undecided when she opened the bathroom door, gasped in surprise when she saw him leaning against the wall in the hallway, his arms folded across his chest. His bare chest.

"Good Lord, you scared me!" she exclaimed.

"Sorry."

"What do you want?"

He pushed away from the wall. "I'm hungry."

That was a good sign, she thought, though it was hard to think at all when he was standing so close. So close she could feel his breath on her face, feel the attraction that hummed between them.

"What . . . ?" She tried to talk, swallowed to ease a throat gone dry. "What would you like to eat?"

It was a bad choice of words.

Desire flared in his eyes, but he didn't answer, at least not vocally. Instead, his gaze moved over her, slow, heated, leaving her feeling naked and vulnerable.

"I don't know," he replied, his voice low and raspy and suggestive. "What have you got?"

It was suddenly hard to breathe. Her heart was pounding wildly. She felt warm all over, her body tingling with anticipation.

He took a step toward her, closing the distance between them. His gaze held hers, fathomless brown eyes that seemed to see into her very soul. She could feel the heat radiating from his body.

She licked her lips. "Trey . . . I . . . we . . ."

"Tell me you're not hungry, too."

She put her hands against his chest to hold him at bay. Big mistake. His skin was warm and firm beneath her palms. She fought the urge to run her hands along his shoulders and down his arms, to run her fingertips over the taut muscles.

"Are we still talking about food?" She tried to keep her tone light, and failed miserably.

"We were never talking about food." His voice moved over her like lush black velvet, warm and smooth. Desire burned like a dark flame in the depths of his eyes, and with it, the knowledge that his nearness was playing havoc with her senses.

If he didn't stop looking at her like that, she was going to fall into his arms, drag him down on the floor, and beg him to make love to her.

She jumped when the telephone rang. Saved by the bell, she thought, wondering when they had fixed the line. She'd been so caught up in caring for Trey, she'd never thought to see if the phone was working again.

"I'd better get that," she said, and turning on her heel, she ran down the hall to her bedroom. She scooped up the receiver, aware that Trey had followed her, that he was standing in the hallway, waiting. Listening.

"Hello?"

"Hey, 'Manda. You been working out? You sound all out of breath."

"What? Oh, yes, working out." She took a deep

breath, trying to still the pounding of her heart. "How are you, Rob?"

"I'm doing okay. I'd be a lot happier if I could get a lead on Bolander. And even happier if I was done with this little job of work and back there with you. I miss you."

She hesitated. "Yes, I . . . I miss you, too." The words sounded flat in her own ears.

Rob noticed it, too. There was a silence on the other end of the phone. Then, "Are you all right, Amanda?"

"Oh, yes, I'm fine. Really. How's the weather back there?"

"Cold," he said. "Like this conversation."

"Rob—"

"I'll call you tomorrow night," he said, and hung up.

She stared at the receiver, then gently put it down. When she turned toward the door, Trey was gone. She hadn't heard him leave, knew she didn't dare go after him.

"Oh, Rob," she murmured. "What am I going to do?"

It was a question that followed her into uneasy sleep that night, and greeted her in the morning. What was she going to do about Trey?

Rising, she dressed in jeans, a heavy sweater, and a pair of boots and went downstairs. The rain had stopped during the night; the sky was a bright, clear blue, the trees around the homestead a vibrant green, their leaves sparkling with raindrops. The rolling desert lands beyond glimmered in the sunlight, and she saw random bursts of color where winter-blooming flowers had responded to the life-giving moisture.

Trey was nowhere to be seen. Probably still asleep, she thought as she went out the back door, headed for the barn.

The big double doors were open. She heard Trey's voice from inside the barn, and after her eyes adjusted to the shadowy interior, she saw him standing beside the stallion's stall, one arm draped over the stud's neck.

She didn't think she had made any noise, but Trey glanced over his shoulder as soon as she entered the building.

"Mornin'," he drawled.

"Good morning." He looked every inch the cowboy. His brown plaid shirt complemented his hair and emphasized the color of his eyes. His jeans fit well enough, though they weren't cut as snugly as today's designer jeans. Perhaps she would buy him a new pair. . . .

"Were you looking for me?" he asked.

"No. I just came out to feed your horse, but I see you've done that," she replied, and turned to go.

For a man who was still recovering from a bullet wound, he was remarkably quick. She hadn't taken more than a step or two toward the door when his hand closed on her arm. "Don't go."

Her skin tingled where his skin touched it. "I need to fix breakfast."

"It can wait."

She didn't resist when he turned her to face him. She tried not to notice how handsome he was, the way his dark eyes seemed to glow when they looked at her. She had never liked hairy men, but the beard roughening his jaw gave him a rugged, sexy look, and she had an almost irresistible urge to run her hand through his hair, to feel the thick strands slide through her fingers.

"You ran away from me last night," he said. "Why?"

"I didn't run away. I had to answer the phone."

He looked at her, one brow arched.

"I didn't!" she insisted. "Oh, all right, maybe I did," she said when he remained silent.

"Why?"

She lifted her chin. "Because you scare me."

One corner of his mouth lifted in a wry smile. "Really? I wonder why."

"You know why. Now, let me go."

"Oh, I don't think so," he murmured, and lowering his head, he kissed her.

She could have avoided him easily. After all, he was still weak from his wound. She had taken a self-defense class at the Y. She knew how to protect herself. But somehow, all thought of resistance fled the moment his mouth touched hers. She swayed against him, her arms wrapping around his waist, her hands moving restlessly up and down his broad back. He groaned low in his throat. It took a minute for her to realize the sound was edged with pain, not passion.

"I'm sorry." She drew away. "Your wound . . . I forgot . . ."

He grinned at her. "You need to cut those nails."

She blushed to the roots of her hair, embarrassed by the way she had melted in his arms. A look, a kiss, and she was like putty in his hands.

And then he was kissing her again, his mouth slowly

seducing hers, filling her mind with vivid, full-color images of the two of them writhing on her bed amid tangled sheets.

"Stop," she gasped.

He drew back, his deep brown eyes smoldering. "You don't mean that."

"Yes, I do. I can't breathe."

He smiled, a look brimming with masculine self-satisfaction. "Guess we'd better slow down a little."

She shrugged out of his embrace. "I think . . ." She drew in a shaky breath. "I think I'd better go fix breakfast."

"Sure," he said, a knowing gleam in his eye.

Turning on her heel, she left the barn, acutely conscious of his gaze on her back.

He entered the kitchen a short time later, sniffed appreciatively. "Smells good."

"Thank you." She gestured at the table. "Sit down. It's ready."

He sat down, automatically putting his back to the wall. "You're gonna spoil me."

She was pretty sure women had been doing that ever since he learned how to smile.

She served him waffles, eggs, bacon, and orange juice, filled a plate for herself, and sat down across from him. Waffles, she thought. She never made them for herself.

"You're a helluva cook," he remarked.

"Thank you."

"I reckon you're good at just about everything," he said, his voice silky soft.

She had no doubt of his meaning. Heat spiraled through her, pooling deep in the core of her being.

This was ridiculous, she thought irritably. She was a grown woman, but she was behaving like a starry-eyed teenager with her first crush. Probably because that was exactly how she felt.

She watched him eat, fascinated by his hands. They were big and brown, with long fingers and square nails. She imagined them holding a gun . . . imagined them sliding over her bare skin. . . .

She shook her head. Enough was enough! The man was a bank robber, for crying out loud, not Antonio Banderas! She smiled faintly. He had eyes like Antonio's . . . dark and smoldering, filled with secrets that begged to be discovered.

"Amanda?"

"What?"

"I'd like to see more of your world."

"Oh, sure. We can go into town in a few days, if you like."

"Why can't we go today?"

She frowned. "Are you sure you feel up to it?"

"Don't worry about me."

"Okay, we can go today, whenever you're ready."

"I'll need my gun."

"You don't need it here."

"Like hell."

"Well, you don't. Men don't go around wearing six-guns these days."

"No?" he asked dubiously.

"No. Besides, I'm not stupid enough to let a stranger have a gun in my house."

He lifted a quizzical brow. "You afraid I'm going to shoot you?"

"Well, you *are* a bank robber."

"This isn't a bank."

"Very funny."

"Dammit, woman, give me my weapon!"

"No."

"You can give it to me," he said, his voice low and deadly, "or I can tear this place apart looking for it. It's up to you."

He meant it. She didn't doubt him for a minute. With a sigh of exasperation, she relented. "Stay here," she said. "I'll get it."

He watched her leave the room, annoyed that she thought he would do her harm. He had never raised a hand to a woman in his life.

She returned a few minutes later carrying his gun belt and holster. She held it out to him the way she might have held a dead rat. "Here."

"Obliged." He took the gun belt, slid his Colt from the holster, and opened the loading gate to check his ammunition. He spun the cylinder; then, satisfied, he dropped the gun back into its leather.

"Before we go to town, we need to talk about that gun," she said earnestly.

He stood to buckle the belt around his waist, settling it comfortably. "So talk," he said.

"Men just don't carry guns in public anymore," she said. "Not in town anyway."

He nodded. "A lot of cow towns have rules like that. Liquor and firearms don't mix."

"You don't want to attract unwanted attention, do you? Besides, you need a permit to carry one."

He considered it. "Okay, I'll leave the gun belt here and tuck my Colt under my shirt."

"But that's carrying a concealed weapon! That's against the . . ."

"Law?" he finished with a smile.

Exasperated, she threw up her hands. "You won't like modern jails. I can promise you that."

"Hell, I don't like any kind of jail," he said lightly. "I'll be . . . discreet."

"You really don't need to wear it here in the house, either," she said, her eyes twinkling with mischief. "I promise not to attack you."

His gaze moved over her, hot and heavy. "Afraid I can't promise you the same," he drawled, and resisted the urge to smile. "But that hasn't got anything to do with six-guns, now does it?"

She wasn't laughing at him now.

They finished the rest of the meal in silence.

Putting down his coffee cup, Trey pushed away from the table. "Is it all right with you if I use the bathtub?"

"Of course. There are clean towels in the cupboard."

He nodded. "I don't reckon you'd wanna wash my back?"

"I reckon not," she retorted.

Smothering a grin, he sauntered out of the room.

He was trouble. More trouble than she had ever imagined, she thought as she watched him walk away.

But he came wrapped in a mighty nice package.

Chapter Nine

Trey stood in the bathroom, watching the tub fill with water. It was nothing like the bathtubs he was used to. It was oval shaped, and made of some slick material he didn't recognize. And it was sky blue. Amanda had shown him how to adjust the water to whatever temperature he preferred. He shook his head. Hot running water piped right into the kitchen and the bathrooms. He had never heard of such a thing.

Earlier, he had grabbed his razor from his saddle-bag, noting as he did so that while all his gear was still there, the money was missing. He would have to ask Miss Amanda about that, he thought. He had risked his life for that money, and he didn't intend to lose it now.

He shaved over the sink while he waited for the tub to fill. Removing his gun belt, he wrapped the belt around the holster and sheath and laid it on top of the sink. He put the lid down on the toilet, sat, and pulled off his boots, then stood up and shrugged out of his clothes. He carefully unwrapped the bandage swathed around his middle. The wound ached, especially when he moved too quickly or forgot about it and bent over, but he had no complaints. Hell, he was lucky to be alive.

He lowered himself into the tub, sighed with pleasure as the hot water enveloped him. Leaning back, his head resting against the wall, he closed his eyes. Heaven, he thought. Pure heaven.

Amanda finished making her bed, trying not to think of Trey. Downstairs. Naked. In her bathtub.

The thought brought a rush of heat to her cheeks. What was wrong with her? She shied away from the answer. Tried to think of something else, but it was useless. He had been in her house a matter of days and had taken over her every thought. And her dreams, as well, she thought irritably. Oh, but what dreams!

Going downstairs, she took a load of towels out of the washer and tossed them into the dryer, then went into the kitchen to wait for him. Pouring herself a cup of coffee, she glanced out the window, wondering what he would think of her car, of the town.

He entered the kitchen a few minutes later. It was all she could do to keep from staring at him. He had shaved, revealing a strong, square jaw, and had put on the shirt she had seen in his saddlebag. The dark red accented the black of his hair and made his brown eyes seem even darker.

"You ready to go?" he asked.

She noticed he was wearing the shirt loose, square tails outside his pants. Quite casual, she thought, until she remembered his remark about concealing his six-gun. Now that she was looking for it, she could see the slight bulge beneath his shirt.

"Must you?" she asked.

He grinned. "You worry too much. I'm not here to rob any of your banks."

"You won't consider leaving it here?"

"No." It was a flat negative and brooked no argument.

She sighed. "All right, but if you get arrested, I don't know you."

"Why would I get arrested?"

"You ever hear of metal detectors? No, of course you haven't."

He frowned, suspicious. "What the hell are metal detectors?"

"A way to tell if you're carrying a gun, even if it's hidden. They have them in all the courts these days. Maybe in banks. Some schools, even."

"Schools? What the hell for?"

"We live in a complicated and violent world," she replied with a shrug.

"Well, I guess things really haven't changed all that much, then," he commented. "You aren't planning on us going to any courts or banks, are you? And I'm sure not going to school! So, now we've got that settled, are you ready to go?"

"All right." Maybe she could persuade him to leave

the gun in the car, once she showed him that it could be locked away safely.

He followed her outside, his expression puzzled when he glanced around the yard. "How are you aiming to get to town? I don't recall seeing a buggy in the barn. And the only horse here is 'Pago. You planning on us riding double?" He flashed her a roguish grin. "Not a bad idea at that, especially if you hang on real tight."

She felt a rush of heat sweep into her cheeks. "We'll take my car, of course."

"Car? What sort of animal is that?"

"You'll see. Wait here."

Leaving him waiting on the porch, she went down the stairs and crossed the yard to the garage. Opening the door, she went inside, smiling as she imagined his reaction.

The Jag was only a year old. Her uncle had bought it on a whim. She had tried to talk him out of it. Sick as he was, he rarely left the house except to go to the doctor, but he had insisted. He had always intended to buy one before he died, he had told her, and time was running out. He had let her pick it out. She had chosen the cheapest one available, which was far from cheap, but he had waved her choice aside. "Pretend you're buying it for yourself," he had said. "Which one would you choose?" Without hesitation, she had picked a convertible. Platinum, with butter-soft ivory leather interior, walnut trim, walnut gearshift knob, wood and leather steering wheel, all for a mere $66,000 before tax and license. Uncle Joe had insisted on chrome sports wheels, another $1,295. Premium Alpine Sound system with six CD disc autochanger? Only $1,800.

When she saw the total, with tax and license, she had almost fainted dead away. The Jag cost more than three times what her parents had paid for their first house! Uncle Joe had waved her protests aside. "It's only money," he'd said with a grin. And while that was true, it was more money than most people made in a year.

She ran her hand over the hood. She had considered selling the Jag after her uncle died, but not for very long. Sleek and silver, it was poetry in motion. And fast. So darn fast. It looked like it was moving even when it was standing still. "A silver bullet," the salesman had said. Something like zero to sixty in less than seven seconds. She had gotten a ticket for speeding the day she drove it off the lot.

Sliding behind the wheel, she slipped the key into the ignition, put the top and windows down. The engine purred like a well-fed cat as she backed out of the garage.

Trey was staring at the car, eyes wide, when she drove up.

"Well," she called, "what do you think?"

"What the hell is that?" he asked, backing away from the edge of the porch.

"It's an XK8 Jaguar convertible. Come on, get it."

He looked dubious as he descended the stairs and walked around the car to the passenger side.

She leaned across the seat and opened the door for him. "Well? Are you going to get in?"

He shifted his weight from one foot to the other.

"You're not afraid, are you?"

"Hell, no," he retorted. "Just figuring out how to mount this thing." He slid into the passenger seat and jammed his worn boots one at a time into the passenger side footwell.

He was a good liar, she thought, smothering a grin. "This is the steering wheel," she said, tapping it with her finger. "This is the dashboard. This is the radio." She sighed, thinking of all the things he had to learn. "A radio plays music." She turned it on, and the voice of Conway Twitty filled the air.

Trey frowned as music surrounded them. "How is that possible?" he asked.

"It comes from a radio station. A building. A place that has to do with airwaves and radio signals, and . . . oh, I don't know how to explain it. Kind of like a telegraph without wires, I guess. You did have telegraphs back then, didn't you?"

"I know what a telegraph is," he said grimly. "But they don't play music!"

She turned the radio down. "This is a CD player. It plays music, too." She slid a Kenny Rogers CD into the player. "This is the temperature gauge. And this—" She reached across him. "This is a seat belt. You fasten it like this."

"What's it for?" he asked, tugging on the strap across his chest.

"To keep you from flying out of the car if we get in a wreck."

"Wreck?"

"An accident," she said, putting the car in gear. "Don't worry about it. I'm a good driver."

He muttered an oath as she pulled away from the front of the house.

"Hang on." She grinned as she accelerated, loving the feel of the wind in her face and hair.

He didn't say anything for a few minutes. He didn't look scared, exactly, more like wary.

He had just settled back in his seat when a plane flew overhead.

"What the hell is that?" he exclaimed.

"It's an airplane. A jet. It's a way to travel when you're in a hurry, or you're going a long way and you don't want to drive or take the train."

He shook his head. "I see it, but I don't believe it. People are in that contraption?"

She laughed. "Yes, lots of them."

"Voluntarily?"

She wanted to laugh harder, but one look at his face changed her mind. She placed a hand on his shoulder. "I know it's an awful lot to take in, especially all at once. I know I'd never do as well in your time if our situations were reversed."

His answering smile was her reward.

The road was straight for the first few miles, lined by imported trees that had been planted years ago as windbreaks. The rolling desert alongside the road was in full bloom after the winter rains. There was a wide, pleasant hollow off to the right. She always expected to see the delicate desert whitetail deer for which the area was noted browsing there, but she never had, though she had seem them in other places now and then.

"Nice-looking buck," Trey commented as they sped by. "Too bad I didn't bring my rifle."

"What?" Her foot lifted off the accelerator. "Where? I didn't see . . ."

"Back there a ways," he said. "Bedded down by those cactus on the ridge." He grunted softly. "A long ways back now, fast as we're going."

"I've never seen any deer there!"

"You've gotta know how to look," he said, and grinned at her. "I guess there are some things I could teach you after all."

For once, his comment didn't seem to have a double meaning, and she smiled. "I guess there are."

The wildlife was one of the reasons she had bought the house. She had grown up in the city, where the only wildlife she had seen had been a dead possum in the road from time to time. But here, there were deer, javelinas, ground squirrels, raccoons, eagles, and an occasional coyote. In the short time she had lived here, she had seen them all, and heard the coyotes singing at night. The forty-five-minute drive to town seemed a small price to pay.

They rode in silence for a while. She glanced at Trey's stern profile. "You okay?"

"Just thinking. Does everyone have a . . ." He gestured at the car. "One of these?"

"Most everyone. Cars replaced the horse and buggy in the early part of the twentieth century. Horses are a luxury few people can afford these days. Mostly they're used for pleasure riding and horse racing. Oh, and some of the police departments have mounted divisions."

He fell silent again as he pondered that. Once his initial trepidation wore off, he found himself enjoying the ride. The speed was exhilarating. He ran his hand over the outside of the door, tapped it with his finger.

"What is your . . . car . . . made of?"

"Gee, I'm not sure. Aluminum, maybe? I really don't know."

"Whatever alum-inum is," he muttered, and then asked abruptly, "Why do you live alone?"

"Why shouldn't I?"

"In my time, young women didn't live alone unless they were . . ." His voice trailed off.

"Go on," she urged. "Unless they were what?"

"Never mind," he said gruffly.

"I live alone because I prefer it," she said. After spending two years being with her uncle almost day and night, she needed the solitude.

His next question caught her off guard. "Why aren't you married?"

"Why aren't you?"

"How do you know I'm not?"

"Are you?" It had never occurred to her that he might be married. She wasn't sure why. Thinking of it now stirred something within her, something that felt very much like jealousy.

"No."

"Too busy robbing banks?"

He glowered at her. "That's none of your business."

"And my marital status is none of your business. But if you must know, I'm engaged."

She slowed as the road curved. When they rounded the second bend, the city came into view. It was a pretty sight, nestled in a valley among the trees and red cliffs. The sun played hide-and-seek behind a scattering of fluffy white clouds that drifted across the powder blue sky.

Trey jerked his chin toward the town. "Is that where we're headed?"

"Yes. That's Canyon Creek."

"I've been there a time or two."

She grinned at him. "Well, I'll bet it's changed some since you saw it last."

He grunted. "Reckon so."

Ten minutes later, she pulled into a parking place on Main Street. "Well," she said, switching off the ignition. "We're here."

He grunted softly. On horseback, the journey would have taken hours.

Unfastening her seat belt, Amanda took the keys from the ignition. She started to get out of the car, then paused.

"Trey?"

"Yeah?"

"We can put your gun in the trunk and lock it. No one will know it's there, or be able to get it out."

He glanced in the backseat, which wasn't big enough to hold a satchel, let alone anything bigger. "What trunk?"

"Come here, I'll show you."

He got out of the car and followed her around to the back. She slid a key into a lock and lifted a part of the car. "See?"

He blew out a breath. "You never let up, do you? All right, this one time."

He pulled the Colt from under his shirt and put it in the trunk. She smiled her thanks as she closed the lid. Grabbing her handbag from the backseat, she dropped the keys inside.

Trey glanced around. There were buildings on both sides of the street, a street that in his time had been dusty in summer and muddy in winter. Now, it was covered with some hard black substance. There were cars parked up and down the street, different in shape and size and color from Amanda's. He noticed most of them had tops of some kind.

The sidewalks were crowded with people. He stared at a woman who passed by clad in a bright orange dress, the hem of which was shorter than any whore's costume. Her hair, an outrageous shade of pink, was short and spiky. Her shoes were the same color as her dress, but unlike anything he had ever seen before.

He saw men in city suits, women in pants that were cut off well above the knee, men in short pants and sleeveless shirts and tinted glasses, women in sleeveless dresses with full skirts. A few of the men were dressed as he was, in trousers, shirt, and boots.

As Amanda had said, none of the men wore guns, or weapons of any kind that he could see.

She moved up beside him. "Well, here we are. What do you want to see first?"

He shrugged. He felt naked without his gun, lost in a town that was familiar in some ways and totally foreign in others. He recognized the courthouse at the end of the block. A building that had once been a brothel had been painted white. A sign on the side of the building read "Nelly Blue's Bed and Breakfast. Cable in every room." The firehouse across from the courthouse was still red. But the fire wagons behind its big open doors looked far too heavy for the stoutest draft horses. A sign on one roof proclaimed "Cobb's Steak House." There were hitch rails in front of some of the stores, but no horses to be seen anywhere.

"Come on," Amanda said.

He fell into step beside her and they walked down the sidewalk, stopping now and then to peer into the shop windows.

One thing hadn't changed. The Four Deuces was still a saloon. He'd been in the place several times in the past and he stepped inside, hoping to find something familiar. He stopped just inside the batwing doors and glanced around. The curved mahogany bar and brass foot rail were still there, but everything else looked different. The gaming tables were gone, replaced by small walnut tables and long-legged chairs. The wagon-wheel chandelier was still there, but the candles were gone, replaced by electric lights. A couple clad in jeans and cowboy shirts danced in a corner of the room.

"Do you want something to drink?"

He turned to see Amanda standing behind him.

"I'm going to get a Coke," she said. "Do you want anything?"

"Coffee," he said, and followed her to the bar.

They stood there a moment, sipping their drinks while they watched the couple on the dance floor do the two-step.

The song ended, and the strains of "Amarillo" sung

by George Strait filled the air. It was one of her favorite songs.

Amanda placed her glass on the bar, then tapped Trey on the shoulder. "Would you like to dance?"

He had never been big on dancing in the white man's way, but he was in favor of anything that put Amanda in his arms. Setting his coffee cup down, he took her hand and led her onto the tiny dance floor. There was no awkwardness between them. He held her close, his hand spread across the small of her back. She followed his lead effortlessly, and they glided around the floor as though they had danced together for years instead of minutes.

Amanda had always loved dancing, and never more than now. She rested her cheek against Trey's shoulder, thinking how natural it felt to be in his arms. He was a wonderful dancer, light on his feet. His hand was warm and firm against her back; she felt a tingle of desire as his body brushed against her own.

The song ended all too soon, the ballad replaced by a lively tune by Brooks and Dunn.

"That's beyond me," Trey said, watching the line dancers take the floor again.

"Shall we go?" she asked. "There's lots to see."

With a nod, he followed her outside. They strolled down the sidewalk, passing several stores before Amanda tugged on his arm.

"Let's go in here," she said.

The sign said "Carl's Cowboy Corral." Frowning, Trey followed her into the store. The first thing he noticed was the head of a white buffalo mounted on the wall across from the door. Shirts hung from round metal racks. Dozens of shirts, long-sleeved and short, in checks and plaids, wool and chambray. Levi's hung from racks or were folded on shelves. Another rack held dusters in black or tan, another rack held a variety of jackets: jean jackets lined with flannel, leather jackets, sheepskin jackets.

One wall was lined with rows and rows of boots. He stared at them in disbelief. Black and white boots that looked like the hide of a cow, red boots, blue boots, boots with fringe, boots with stars. He shook his head. What the hell kind of cowboy would wear boots like that?

Another wall held hats: black, tan, brown, gray, blue. Red! Trey ran a hand through his hair. He'd lost his battered old slouch hat somewhere along the way.

Crossing the room, he plucked a black Stetson from the shelf and settled it on his head. It had a low crown and a braided band. He ran his hands along the edge of the brim, curling it down a little in front.

"Looks great," Amanda said, coming up behind him. "You should buy it."

"Yeah?" He arched a brow at her, thinking of the loot that had mysteriously disappeared from his saddlebag. "With what?"

"I'll buy it for you. Think of it as a kind of 'welcome to the twenty-first century' gift."

"I don't think so."

"Why not?"

"What kind of man do you think I am?"

"One who doesn't have any money."

"Yeah, I meant to ask you about that," he said. "Where's the money that was in my saddlebags?"

"Safe at home. You couldn't spend it here anyway," she said, and before he could argue further, she plucked the hat from his head and carried it to a counter at the front of the store.

Trey followed her, frowning as she handed the clerk a piece of what looked like hard paper. "What's that?"

"My Visa card. You can use it instead of cash."

"I don't understand."

"It's a credit card. I charge all my purchases on it, and then I get a bill at the end of the month."

"Do you not use money anymore?"

"Oh, yeah, for some stuff."

The clerk handed Amanda a piece of paper and a funny-looking shiny pencil and she signed her name, then handed the paper and pencil back to the clerk. "I'll just put this in a bag for you," the clerk said.

"Never mind," Amanda said. "He'll wear it."

The clerk smiled. "Here you go, sir." He handed Trey the Stetson, gave Amanda a copy of the receipt. "Thanks for shopping at Carl's."

Amanda smiled at him. Tucking the receipt into her bag, she started for the door, then stopped. "You need some new jeans, too."

"What's wrong with these?"

"Well, aside from the fact that they're over a hundred years old, and out of style, nothing at all."

He could see she had her mind made up, so he followed her to where the Levi's were and rummaged though a stack, holding up one pair after another until he found a pair that looked about right. She insisted he try them on, and pointed him toward a tiny room at the back of the store.

116

Off with the old, on with the new. At first, he thought he had the wrong size, they were so snug, but they didn't feel too tight in the waist. The material was different from anything he'd ever felt, and seemed to move when he did.

"Hey," Amanda called, tapping on the door. "Let me see."

"I've been buying my own clothes for years," he muttered, but he opened the door and stepped out, felt a wave of heat climb up his neck when she whistled at him. "Quit that," he hissed.

"We'll take those, too," she said. "And a pair of black ones just like them." Before he could stop her, she had grabbed his old jeans.

"Dammit, Amanda—"

But she was already gone, headed for the counter with his old pants and a pair of black Levi's tucked under her arm.

Trey shook his head. She was a woman used to getting her own way, there was no doubt about that. Going back into the tiny room, he pulled on his boots, then took another look at himself in the mirror. Damn jeans fit almost like a second skin. He grinned at his image. But they looked good on him.

He took hold of her arm when they left the store. "How much do I owe you?"

"You don't owe me anything."

A muscle worked in his jaw as he fought to control his temper. "I'm already beholden to you for savin' my life. I said I'll pay you back, and I will. Now, how much do I owe you?"

"Well, the hat was a hundred and forty dollars—"

"A hundred and forty dollars! For a hat?" He was shocked out of his anger momentarily. "That's worse than robbery! That's . . . that's . . ." Words failed him.

"Western wear is popular these days," she said. "And expensive."

"How much for the jeans?"

"About seventy dollars."

"For both?"

"No, for one."

He looked totally shocked.

"I guess prices have gone up some in the last hundred years," she remarked.

"You can say that again," he muttered.

"Well, don't worry about it," she said. "I can afford it."

"It's not right, you payin' my way. I'll pay you back for what you spent today. Even if I have to rob another bank to do it."

He continued to brood about the outrageous prices as they strolled down the street. So much had changed, it was hard to believe he was in Canyon Creek. Amanda showed him video stores and music stores. They stopped at a pet shop that had once been a boardinghouse and she cooed over a fluffy gray kitten and a pot-bellied pig.

They wandered through a gift shop that carried plates and cups, toothpick holders and shot glasses, shirts of all kinds emblazoned with the name of the town. Row after row filled with more knickknacks than he had seen in a lifetime.

He paused, realizing she wasn't with him. Turning, he saw her standing next to a pile of stuffed animals:

dogs and cats, lions and tigers, horses and cows. He had to admit they were kind of cute. Totally useless, but cute.

He stepped back as a tall, willowy girl clad in a pair of skin-tight red jeans and a white sleeveless shirt came down the aisle toward him.

He tipped his hat automatically.

"Hi, cowboy," she said in a throaty voice.

"Ma'am."

"Ma'am?" She smiled at him, batting her eyelashes prettily. "Are you all alone, handsome?"

He grinned at her, flattered and amused by her attention. "Honey, I've got a saddle older than you."

She winked at him. "I'd be glad to let you break me in."

He laughed out loud at that, wondering if all the women in this day and age were as forward as this one.

"Having fun?"

Trey met Amanda's inquiring gaze over the top of the girl's head.

Glancing over her shoulder, the girl looked Amanda up and down. "Is he with you?"

"Yes," Amanda said curtly.

"Well, if you ever get tired of him, let me know."

"Yes," Amanda replied dryly. "I'll do that. Run along now."

The girl winked at Trey. "So long, cowboy."

He touched the brim of his hat with his forefinger, laughed softly as she sashayed down the aisle.

"Don't let me keep you, if you'd rather be with her," Amanda said.

He didn't miss the slight edge in her tone, couldn't resist asking, "You jealous?"

She tossed her head. "Of course not."

"Well, don't worry, sweetheart, I never change partners in the middle of a dance," he assured her with that now familiar roguish grin.

Amanda felt her heart catch in her throat. He was far too handsome, his smile far too devastating. And he knew it, too. She hadn't missed the way women stopped to look at him as they walked down the street. He had a long, easy stride, an aura of self-confidence that was almost palpable. He was a man who knew who he was, a man comfortable in his own skin, her uncle would have said. But it was his face that drew the eye of every woman past puberty. Smooth, copper-hued skin, finely sculpted cheekbones, a strong, square jaw, that sensual lower lip that even now tempted her touch. It didn't hurt that he filled out those new jeans like a Hollywood model, or that his shoulders were as broad as a barn door. And he oozed sex appeal. She grinned. Sex on a stick, she thought, remembering her girlfriend's apt but humorous description of Russell Crowe in last year's hit movie.

He was looking at her, one brow raised inquisitively.

"Shall we go?" she asked.

With a nod, he followed her out of the shop.

"I'm hungry," she said. "Do you want to get something to eat?"

"Sure."

She took him to her favorite restaurant, a little place that served the best Mexican food she had ever tasted. They took a table by the window.

The waitress wasn't immune to Trey's good looks, either. The woman had to be forty if she was a day, but she simpered and smiled while she took their order as if she had never seen a man before. Amanda couldn't blame her. There was something about a long-legged, good-looking man in tight-fitting jeans and a cowboy hat.

"So, tell me," Amanda said when they were alone. "How'd you get into robbing banks?"

"It's a long story. And not very interesting."

"Tell me anyway. I'd like to hear it."

"Some other time. You said you're engaged. When do I get to meet the lucky man?"

"I don't know. He's out of town." She paused a moment, savoring her next words. "He's a bounty hunter."

Trey stared at her. "You're kidding."

"No, I'm not. I'm sure he'd love to meet you. Professionally speaking, of course."

"You think he'd take me in for a crime I committed a hundred and thirty-two years ago?"

She laughed. "I doubt it. I'm sure there's some sort of statute of limitations on robbery."

"Statute of what?"

"Limitations. You know, some sort of limit on how long you can be prosecuted for a particular crime."

"Well, that's good to know," he replied dryly. "So, when's the big day?"

"We haven't set a date yet. We only met a short time ago."

His gaze met hers, hooded and indecipherable. What was he thinking? And why did she feel as though she had somehow betrayed him?

Chapter Ten

It was sprinkling when they left the restaurant.

Shivering, Amanda rubbed her hands up and down her arms. "Looks like we're in for another storm."

Trey glanced up at the sky and nodded. Judging by the dark clouds rapidly gathering overhead, they were in for a real gully washer.

"I think we'd better head home," she said. "I hate driving that winding road in the rain."

"Okay by me," Trey said. He'd seen enough of the town; his back was aching. He looked at Amanda's car. It was going to be a long, wet ride back to her place, he thought.

Amanda tossed her purse and Trey's jeans on the backseat, then slid behind the wheel and put the key in the ignition. She watched Trey fold his long length into the passenger seat, saw him grimace as he did so. Sometimes she forgot he had been wounded.

She put on her seat belt, and, after watching her, he did the same.

She pushed something on the dashboard. There was a soft whirring noise.

Trey glanced over his shoulder, alarmed to see a part of the car unfolding and rising over him.

"Relax," Amanda said. "It's just the top."

He had to hunch over to keep the top from hitting his head. Taking off his hat, he tossed it onto the backseat. That afforded him a little more headroom, but not much.

She released the button when the top clicked into place. "Are you ready?"

He nodded, not certain he liked this new closed-in feeling.

"I'd better get some gas. For the car," she explained, seeing his puzzled look. "It's what the car runs on, what makes it go."

He grunted softly. "Where do you get it? Gas."

"There," she said, pointing at a building across the street. "You can buy gasoline there, as well as bread and milk, beer, that kind of stuff." Pulling up in front of several strange-looking objects, Amanda stopped the car and turned off the engine. "I'll be right back."

He watched with interest as she inserted her credit card in a slot, then removed a long hose from a hook. Curious, he got out of the car to watch as she shoved the end of the hose into a hole in the side of the car.

"This is a gas station," she explained. "This is a gasoline pump. These numbers"—she pointed to a window on the pump—"tell you how many gallons of gas have been pumped into your car."

"All cars run on gas?"

"Yes. Some get better mileage than others. I get about seventeen miles to the gallon in the city, more on the highway."

"Highway?"

"The open road."

"Is that good?"

She shrugged. "About average, I guess. Usually, the bigger the car, the worse the mileage." She put the hose back on the hook. "Let's go."

"Your credit card?" he said as he got into the car. "You can use it for gas, too?"

"Yes, you can use it for just about everything—food, clothes, whatever you want."

It was raining harder now. Amanda switched on the windshield wipers.

Trey gazed out the window. The clouds were dark, ominous. A brilliant flash of lightning was followed by a clap of thunder. Soon, they had left the town behind.

"I love thunderstorms," Amanda said, both hands gripping the steering wheel as she maneuvered the car around the first curve in the road. "When I'm at home in front of a cozy fire."

Trey nodded. He had always loved storms. The sound of the rain and the thunder, the sharp crackle of lightning sizzling across the sky. He loved the power of it, the wildness. It called to something deep inside him, something feral and untamed.

Another flash of lightning cut across the sky. Thunder followed hard on its heels. Another bolt rent the heavens. Amanda screamed as it struck a tree just ahead. Sparks lit the sky as, in seeming slow motion, the big tree buckled near its roots and toppled over, crashing onto the roadway. Amanda rode the brakes as the Jag hydroplaned on the wet surface, until, after what seemed like an eternity, the car came to a stop within feet of the tree's tangled limbs.

She sat there a moment, breathing heavily, her hands in a death grip on the wheel, her knuckles white. She slid a glance over at Trey. "Now you know what seat belts are for."

He nodded. The rain was coming down in sheets now, the heavy drops making a loud tattoo on the top of the car.

She was shivering. Nerves, he thought, in reaction to what had almost happened. He couldn't blame her. It had scared the hell out of him, too. They had missed plowing into the sudden road block by no more than a couple of feet. She had good reflexes, for a city woman.

He put his hand on her shoulder and gave it a squeeze. "You okay?"

"Y . . . yes."

He glanced at both sides of the road. Trees grew thick on either side. There was no way around the tree, and no way he could move it.

The rain pounded on the roof of the car.

When she regained her composure, Amanda carefully backed her car around in the two-lane road, and drove slowly back the way they had come.

"Where are we going?" Trey asked.

"I don't think I want to try the side road up to the house," she said, her voice still a little shaky. "It's very narrow, hardly more than a dirt path. It's probably washed out, anyway. There's a motel about a mile this side of town. We can spend the night there."

"What's a motel?"

"It's like a hotel, except people usually stay only for a night."

Trey nodded. She had said she hated driving in the rain. He could see by the taut line of her jaw, the way her hands clenched the wheel, that she was tense.

He felt a sense of frustration. With a wagon and team, he could have taken over and gotten them home safely. But he had no knowledge of her car, no understanding of what made it go. He longed momentarily for 'Pago. The stallion shrugged off storms with equanimity, had no need of roads or trails.

Lightning continued to slash across the skies. The rain continued to come down in heavy sheets, making it difficult to see more than a few feet ahead.

Silence enfolded them, broken only by the sound of the rain, the rumble of thunder, and the swish of the windshield wipers against the glass.

Night spread her cloak across the land, cocooning them in deepening darkness.

A man's voice came over the radio saying the storm was expected to last through the night and warning motorists to drive carefully.

"What does that mean?" Trey asked. "Motorists drive carefully?"

"We're motorists," Amanda replied, not taking her gaze off the road. "And driving is what I'm doing."

"And who is the man on the radio?"

"He's a DJ. A disc jockey. It's his job to play the music and make public service announcements."

"Where is he?"

"At that radio station I told you about."

She fell silent as the road curved again.

He heard her sigh of relief when the road straightened out and the lights of the town became visible.

A few minutes later, she pulled up in front of a long, low building. The sign said "Cactus Tree Motel. Vacancy."

"I'll be right back." Reaching into the backseat, she grabbed her handbag. Opening the door, she got out of the car and hurried into the office.

Through the window, Trey could see her talking to a pudgy, gray-haired man. She emerged a short time later, and they drove around the side of the building. She stopped the car and turned off the engine. She sat there a moment, then got out of the car.

Grabbing his hat, he followed her out, hunching his shoulders against the rain.

"Here's your key." She thrust it into his hand, her fingers brushing against his. "See you in the morning."

She opened the door to the room next to his and stepped inside. "Good night."

"Good night."

He waited until she closed the door, then looked at the key in his hand. It was attached to an oblong disk with the number 31 on it. Unlocking the door to Room 31, he stepped inside. It was dark and cold. In the dim light coming through the open door, he could make out two beds with a table in between. Remembering Amanda's house, he felt along the wall beside the door until he found the light switch. He flicked it on, shook his head as the room filled with light. Amazing. The walls were a faded green, reminding him of the color of sagebrush in the spring. There was a small lamp on the table, one of those telephones people in this century seemed so fond of, a small chest of drawers across from the beds, and a single overstuffed chair.

He tossed his hat on the dresser, then stretched out on the bed, hands clasped behind his head, and listened to the steady drumming of the rain against the window. He thought briefly of Relámpago, though he was not really concerned. The stud had shelter and water, and would have been fine even if he didn't. It wouldn't hurt the stallion to miss a meal, Trey thought wryly. They had both done it in the past. He was a sight more concerned about how he was going to get back where he belonged. Damn.

Feeling restless and closed in, he stood and began to pace the floor. What was she doing? he wondered. Maybe he should just go check to make sure she was all right.

He headed for the door, stopped, his hand on the knob. Muttering an oath, he went back to pacing the floor. She was probably asleep by now.

He was thinking about trying to get some sleep himself when he paused, his head cocked to one side, listening. Had he imagined it, or was someone knocking on the door? It could only be Amanda.

He hurried to open the door when the knock came a second time.

She smiled tentatively. "Can I come in?"

"Sure." He stepped back, closed the door behind her.

She stood in the middle of the floor, her arms crossed over her breasts. "I can't sleep."

Trey nodded.

"Do you mind if I sit down?"

"Make yourself at home," he said with a wry grin. "You're paying for the room."

She glanced around, started toward one of the beds, then changed direction and sat down in the chair. "It's cold in here."

"Yeah."

"Why don't you turn on the heat?" she asked, and then grinned. "Because you don't know how," she said, answering her own question.

Rising, she walked across the room. "This is the thermostat," she said. "You turn it this way for heat, and this way to turn on the air. Heating and air-conditioning," she elaborated. "One heats the room when it's cold, and the other cools the room when it's hot."

"Handy." He came up behind her, peering over her shoulder.

"Yes." She turned to face him, her breath catching in her throat. She hadn't realized he was so close. Coming in here had been a mistake. He was too close. Too virile. Too much on her mind. And far too tempting. But she had come here anyway, hoping for . . . what? She shied away from the answer that came quickly to mind.

"Well," she said, "I'd better go. I just wanted to make sure you found everything. I mean, you've never been in a motel before, and . . . and I need to check on your wound. And—"

"Relax. My back is fine. Just a little sore, that's all."

He whispered her name, his hand cupping her cheek. His callused palm was warm against her skin.

She met his gaze, felt the attraction sizzle like lightning between them, vital and alive and irresistible.

His arms slid around her waist and he drew her up against him.

She rested her cheek against his chest, acutely aware of his arms around her, of the smooth texture of his shirt against her skin, the way her body seemed to fit to his. They stood that way for several minutes, not moving, not speaking. There was a sudden hum as the heater came on.

He tilted her head up, his gaze moving over her face, lingering on her lips. Was he remembering the kiss they had shared, as she was? Was it making his mouth dry and his palms damp? Was his heart pounding as loudly as the thunder rattling overhead? And if he tried to kiss her, what then?

And then there was no time for thought. Trey's fingers were on her hand, sliding slowly up her arm, curling around her shoulder to draw her closer. How was it possible for her to feel this way? One look, one touch, and her whole body came alive. Her heartbeat increased, happiness and excitement welled within her, bubbling up from the deepest part of her being. She felt like laughing, singing. Shouting for the sheer joy of it.

Lifting her into his arms, he carried her to the overstuffed chair and sat down.

"Amanda."

She took a deep breath, but before she could speak,

he was kissing her, his arms strong and sure around her. There was no doubt, no hesitation. He knew what she wanted better than she knew herself.

The rain, the room, everything seemed to fade away as Trey's mouth moved over hers, never rough, never demanding, ever gentle.

She surrendered to him with a sigh, every fiber of her being caught up in the sweet fire of Trey's lips on hers. Impossible. Magical. Heat flowed through her.

His hand slid under her sweater, encountering warm flesh, making her quiver with desire as he cupped her breast. An image of the bed only a few feet away flashed across her mind.

He murmured her name, his voice sandpaper-rough with desire as he kissed her again, his tongue sliding over her lower lip in silent entreaty. Like a flower opening to the sun, she opened for him, aching, yearning. No one had ever made her feel like this before. Not her high school boyfriend. Not Rob . . .

Rob! An image of his face, his eyes filled with silent accusation, rose up in her mind. His ring on her finger was suddenly an unwelcome weight.

Pushing against Trey's chest, she stood up, her breathing ragged. What was she doing here?

Trey rose to his feet in a single, fluid movement, reaching for her.

Amanda shook her head. "No. I can't do this."

His eyes were hot. "You were doing just fine, sweetheart."

"No!"

"No?"

"I can't do this. I'm engaged. To Rob."

"You weren't thinking about Rob a few moments ago."

It was true, and she couldn't deny it. What did that say about her relationship with Rob? She touched the ring on her finger, turning it around and around. If she loved him, really loved him, would she have been so quick to fall into the arms of another man? A man who was, for all intents and purposes, a complete stranger?

"I'd better go," she said hoarsely, and ran out of the room.

For a moment, she stood outside in the rain, letting it cool her heated cheeks. What had she done? How was she going to explain it to Rob?

And how was she going to face Trey in the morning?

Chapter Eleven

Trey climbed out of bed and ran a hand through his hair. It had been a long, sleepless night. Every time he closed his eyes, he had seen Amanda, remembered how her kisses had aroused him, how good she had felt in his arms. Angered by her abrupt departure, he had paced the floor far into the night. Hell, he could have walked back to her house with all the miles he had put on the rug.

Crossing the floor, he drew back the curtain and looked out the window. He wouldn't have been surprised to discover she'd taken off without him, but her fancy car was still there, as sleek and beautiful as the lady herself. It had stopped raining. The sky was clear and blue, the sun shining brightly.

Damn! What was he going to do about Amanda?

Another half hour passed before he heard her knock on the door.

There was an awkward moment of silence when he opened the door.

"Are you ready?" she asked, not meeting his eyes.

"Yeah. Just let me get my boots."

She waited in the doorway while he sat on the edge of the bed and pulled them on. Grabbing his hat, he settled it on his head, then followed her out to the car, waited while she unlocked the door and slid behind the wheel.

He ducked inside and closed the door, watched while she backed up and drove out onto the street. He wondered if she'd ever let him have a try at driving the car.

"Are you hungry?" she asked.

He shrugged. "If you are."

"I'm not."

"Okay by me." He swore silently, angered by the wall she had erected between them. Last night, she had been like a living flame in his arms; this morning, she was like ice. "What are you gonna do about that tree?"

She shrugged. "Hope that it's been cleared away."

"Cleared away by who?"

"The road maintenance people."

"And if it hasn't?"

"I don't know. Go back to the motel and call for help, I guess," she replied, her voice cool. Taking one hand from the wheel, she turned on the radio.

He grunted softly. If she didn't want to talk, that was fine with him. He'd try to catch up on the sleep he had lost the night before.

He sat back, his hat pulled low over his eyes, listening to some gravel-voiced singer lament over a love that had gone bad. Interesting thing, radio, he thought. And television. And all the other things she had shown him. Things he had never imagined, things he would never have believed existed if he hadn't seen them with his own eyes. Her car, for instance. It was comfortable. It was fast. But the car was just a machine, cold, unfeeling. Give him a good horse any day. Like Relámpago.

He sat up, pushing his hat back, as the car came to a stop. "Something wrong?"

"No. I need to go to the store. I'll be back in a few minutes."

She exited the car. He watched her walk across the blacktop toward Tom's Market; a moment later, he followed her.

It was kind of like a general store, he thought. Looking around, he spotted Amanda pushing some sort of cart down the aisle. She didn't look happy to see him when he fell into step beside her.

He studied the boxes stacked on the shelves that lined both sides of the aisle. Cocoa Puffs. Rice Krispies. Count Chocula. Mini-Wheats. He shook his head. "What is this stuff?"

"Cereal." She picked a box of Rice Krispies off the shelf and tossed it in the cart.

The next aisle held shelf after shelf of bread. Old-fashioned Rye. Country Potato. Hawaiian. Homestyle White. Country Wheat. Wheat Berry. Wheat and Honey. He shook his head. He'd always thought bread was bread. He picked up two loaves. One was whole; one was sliced. He shook his head again. Seemed peo-

135

ple in this day and age didn't even have to slice their own bread unless they had a mind to.

Amanda dropped a loaf of wheat bread into the cart.

They walked down an aisle of canned goods and bottles of fruit juice; an aisle filled with various kinds of paper goods; an aisle filled with candy and cookies, nuts, coffee and cocoa, marshmallows and puddings.

The next aisle held frozen foods. Trey stood there wide-eyed. There was a long double row of glass-fronted cupboards, some of the glass looking kind of frosty. The temperature along the aisle was colder than in the rest of the store. Amanda opened one of the doors, and a puff of cold air touched his skin. She pulled a carton of chocolate ice cream off the shelf and closed the door. It closed with authority, like a bank vault.

A little further on, she selected several packages of vegetables. Trey picked one up, feeling the chill sink into his fingers. The package said "Frozen," and it was as cold and hard as a block of ice. He marveled that it was possible to keep food frozen when there was no ice in sight.

"It works like my refrigerator back home," Amanda explained, seeing his puzzled look.

He nodded. Electricity again.

Perhaps most remarkable of all was the meat section. He stared at package after package of meat. Steaks, pork chops, chicken, and all kinds of fish and what was labeled as seafood. They were a long way from any ocean, and he read the labels and signs with interest: crab, shrimp, shark, albacore. At least he recognized the ice. A sign over a large tank read "Fresh lobster." In another case, there were whole turkeys and whole chickens, neatly cleaned and plucked, and cans that said they had smoked hams inside them. Smoked ham he knew, and his mouth watered at the thought.

Amanda put some slabs of steak, red and heavily marbled, in her cart. They were in individual packages, wrapped in transparent coverings. The pork chops and the whole chicken she selected were packaged the same way.

The last stop was the dairy section. He read the cartons. Buttermilk. Whole milk. Lowfat milk. Nonfat milk. Butter was in this section, as well as items he had never heard of: margarine, cottage cheese, yogurt.

"Unbelievable," Trey muttered. Didn't anyone milk their own cows anymore?

He followed her to the checkout counter, watched in awe as the clerk added up her purchases. She paid with her credit card, a young boy put the groceries into some kind of bag, then placed them in her cart.

"I'll do that," Trey said when Amanda started to push the cart toward the door.

"I can do it," she retorted. He didn't argue, just placed his hands over her.

She relented without another word and led the way out to the car. She unlocked the trunk and he put the bags inside. She watched with obvious disapproval when he reached for his Colt.

A few moments later, they were on the road again.

Knowing his gun made Amanda nervous, Trey slid it under his seat.

"Where does all the food in the store come from?" he asked.

"Farmers, ranchers. I think most of it is brought in by truck."

"Damnedest thing I've ever seen. Don't people grow their own food anymore?"

"Not many. Farming and agriculture is a huge business."

With a shake of his head, he settled back in his seat.

She slowed the car as they reached the curve in the road. The tree had been dragged away. Two men clad in strange hats and bright orange overalls waved as they drove past.

Amanda waved back.

A short time later, she pulled up in front of her house.

Trey unfastened his seat belt and slid out of the car. He helped Amanda carry the groceries into the house, then headed for the barn.

Relámpago let out a shrill whinny as Trey opened the door and stepped inside.

"Hi, fella," Trey said, scratching the horse's ears. "Bet you thought I was never coming back."

The stud tossed his head, then shoved his nose against Trey's arm.

"Coming up," Trey said, and scrambling up the ladder, he dropped two flakes of hay into the horse's feeder.

He was filling the stud's water barrel when Amanda entered the barn.

"Is he all right? I feel awful," she remarked. "Leaving him locked up in here for so long."

"He's been through worse," Trey replied with a shrug. "I'll turn him out later."

"Whatever," she said, and left the barn.

Trey stared after her. Damn! What the hell was "whatever" supposed to mean?

Filled with sudden restless energy, Trey grabbed a shovel. Opening the stall door, he began shoveling manure into a wheelbarrow.

When he was finished, he dumped the manure out behind the barn and spread it around with a rake. He stood there for a moment, gazing into the distance, one arm propped on the tip of the handle. He grunted softly, wondering, for the first time, what the posse had thought when he vanished without a trace. He thought about his grandfather. He had promised Walker on the Wind he would return home when he had avenged Louis's death. But Hollinger still lived. And now he was here, in the far distant future, with no idea how to get back where he belonged. And then there was Amanda . . . Amanda, with her silky red hair, luminous green eyes, and a body that he couldn't stop thinking about. Damn, but she had felt good in his arms! Women had never been a problem for him. He didn't know why they were drawn to him, but they were. Maybe it was his love 'em and leave 'em attitude. He knew some women saw it as a challenge of some kind and longed to prove he couldn't live without them. Maybe it was his Apache blood that made him attractive—the lure of the forbidden, the dangerous, the unknown.

He laughed out loud. Damn, she must be driving him crazy for him to be having thoughts like that. The long and the short of it was, he liked women and they liked him. And Amanda had been no different until she suddenly remembered she was engaged. What kind of man was . . . what was his name? Rob?

Muttering an oath, he took the wheelbarrow and rake back to the barn. Removing his hat, he wiped the sweat from his brow with his forearm. Settling his hat back on his head, he opened the door to the stallion's stall, and went outside. Relámpago trailed after him like a puppy. He put the stud in the corral, gave him a pat on the shoulder, and went up to the house.

He found Amanda in the kitchen, laying out enough grub to feed the Seventh Cavalry. Bacon and eggs. Waffles. Sausage. Fried potatoes. Something called cantaloupe. Orange juice. Coffee.

"You expecting company?" he asked dryly.

"Just sit down and eat."

"Yes, ma'am." Removing his hat, he tossed it on the counter.

She was a good cook, and he was hungry now. So was she. Between them, they finished up everything except the potatoes and half a sausage. All in silence so thick he could have cut it with a knife.

As soon as she finished eating, she stood up and began to clear the table. He sat back in his chair, a cup of coffee cradled in his hands, and watched her. She was angry. It was obvious in every taut line of her body, every movement as she rinsed the dishes and shoved them in the dishwasher, then filled the sink with water and began to wash the frying pans.

She gave a little cry of dismay as she reached into the sink. Pulling her hand from the water, she stared at the blood filling her palm.

Trey was on his feet in an instant. Setting his cup on the table, he snatched the towel from the back of a chair and wrapped it tightly around her hand. "What happened?"

"I must have cut it on a knife. I'm all right." She tried to pull her hand from his.

"Yeah, you look all right. You look like you're gonna faint."

"I feel that way, too," she murmured, swaying against him.

He sat down, drawing her down on his lap. "Let me take a look at it."

She glanced away while he studied the cut in her hand. It was long, but not too deep.

"How'd you ever manage to cut a bullet out of me?" he asked.

"Oh, I don't mind the sight of blood," she said weakly, "as long as it's not mine."

He laughed at that as he wrapped the cloth around her hand again. Rising, he sat her down in his chair. "Stay here. I'll be right back."

Amanda stared after him. He was a rogue, she thought, with a killer smile and a laugh that made her insides curl. He was a stranger, a man from another time, and he made her feel more alive, more feminine, than any man she had ever known. How dull her life had been without him! Though she hated to admit it, she knew she would miss him terribly if he was suddenly zapped back to his own time.

He returned a few minutes later carrying the roll of gauze, tape, and the bottle of disinfectant she had left on his bedside table, along with a wet washrag.

She looked up at him, a question in her eyes.

"Don't worry," he said. "I know what I'm doing."

Kneeling in front of her, he unwrapped the towel from her hand and spread it on her lap. Then, very gently, he washed her palm and coated it with disinfectant. Next, he wound several layers of gauze around her hand, and then taped it in place.

She checked the bandage. "You do know what you're doing," she allowed.

Still on his knees, he looked up at her. "Why'd you run away last night? What were you afraid of?"

On the way home, she had vowed to put some distance between them, but now, gazing deep into his eyes, it was all she could do to keep from running her fingers through his hair, to keep from bending down and pressing her lips to his.

"Amanda?"

"Nothing," she said. "I wasn't afraid."

"No?"

"No. Ohmigosh, look at the time!" she exclaimed, and jumped to her feet.

"What the . . . where the devil are you going?"

"I've got to go . . . go . . . wash my hair," she said, and hurried out of the room and up the stairs.

Trey stared after her. Wash her hair? Not likely!

Amanda hid in her room the rest of the morning. It was a cowardly thing to do, and she knew it. What was worse, she knew he knew exactly what she was doing, and why. But she couldn't help it. Every time he looked at her, she melted like ice cream on a summer day. Never before had a man affected her so strongly.

Why had he come along now, when she was engaged to someone else?

She looked at the picture of Rob she kept on her dresser. Had his eyes always been that close together, his nose that sharp, his lips that thin? She thought of Trey's full lower lip, remembered the touch of it, the taste of it.

"Stop it!" she muttered. "You love Rob, and he loves you."

But did she, really? How could she truly be in love with Rob if another man attracted her so? She'd hardly spared Rob a thought since Trey's mysterious appearance. Of course, she could make excuses for that. Trey had been hurt. She had been naturally curious about who he was and where he came from. She had been worried about him, afraid he might die.

Curious? her conscience chided. *Is that why you kissed him? Because you were curious?*

"Oh, shut up."

She'd said she was going to wash her hair, so she went into the bathroom and turned on the shower. Maybe she should make it a cold one, she thought. Maybe that would drive him out of her mind.

It didn't.

She washed her hair. She put a fresh Band-Aid over the cut in her hand. She did her nails. She applied her makeup carefully, and refused to think of why she was going to so much trouble. She pulled on a pair of stretch jeans and a tank top, put on her shoes, and then, with a sigh, she sat down on the edge of the bed. How could she face him after the way she had run out of the room?

143

She almost jumped out of her skin when he knocked on the door.

"You ever coming out of there?" he called, and she heard the laughter in his voice. "I'm getting hungry."

Just like a man, she thought irritably, always expecting to be waited on. Taking a deep breath, she stood up and opened the door. "I was just coming down."

He looked at her, one brow arched.

"Well, I was!" she snapped.

He wisely refrained from saying anything further as he followed her down the stairs and into the kitchen.

He stood in the doorway, his arms folded across his chest, while she opened the refrigerator and slammed things down on the counter.

She had just finished making two sandwiches when the doorbell rang.

Trey automatically reached for his Colt, swore under his breath when he realized it was still under the seat in the car. He was getting damned careless, his mind too much on this woman. He pulled the big Bowie knife from its sheath on his gun belt, which was still draped over the chair where he'd left it the day before.

"What are you doing?" she asked, her eyes wide. "This isn't the Wild West, you know. Put that thing away."

The doorbell rang again.

Amanda looked at Trey, who was still holding the knife. With a shake of her head, she went to answer the door.

"Rob!" Dressed in a white sport shirt, a pair of gray

slacks, and black loafers, his blond hair freshly cut, he looked as handsome as always.

"Hi, honey bunch. Thought I'd surprise you." Pulling her into his arms, he kissed her soundly, then grinned at her. "I see the horse came back."

"Yes," she said, her mind whirling. How was she going to explain Trey to Rob?

"You got anything to eat?" Rob asked, closing the door behind him.

"Sure, I was just making lunch." Taking a deep breath, she went into the kitchen.

Trey looked up as she entered the room. "Who was at the . . ." His voice trailed off at the sight of the man entering the kitchen behind her. Trey stared at the stranger, certain they had met before, but of course that was impossible.

"Trey, this is my fiancé, Rob Langley. Rob, this is Trey. He's . . . he's a friend of . . . of my family's. From Montana."

Trey looked at her, one brow arched. Montana?

Rob glanced casually at the wicked-looking blade in Trey's hand. "Heck of a mayonnaise knife," he said.

Trey wasn't sure what mayonnaise was, but he certainly understood the casual challenge in the other man's words. He shoved the Bowie back into its sheath as Rob stepped forward, smiling, one hand outstretched. "Whereabouts in Montana are you from?"

"Billings," Trey answered, shaking Rob's hand. At the moment, it was the only Montana town that came to mind.

"Always a pleasure to meet a friend of Amanda's."

Rob sat down at the table. "I didn't catch your last name."

"Long Walker," Trey said.

"Sounds Native American," Rob said. "Or do you prefer Indian?"

"It's Apache," Trey said. *Native American? What the hell was that?*

Rob grunted. "Apache, you say? I've met a few in my time." He glanced at the gun belt draped over the chair. "I reckon that's yours. Looks like fine old hand-tooled leather. Mind if I have a look?"

Trey handed it across.

Rob examined the leather work with appreciation, touched the haft of the knife. "Do you mind?"

Trey hesitated a moment, then shook his head. Rob slid the knife from the sheath, handling the blade in the manner of a man familiar with weapons.

"Handmade, or I miss my guess," Rob said. "And by a master smith. Impressive." He slid the knife back into the sheath and turned his attention to the empty holster. "Authentic—not one of those stiff-leather Hollywood things. Is there a six-gun that goes with it?"

"It's . . ." Trey paused, wondering how to explain that his Colt was in Amanda's car.

"I'll go get it," Amanda said quickly, and left the kitchen.

Rob raised his eyebrows. "You let her handle your firearms?"

"Seemed safe enough," Trey ventured. "Although she said they make her nervous."

"Weapons make her nervous?" Rob said with a chuckle. "Do tell. That's something she'll have to get over, since she's marrying a bounty hunter."

Before Trey could come up with a suitable reply, Amanda was back, holding his Colt with both hands. Rob held out his hand expectantly. She glanced at Trey for approval, then offered Rob the pistol, butt first.

"Good girl," he said with a smile of approval. He thumbed open the loading gate, spun the cylinder with familiarity. "One empty chamber under the hammer," he said. "You're a careful man. I like that. So am I." He punched the five live rounds out into his palm and stood them neatly in a row on the table, then turned the weapon over in his hands, aimed it at the far wall, checking its balance.

Next he examined the barrel, reading the patent and proof marks. His brows furrowed thoughtfully.

"I took this for a replica," he said. "Look at that bluing. Damn thing looks almost new, just a little holster wear. But the barrel markings—is this an authentic Colt's .45?"

"I don't use any other kind," Trey said.

"Well," Rob said, looking at Amanda, "I am very impressed. Your friend walks around using an authentic Colt for his Old West getup." He hefted the gun again. "I could get three thousand dollars for this if I could get a dime." He looked at Trey. "I don't suppose you'd consider parting with it? How long have you had it?"

"I'll hang on to it," Trey said. "I got it in Tucson a few years back."

He didn't say he'd paid forty dollars for it brand-new. This man knew too much about guns. Like everything else in this century, the price of weapons seemed to have gone sky high, though he couldn't imagine anyone paying three thousand dollars for a gun.

Rob nodded as he handed the weapon to Trey. "I'll be going to Tucson on business in a couple of days. What's the name of the dealer where you bought that Colt? I'd like to pick one up. I collect old guns. The real thing when I can find them; reproductions when I can't."

Trey stepped to the table, opened the gun's loading gate, and replaced the ammunition. He wasn't sure what a reproduction was, but he sure as hell wasn't going to let good old Rob know that.

"I'm sorry," he said. "The fella I bought it from is dead." Bound to be, Trey mused, since the sale had taken place over a hundred years ago.

"Too bad," Rob said. "Guess I'll just settle for lunch."

"And it's ready," Amanda announced as she finished making Rob's sandwich. She put a plate in front of Trey and one in front of Rob. "What would you two like to drink?"

"Iced tea if you've got it," Rob said.

Trey looked up at Amanda, a question in his eyes. She frowned at him, her expression clearly saying, "Don't ask."

"I'm having coffee," she said. "Trey, would you like some?"

"Sure." He watched as she opened the refrigerator door, took out a pitcher, and filled a tall green glass with what looked like weak coffee. She added a spoonful of sugar, stirred it, and set it on the table in front of Rob.

"Hey," Rob said, taking hold of her bandaged hand. "What happened here?"

"It's nothing," she said. "I cut it on a knife."

"You sure it's okay? Did you have a doctor look at it?"

"It's fine." Sliding her hand out of his grasp, she poured two cups of coffee and put them on the table, then grabbed her own plate and, with a smile, sat down between the two men. "So, Rob," she said brightly. "Tell us about your trip. Did you catch your man?"

"Honey, don't I always?" Rob took a bite of his sandwich and washed it down with a long swallow of iced tea. "He's cooling his heels in jail where he belongs."

Trey grunted softly. "Bounty hunting pay good these days?"

"Not bad," Rob said, turning his gaze on Trey. "Bail bondsmen have a lot of bail money at stake when some dirtbag skips out on a court appearance. What line of work are you in?"

"Banking," Trey replied calmly. He bit back a grin when he saw Amanda's eyes widen.

"Good steady work," Rob said, though it was clear, from the tone of his voice, that he thought banking was about as exciting as working in a shoe store.

Trey glanced at Amanda. "I've found it to be profitable."

Amanda almost choked on her coffee at that. Rob leaned over and pounded her on the back.

Trey took that moment to make his exit. "I'll give you two a little privacy," he said.

Slinging his gun belt over his shoulder, he clapped his hat on his head and picked up what was left of his sandwich. Turning away from the table, he grabbed an apple out of the bowl on the counter and headed out the back way.

The stallion whinnied softly when he heard the kitchen door open.

"Hey, boy," Trey said, approaching the corral. He held out the apple. "Here ya go."

The stallion tossed his head, then plucked the apple from Trey's hand. Juice dripped from the stud's mouth as he noisily ate the fruit, core and all.

Trey leaned against the fence post. "Did you see him, that bounty hunter?" he asked the stallion. "Hell, he was so pretty, I felt like tippin' my hat."

The stallion blew out a breath, which sounded strangely disdainful.

Trey ginned. "Yeah. What does she see in that ten-derfoot?" Finishing his sandwich, he wiped his hands on the sides of his jeans. "He doesn't look like any bounty hunter I ever saw. Not like old Wolf Langley. Now, there's a man to be reckoned with, but . . ."

Trey cursed as his mind made the connection. Langley! No, it couldn't be. . . . No wonder the man looked familiar.

Impossible as it was to believe, Trey would swear that that greenhorn up at the house was related to Wolf Langley.

Chapter Twelve

Amanda sat back in her chair, listening to Rob as he related how he had tracked Jeb Bolander to his family's house in West Virginia.

"You should have seen that place," he said. "Looked like something out of *Deliverance*. His old lady came after me with a rolling pin. And his two brothers threatened to skin me alive."

"Rob, that's awful!"

He brushed off her concern with a wave of his hand. "Not really. It happens all the time."

"Well, I'm glad you made it home safe."

Her mind wandered as he reminisced about other cases he had been on. Once, she had been fascinated by his stories; now, she found herself wondering where Trey had gone. Trey Long Walker. She recalled wondering if he had Indian blood when she first saw him. Now she knew.

Once, she had thought Rob the handsomest of men; now, she found herself comparing him to Trey; now Rob came in a poor second.

Once, she had been excited at the thought of being Rob's wife; now . . .

"What?" She gave a guilty start as she realized Rob had asked her something and she had no idea what it was.

"I said where would you like to go tonight?"

"Go?"

"Sure. We always go out to dinner when I get home. What are you in the mood for tonight? Italian? Chinese? Hey, there's a new sushi bar in town."

"Sushi!" She grimaced.

"I'll get you to try it sooner or later."

"I doubt it. Anyway, I probably shouldn't go . . ."

"Why not?"

"Well, I have company, and—"

"I'm sure he'll understand."

"I'm sure he would, but it would be rude of me to go off and leave him here alone."

"I see. So, you're more concerned about his feelings than mine, is that it?"

"Of course not," she said quickly. "But . . ."

"I wasn't going to mention it, but you didn't sound too happy to hear from me when I called the other night."

"Oh, that."

"Yes, that."

"I was just . . . you know, just distracted."

"By Long Walker?" he asked sharply.

"Yes. No. I . . ." She looked at Rob helplessly, not knowing what to say.

"So that's the way it is. I think I'd better be going," he said, pushing away from the table. "I wouldn't want to keep you from your 'guest.' "

"Rob . . ." She stood, torn between asking him to stay and wanting him to leave so she could go out and see what Trey was doing.

He brushed a kiss across her cheek. "I'll call you next week," he said.

"Fine."

She watched him walk out of the room. Why wasn't she more upset that he was leaving? Why hadn't she tried to placate him, the way she usually did? She hadn't seen him in almost a week, yet she wanted to be with Trey more than she wanted to be with Rob.

"I don't love him," she murmured. "Maybe I never did." She looked at the ring on her finger, then slowly slid it off and put it in the empty candy dish on the mantel. Surprisingly, she felt suddenly light and carefree.

Going to the window, she looked outside. Rob's car was a distant cloud of dust, but it was Trey who held her attention. He was standing inside the corral, talking to the stallion. Her gaze moved over him. He was tall and lean and rugged, a feast for her eyes from his thick blue-black hair and broad shoulders to his slim hips and long, long legs. He had strapped on his gun belt and the wicked-looking knife. The Colt looked good on his hip, as if it belonged there. A few years back, he would have been the perfect model for the Marlboro man.

She glanced at the dishes on the table. They could wait, she decided, and went outside, her heart pounding, her stomach fluttering with excitement.

"He didn't stay long," Trey remarked as she approached.

She shrugged. "I think he's mad at me."

"Why?"

"Well, he asked me to go out with him, and I said no, that I didn't want to leave you here alone."

Trey raised one brow. "Afraid I'll steal the family silver?"

"Of course not. The truth is, I just didn't want to go."

Trey grunted softly. "I thought you were in love with the guy."

She lifted one hand and studied her nails for a moment before replying, "I thought so, too."

Trey's gaze moved over her. She was prettier than a little red heifer in a field of flowers. "He'll be back."

"Maybe."

Trey fought down an unreasonable wave of jealousy. "No maybe about it. The man would be a fool to . . ."

She looked up, meeting his eyes. "To what?"

"Nothing."

"Why the gun?"

"I thought I'd take Relámpago out for a while."

"Oh." She hesitated a moment. "Would you mind . . . can I come along?"

"We'd have to ride double."

"I don't mind."

"Okay by me." Trey opened the corral gate and whistled softly.

Relámpago followed him back to the barn, and whiskered when Trey saddled the stallion. Returning to the corral, Trey lifted Amanda onto Relámpago's back, then swung up behind her and took up the reins. "Where shall we go?"

She glanced at him over her shoulder. "Where were you going?"

"No place in particular."

"Sounds good to me."

Trey clucked to the stud and the horse moved out. Once clear of the yard, he followed what looked like a game trail.

"What are you doing living out here by yourself?" Trey asked. "It's not safe for a woman alone."

"I'm just as safe here as anywhere else. There's violence everywhere these days, especially in some of the bigger cities. Gangs . . . young men with guns and a grudge against society are a big problem. Lots of kids, and adults, too, are doing drugs—"

"Drugs?"

"Yes. There's all kinds of things out there that are illegal that make you feel good—marijuana, crack, heroin. Unfortunately, some of them also make you crazy in the head." She laughed softly. "Life was probably safer, and saner, in your time than it is now."

Trey grunted softly. His time. How was he ever going to find his way back to his own time? And did he really want to?

They rode in silence for a while. Trey tightened his arm around her waist a little, and she leaned back against him. Her scent filled his nostrils. A few strands of her hair fluttered against his cheek. He moved his arm a little, and felt the warmth of her breasts.

He shifted in the saddle as his jeans grew suddenly tight in a particular area of his anatomy.

It was pretty country. Red hills, blue sky, the desert blooming from the recent rains. For the first time in years, he felt tongue-tied, awkward, like some green kid with his first girl. Hell, he hadn't been this nervous with his first girl. Of course, she hadn't been a girl, but a woman in her prime, a little overblown, with a lot of experience where men were concerned. She had been patient with him, and after he had taken her, rough and quick the first time, she had shown him there was a better way.

Amanda looked at him over her shoulder. "What are you thinking about?"

And he blushed like a kid caught with his pants down behind the barn.

"Well, come on, tell me," she said, grinning.

"We'd better stop here." He slid over Relámpago's rump, and then lifted Amanda from the stud's back.

"Why are we stopping?"

"My back's a little sore." It wasn't the truth, but he couldn't tell her that her nearness was playing havoc with his senses.

She sat down on a flat rock. "Tell me about your life," she said. "I don't know anything about you."

He sat cross-legged on the ground facing her. "There's not much to tell."

"Oh, come on. A bank robber from the past, and there's nothing to tell!"

He grunted softly.

"You told Rob you're Apache," she remarked. "On whose side?"

"My mother's. Is that a problem?"

"No. I've always loved Indians."

"Yeah?"

She nodded. "They fascinate me. Their way of life and beliefs. I've read a lot about them."

"It's a good way to live."

"Why did you rob that bank?"

As briefly as possible, he told her about Hollinger, and how the banker had refused to grant his father an extension on their loan. "And then, when I had the man in my sights, I couldn't do it," he said, his voice thick with self-disgust. "I couldn't pull the trigger."

"I'm glad."

He looked at her askance, one brow raised.

"Bank robbery is one thing, murder is another."

"Hollinger murdered my old man, and no one did a damn thing about it."

"Trey—"

"Why would they?" he said bitterly. "He was just a drunk, a squaw man."

Leaning forward, she placed her hand on his knee. "I'm sorry, Trey."

He looked up and met her eyes, and suddenly the past didn't matter. Nothing mattered but now, and the woman sitting across from him, her green eyes dark with compassion.

"Are you gonna marry that tenderfoot?"

Amanda stared at Trey. It was a question she had asked herself ever since he rode into her life.

She was still trying to form an answer when Trey

dragged her onto his lap and kissed her. At the first touch of his lips on hers, her eyelids fluttered down, her heartbeat increased. The world and its troubles fell away. Her arms went around him, holding him tight. His tongue slid over her lower lip, tantalizing, softly entreating, and she opened for him, shivers of delight coursing through her. She pressed against him, wanting to feel the hardness of his body against her own. Her hands moved restlessly up and down his back, then slid under his shirt, reveling in the touch of his skin, the way his muscles rippled beneath her fingertips.

She drew back as her hand encountered the bandage swathed around his middle. "Did I hurt you?"

He groaned deep in his throat. "I'm hurting, sweetheart, but not there."

He wanted her. The knowledge filled her with pleasure and a sense of power. She dragged her fingertips lightly up and down his spine. When his hand brushed against her breast, she moaned with pleasure, leaning into his touch, wanting more. More.

She shifted uncomfortably as her hip pressed against the butt of his gun, and she burst out laughing.

Trey drew back. "What's so funny?

She shook her head, unable to stop laughing. "Is that a gun in your pocket," she gasped, wiping the tears from her eyes, "or are you just glad to see me?"

He frowned at her. "What?"

"Nothing. It's an old joke."

"Heck of a time to be making jokes," he muttered.

But it had come at just the right time, she thought, before things between them went any farther. There was too much standing between them now, and Rob was the least of her worries. She was afraid she was falling in love with Trey, afraid he'd suddenly disappear from her life and take her heart with him. That would be bad enough, but if they were intimate . . . she shook her head. Now was not the time to be falling head over heels into his arms. Not until she knew if he felt the same. Not without some kind of commitment, though promises of forever seemed out of the question, given the circumstances.

Rising, she brushed off her jeans. "I think we'd better go."

He rose to his feet in a lithe, easy motion. "If that's what you want."

"Trey—"

He waved a hand, silencing her. "You changed your mind. Hey, I understand."

"I don't think so," she muttered dryly.

He moved toward her, a hungry look in his eye. "Wanna explain it to me?"

She held out her hands to hold him off. "Trey, this is all happening way too fast. And—"

"Not too fast for me," he said, a wicked gleam in his eye.

"And we don't know how long you'll be here—"

"All the more reason to hurry."

"No!" She stamped her foot. "Listen to me!"

"Sweetheart, you're not saying anything I wanna hear."

"Trey, I can't just fall into your arms. I want more than just a . . . a . . . quick roll in the hay."

He came to an abrupt halt. "Is that what you think this is?"

"I don't know." She lifted her chin. "Is it?"

Trey muttered an oath. Women always wanted to talk at the wrong time. "I don't know what to tell you. All I know is I want you, and as near as I can tell, you want me. Why complicate it with a lot of talk?"

"I don't know what kind of women you're used to," she retorted, her cheeks flushing, "or what kind of woman you think I am, but I'm not in the habit of falling into bed with every dusty cowhand who rides up to my door."

Trey held up both hands. "Easy now."

She took a deep, calming breath. "I think we'd better go back before we both say things we might regret."

"Yeah," he muttered. "I think you're right."

He lifted her onto Relámpago's back and swung up behind her. Taking up the reins, he clucked to the stud.

It was a long, quiet ride back to the house.

There was a battered red pickup truck with a dented fender parked near the barn when they rode into the yard.

Amanda frowned. "Wonder who that belongs to," she murmured.

Trey shrugged. He was about to dismount when he noticed two men in baggy overalls standing in the shadowy interior of the barn.

A third man, dressed in faded blue jeans, a black tee shirt, and a battered felt hat, stepped out of the house onto the front porch.

"What are you doing in my house?" Amanda exclaimed. Trey's arm tightened around her waist. She could feel the coiled tension in him.

"Just waiting for you to get home," the man drawled. He glanced at Trey. "Where's the bounty hunter?"

"Rob?" A shiver of unease slid down her spine. "Who are you?"

"Name's Bolander," the man on the porch said.

Bolander! Amanda shifted uneasily in the saddle. She felt Trey's breath fan her cheek as he whispered, "Easy, sweetheart."

The man on the porch smiled, revealing a mouthful of crooked yellow teeth. "Name rings a bell, I see. Why don't you two just step down from that there horse and we'll have us a talk about old Langley?"

"We're fine right here," Trey said over Amanda's head. "Say your piece."

She saw the man's expression go flat and hard. "Tough cowboy, huh?"

"Please . . ." she said. "What do you want?

"I ain't the Bolander that Langley went after, if that's what you're wonderin'," the man said grimly. "I'm his brother Nate. And that there's our brother Arnie, and our cousin Cletus." He scowled past her, his eyes narrowing as he looked at Trey. "Name mean anything to you, cowpoke?"

"Is it supposed to?" Trey drawled.

"It will," the big man promised. "It will."

Amanda glanced at the two men standing near the barn, then looked back at the man on the porch. "What do you want?" she repeated, hating the frightened quaver in her voice.

"Where's the bounty man?" Nate demanded. "Tell

161

us now, and we'll be on our way. Otherwise . . ." He crossed the porch and started down the stairs.

She felt Trey move behind her, heard the oily snick of his Colt being cocked.

"No," she murmured.

"He's not coming over here to shake your hand," Trey muttered, "and neither are those two hombres."

It was then she saw what Trey had obviously noticed earlier. One of the men was holding a sawed-off shotgun down along his pant leg, the other was carrying a short rifle the same way, one-handed. Her eyes widened and her heart seemed to jump into her throat. She swallowed hard.

Trey lifted the reins just a little. She heard him murmur something to Relámpago in what she assumed was Apache.

At the foot of the stairs, Nate Bolander reached under his shirt and produced a flat black automatic pistol. Before Amanda could quite take it all in, the stallion leaped forward. Nate let out a cry and fell back, his gun going off with a flat crack. But it was too late. The stallion was on him, slamming into his shoulder, tossing him back on the stairs.

A rifle barked from the direction of the barn, and Trey's revolver exploded thunderously from behind her.

Amanda screamed, her hands going over her ears. She fell back against Trey's chest as Relámpago broke into a dead run away from the house. Trey's rein arm steadied her like a living band of warm steel.

She risked a glance over her shoulder. Nate and Arnie were running for the truck. The third man, the one who had held the rifle, was on his hands and knees in the yard, rifle forgotten, his head hanging low.

The men running for the truck didn't spare a glance for their fallen comrade. The engine roared to life. The man on the passenger side leaned out the window, his shotgun tracking them.

It was hopeless, she thought. Relámpago would never be able to outrun the truck.

Trey's left arm stretched out to its full length, and the Colt in his hand barked twice in quick succession. She saw the windshield on the passenger's side of the truck web with cracks and sag inward. She couldn't see the man who had been hanging out the window anymore. Had he been hit?

An Apache war cry rose up in Trey's throat as he cranked off another round that ricocheted off the side of the cab.

Amanda felt suddenly numb. This couldn't be happening. Things like this happened to other people.

She screamed again as the truck drew closer. She could see the contorted face of the driver as he closed in on them, the concentrated fury in his eyes. He was going to ram the stallion with the truck!

They were going to die. The reality hit her with stunning force. She clung to Relámpago's mane, her ears ringing loudly from the gunfire and the roar of the truck's engine. Abruptly, uncannily, the noise in her head faded to a soft buzz, like bees in a field of wildflowers on a sleepy summer afternoon. Long fingers of swirling gray mist rose up out of the ground. And then everything went black.

Chapter Thirteen

Amanda shook her head. Awareness of her surroundings returned slowly. The buzzing inside her head faded, and she became aware of the sound of Relámpago's hoofbeats, walking now, not galloping wildly. The thick gray mist had disappeared. She was aware of Trey's arm, still around her, though not as tight as before.

There was no sign of the truck that had been pursuing them.

Amanda glanced around. The landscape looked the same, yet not the same. The most startling change was the grass, stirrup high, spreading off around them, dotted with clumps of creosote and sage, and the ever present, towering saguaro. She remembered a local environmentalist telling her that the patchy grass and bare eroded earth of the desert near her home were the result of a century of overgrazing. She had never seen the grass this lush, this high.

She shook her head again. It had been late afternoon before; now, the sun was just climbing in the sky. How was that possible? Had she been unconscious for more than a day?

Feeling more than a little disoriented, she looked over her shoulder at Trey. "What happened? I felt so strange for a minute there. Kind of dizzy."

He shook his head, looking as confused as she felt. "I'm not sure, but . . ."

His arm fell away from her waist and he leaned back a little, bringing his arm behind her. In between the muffled thuds of the stallion's hooves she heard a snick-snick as he rotated the cylinder of his gun, one chamber at a time. Empty cartridges rained down the saddle leather and disappeared in the grass below. The cylinder snicked through its cycle again, and she knew he was reloading. A moment later, his arm slid around her waist again.

"But what? Tell me."

"I had that same feeling once before."

A shiver went down her spine. "When was that?" She felt compelled to ask, though she was sure she didn't want to hear the answer.

"Just before I showed up in your yard."

"I was afraid you'd say that."

"Those old boys vanished in a heartbeat when that mist came up," he said. "Just like that posse that was chasing me did the last time. I think we're back, Amanda—back where I belong."

"Oh, no. No." She shook her head in denial. Glancing around again, she tried to find something, some point of reference that would prove him wrong. She couldn't, but she couldn't accept it. "What makes you think we're in your time?"

He laughed softly. "I don't know. It just feels . . . right."

"Right? How can it be right? If you're correct, I don't want to be here! Turn around. Let's go back."

"I'm not sure it works like that."

"What are you talking about?"

"I don't know if I can go back and forth at will. It wasn't something I was trying to do before, and it wasn't something I tried to do this time. It just happened."

"How did it happen before? You never told me."

"I was running from a posse."

"So that's how you got shot."

"Yeah. Almost as soon as I did . . . it happened. It was like 'Pago knew how to get me out of danger. I know that sounds crazy, but my grandfather told me 'Pago would always carry me to safety. I guess 'Pago knew you'd look after me."

"Well, turn Relámpago around. Let's go back to where it happened this time and at least try."

He did as she asked. Wheeling the stud around, they followed their back trail.

The wind stirred the tall grass; a cactus wren flitted across the sky.

Nothing else happened.

"Try again!" she said.

He reined the stallion around and did so. Again, nothing happened.

He tried it again, unbidden. And yet again.

"It's no use," he said. "Maybe it's still dangerous back there. That fella driving that truck was—crazy. And I'm only sure I got one of them. The other one, the one with the shotgun, he might still be alive and kickin'."

"But I don't want to stay here," she wailed. "You don't even have indoor plumbing." Or toilet paper, she thought.

"Sure we do," he said, grinning. "We call them chamber pots."

"Very funny."

He reined the stallion around once more and struck off in a new direction. She thought it might be south, but she'd never had a very good sense of direction.

"Where are you going?"

"Canyon Creek." He glanced up at the sky. "If we ride hard, we can be there by nightfall."

"But . . ." Canyon Creek! For a moment, she thought it might be fun to see the town the way it had been over a hundred and thirty years ago. But only for a moment.

He looked at her and grinned. "Don't know what we'll use for money, since you took all of mine."

"It wasn't yours," she retorted.

"Sure as hell was. I stole it, didn't I? And we could use some of it now."

Before she could argue further, he clucked to the stud and Relámpago broke into an easy, mile-eating lope.

167

Amanda watched the countryside slip by. It couldn't be real. She couldn't have been transported to the past. It was unthinkable, impossible. And maybe it wasn't true anyway. Just because Trey said "it felt right" didn't make it so. Maybe she was just imagining that the landscape looked different. Maybe the recent rains had caused the grass to come back so strongly, though she hadn't noticed it on their earlier ride.

They rode for several hours, not saying much. Her legs and seat began to ache from the saddle. But that was minor compared to her whirling thoughts. What if it was true, and she was in the past? How would she ever get home again? What about her house? The door was wide open. And her car? And what about those awful men who had come looking for Rob?

She shuddered at the thought of one or more of them lying dead on her property. No, the survivor or survivors would probably take the body. Would they trash her house for revenge? Take the Jag? And Rob— he was in danger. She had to get back, had to warn him! But how?

Her thoughts chased each other endlessly. When the buildings of a town finally showed in the distance, she realized that she was very tired. She stared at the town blankly. "That can't be Canyon Creek!"

He chuckled softly, his breath warm on her neck. "Yep, that's it. Just the way I remember it."

It was near dusk when they reached the outskirts of town. It didn't look like much from a distance, and looked even worse the closer they got. A sign read "Canyon Creek. Population 853." The dirt road they had been following for the last hour or so widened out, rutted like an old washboard. Fresh wheel tracks scored its surface. Wagon wheels, not tire tracks. Buildings lined both sides of the street. Most of the structures were made of raw, unpainted wood with false fronts and fancy names. The Monarch Hotel. The Emperor's Saloon. The Bon Ton Millinery Shoppe. She shook her head. They were in an untamed Western town, for crying out loud, not New York City. At any other time, she would have laughed, but not now, not with the reality of her situation bearing down on her.

A few side streets branched off the main road. She could see houses scattered beyond the town: a few large ones on the east side of Main Street, smaller dwellings on the west side.

If it had been shocking for Trey to see the town the way it was in her time, it was no less of a shock for her to see it as it was now. Every other building seemed to be a saloon: One Eyed Jack's, the Painted Lady, the Ace High, the Red Queen. Women in scanty attire lounged in front of the saloons, or hung over the second-floor balconies, flirting outrageously with the men who passed by on the boardwalk below.

Horses were tied to hitch racks in front of the various businesses. Sandwiched in among the saloons were a number of other stores and shops: a shoemaker, a dentist, a dressmaker, two barbershops, three laundries, a lawyer's office, a bank, a tailor, a bathhouse, a doctor's office, a drug store, several restaurants, a post office. There was a livery stable at one end of the street and a jail at the other. She recognized a few of the buildings, like the firehouse and the courthouse.

Beyond the town, there was nothing but wide-open

spaces as far as the eye could see. Near the outskirts of town were a number of corrals filled with cattle, and across from them a railroad station. There was a church in the center of town, and beside it a red schoolhouse. And further down the street a theater, of all things. The sign out front read "Canyon Creek Opera House. Now Starring Lily Victoria, the Louisiana Songbird."

Trey reined the stallion to a halt in front of a saloon that looked vaguely familiar. Amanda gasped as she read the red and white sign. "The Four Deuces." It seemed like only yesterday she and Trey had danced there. And in some reality, it *was* only yesterday, she realized. But terms like yesterday and tomorrow were hopelessly blurred now.

Sliding down the stud's rump, Trey looped the reins over the hitching post, then lifted her from the saddle.

"What are we doing here?" she asked.

"I'm broke."

She looked at him blankly.

"We need money," he said. "I aim to get some the best way I know how."

She looked at the saloon. "You're not going to rob the place, are you?"

"No, sweetheart. Just play a little poker."

"You're a gambler, too?"

"Well, it's a sight easier than robbing banks. Safer, too."

"Very funny," she muttered. She frowned as a man on the boardwalk stopped and stared at her. "What are you looking at?"

The man tipped his hat. "Sorry, ma'am, I was

just . . ." He glanced at Trey and cleared his throat uneasily. "I didn't mean no disrespect, ma'am," he said quickly, and hurried down the street.

"What was that all about?" Amanda asked.

"Your getup, I reckon."

"What do you mean?"

"Well, those pants, for one thing. And that there, ah, shirt, or whatever you call it."

Amanda glanced down at her clothes. She was wearing a pair of red stretch jeans, a white tank top, and white sneakers. "What's wrong with what I'm wearing?"

"Well, those duds might be all right for your time, but they're pretty scandalous for mine. That top is a mite revealing, and those jeans aren't like any that people hereabouts have seen before. Besides being red, they fit right snug. Not that I'm complainin', mind you, but—"

"They aren't that tight," she retorted.

He shrugged. "Wait here. I won't be long."

"I'm not sitting out here in the sun. I'm going with you."

"Decent women don't go into saloons."

"What are you going to use for money? I thought you were broke."

"Don't fret your pretty head about it." Turning, he climbed the stairs and disappeared through the saloon's swinging doors.

Amanda stood there a few minutes, idly patting Relámpago's neck while she watched the people on the street. And they were watching her. She noticed all the covert glances, as if she were a freak in a side show,

171

and felt her cheeks begin to burn. Their disapproval was almost tangible, though they pretended to ignore her as they went about their business.

She stared at the women strolling past. They wore high-necked, long-sleeved dresses made of calico and gingham and serge. Bonnets shaded their faces. They wore gloves and carried parasols. Dainty handbags that weren't big enough to hold her wallet, much less a cell phone, comb, brush, lipstick, checkbook, and day planner, dangled from their wrists. How did they endure being smothered in yards and yards of cloth when it was eighty degrees outside?

Men nodded and tipped their hats to these modestly clad women as they passed by, held doors open for them. If she hadn't believed she was in the past before, she believed it now.

The men all wore hats and boots and spurs. Most wore vests of some kind over long-sleeved cotton shirts, and trousers made of canvas or whipcord or wool. And they all carried guns.

She glanced at the saloon, gave the stud a final pat on the shoulder, and made her way up the stairs and into the saloon.

It took a moment for her eyes to adjust to the dim interior. The air smelled of tobacco smoke, alcohol, cheap perfume, and stale sweat. She grinned as she glanced around. It was like being in the middle of a Western-movie set. There was the typical long bar on one side of the room, complete with brass rail and spittoons. A number of gaming tables covered with what looked like green felt were situated in the center of the floor; there was a faro table in the back of the house. The floor was covered with sawdust. A trio of girls in short dresses and high-heeled boots wandered from table to table, laughing and smiling at the customers.

Trey was seated at a table near the back of the room. A guttering oil lamp hung from a chain above the table.

Skirting the room, she moved up to stand behind him, acutely aware of the men who turned to stare at her as she threaded her way through the crowded floor. There were three other men sitting at Trey's table, all concentrating on the cards in their hands.

Leaning forward a little, she saw that Trey held a pair of kings and a pair of tens. There were no numbers on the cards, just pictures and spots.

"I'll raise," said a man wearing a black bowler hat and string tie. He tossed a silver dollar into the pot.

"I'll see your raise," said the man beside him, "and kick it up another dollar."

"Two dollars to me," mused a man with a red handlebar mustache. He tossed his cards into the center of the table, face down. "Too rich for my blood." Looking up, he saw Amanda standing behind Trey. And winked at her.

Unable to help herself, she grinned at him.

Trey threw two silver dollars into the pot and added a third. She wondered where he'd got the money to bet with.

"All right," Black Bowler said. "What have you got?"

Trey laid his cards on the table. Two pair.

"Damn!" Black Bowler said. "I thought you were bluffing."

"Not me." Trey raked in the pot, sat back as Red Mustache dealt a new hand.

Amanda backed up a step as one of the saloon girls sashayed up to the table. The girl wore a short, low-cut red dress, black net stockings, and high-heeled shoes. Her eyes were lined with kohl, her cheeks rouged. Putting a hand on Trey's shoulder, she leaned forward, giving him a glimpse of her ample cleavage.

"How ya doin', honey?" the girl purred.

"Fine as a flea in a doghouse," Trey replied with a grin.

"Anything I kin get ya?" she asked.

"A glass of beer would just hit the spot."

The girl smiled at him and batted her lashes. "Sure thing, honey." Straightening, she looked at the other men. "Can I get you gents anything?"

Black Bowler ordered whiskey with a beer chaser, Red Mustache asked for beer, the third man shook his head.

"Be right back," the girl said, her hand trailing over Trey's shoulder.

"Be right back," Amanda mimicked under her breath. Unable to help herself, she moved up beside Trey and put her hand on his shoulder. "Hi, honey," she purred. "Can I get you anything?"

Startled, Trey stared up at her. "What the hell are you doing here?"

"I got bored waiting outside."

"You shouldn't be here." He glanced around the room. "Dammit, decent women don't frequent saloons."

The other men at the table were staring at her with avid curiosity.

"Who's your friend?" Black Bowler asked.

"Yeah," Red Mustache said. "Introduce us."

"Mind your own business," Trey said curtly. Pushing his chair away from the table, he stood and scooped up his winnings, which he shoved into his pocket. "Come on, let's get out of here," he said, and grabbing her by the arm, he practically dragged her out of the saloon.

"For goodness' sake," Amanda exclaimed, jerking out of his grasp. "You don't have to yank my arm off."

Trey muttered an oath. "What's the matter with you?"

"Me? What's the matter with *you*? I've never been so embarrassed in my life. How dare you drag me out of there like some . . . some—"

"You *should* be embarrassed, letting people see you in a place like that."

"*You* were in there."

"I'm a man."

She made a face at him. "What difference does that make? I'm over twenty-one."

He glared at her. "I told you—"

"Oh, just forget all that macho chauvinist stuff!"

He looked at her, one brow raised, a look of amusement dancing in his dark eyes as he stepped on to the street and untied Relámpago. "Chauvinist?"

"Never mind. Can we go get something to eat? I'm hungry."

"Sure." He settled his hat on his head and started walking down the street, leading the stallion.

She was aware of the looks that came her way from the people they passed. The men stared at her, their eyes filled with curiosity or lust. The women looked at her speculatively, or with obvious disdain. A few looked envious, no doubt because she wasn't weighed down by layers and layers of petticoats. Or maybe because she was with Trey. She didn't miss the looks they cast his way, or the envy in their eyes.

Trey tied the stallion to the hitch rail in front of Gordon's Restaurant, then stepped up on the boardwalk. Amanda followed him into the restaurant and they found an empty table near a window. It looked like a nice enough place. There were bright yellow cloths on the tables, frilly white curtains at the windows. The air was heavy with the odor of grease and onions.

Trey ordered a steak, rare, with all the trimmings. Amanda ordered a steak, too, thinking there wasn't much you could do to ruin a steak.

"So," she said, "how'd you get enough money to join the poker game?"

"Put my knife and my hat into the pot."

"I see you're still wearing both, so I guess you must have won. Do you play a lot of poker?"

"Some, now and then."

"I'll bet you cheat."

"Why the hell would you say that?"

"Do you?"

A slow smile spread over his face. "Only when I have to."

She couldn't help it. She laughed, and then grew thoughtful. "Do you have any family here?"

"In Canyon Creek? No. My Apache grandparents are still alive, though."

"Did you like living with the Apache?"

"I liked it fine. But I said I wouldn't go back until J. S. Hollinger was dead."

"You had your chance when you robbed the bank," she said. "Why didn't you do it then?"

"Beats the hell out of me." It was a question he had asked himself a hundred times.

"You're going to try again, aren't you? What if he kills you, instead?"

Trey shrugged. "It's a chance I'm willing to take."

And if he was killed, where would that leave her? she wondered.

The waitress brought their order. Amanda stared at her plate. The steak was the biggest one she had ever seen. There was hardly room for the mound of mashed potatoes and green beans that came with it.

Amanda cut into her steak and took a bite. It was not as rare as she liked, and would have benefited from a little A-1 Sauce, but, all in all, it wasn't bad.

Trey finished his before she was a third of the way through hers.

Amanda gestured at her steak. "Do you want the rest of mine?"

"Don't you want it?"

"No."

"Sure." He speared it with his fork and dropped it on his plate.

Amanda sat back, sipping her coffee, while he finished her steak. This couldn't be real, she thought. She wasn't cut out for life in the 1800's. She was a city girl through and through. She liked shopping and malls and movies and wash-and-wear clothes. She liked flush toilets and running water and microwave ovens and dishwashers, and television, even when there was nothing on. Women in the 1800's were little more than chattel, subject to their husbands' will, with few rights of their own. They did their laundry in rivers or washtubs and spent all day cooking and cleaning and sewing and making bread, not to mention caring for their children. They never had any time to themselves. They looked fifty when they were thirty.

Trey dropped some money on the table and rose to his feet. "Ready?"

"Yes." Rising, she followed him out the door. "Now what?"

"I'll get us a room." He took up the stud's reins and walked across the street to the Delaware Hotel.

Amanda hurried after him. "Us a room?" she said. "What do you mean, us?"

"Us, as in you and me, what do you think I mean? Oh," he said, "I reckon you want a room of your own." He tethered the stud to the hitch rack and they went into the hotel.

Amanda glanced around. It looked just like every hotel in every Western she had ever seen.

Trey stopped at the desk and asked for two rooms adjoining, one with a bathtub. He paid for the rooms, and the clerk handed him two keys.

"I'll have some hot water sent up right away," the clerk said. He stared surreptitiously at Amanda.

Trey nodded. "Obliged." He handed some greenbacks to Amanda. "I'll see you later."

"Where are you going?"

"I'm gonna get Relámpago settled in down at the livery, and then I'm gonna go find me another poker game, now that I've got a decent stake."

She yawned. "What am I supposed to do while you're gone?"

"It's been a long day. Why don't you go upstairs and get some sleep? In the morning, maybe you can go out and find yourself something to wear."

She wasn't crazy about the idea of staying in the hotel alone, but he was right. It had been a long day. She was exhausted and still a little befuddled from all that had happened since their run-in with the Bolanders.

"All right," she said, and taking the money from his hand, she went up the stairs.

Chapter Fourteen

Feeling at a loss, Amanda stood in the middle of the floor and looked around. It was a nice enough room, with a brass bed, a ladder-back chair, and a chest of drawers with a white pitcher and bowl on top. There was a colorful rag rug on the floor, a small oval mirror on one wall, three hooks for clothes, and a chamber pot under the bed.

"Indoor plumbing, indeed," she muttered.

A garish floral print wallpaper covered the walls. White lace curtains hung at the single window, which looked out over Main Street. She found a zinc tub behind a screen.

"All the comforts of home," she said, and wondered if she would ever see home again.

Crossing the floor, she opened the adjoining door. Trey's room looked much the same as hers. She started to shut the door, then decided to leave it open.

Going to the window, she gazed down into the street. A layer of dust, churned up by the wheels of several wagons and carriages, hung in the yellow lamplight spilling out of the saloons. She shook her head in disbelief when she saw a cowboy leave one saloon, mount his horse, ride across the street, dismount, and enter another saloon.

Further down the street, she saw a buxom blonde clad in a gaudy pink robe leaning over the balcony of a second-story building. A young freckle-faced cowboy stood on the street below, gawking up at her.

Amanda turned away from the window when someone knocked at the door. "Who is it?"

"We brung water fer yer bath."

"Oh." Opening the door, she saw a teenage boy and an elderly man standing in the hallway, each carrying two buckets of steaming water. "Come in."

She stood aside so they could enter the room, watched as they emptied the buckets into the tub.

She smiled as they finished their task. Plucking a dollar from the dresser, she handed it to the man. "Thank you."

The man smiled broadly as he pocketed the money. "A whole dollar! Why, thank you, ma'am. Anything you want, just let out a holler!" He nudged the boy. "Let's go, Johnny."

Amanda shut and locked the door behind them. She had no idea how much she had overtipped the man, but perhaps it had been a good idea. She would have to ask Trey about things like that.

With a sigh of resignation, she undressed and stepped into the tub. The water could have been hotter, and there could have been more of it, but at least it was clean. She bathed quickly and felt better for it.

Stepping out of the tub, she wrapped herself in a towel. The rough fabric was dingy, but it smelled clean. After rinsing out her underwear, she hung it over the back of the chair to dry. When that was done, she pulled on her jeans and shirt and crawled into bed. There was no way she was sleeping naked in a strange bed in a strange room in a strange town.

For all that she was exhausted, sleep was a long time coming. The sounds that filtered into the room from outside were strange, the bed was unfamiliar. What was she doing here? She was a city girl. She had never been one for roughing it. She hated camping, though she loved driving through the countryside. Her idea of a vacation was a hotel with room service. She liked clean sheets and fast food and expensive restaurants. She liked having her nails done, and lunch with the girls. What would her parents think when her phone went unanswered? What would Rob think when she didn't return his calls? When he came to the house and her car was there but she wasn't? Always supposing those ruffians hadn't stolen it, of course. She bit her lip. Somewhere in her time, the surviving bad guys were searching for the man she had promised to marry. And there was no way she could warn him.

The sheets were rough against her skin, and the blanket smelled faintly of mildew. The mattress was hard and lumpy compared to her Posture-Pedic. She shifted restlessly, trying to get comfortable. Her body ached from all the unaccustomed riding and she was very tired, but her mind kept racing. She didn't see how she was going to be able to sleep. . . .

She woke to bright sunlight streaming through the window. For a long moment, she was totally confused, wondering where she was, and then it all came rushing back. She sat up so quickly her head spun. It wasn't a dream. She was in the past. In Canyon Creek. She wondered what time it was. It felt late.

The door connecting her room to Trey's was open. She padded barefoot to the door.

He was asleep in the next room, fully clothed, on top of the covers. At least he'd removed his gun belt and boots. His room reeked of tobacco and stale beer—evidence of where he had spent much of the night. She wrinkled her nose, wondering if all the strong odors of this time period would eventually fade into the background.

He was sleeping peacefully, his strong features completely relaxed. She forgot the odors, thinking again how handsome he was, how dark his face and hands looked against his clothing and the dun-colored blankets.

Going back into her room, she closed the door. Undressing, she put on her underwear, dressed again, and then put on her socks and shoes. Looking in the cracked mirror, she grimaced at her reflection as she ran her fingers through her hair. She needed a lipstick, a comb, a brush. Toothpaste. She glanced at the chamber pot under the bed. Toilet paper.

A short time later, more appreciative than ever of flush toilets, she tiptoed into Trey's room. His boots stood in front of the dresser in his room, and his gun belt was coiled on top, the holster empty. Knowing him as she was beginning to, she realized the revolver was probably under his pillow. There was a pile of crumpled greenbacks beside the gun belt. He must have had a run of good luck, she thought. Moving on tiptoe, she approached the dresser. Taking a twenty and a ten from the pile, she shoved the bills in the pocket of her jeans. He didn't stir as she left the room, quietly closing the door behind her.

She was aware of the clerk staring at her as she walked across the hotel lobby to the front door. She definitely needed a change of clothes!

Outside, she glanced up and down the boardwalk, then turned left because it put the sun at her back.

Sounds and images imprinted themselves on her mind. The ringing of a blacksmith's hammer, the dust-muffled clop of hooves, the rattle of horse harness and creak of wagon wheels as a stage rumbled through town, the chiming of a distant clock.

The Old West. It was certainly different from what she had imagined. Noisier. Dustier. And it reeked to high heaven. Steam rose from fresh mounds of horse manure; the people on the boardwalks smelled as if a bath every Saturday was not something they truly believed in.

She paused when she came to Weston's Dry Goods. Taking a deep breath, she pushed open the door and stepped inside. A bell tinkled to announce her arrival.

She nodded at the man behind the counter, hardly noticing his inquisitive stare. She walked up and down the aisles. There were shelves filled with bolts of cloth:

muslin and linen, cotton and corduroy, gingham and serge. The odors of new cloth were a welcome contrast to the stench of the street. Even the clerk's cigar smelled clean in comparison. Moving on, she saw spools of thread and packages of needles, buttons, yarn and knitting needles, tape measures and patterns. She saw a pile of blankets on a table in one corner. And in the back of the store, several racks of ready-made dresses, petticoats, pantalets, and long cotton stockings.

She went through the dresses one by one. Most were plain cotton, with high necks and long sleeves. She paused when she came to a pretty blue gingham with a square neck and short, puffy sleeves edged with lace. She picked out a petticoat from a pile on a shelf and carried the dress and petticoat to the front counter.

"Afternoon, miss," the clerk said, his gaze darting over her attire. "Will that be all?"

"Is there a place where I can try this on?"

"Try it on?" He gulped and looked around. "Ah, back there." He waved to a doorway behind the counter.

"Thanks."

It wasn't a dressing room, but a storage room. Closing the door, she slipped off her shirt, took off her shoes and jeans, and stepped into the dress. There was no mirror, but the dress seemed to fit well enough. Lifting the skirt, she pulled on the petticoat, then put her shoes on and laced them up.

After running a hand through her hair, she rolled her old clothes into a ball, tucked them under her arm, and left the storage room.

"I'll take it," she said.

"You want to wear the dress and the, uh . . ." He cleared his throat and blushed. "The petticoat?"

"Yes, thank you. How much do I owe you?"

"Three dollars for the dress," he said, "and one dollar for the petticoat."

"Four dollars!"

"I'm sorry," he said quickly. "Prices have gone up a little."

Amanda stifled the urge to laugh as she dug four dollars out of her balled-up jeans. The last dress she had bought cost a heck of a lot more than three dollars.

The man wrapped her old clothes in brown paper and tied it with string. "Thank you, miss. Come again. Uh, say . . ." He paused, his color still high.

"Yes?"

"Are you the new one down at the Four Deuces?"

"The new one?" she asked. "The new what?"

His faced reddened even more. "Folks talk," he said. "I hear tell you made quite an entrance down there last night. It's all over town."

"I see," she said, her voice suddenly cool. "Well, 'folks' should mind their own business, shouldn't they?"

"Yes, ma'am," he said, chastened. "Hope you like the dress."

"Thank you," she said, and taking the parcel, she swept out of the store.

She strolled down the boardwalk and then crossed the street. The dress swished around her ankles when she walked. Right away, she noticed that she was not drawing the same kind of critical attention she had earlier. Men passing by tipped their hats at her; the women smiled.

It was after noon when she returned to the hotel. Trey was awake, but still in bed. He lifted one brow when he saw her. "Nice dress."

"Glad you like it, since you paid for it." She frowned at him. "Are you okay?"

He grunted. "I think I've got a bit of a hangover."

"Really? What time did you get in last night?"

"You mean this morning?" He sat up, groaning softly. "But it's not so bad I can't appreciate a pretty new dress like that one. You look right nice."

She smiled. "Like a proper lady now?"

His answering smile was pained. " 'Cept for them shoes." He held his head in his hands. "I need some coffee. Maybe about a gallon of it. Let's go get something to eat. Want to hand me my boots?"

"Anything for the lord and master." She effected a small curtsey.

He muttered something under his breath as she handed him his boots.

"I think the dress is long enough to hide my shoes most of the time," she remarked. "Don't you?"

"I reckon. No point in causing unwanted attention." He stamped his feet into his boots, stood, and buckled on his gun belt. And then he reached under his pillow and produced his Colt, checking that it was still loaded. She was sure it was a long-ingrained habit. She thought about teasing him about who would sneak in and unload it and put it back under his pillow, but decided he was in no mood for jokes.

"How's your hand?" he asked.

She shrugged. "All right, I guess."

"Let me have a look."

Her heart skipped a beat as he took her hand in his and carefully lifted the large square Band-Aid that covered the cut. "It's healing just fine," he said, and dropped a kiss on her palm. A kiss she felt clear down to her toes.

She jerked her hand away, flushed at his knowing grin. Darn him. He knew exactly what effect he had on her.

"You ready to go?" He shoved the wad of greenbacks in his jeans.

With a nod, she smoothed the Band-Aid back over the cut.

They went to the same restaurant they had eaten in the night before. Trey asked for a cup of coffee as soon as they were seated. Amanda ordered bacon and eggs. Trey decided all he wanted was coffee.

"I thought you were hungry."

"I thought so, too."

Amanda shook her head. "You must have had some night."

"Yeah. Profitable, though." He nodded his thanks as the waitress brought their coffee, sipped his gratefully. "I won about three hundred bucks, I think." His gaze moved over her. "Did I tell you that you look right pretty in that dress?"

"Yes, thank you."

The waitress brought Amanda's breakfast a short time later, then refilled both their coffee cups. "Are you sure I can't get you something to eat, sir?" she asked.

He started to shake his head, and thought better of it. "No. Thanks. Just keep the coffee coming."

The waitress smiled sympathetically. "Yes, sir."

He had finished five cups of coffee and was feeling a lot better by the time Amanda finished breakfast. He had one last cup, and then they left the restaurant.

Trey paused outside. "I need to go check on 'Pago." He dragged a hand over his jaw. "I think I'll go get a shave, too. Why don't you go have a look around, and I'll meet you back at the hotel at, say, six o'clock?"

"Six! How long does it take to get a shave?"

"I thought I'd add a few more dollars to our stake, as long as the cards are falling my way."

"Oh."

"Here." He handed her two tens and a twenty. "We need some supplies for the trail."

"Where are we going?"

"I've got some business to take care of."

She waited for him to explain. Instead he said, "We'll need matches, some jerky, couple cans of beans, coffee and a coffeepot if you want it, couple of canteens. Oh, and a couple boxes of .45 cartridges. Can you remember all that?"

"Not to worry," she said with a smile. "Shopping is what I do best."

She watched him walk down the street toward the livery, wondering what kind of business he meant. She supposed he'd tell her when he was ready. Turning, she strolled down the boardwalk. She crossed the street at the corner, drawn by a sign that read "Green's General Store."

A small bell tinkled above the door when she opened it. A heady blend of coffee and fresh tobacco and kerosene and foodstuffs engulfed her. The stock seemed to be organized in sections. With lots of time to kill, she wandered through the store, looking at everything.

The left side of the building held grocery items and kegs and barrels filled with sugar and flour and coffee, beans and salt, pickles and sauerkraut. There were fifty-gallon barrels of vinegar and coal oil. There was a set of balance scales on the counter, and she watched as the clerk weighed two pounds of sugar, poured it into a brown paper bag, and tied it with string.

Another clerk pulled a box of cigars from under the counter and opened it for a portly man in a battered straw hat who picked out several cigars. The clerk snipped the ends of one of them for him, and lit it with a large wooden kitchen match that he struck on a rough support beam. Amanda thought she remembered reading somewhere that such matches were called Lucifers in frontier days.

Pots and pans, straw hats, whole hams wrapped in muslin, bridles and bits for horses hung from the rafters. The hams smelled wonderful, and so did the oiled leather of the tack.

She took a deep breath, her nostrils filling with the scent of tobacco and leather and fresh-ground coffee.

A huge cracker barrel stood near a cold pot-bellied

stove. Two men stood there, helping themselves to crackers.

She saw a handful of women sitting on benches near the door, talking and laughing. Others were bent over a mail-order catalog.

Near the back of the store was the hardware department. She saw zinc tubs in three sizes, stacked one inside the other. Nearby she saw chamber pots and coffeepots, dishpans and coffee grinders, milk pails and flour sifters, dustpans and bread pans, washboards and teakettles.

There was a case filled with knives of all sizes. A rack of rifles and shotguns behind the counter, and a glass display case full of gleaming revolvers. Boxes of cartridges on a shelf. Remembering Rob's comment about the modern value of Trey's six-shooter, she realized she was looking at a fortune's worth of firearms by twenty-first-century values. For that matter, everything in the store would have commanded exorbitant prices as treasured antiques. She couldn't help smiling to herself. If Relámpago could just be hitched to a wagon full of this stuff . . . she shook off the thought as silly. If the big white horse could get *her* home again, that was all she cared about.

A large black and white cat slept on a pile of bedding.

She had spent a good hour wandering through the store when she went back to the front and approached the counter. A portly, balding clerk moved toward her. He had green garters on his shirtsleeves and wore a black vest whose buttons were threatened by his paunch. His smile was friendly. "Afternoon, ma'am. How can I help you?"

A half hour later, the counter was piled high with her purchases: a blue-speckled enamel coffeepot like the one she had seen in Trey's saddlebag, a pair of matching plates, knives, and forks; a can opener; several boxes of what she would have called kitchen matches; the ammunition; canned beans; two canteens, and a package of jerky the clerk had sliced from a hanging slab with a sharp butcher knife. In addition to the items Trey had asked for, she'd added a hairbrush, a package of hairpins, and a bar of lavender-scented soap.

With the clerk's help, she loaded everything into the new saddlebags she had purchased. She draped the two blanket-wrapped canteens over her shoulder and pocketed her change, amazed that there was still quite a bit of her forty dollars left.

Leaving the general store, she crossed the street gingerly, holding the hem of her skirt out of the thick dust and stepping carefully as she glanced up and down the street, wondering if Trey's luck was holding. The chiming of a distant clock told her it was four. She still had two hours before she was supposed to meet him.

She was on her way back to the hotel to drop off their supplies when she saw the wanted poster nailed to a post supporting the boardwalk overhang. Printed on thick stock, it wasn't very big, about the size of a sheet of stationery. She read it once, then read it again.

Wanted for Bank Robbery and Murder
Trey Long Walker
Hair: Black

Chase the Lightning

Eyes: Brown
Reward $1,000
Anyone having information
Contact J. S. Hollinger
First National Bank
Wickenburg, Arizona

There was a crude sketch, which didn't do Trey justice. She wondered how many other posters were plastered around town. No doubt bounty hunters were scouring the West for him, and who knew how many armed men with a need for ready cash had read this poster or one like it. Yet he was sitting in a saloon somewhere on this street, playing cards as if he didn't have a care in the world.

Trey leaned back in his chair and regarded his cards. A pair of aces and three sixes. Face impassive, he laid his cards face down on the table and tossed five dollars into the pot. The other three men at the table met his raise. Two of the men were shrewd poker players, showing little emotion whether they won or lost. The third man, sitting to Trey's left, managed to keep his face blank during the play, but wasn't shy about letting his feelings show when a hand was over.

When the pot was right, Trey turned his cards over one by one.

"Full house," exclaimed the man on his left. "Damn!"

With a shrug, Trey raked in the pot. He glanced out the window while the man to his right shuffled the cards. It was almost time to meet Amanda. He wondered how she had spent the day. Why the hell was he sitting here, when he could be with her? Overcome

193

by a sudden urge to see her, he drained the one beer he had permitted himself. Damn, it tasted good.

Gathering his winnings, he stood up. "Thanks, gents, but I think I'm gonna call it a day."

"Good," muttered the man on his left. "Maybe I'll have a chance to win a hand for a change."

Trey tossed a five-dollar gold piece back on the table. "Drinks and dinner on me, boys. Thanks for the game."

Outside, he took a deep breath. There was a smell of rain in the air. Settling his hat on his head, he struck out for the hotel. He shouldn't have left her alone so long—not that there was anything to worry about. Canyon Creek was a law-abiding town. Still, she was a stranger here and had some outlandish notions about a woman's place. It could have caused some difficulty.

He was approaching an alley when that sixth sense that had served him so well in the past caused the short hairs to prickle on the back of his neck.

He dropped his hand casually to the butt of his gun and paused, his gaze searching the long shadows on both sides of the street. The sun was well down, and the shadows between the buildings were deep and dark. He saw no movement, heard nothing, but the feeling of danger persisted. He backed up a few steps slowly, and turned into the last saloon he had passed. He walked straight to the bar.

"What can I get for ya?" the bartender asked.

"You got a back entrance to this place?"

The bartender grunted. "Somebody lookin' for ya?"

"Could be," Trey allowed.

The bartender jerked his thumb over his shoulder. "Back there."

"Thanks. And if anyone—"

"I know the drill. If anyone asks, you were never here."

Grinning, Trey headed for the door.

It opened onto a short side street. After glancing up and down, Trey turned left and took the long way back to the hotel.

He entered the lobby cautiously. There was only one man there, an elderly gent reading a newspaper.

Keeping his hand close to the butt of his Colt, Trey crossed the floor and climbed the stairs to the second floor. He knocked on Amanda's door, glanced over his shoulder while he waited for her to answer it. Damn, he was as nervous as a whore at a prayer meeting.

She opened the door just as he was about to knock again. "Hi, I got all the stuff you wanted—"

He pushed past her, closed and locked the door behind him.

She looked at him, one brow raised.

Trey shrugged. "I think I'm being followed."

"I'm not surprised. Did you know there's a wanted poster out with your name on it? A bank in Wickenburg is offering a thousand-dollar reward."

Trey whistled softly. "Old Hollinger must be scared shitless."

Amanda nodded. "His name was on the poster. I guess he put up the reward."

"Yeah. Damn." He ran a hand over his jaw, then

went to the window. Standing to one side, he peered down at the street.

"Maybe we'd better leave?" Amanda suggested.

"You're reading my mind, sweetheart." Moving away from the window, he began to pace the floor. "As soon as it's full dark, I'll be on my way. I think you'd better stay here."

"Not on your life!" she exclaimed. "You're not going off and leaving me behind. No way!"

"You'll be safer here."

"I don't care. I don't know anybody in this town. Hell, I don't know anyone in this *time*. Besides, I want to go home! You and that horse got me here, and I'm counting on the two of you to get me back."

"There's no time to worry about that now," he said.

He went to the window and looked down at the street again. Amanda was right in what she said, but it just wasn't smart to take her with him into possible danger. He smiled wryly. Sometimes he just wasn't smart. He ran a hand through his hair. Who was it down there on the street? Langley and his men? Or just some cowboy looking to make some fast money?

Out of nervous habit, he pulled his Colt and checked his ammunition, then settled the gun in his holster. After a moment's hesitation, he added another round to the chamber he usually kept empty. He might need every edge he could get. His every instinct for survival was screaming at him to get out of town. Fast.

"All right," he said. "Get your stuff together. We're leaving."

She picked up the bundle holding her jeans and top. "This is all the stuff I have. Remember?" Unfastening the flap on one of the roomy saddlebags lying on the bed, she stuffed the clothing inside.

Trey took a minute to examine the contents of both bags and then buckled them shut. "Good work," he said. "We'll fill the canteens at the first clean water we come to. You carry them. And don't let them knock together!" He slung the saddlebags over his left shoulder. "Stay behind me," he warned, "and keep quiet."

She nodded, then followed him out the door into the hallway. She frowned when he turned right instead of left toward the stairs. "Where are we going?" she called softly.

"Out the back way."

He stopped at the back door, opened it a few inches. The sun was down now, and dusk had settled in. He stood stock still, all his senses alert then beckoned for her to follow.

She tiptoed down the outside staircase behind him, his unease communicating itself to her. The whisper of her Nikes' soles seemed loud; she wondered how he could move so silently in those clunky boots. She glanced nervously from side to side. Every shadow seemed fraught with menace. Who was out there that had spooked him so?

Bypassing the main street, they made their way down an alley toward the livery. Trey rapped on the rear entrance.

A moment later, a brawny man wearing overalls opened the door. "Whaddya want?" he asked gruffly.

"I need to buy a horse."

"Come back tomorrow."

Madeline Baker

"I need it tonight, Abe. And a saddle and bridle, too."

The man regarded Trey for a moment, then nodded. "Come on in." He stood away from the door so they could enter the barn. "I got a pretty little gelding for sale. He's ten years old. Sound as a dollar. I'll let you have him for, oh, say, sixty dollars. Throw in the tack for another fifty."

Trey narrowed his eyes. "Must be a good horse. And a mighty fine saddle."

The other man spat a stream of tobacco juice. "Them's nighttime prices, Trey."

"Done," Trey said. "Saddle the gelding for me, will ya?"

"Sure. As soon as you pay for it."

"You've made your sale," Trey said flatly. "Saddle the horse."

Abe lowered his gaze. "Sure, sure."

Trey pulled his winnings out of his pocket, counted out a hundred and ten dollars while the man went to get the horse.

When Abe led the bay gelding out of its stall, Trey exchanged the money for the reins, and turned them over to Amanda. She noticed the horse had one white sock and a narrow blaze from its forehead to its nose. So now she had a horse, just as she'd been thinking about—but hardly the way she had planned! She rubbed its muzzle distractedly.

"I'll get 'Pago," Trey said. He found his gear in the tack room. He saddled and bridled the stallion, secured the saddlebags behind the cantle quickly and efficiently.

"Mount up, miss," Abe said. "I'll adjust them stirrups for you."

Amanda draped the canteens over the saddle horn, then put her foot in the stirrup and pulled herself into the saddle—no easy task in a skirt and petticoat. She would have liked to change into her jeans and shirt, but Trey had been in such a hurry, she hadn't suggested it. Leaning forward, she patted the gelding's neck. "Does he have a name?"

Abe shrugged as he deftly adjusted the stirrups for her. "If he does, he never told me." He handed her the reins. "Them's mighty funny-looking riding shoes," he said. "Be careful you don't let your foot slip through the stirrup."

Trey swung into the saddle. "You ready?"

"I guess so."

"You do know how to ride, don't you?"

"I've ridden." She didn't tell him it had been years ago.

"Good."

Trey pulled twenty dollars out of his pocket and handed it to Abe.

"What's that for?" the livery man asked, looking surprised.

"If anyone asks, we were never here."

Abe nodded. "Right."

"This is serious business, Abe," Trey said. "Anyone picks up our trail tonight, I won't take it kindly."

Abe pocketed the money. "Don't worry." He led the way to the big double doors and slid one back just enough for the two of them to leave single-file. Before he rode through, Trey looked back at Amanda.

"Stay close," he said. "If there's any shooting, you take off running, you hear? Don't wait for me. Don't look back. Just ride like hell. I'll catch up when I can."

She nodded, her heart pounding as she followed him out into the deepening night.

Chapter Fifteen

Amanda braced her Nikes carefully in the stirrups and stood in the saddle, stretching her cramped legs and arching her back, rotating her shoulders. Didn't Trey ever get tired? They had been riding for what seemed like forever. It was eerie, moving through the darkness with only the muffled sound of hoofbeats and the occasional chirp of a cricket to break the quiet of the night. Back home, she had never noticed just how *dark* dark really was. The cloud cover made it darker. Even she could smell the rain Trey had told her was coming.

Trey rode ahead of her. He was nervous and on edge, and because of that, so was she. She saw danger lurking in every passing shadow, hiding behind every shrub that rose up out of the darkness. Every time her horse twitched his ears, her hand tightened on the reins, and soon her nervousness had transmitted itself to her horse.

She kept her gaze fixed on the stallion. Relámpago was easy to follow. His coat shimmered like new-fallen snow even beneath the cloud cover. A ghost horse, she mused; that was what the stallion looked like. A ghost horse with a very special gift? Perhaps the ability to get her home again?

Home: the very word made her ache with longing. She wondered where Trey was headed, where he considered a safe haven. Her apprehension grew with each passing mile. It seemed they were getting farther from that spot in the desert where they had arrived in this time period. Was there some sort of key, some kind of time portal or gate there? She had never been a fan of science fiction, considering it too wildly improbable to enjoy. But if there was a place, one particular spot that was somehow the link between his time and hers, then they needed to go there.

But what if the link wasn't a place at all? What if the link was the stallion?

She frowned thoughtfully, remembering how Relámpago had mysteriously arrived in her corral, with no hoofprints leading in from the desert. He had arrived in her front yard with his injured rider the same way. Out of the blue, so to speak, with no tracks to indicate from which direction he had come. Though she hadn't discussed it with Trey, she was pretty sure he hadn't been sitting in one spot between the stallion's visits. So perhaps the horse could take her home from just about anywhere.

If so, she was going to stay close to that white rump if it killed her!

With thoughts of returning home filling her mind,

she was caught off guard when her horse stumbled. She grabbed the pommel and jammed her feet hard into the stirrups. The nonskid soles of her athletic shoes gripped securely.

"Easy," she murmured, leaning forward to pat the gelding's neck. Clucking to the horse, she rode up beside Trey. "I want to go back home," she said. "Now."

"Are you crazy? We're busy right now just trying to stay alive."

"I understand that, and I want to get out of this crazy time of yours just as fast as I can. I want to go home, and I need Relámpago to take me."

"So you figured that out, did you?" He patted the stallion's arched neck. "He's the key to it all. I can't say as I understand it, but it's the only answer that makes any sense."

"I see that now. Can't you make him do it?"

"Sweetheart, I didn't even know he *could* do it. My grandfather always said 'Pago would carry me out of danger, and he has, on more than one occasion, but never anything like that before. It was . . ." He shook his head.

"Unbelievable," she supplied.

"Yeah. Even though he's done it twice now, I can't credit my own senses anymore."

"I want to go home!" she said, her voice rising.

He shushed her. "Voices really carry on this still air," he said quietly. "There's a man back there who's looking to collect a reward on my hide. Maybe a lot of men. Have you forgotten that?"

"I'm sorry—I . . . I'm not used to this."

"I hope you never do get used to it, sweetheart."

She brightened. "But . . . but Relámpago took you away from the posse before, right? And brought you to me?"

"He did that," Trey admitted. "And he brought us back here to get us away from those hard cases looking for your boyfriend. What if those three had friends, or more relatives? What if they're camped out at your place, waiting for us? Somehow I don't think 'Pago will take us back there if they are."

She wanted to argue with him, assert that those men would be long gone. But how could she? There was no way to know for sure. She might not be happy here, but for now she appeared to be stuck, unless . . .

"What if we get chased again?" she said. "Would he take us back then?"

"The only way to find that out is to let them find us," Trey said. "You willing to risk it? I'm not! Langley might shoot straighter this time. And you might find yourself in the way of a bullet."

There wasn't anything she could say to that. They rode silently for a while before she asked him where they were going.

"Diablo Springs."

"Where's that?"

"Not far from Tucson."

"What's in Diablo Springs?"

"Not much, but it's a good place to hole up for a while."

"Is it very far?"

"Three, four days from here."

Four days on horseback. She closed her eyes, thinking of her Jag parked in the garage. If it was still there.

If those creeps hadn't stolen it or driven it off a cliff out of spite. She opened her eyes as a new thought came to her. Four days on the trail, and probably not a rest stop the whole way. "Where are we going to spend the night?"

"This is as good a place as any," he said, and reined the stallion to a halt.

"Here?" She glanced around.

"Yep." Trey dismounted and dropped the stud's reins.

Amanda stared at him as he walked toward her. "Here?" she asked again.

He lifted her from the back of the gelding. "You wanted to come."

Reaching under the horse's belly, he loosened the cinch and lifted the saddle. Holding it up with one hand, he rubbed the horse's back, back and forth, with the saddle blanket, then smoothed the blanket back into place and resettled the saddle without tightening the girth.

"Not a good idea to off-saddle, in case we have to leave here quick," he explained as he performed the same chores on the stallion.

He tied the gelding's reins to a low-growing bush, close enough to the ground so the horse could crop the grass. He left the stallion free.

"What about Relámpago?" Amanda asked. "Aren't you afraid he'll wander off?"

Trey shook his head.

She looked around. "Where are we going to sleep?"

"Right here."

Amanda watched as he kicked the hardpan loose

in several places with his boot heels, then took his big knife and hacked off several handfuls of branches from the surrounding brush.

"You can use your bundle for a pillow," he said.

"What about you?"

She could barely see his grin in the darkness. "I got me these fancy new saddlebags. Not as soft as your bundle, but I've had lots worse for a pillow. Best turn in. We'll be moving out at sunrise."

She couldn't believe he meant to sleep out here, in the back end of beyond. But he did. Sitting down on one side of the springy brush pile, he tipped his hat over his eyes and rested his head on the saddlebags.

Amanda realized he'd prepared only one brush pile, and it wasn't nearly as wide as her queen-size bed back home. She lowered herself carefully on the other side, as far away from him as she could get. The brush tickled her through the gingham, and released pungent odors. There was no way she could sleep like this. She wanted to wash the dust out of her hair. She wanted to brush her teeth. She wanted to go home.

With a sigh of despair, she lay down, her head pillowed on her bundled jeans and shirt and stretched out on the crackling brush. Carefully, she tucked her feet up under her skirt, and steadfastly tried not to think of creepy crawly things that might call the desert home.

It was going to be a long night.

She dreamed of horses running wild across a vast sunlit prairie, of a tall man with copper-hued skin and long black hair astride a white stallion. At first, she thought the man was Trey, but as he rode closer, she realized it wasn't Trey, though the resemblance was striking. The man wore only a breechclout and moccasins. Two eagle feathers were tied in his waist-length black hair; jagged streaks of black paint adorned both cheeks.

He rode toward her at a gallop, his black eyes fierce, the lance in his hand held high overhead. Too frightened to move, she stood there while he thundered toward her. A shrill cry rose on the warrior's lips as he closed the distance between them. He was going to run her down . . .

She woke with a start, her heart pounding.

Relámpago grazed nearby. The stallion lifted his head and whinnied softly.

With some effort, she managed to gain her feet. Every muscle in her body seemed to be complaining. Her teeth felt furry.

She went to stand beside the horse. "I dreamed about you last night," she said, stroking the stallion's neck. "Did you know that?"

The stallion tossed his head.

"How about me?" Trey asked, coming up silently behind her. "Did you dream about me, too?"

"No."

"Damn the luck," he muttered with a wry grin. "Here." He offered her a cup of coffee.

She sipped the hot, bitter brew. When she was finished, she dug her hairbrush out of a saddlebag and brushed out her hair, then pinned it back, out of her face.

By the time she felt halfway presentable, Trey had

207

put out the fire, scattered the ashes, and packed up the coffeepot and cup. "It's time we were moving on."

"I'm hungry. I ache in places I didn't even know I had, and I'm starving."

"There's a town a few miles ahead. We'll get some grub there."

"Why didn't we go there last night? We could have got a room somewhere."

He didn't bother to answer her, just busied himself tightening the cinches. She stared at him in exasperation. Impossible man, she thought, making her sleep on the ground when there was a town ahead. As she watched, he broke up the brush bedding, scattering it among the undergrowth.

She was putting her foot in the stirrup when she felt Trey's hands at her waist. He lifted her effortlessly into the saddle, checked the cinch and stirrups, then swung aboard Relámpago and clucked to the stallion.

With a sigh, Amanda tapped her heels to her mount's flanks.

They stopped near a quiet stream a short while later. Trey held her horse while she knelt on the bank. Scooping water into her hands, she rinsed out her mouth, then bent down and took a drink. The water was clear and cool, and even as she drank, she wondered if it was safe to do so. When she was finished, she held the horses for Trey to drink, and then they let the horses drink. Finally, he went a few paces upstream and filled both canteens, looping one around her saddle horn and the other around his.

Her stomach growled loudly as Trey helped her remount. "You did say there was a town ahead?"

He chuckled as her stomach growled again. "If you can't wait until we find a place to eat, I could let you nibble on me for a while." He looked up at her, grinning roguishly, one hand resting just above her knee.

Her stomach turned over, but it had nothing to do with hunger and everything to do with the heat of his hand on her leg, and the look in his deep brown eyes. It was sinful, she thought, what that man could do to her with just a look. She couldn't fall in love with him! She couldn't! She didn't belong here, would never belong here. Not only that, she was engaged to Rob . . . but somehow none of that seemed to matter, not when Trey was looking at her like that, as if she were a tasty morsel.

His grin widened, as if he knew exactly what she was thinking. Giving her knee a squeeze, he took up Relámpago's reins and swung into the saddle.

"You can always chaw on some of that jerky you bought, if you find that more to your taste."

The weathered sign outside the town read "Welcome to Walker's Well, population 235."

Amanda grimaced as they rode side by side down the wide, dusty street that ran between two dozen or so ramshackle buildings. Calling the dwellings that were scattered beyond the main street houses was paying them a compliment. They were little more than hovels.

Trey reined his horse to a halt in front of a large, raw plank building with a peaked roof and unpainted shutters at the windows. The sign above the door read "Ma's Place. Best food this side of the border."

"You want to eat here?" she asked skeptically.

Dismounting, Trey jerked his thumb toward the sign. "Best food this side of the border," he said, reading aloud.

"Yeah, right."

Chuckling softly, Trey lifted her from the saddle. Tossing the gelding's reins over the rack, he took her by the hand. "Come on."

The inside of the restaurant was dim. There was sawdust on the floor. Faded red-and-white-checked curtains hung at the windows. Faded cloths covered the tables, most of which were occupied by rough-looking men who didn't smell much better than they looked.

Then, through the miasma of Bull Durham smoke, she got a whiff of something wonderful emanating from the kitchen, and she knew why the place was so crowded.

Trey sat down at a vacant table in the far corner of the room, his back to the wall, and she sat across from him. "I take it you've been here before?" she remarked.

He nodded. "Best grub this side of the border, just like the sign says."

Amanda nodded. "Whatever's cooking in there smells heavenly."

Trey lifted his head and sniffed the air. "Beef stew," he said. "Fresh biscuits. And apple pie."

"Beef stew for breakfast? Are you making that up?"

"Wait and see."

Her heart did a somersault as his gaze met hers across the table. She loved the way he looked at her, as if she were something incredibly special; loved the intensity in his eyes, the way his mouth curved in a smile that seemed to be for her alone. Had she designed him herself, he couldn't have been more perfect, except for two little things: He lived in the past, and he was a bank robber.

The thought made her grin.

"What's funny?" he asked.

"Oh, nothing," she said, and laughed out loud.

Trey frowned at her. "Come on, spill it."

It was obvious he wasn't happy that looking at him made her laugh. And that made her laugh harder.

He was still scowling at her a moment later when a harried-looking waitress wearing a brown dress and a remarkably clean white apron came to take their order.

"Howdy, Martha," Trey said. "What's the special of the day?"

"Beef stew, hon." She brushed a lock of hair from her forehead with the back of her hand.

Trey winked at Amanda. "Told you so. Give me a big bowl, and some of those fresh biscuits, too. Maybe about a half dozen for starters."

The waitress grinned. "And coffee, black, and apple pie."

"Martha, you're an angel."

Martha gave him a friendly slap on the shoulder, then turned to take Amanda's order. "What'll you have, dearie?"

"The same I guess, but could I have some cream and sugar for my coffee?"

"Sure enough, dearie. Coming right up."

"I take it you come here often," Amanda remarked after Martha moved to the next table.

"Now and then. You can't go wrong with Ma's cookin'." He smiled at her. "Although even she can't cook up a steak as good as yours."

"Well, that's nice to know. I guess if I can't get back where I belong, I can always open up a steak house."

Trey laughed. "I'll be your first customer."

"I was kidding! I don't want to stay here. I want to go home."

"Yeah," he said, suddenly sober. "So do I."

"Where is your home?"

He grunted softly. "I don't have one, at least not yet. I guess now I never will."

"What do you mean?"

"That money I stole, it was to buy some land, start a ranch."

"With stolen money?"

He shrugged. "I didn't think of it as stolen. I thought of it as getting back what was rightfully mine."

"What do you mean?"

"Hollinger refused to extend the deadline on my old man's loan because he wanted the property for himself. And when my old man went to talk to him about it, Hollinger killed him."

"I can't believe that. It's just so awful, so unfair."

"It's what happened." He shrugged. "Hollinger owned the bank, and pretty much owned the town. He said he shot in self-defense. Nobody was gonna argue with him."

"What about the law?"

Trey snorted. "The law was married to Hollinger's sister."

"I'm sorry."

"Yeah. Not as sorry as I am that I didn't blow his head off when I had the chance."

Before Amanda could frame a suitable reply, the waitress was back.

"Here we go," Martha said. "Two bowls of stew." She blew a lock of hair from her brow. "You wanted cream and sugar, right, dearie?"

"Yes, please," Amanda said.

"Coming right up." She tapped a finger on Trey's shoulder. "Careful now, it's hot."

The stew was, indeed, the best Amanda had ever tasted. The biscuits were hot and fluffy; the coffee, even with cream and sugar, was strong enough to peel paint off a wall.

Amanda was still working on her first bowl of stew when Trey finished his and ordered a second. And then a third.

"I love a man with a hearty appetite," Martha said. She beamed at Trey a moment before glancing back at Amanda. "Can I get you anything else, dearie?"

"Another biscuit, please," Amanda said. "They're wonderful."

Martha beamed at her. "Coming right up. More coffee, Trey?"

He nodded. "Thanks."

"Better save room for some of Ma's apple pie," Martha warned.

"Always room for that," he said.

"Are you going to have three helpings of pie, too?" Amanda asked.

Trey sat back in his chair and grinned at her across the table. "You never know."

"Wouldn't be the first time," Martha said. She looked at Amanda and winked. "Never seen anyone, man or boy, who can put food away like he can. I'll be right back with that pie."

"I think she likes you," Amanda remarked.

Trey shrugged. "Martha? She likes everybody."

The pie was every bit as good as Trey had promised. The pie was still a little warm, the crust light and flaky.

"I make a pretty good apple pie myself," Amanda said, "but I have to admit, this is the best I've ever tasted. One of these days I'll have to—"

"Trade places, quick!"

"What?"

"Just do it!"

"What was that all about?" she asked when they had changed seats.

"That man who just came in the door, Wolf Langley—I'd rather he didn't see me."

"Langley!" She glanced over her shoulder. "My gosh, he looks a lot like Rob, doesn't he?"

"What's he doing?"

"Talking to Martha. I can't believe the resemblance. You don't suppose he's—"

"Is he alone?"

"Yes, why?" Her eyes widened. "He's after you, isn't he?"

"Is he coming this way?"

"No. Martha's talking at him a mile a minute. He's looking around the room."

Trey swore. He should have left Relámpago down at the livery. The stallion was a dead giveaway. But who'd have thought Langley would show up this early in the morning? The man had the instincts of the wolf he was named for. "What's he doing now?"

"Martha gave him a piece of pie."

Trey grunted. "So, even Wolf can't resist Ma's apple pie. Maybe he's human, after all."

"It's easy to see he's related to Rob. They look so much alike."

Trey grunted softly. "Some say he's related to the devil himself."

"Rob told me once that he had a relative who was a bounty hunter in the Old West. His great-great-grandfather, I think. I never thought I'd meet him."

"What's he doing now?"

"Eating."

"Is he facing this way?"

"No."

"All right, get up real slow and get out of here."

"What are you going to do?"

"Damned if I know." There was only one way in, and one way out.

"Trey—"

"We don't have time to discuss this. Just do as I say. Now!"

Heart pounding, Amanda stood up and walked toward the door. She met Martha's gaze as she skirted the bounty hunter. He scrutinized her as she passed by, then turned his attention back to Martha.

"How long ago did he leave?" Langley asked.

Amanda paused, pretending to read the handwritten menu tacked to a bulletin board just inside the door.

"Not more than a few minutes," Martha replied.

"Said he was going on down the street to the Palace. Shameful place! Can I get you another piece of pie, Mr. Langley?"

"No thanks."

"Are you sure? It's no trouble."

"Obliged, but I'd best be on my way."

"Here," she said, reaching behind her. "Have a cup of coffee . . . oh!"

Langley swore as Martha spilled hot coffee down the front of him.

"I'm so sorry!" Martha exclaimed. "Come in the kitchen and dry that off." She didn't wait for an answer. Reaching for his hand, she pulled him behind the counter and into the kitchen.

As soon as Langley was out of sight, Trey headed for the door. Grabbing Amanda by the arm, he hustled her outside and lifted her onto the gelding's back. He thrust the reins into her hand, then took up the stallion's reins and swung into the saddle.

Trey drummed his heels into the stallion's flanks, and Relámpago took off at a gallop. The gelding followed without any encouragement at all.

They had only gone a short distance when she heard Langley's voice holler, "Long Walker!"

The bounty hunter's outraged cry was followed by a pair of gunshots that echoed in Amanda's ears like thunder. She screamed as her horse reared, unseating her. She landed on her rump, hard.

Things seemed to happen in slow motion after that.

Langley took a step forward, smoke curling from the muzzle of the gun in his hand.

People on the street ducked for cover.

Trey wheeled his horse around in a tight circle and raced back toward her. There was something almost otherworldly in the sight of him riding toward her. Relámpago's coat seemed to blaze in the morning sun, and sparks seemed to fly from his hooves.

Langley fired again, and Trey's hat went flying. Amanda felt her stomach drop. That was close. Too close!

She watched with a sort of horrified fascination as Trey drew his weapon and fired in one smooth, easy motion.

Langley staggered backward.

Trey was almost upon her now. He leaned forward in the saddle, his arm outstretched. She reached toward him, and he swept her from the ground and swung her up behind him. Her arms went around his waist, hanging on for dear life as they galloped down the street.

She buried her face against Trey's shoulder, certain she was about to get a bullet in the back. Oh, Lord, she wasn't ready to die! Not now! Not here!

Her arms tightened around Trey's waist. Closing her eyes, she clung to him, tried to pray, but she was too afraid to think coherently, too afraid to do anything but hold on to Trey. And in that moment, with death breathing like a dragon down her neck, she realized she was falling in love with Trey Long Walker.

Chapter Sixteen

Though they'd been running for a long time, Relámpago had barely broken a sweat when Trey reined the horse to a halt. But for Relámpago's smooth, effortless gait, Amanda was sure she would have been jarred senseless by now. She was amazed by the stallion's stamina.

She loosened her death grip on Trey's waist, flexed her aching arms, and leaned back a little to look around. The terrain was wide and rugged, covered with cacti and brush. A roadrunner dragged a small plume of dust up a dry wash off to the left. It was the only movement, other than high clouds moving toward the sun. The threat of rain the night before had yet to materialize.

Trey dismounted and lifted her from the saddle, then whirled around, gun in hand.

Amanda stared at him, startled, and then she heard

it, too. The sound of hoofbeats coming hard and fast toward them.

Trey grabbed her by the arm and thrust her behind him.

Oh, Lord, she thought, would this nightmare never end?

The hoofbeats drew nearer, slowed, stopped. She heard Trey swear softly as he holstered his gun.

She peered around him, a bubble of hysterical laughter rising in her throat as her gelding trotted into view.

The horse stood there, sides heaving and covered with sweat, holding his head high and to the side to avoid stepping on the reins. The gelding blew softly as Trey caught up the reins.

He thrust them into her hands. "This critter needs a rest," he said. "But we need to keep moving. Langley might have followed him. We'll walk awhile, give your mount some time to cool out."

"All right."

It was unsettling to walk across the rugged, wide-open terrain. She felt very conspicuous. Being hunted was *no* fun. Her gaze darted from side to side. This was Indian country. She envisioned paint-streaked Indians lurking behind every bush and rock, just waiting to ravish her and take her scalp. And what about that bounty hunter Trey had shot?

"Do you think he's dead?" she asked.

"Who, Langley? I couldn't be that lucky. I think I might have nicked him, though."

"Oh! I just thought of something!"

"What?"

219

"You can't kill him!"

"Why the devil not?"

"Because of Rob."

"What are you talking about?"

"Don't you see? If you kill Langley, Rob will never be born!"

Trey grunted. That might not be so bad, he thought. At least then he wouldn't have to worry about Amanda marrying that two-bit greenhorn if she made it back to her own time. He slid a glance in her direction. If he had his way, she would never make it back.

Amanda took hold of his arm. "You won't kill him, will you?"

"Not if I don't have to."

She seemed satisfied with his answer. He was sorry when she let go of his arm.

"Have you killed many men?"

"A few, in self-defense." But not the one who needed killing most, he thought bitterly. Not J. S. Hollinger. His failure gnawed at him.

They walked the horses for half an hour or so before Trey told her to mount up. She swallowed a groan as she stepped into the saddle. Even though the gelding had a nice easy gait, spending so many hours in the saddle was tiring.

For the rest of the day, Trey set an easy but steady pace, only pausing now and then at hidden water holes he seemed to find by dead reckoning. He seemed to know his way around the wilderness the way she knew her way around her house. Several times he had her wait while he doubled back to check for pursuers from some high point. Each time, he was satisfied to find their back trail clear. During one break, she rinsed off her face and hands. The Band-Aid on her palm had come loose and she peeled it off, dug a hole, and buried it.

Another long afternoon twilight was descending, and the clouds were massing again, when he decided to call a halt for the night.

This time he stripped the rigging from the horses and rubbed them down with their blankets, before spreading the blankets over a patch of brush to dry out.

"They'll dry quick in this air," he said. "I'm going to scout on foot. You might gather up some of that dead brush. I think we can risk a fire tonight." He loosened his six-gun in its holster and faded from sight like a . . . like an Indian, she thought.

She gathered an armful of dried branches. She layered some of them on the most level patch of ground she could find and then spread the blankets over them. She dragged the saddles over for pillows, and then, after a quick look around, she hurriedly changed out of her dress and petticoat and into her tank top and jeans, wondering why she hadn't done it sooner.

She rolled the dress and petticoat into a ball and shoved them inside one of the saddlebags. She spent a few minutes brushing the dust and tangles out of her hair and then, with a weary sigh, sank down on the impromptu bed, her head resting on the saddle. She pulled a corner of the top blanket up over her and lay there shivering, partly from the chill creeping into the air and partly from nerves as she relived their close escape from town. Trey could have been killed. She could have been killed.

"I don't belong here," she whispered. "Please, just let me get back home."

"You say something?" Trey asked, startling her. He had materialized as quietly as he had disappeared.

She sighed tremulously, determined not to cry. "No."

But Trey heard the unshed tears that made her voice tremble. "Amanda?"

She sniffed.

He knelt down beside her and pulled her into his arms. "What's wrong?"

"I want to go home," she wailed softly.

"Yeah, you said that before."

"Well, it's still true." She sniffed again, wishing she had a tissue.

All her misery seemed to evaporate as Trey's hand stroked her back, making her forget everything but how good it felt to be in his arms. His chest was solid, comforting, his touch light, soothing, his breath warm against her cheek. Only a moment before, she had been feeling afraid and alone, but no more. She relaxed against him, content to be in the past, for the moment, if it meant she could be in his arms.

She closed her eyes as he continued to rub her back, massaging away her tension, easing muscles that ached from spending a long night on the ground the night before, and a longer day in the saddle.

Trey's arm tightened around her as sleep claimed her. He couldn't blame her for wanting to go home. For a woman accustomed to fancy cars and indoor plumbing, life in his time must seem primitive indeed. If it wasn't for the woman in his arms, he might have thought he'd dreamed all of it: the electric lights, the indoor privies, hot running water, machines that washed and dried clothes, machines that made ice and kept food cold, pictures that moved and talked. He had never imagined such things.

He should have left her in Canyon Creek. It was a good-sized town. She would have been happier there, staying in a decent hotel, than tagging along with him. At least there she would have had three hot meals a day and a warm bed to sleep in. If he couldn't hunt up some game, they'd have to make do with jerky and beans, and she would have to get used to sleeping on the ground until they reached Diablo Springs.

He shook his head ruefully. How could he take her there? The place was populated by whores, horse thieves, murderers and . . . he swore softly. Bank robbers.

He stared into the darkness. Why hadn't he left her behind? She stirred in his arms, and he knew why he hadn't left her. Her breasts were warm and soft against his chest. Every time he inhaled, her scent filled his nostrils. Lowering his head, he brushed a kiss across her cheek. Her skin was soft and warm; her hair still carried the faint scent of fresh peaches, even after all this time on the trail. Looking at her, holding her, made him ache with desire, filled him with the need to protect her, even if it meant protecting her from men like himself.

She felt good in his arms, and he held her for a long while before he lowered her onto the blanket. Awake or asleep, in a pretty blue dress or tight jeans and a shirt like she was wearing now, she was the most beautiful woman he had ever seen. And yet, it wasn't just her beauty that attracted him. He recalled the tenderness of her touch when she had tended his wound, her willingness to take in a stranger, the mischievous light in her eyes when she had insisted on buying him a hat and new jeans. She made him feel good, he thought, inside and out, made him think about settling down—damn! Where had that thought come from? As if he could settle down now, with Wolf Langley on his trail and his stake 132 years in the future.

A sigh escaped Amanda's lips and she smiled in her sleep. Trey stared at her mouth, remembered the taste of her, the way she fit into his arms. His new jeans felt suddenly tight in the crotch and he stood up, restless and aching.

Relámpago whinnied softly as Trey approached. "Hey, boy," he murmured. "What the devil are we going to do about her?"

Amanda awoke with a groan. The sky was pale with a new dawn, and it still hadn't rained. Her neck ached, her back ached, and she was hungry enough to eat her Nikes, dirt and all. Cracking one eye open, she glanced around. There was no sign of Trey, but she saw Relámpago and the gelding standing head to tail a little ways off, so she figured Trey hadn't gone far.

She sat up slowly, stretched her arms and legs, and then stood up. Where was he?

Even as the thought crossed her mind, she saw him walking toward her. He moved with lithe grace, supple and silent. Just looking at him made her heart do a little dance, sent a warmth spreading through her that had nothing to do with the heat of the sun.

"Morning," he said.

"Morning. Where'd you go?"

He lifted his arm. A rabbit dangled from his hand.

Amanda grimaced. "What's that for?" she asked suspiciously.

"Breakfast. Something to go with a can of those store-bought beans. Let's saddle up. I found a water hole not far from here. The horses can graze while we eat."

"Eat? The rabbit?" She shuddered. "Raw?"

He laughed softly, amused by her horrified expression. "Guess you've never cooked rabbit over an open fire."

"No."

"Good eating," he said. "You'll see. There's plenty of firewood around the water hole. We can heat the beans, too." He thrust the carcass into her hand and began to saddle Relámpago.

She felt dampness under her hand. Blood, already congealing. She swallowed a gasp and held the rabbit the way she might hold a live snake. "Where'd you get this, anyway?"

"Shot it." He reached under the stallion's belly for the cinch and drew it up tight.

"You're a regular Daniel Boone, aren't you? Where'd you learn to hunt like that?"

"My grandfather taught me."

"The Indian one, I guess."

He chuckled as he smoothed the blanket over the gelding's back. "Sure as hell wasn't the other one."

"You didn't like him?"

"I never met him." He cinched the saddle in place,

took the rabbit from her hand, and draped it over Re-lámpago's withers. "Ready?"

She wiped her hand against her pant leg. "I guess so."

"Need a leg up?"

"No. I can manage."

The water hole was less than a mile away. Several patches of yellow-green grass grew nearby. Dismounting, Trey tethered the horses to a sturdy bush. Amanda knelt at the water hole. Dipping her hands in the water, she took a drink, swallowing just enough to quench her thirst. She watched Trey gather tinder and some dry wood from beneath a stunted mesquite tree and start a small fire. She grimaced while he skinned the rabbit. "Aren't you supposed to take out its . . . its innards before we eat it?"

"I already did that."

He cut the carcass into pieces, tossed the skin away from their camp, "for the coyotes," he said, and then put the meat on a stick. Hunkering down on his heels, he held the stick over the fire. Sort of like roasting marshmallows, she thought.

"Open up a can of those beans and set it here, at the edge of the coals," he told her.

She did so, having a little trouble with the manual can opener. She dragged one of the saddle blankets over for a table, and put out the two enamel plates and the flatware. She wasn't keen on the idea of eating a freshly killed creature, but her stomach began to growl as the air filled with the aroma of warming beans and roasting meat.

"Won't be long now," Trey said, grinning as her stomach growled loudly.

She glared at him. Even though she liked living in the country, she was, by no stretch of the imagination, a country girl. She had gone on one camp-out when she was nine or ten years old, but when she found out she had to sleep on the ground, she had called her mother to come and get her.

Oh, Mama, she thought. *If you could only come and get me now!*

Amanda arched her back, then stood in the stirrups for a moment. Who would have thought horseback riding could be so tiring? She didn't remember getting so stiff and sore when she rode on the farm. Of course, she had been a lot younger then. And she had only ridden for a couple of hours at a time, not all day and into the night.

The land stretched ahead of them, seemingly endless, flat in every direction save for the mountain that loomed in the distance. For all that the country seemed to be populated by little more than salt scrub and cacti, roadrunners and beady-eyed lizards, Trey managed to find food enough to stretch out the meager supplies in their saddlebags. Another rabbit, a prairie chicken, a cute little squirrel she refused to eat, a small deer. He'd also found some wild onions and cabbage to break up the constant diet of meat and beans.

The black coffee he brewed was strong enough to float a bullet, which was apparently just the way he liked it. Her only recourse was to dilute it with water from her canteen.

By the third day, she was dying for a Caesar salad, a cappuccino, and a big bowl of chocolate ice cream.

She urged her horse up alongside Trey's mount. "How much longer until we get to Diablo Springs?"

"We're not going there."

"We're not? Why not? Where are we going?"

"Bonita Canyon."

"Where the heck is that? Why are we going there?"

"It's about a two-day ride from Diablo Springs, and we're going there because it's the only place I can think of where Langley won't follow us."

"What's in Bonita Canyon? I'm afraid to ask."

"My people."

She stared at him a moment. His people. "You don't mean . . . you can't mean . . . Indians?"

"Yeah."

She looked at him, speechless. Going to an Old West town had been bad enough, but this . . . She reined her horse to a halt. She'd had enough.

" 'Pago, whoa." Trey reined the stallion around to face her. "What's wrong?"

"Wrong? Wrong? I'll tell you what's wrong. Everything!"

He leaned forward, his forearms braced on the pommel. "Well, I can't argue with that."

"It's not funny."

"No, I reckon not."

"Let me take Relámpago and go back. You can take my horse."

"Have you taken leave of your senses, woman? You can't go traipsing around out here by yourself."

He was right, and she knew it. But she didn't have to like it.

Chapter Seventeen

Rob Langley parked his big Ford Expedition in front of Amanda's porch. Switching off the ignition, he climbed down and stood listening to the engine tick in the silence. Instincts honed by years of bounty hunting were at once alert; something wasn't right. Not by a damn sight.

Opening the driver's door, he reached under the seat for his 9mm Beretta. He never wore a gun around Amanda because she seemed finicky about it. But something wasn't right, he could feel it in his gut.

He stood by the fender of the Expedition, which reached halfway up his chest. Good cover in a firefight. He kept the Beretta down along his leg, thumb on the safety.

Amanda and he hadn't parted on the best terms the last time he had been here. Since then, she hadn't answered her phone or returned his calls. Despite the tension that had come up between them, that just wasn't like her. At first, he'd felt an unfamiliar jealousy take hold, thinking she was spending all her time with that odd cowboy with the three-thousand-dollar six-gun. But his annoyance had quickly turned to concern. What did she really know about that half-breed, anyway? Knowing Amanda, she would have taken the cowboy at his word without a second thought.

What if the half-breed was some kind of predator who knew how to get next to lonely women? He certainly had the looks for it. That hadn't been Rob's first impression of the man, but he had been man-hunting long enough to know that appearances could be deceiving.

Eyes narrowed, he scanned the yard, focusing on details. Days-old hoofprints left the yard, and returned—and then left again, deep dug and wide spaced. Running. That big white horse?

There were also strange tire tracks, a mud-and-snow tread typical of trucks and SUV's like his Expedition. Though several days old, the tracks were relatively easy to read: the truck had come into the yard, parked over there near the barn, and then left in a jackrabbit start, digging deep furrows, slinging dirt far and wide. The tire tracks overlay the running hoofprints.

Rob strode along beside the tire tracks, careful not to disturb the scene. He was some distance from the house when he found where the truck had skidded to a halt, going almost sideways. Sunlight glinted off a scatter of bright fragments. Squatting down, he turned one over with his finger. Safety glass from a shattered car window. Probably the truck window.

He saw where the truck had turned around and then arced off across the desert to go behind Amanda's house. He followed the tire tracks back. The truck had stopped on the far side of the house, and one set of boot tracks led away from the driver's door—and back, followed by a pair of uneven furrows which smeared the footprints. Irregular blotches glazed the dust here and there between the furrows. Rob swore and backtracked the furrows to just in front of the barn. A large blot of dried blood there had turned brown in the sun's heat.

Going around to the front of the house, he saw that the door stood open. He didn't like the looks of that. He pressed against the doorjamb and peered through the screen door. Whatever had happened in the yard had happened a day or more ago. Where was Amanda?

The house was quiet. Too quiet. She usually had the radio or TV on, sometimes both at the same time. To his straining senses, the house felt empty.

He went through the doorway in one smooth move and put his back to the wall inside, his Beretta up, held rock solid in both hands.

Nothing moved.

With the caution born of too many close calls, he went from room to room, always keeping the staircase in the periphery of his vision.

In the guest bedroom he found where the cowboy had been sleeping. Well, that answered one thing he'd wondered about. There was a ratty pair of clean jeans folded on a chair, and a rough flannel shirt hanging over its back. That was it for clothing. The man clearly traveled light.

Going back down the hallway, Rob moved quietly up the stairs and went through the rooms on the second floor.

Amanda's bedroom smelled of her perfumes and shampoos—peaceful, ordinary, as if she had just stepped out for a moment.

Returning to the first floor, he called her name.

"Amanda? Amanda?"

Silence answered.

Leaving the house, he headed for the barn. Her Jag was in the garage. She never left this place except in her car.

The doors to the barn were open, but there was no one inside. The horse was gone, too. He grunted softly.

He could be overreacting. It could be that she had just gone riding with the cowboy. Riding double. Cozy. His jealousy returned at the image, but it was forced out by everything he'd seen in the yard. Violence had been done here. He could read that much. And he could read enough to know that experts were called for.

He went back into the house and picked up the phone, dialing the county sheriff's number from memory. When dispatch came on the line, he mentioned the name of a detective in Crimes Against Persons that he had worked with on several occasions. He was patched through, identified himself, and told the deputy what he'd found.

The deputy promised a car shortly. And a crime-scene team.

Chapter Eighteen

Trey found himself looking forward to seeing his grandfather again, though he wondered if he would still be welcomed by the People. He had been away a long time; he was afraid he had forgotten much of what he had learned as a child. He had promised he would return to the People when he had avenged his father's death. How could he face Walker on the Wind and tell him he had failed? And yet, everything within him urged him to go home.

He was aware of Amanda riding behind him, could almost feel her scowl on his back. He should have left her behind, but he felt responsible for her being here. More than that, he wanted her here in his time with him, even though he was pretty sure she wouldn't like living with his people. She was used to the ease and comfort of her own time. By her standards, Walker's Well had been primitive. What would she think of the

People's lifestyle? He shook his head. Maybe it was a mistake, bringing her here. The threat of war was something the Apache lived with constantly—war with the Comanche, war with the Army. Not long ago, he had been in a saloon in California where he had overheard a couple of troopers talking about orders issued by General Ord, who had succeeded General McDowell as Commander of the Department of California. Ord's instructions had been to destroy the Apaches by any means, to hunt them down like he would any wild animal. According to the troopers, those orders had been carried out vigorously. Over two hundred Apaches had been killed by soldiers who had trailed them for days and weeks, burning villages, clothing, and provisions. Twenty-eight women, two men, and twenty-four children were reported captured. The troopers had noted that the Indians had killed more than fifty whites.

Things hadn't been much better in Arizona. Under the direction of General Thomas C. Devin, the cavalry had invaded the very heart of the Apache homeland, scouting south of the Mogollons, north of the Gila, where they were now, and throughout the region of the Salt River. Devin had broken new trails and made maps leading to some of the Apaches' almost inaccessible strongholds. Trey frowned, wondering if his grandfather's band had been one of those attacked.

But it was too late for second thoughts, Trey mused. Too late to turn back now.

Amanda rode up alongside him. "How much farther?"

"We should be there tomorrow morning."

She groaned softly. "I guess that means spending another night on the ground."

"Get used to it, sweetheart. There aren't any beds like you're used to where we're going."

"I didn't think there were. But you do have tipis or something, don't you? We can at least sleep inside."

"Sure." Apache lodges were warm in winter and cool in summer. He'd never had any trouble sleeping on a bed of soft furs, and looked forward to it now.

His grandfather would be surprised to see him, he thought, and then again, maybe not. They were in Apache territory now. Walker on the Wind might have already received word that his grandson and a white woman were on their way. If he was even still alive . . .

Trey pushed the thought aside, refusing to consider the possibility that his grandfather might have passed on. Walker on the Wind had always been as strong as the Chiricahua Mountains, reliable as the sunrise.

His gaze roamed the countryside; it was a harsh land with a beauty all its own. The whites saw only desolation and barrenness in the desert, but the Apache knew every stream, every river, every water hole, every mile of sand and cactus. He had not been here in five years, yet the very air seemed to welcome him home.

Even Relámpago seemed to know where they were headed. The stallion's pace quickened and he tugged against the reins, eager to run. Finally, tired of holding him in, Trey gave the stallion his head and the horse broke into a gallop.

Trey glanced over his shoulder to make sure Amanda was with him, and then he lost himself in the sheer pleasure of racing across the desert.

Amanda grinned as the gelding gave chase. She loved her Jag, loved driving fast along an open stretch of highway, but there was nothing quite as exhilarating as a wild gallop across open ground, nothing to compare with feeling the power of the horse beneath her, or the wind's fingers going through her hair. Caught up in the sheer joy of the ride, she laughed out loud as the gelding jumped across a dry stream bed.

How had she gone so long without riding? How could she have forgotten how much she had once loved it, how much fun it could be?

She urged the gelding on in a vain attempt to catch Trey and Relámpago. Trey rode with an ease she supposed was inborn, rode as though he were a part of the horse. Man and horse made a beautiful sight as they raced across the desert—the man leaning low over the stallion's neck, his long black hair whipped by the wind; the horse moving like some mystical creature, its hooves hardly seeming to touch the earth, its mane and tail flying like battle flags.

Trey let the stallion run until it slowed of its own accord. Reining the stud to a halt, he turned the horse and waited for Amanda to catch up. She rode well, her body moving in rhythm with the gelding's, her hands light upon the reins, her skin glowing. The late afternoon sunlight cast golden shadows in the wealth of her auburn hair. He knew a sudden urge to run his fingers through her hair, to feel her body writhing beneath his, to bury himself in her warmth.

"That was wonderful!" she exclaimed as she reined her horse to a stop beside his. Leaning forward, she patted the gelding's neck exuberantly.

He had never seen anything more desirable in his life, Trey thought, than Amanda the way she looked just then, with her hair falling about her shoulders in wild disarray and her cheeks flushed with pleasure.

"It is beautiful out here, in a wild, rugged sort of way," she said breathlessly. "I used to wonder why the Indians loved it so much, why they fought for it so hard, but now . . ." She shook her head. "I guess I understand, at least a little."

"It's home," Trey said. "That's why they fight for it, why they love it."

Amanda nodded. "Of course," she said wistfully. "Home."

He heard the longing in her voice, the yearning to return to her own home, her own time, and knew it was the one thing he would deny her, even if he'd had the means to give it to her.

They rode until dusk, then made camp near a shallow water hole. In what had become routine, Trey looked after the horses and Amanda spread their blankets; when that was done, she gathered what fuel she could find for a fire while Trey went hunting.

Taking the box of matches from a saddlebag, she lit the fire, her apprehension growing as it grew darker and darker and he didn't return. She told herself there was nothing to be afraid of. After all, there was nothing in the desert but sand and lizards. And rattlesnakes. But snakes didn't like the cold, did they? Wouldn't they all be holed up somewhere for the night?

Without her watch, she had no way of knowing how long Trey had been gone, but it seemed like well over an hour. He wasn't usually gone so long. No doubt he would be back soon. Feeling suddenly fidgety, she went to stand beside Relámpago.

"He'll be right back," she told the horse, even though she knew she was really trying to reassure herself.

The stallion shook his head, as if in disagreement.

"You'll see." No doubt he was just having more trouble than usual finding a rabbit. Of course, that was it.

She glanced into the distance, but beyond the light cast by the fire, there was nothing to see.

She stood there stroking the stallion's neck, growing more and more afraid that something had happened to Trey. He could have fallen, she thought, broken an arm or a leg or something. He might have gotten lost, though she found that hard to believe. That was *her* thing, she thought, grimacing. She had no sense of direction at all, but Trey seemed to find his way around the desert with no trouble at all.

How long had he been gone? An hour? Two?

Something was definitely wrong. She knew it, could feel it in her bones. She should go after him, she thought. Or maybe not. . . . After several minutes of indecision, she saddled the stallion, mounted, and headed in the direction Trey had gone. She had better find him, she thought ruefully, because she would probably never find her way back to camp on her own.

The gelding snorted and pulled against his tether as she rode away on Relámpago.

In no time at all, the faint glow of the campfire was gone, swallowed up by the darkness.

"Trey?" She called his name softly, some inner voice warning her not to shout.

She reined Relámpago to a halt, having no idea which way Trey might have gone from here. She was about to call Trey's name again when the stallion tugged on the reins.

"Easy, boy." A shiver went down Amanda's spine as she peered into the darkness. "Do you see something out there?" she whispered. "Do you know where Trey is?"

The stallion pawed the earth, then tugged on the reins again.

"All right," she said, giving the stallion his head. "But I hope you know where you're going."

The hulking, red-bearded man backhanded Trey with a huge hairy paw. The force of the blow spun him to the ground, almost knocking the wind out of him. Furious anger surged through him, and he tugged against the ropes that held him, his concern for his own life paling when he thought of Amanda back at their camp, waiting for him.

He stifled a groan when the blunt toe of the second miner's boot exploded against his ribs.

"Where's your camp, half-breed?" Redbeard demanded, kicking him, too. "Where's your horse and outfit?"

Trey glared at the man. He'd die before he told them a damn thing, but there was always a chance they might be trail-wise enough to backtrack him to Amanda. His mind refused to contemplate what would happen then. Alone and unarmed, she'd be helpless.

239

"That's enough for now," the second man said, going to the fire. "Meat's about ready."

"I could shore eat," Redbeard said. He gave Trey a halfhearted kick. "We'll finish with you later."

With his cheek ground into the dust, Trey watched the other man turn a slab of venison over the fire. His venison. The deer he had killed so Amanda could eat.

He had let her down. Of all the times to be careless in the desert . . . he ground his teeth in frustration as Redbeard joined his partner at the fire. The aroma of cooking meat was maddening. He had been so intent on stalking the little Coues whitetail at the desert water hole, he had failed to see the dull blur of two hunters seated below the skyline of that little ridge, rifles ready for whatever came down to water.

Trey had made the shot cleanly. The hunters had waited until he had both hands in the buck's body cavity, cleaning it, before singing out for him to grab some sky. They had him in the open, both of his hands too slick with blood and gore to reach for his gun. Both men had rifles. On top of everything else, one of the men had recognized him. They'd only been thinking about stealing his horse and rig until then.

Of all the rotten luck, his had to be the worst. Nothing but desert for miles around, and he had to run into a two-bit-drifter who memorized wanted posters.

Damn. What a predicament. He tugged again on the ropes that bound his wrists, wincing as the movement cut off his circulation.

To add insult to injury, the two men were hunkered over a small campfire, enjoying *his* venison, rubbing their greasy hands on their pants.

There was a shift in the wind as what had been a gentle breeze began to gust. Surprisingly, the campfire guttered and went out. The two men scrambled to their feet, glancing at each other uneasily as a low keening rode the coattails of the wind.

"Look!"

Trey turned his head, his gaze following the direction of Redbeard's finger. A gray mist swirled up out of the ground, and a horse appeared out of the mist, its long white mane and tail flowing like fingers of cold lightning, its snowy coat shimmering in the moon light.

The horse paused near Trey, then rose up on his hind legs, forelegs pawing the air.

"Damn," whispered the other man. "Look at that."

Trey watched as the stallion dropped to all fours, then reared again. Moonlight glinted off his flashing hooves. Dropping to all fours again, the stallion paced back and forth between Trey and the men.

"What the hell?" Redbeard exclaimed.

"It's a ghost horse!" his partner said, an unmistakable quaver in his voice.

Trey sensed movement in the darkness behind him and tensed, then caught a whiff of a familiar fragrance. Amanda.

"Hold still," she whispered urgently.

He felt her hands fumbling with the rope that bound his wrists. Moments later, he was free.

Relámpago reared again, and as the stallion came down, Trey grabbed a handful of mane and swung onto the stallion's back, ignoring the jolt of pain in his ribs and the tingling in his arms.

One of the men swore, then shouted, "Shoot him!"

as Trey wheeled the stallion around and bent low, scooping Amanda up in front of him, all in one motion. He slammed his heels into Relámpago's flanks, and the big horse launched into a dead run, the whip-crack of futile rifle fire fading behind them.

Trey didn't rein the stallion to a halt until they were back at camp. Her gelding whinnied softly as they rode up.

Trey eased Amanda to the ground, then slid off the stallion's back. "Are you all right?" he asked.

"I'm fine."

He sat down carefully, one arm wrapped around his midsection. "How'd you find me?"

"I didn't. Relámpago did. When we got close to where you were, he stopped and refused to move again until I got off. Then he went to you, and I followed him. It was so . . . so spooky, the way the wind came up and their fire went out." She shivered at the memory. "And that mist . . . if I hadn't seen it, I wouldn't have believed it. Are you sure you're all right?" She held his bloody hands up to the moonlight. He winced.

"That's not mine," he said. "It's from the deer I was cleaning when they got the drop on me. They kicked me around some." He didn't tell her why. "I'm more aggravated than anything. Damn, I must be losing my edge, to let a pair of no-account drifters catch me flat-footed like that. Not only do they have our supper, but they've got my gun and my knife, too." He swore softly.

"What happened?" Amanda asked, dropping down beside him.

"Those two drifters were set up on a water hole waiting for meat. I walked right into them."

"What do we do now?"

"We ride," he said grimly. "There's going to be plenty of moon to see by, and I don't want them catching up to us. We'll bed down after we put some ground between them and us."

"But you're hurt."

"No time to worry about that. Saddle up."

She nodded. They'd be helpless to defend themselves, now that the miners had Trey's weapons. She knew he was blaming himself for being caught off guard, but it could have happened to anyone.

They rode for several hours, until her head was swimming with fatigue. The stallion moved tirelessly, his white coat seeming to shimmer with an otherworldly light.

When Trey finally called a halt in a dense stand of mesquite, he allowed her to remove his shirt and examine his rib cage. He shrugged off her concern about his swollen lip and the bruise on his jaw. But he flinched when she probed his ribs.

"We need to wrap 'em up tight," he said. "So I can keep moving. But—"

"I know. I've seen plenty of Westerns," she said with a grin. Going to her saddlebags, she pulled out her petticoat. "Instant bandages," she said, and ripped off the bottom ruffle.

He nodded. "Smart." He winced as she wrapped the strip of sturdy cotton around his middle. "That's it, good and tight. Can you unsaddle the horses and make up the bed? I hate to ask it—"

She placed her fingers against his swollen lip. "Shh, don't worry. I'll take care of it."

She unsaddled the horses and turned Relámpago loose. Dragging the heavy saddles into place and spreading the blankets took the last iota of her strength. She made Trey as comfortable as she could, then stretched out beside him.

Lying there with her head pillowed on a saddle, she stared at Relámpago through heavy-lidded eyes. Maybe the stallion really was a ghost horse. And if that was so, then maybe he was the best protection they could have. It was her last thought before sleep claimed her.

She woke to a ravenous hunger. A drink from the canteen and a piece of store-bought jerky helped a little, but not much. She looked over at Trey. He was still asleep. Not a good sign, since he usually woke before she did.

Rising, she glanced around as she stretched the kinks from her back and neck. They were sitting ducks out here, and even as the thought crossed her mind, she saw two riders in the distance.

"Trey?" She shook his arm gently. "Trey, wake up."

He jackknifed into a sitting position, swore as pain lanced through him. He wrapped one arm around his middle, his breath coming in painful gasps. "What is it?"

She pointed toward the west. "Riders. Come on," she urged, offering him her hand. "We've got to get out of here."

He climbed heavily to his feet. Amanda had the

gelding saddled and was smoothing the blanket over Relámpago's back when she noticed Trey staring hard at the oncoming riders.

"Trey . . . ?"

"It's okay," he said, smiling.

"How can you be sure it's not those two men?" Amanda asked, glancing over her shoulder.

"I've got eyes is how," he said.

"Are you sure?"

His smile widened. "I'm sure."

Seeing his expression, Amanda frowned. "What are you smiling at? It might be—"

"It might be anyone, up to and including Langley— but it ain't. Help is on the way."

"Help?" Turning, she stared at the two men riding toward them. They were close enough now for her to make out details.

Two men dressed in breechclouts and knee-high moccasins; men with feathers in their hair and paint on their faces.

Indians.

She took a step backward, her heart pounding loudly in her ears. They had dark copper-colored skin, ink-black hair, and deep-set dark eyes. Barrel-chested, they were powerfully built, with well-muscled arms and legs. One wore an amulet suspended from a slender strip of rawhide around his neck. Both were armed with bows and arrows and leading saddled horses. And both were carrying rifles.

Draped across the withers of the lead rider's horse were the hindquarters of a deer, its hooves visible below a bloody hide. The second rider wore a familiar gun belt cinched around his lean waist.

They came to a stop a few feet in front of Trey, their expressions impassive but not hostile.

Amanda stood rooted to the spot, listening as the three men spoke in a language she didn't understand. One of the Indians gestured at her, and there was a rapid exchange, with both of the Indians glancing at her from time to time. The second rider slipped gracefully from his mount, unbuckled the gun belt, and handed it to Trey, who buckled it in place, then nodded his thanks.

"I take it they're friends of yours?" she said.

"Yeah. This one here is Elk Runner. He says I never could stay out of trouble long, and it's a good thing I've got a medicine horse and a white woman to look after me. That's his cousin, Two Horses."

"They . . . they were there?"

"Not last night. They cut our sign early this morning."

He didn't have to tell her they'd also found the two white men. The fact that they had Trey's gun belt and two horses carrying brands proved that. She didn't ask what had happened to the men.

"Looks like our luck has changed," Trey said with a wry grin.

Chapter Nineteen

The young detective from the sheriff's office stood in front of Rob's desk. He was dressed like a prosperous cattleman in a Western-cut suit and polished black cowboy boots. Like many Arizonans, he wore a bolo tie, this one secured by a turquoise stone set in silver. He twisted the brim of his white Stetson in his big hands. "We're plumb out of leads, Rob."

Rob leaned back in the big leather chair behind his desk, which was laden with case files. "I appreciate everything you've done, Sam. If there was anything to find, you'd have found it."

"You'll let us know if you hear anything from her?"

"You bet. But I have a bad feeling about this."

"I understand." The detective shifted from one foot to the other. "I'd better be going. I'll keep in touch."

"Thanks, Sam. I owe you."

After the detective was gone, Rob sat staring at

Amanda's address book, neatly squared atop the active files on the desk. He had called everyone in the book, persisting until he had contacted every one of them, but no one had heard from her since that day he had been out at her house. She had missed her appointment at the dentist; she hadn't started her new job; she hadn't returned her mother's phone calls.

He glanced out the window, wondering if the yellow crime-scene tape was still draped around her porch and the front yard.

The sheriff's crime-scene team had been very thorough. They had found the boot tracks of four separate men in and around the scene, and taken casts of them all. They had taken good casts of the strange tire prints. And they had recovered enough blood from the stains in the yard to ensure a match if they ever came up with a viable suspect.

Using metal detectors, they had dug four slugs out of various walls. One of those had been soft lead, badly deformed, as if it had punched through something or somebody before coming to rest in the barn door. The forensics people were curious about its conformation, and especially curious about a couple of boxes of .45 cartridges they had found in the house: pristine pasteboard cartridge boxes, one full, the other almost so. The printing on the boxes named a cartridge company that didn't exist. Pulling apart one of the rounds had proved it matched the information printed on the box: a black-powder round.

Remembering the perfectly preserved six-gun Trey Long Walker had shown him, Rob had kept his own counsel. The man clearly carried his Old West hobby to extremes that most of the Single Action Shooting Sports aficionados did not. Preliminary research on Rob's part had determined that, yes, some cartridge companies printed old-fashioned-looking boxes for reenactment fans, but if these boxes had been printed by such a company, there would be a legitimate address somewhere on them. Had Long Walker loaded the rounds himself and had the boxes printed with a fake address? That was an idea Rob wasn't willing to share with the authorities. Not yet.

Then there was the stash of well-preserved old money the detectives had found in Amanda's bedroom. If it was authentic, that money was worth far more than its face value in modern dollars. If it wasn't—again, Long Walker had gone to extremes; the kind of presses that could handle such a specialized printing job shouldn't be too hard to find. He would start in Montana.

Normally, such anomalous material at a crime scene would have been marked as evidence and taken in, but the case was too off-center. Since Rob was well known to the local authorities, they had agreed to let him take custody of the cash, for the time being. Amanda's parents had agreed with that decision.

Her mother had flown out, stayed a few days, and left in tears.

Her father called every day, asking Rob if any progress had been made.

Time and again, Rob had walked out to where the horse's hoofprints disappeared, and the truck had turned back. He had plucked a long strand of white hair from a chest-high shrub and wrapped it around his finger. Where had the horse gone? Why had his tracks vanished in plain sight? Or maybe the question was how? It was as if the stud had taken wing.

The sheriff's office had run Long Walker through its computers and come up blank. There was no driver's license on him in Montana. He had never served in the military. He didn't even have a Social Security card.

It was as if the cowboy had materialized out of thin air.

Just like the white stallion had, according to Amanda.

He leaned back in his swivel chair and closed his eyes. The noise of traffic from the busy Tucson street below his window filtered into his consciousness. The horse had appeared, and then the cowboy had shown up, and then something had happened out there, something violent. Now horse and cowboy—and Amanda—had vanished off the face of the earth.

He was missing something. Something right in front of his face. He frowned thoughtfully. He was supposed to be a man-hunter—one of the best. It was in his blood. But he needed a trail, a lead, something to start on.

Those bank notes and the cartridge boxes . . . it was time to do some research.

He spun his chair around to face his computer screen, tugged the keyboard out of the drawer, and logged onto the Internet.

Chapter Twenty

They were on their way to Bonita Canyon. It was a favorite Apache stronghold, Trey told her. Located off a tributary of the Gila River, it was an ideal hideout, hard to find, easy to defend.

The Indians had offered them jerky and cakes made of ground acorns. Amanda had eaten beef jerky before, but it had never tasted like this. When she remarked on it, Trey told her it was made from buffalo, not beef.

And now she rode beside him, feeling somewhat distant from it all, as if she were watching everything through someone else's eyes. How could this be happening? What was she doing here, in the middle of nowhere?

She glanced at Trey. He rode slightly slumped forward in the saddle, one arm wrapped protectively around his midsection. A fine sheen of perspiration dampened his brow; his jaw was rigid with discomfort. In the light of day, she could see he did, indeed, have a black eye, and it was a beaut.

The two warriors rode ahead of them. She had the feeling that they were aware of every plant, every lizard, every grain of sand. They were a fearsome-looking pair. She kept reminding herself that they were Trey's people, Trey's friends. But they looked so . . . so . . . ferocious was the only word that came to mind. Their hair was shoulder length, thick and black and coarse. Their clouts were made of some kind of animal skin that reached to the knee, front and back; their moccasins reached to mid-thigh, to protect their legs from prickly brush and cacti she supposed. One of the warriors had folded his moccasins down to just below the knee. She thought it curious that the toes of the moccasins curled up at the ends.

Amanda shifted her weight in the saddle. They had been riding for several hours, following the river. Now the warriors turned off into a pass that Trey said led to the stronghold. High canyon walls rose up all around. Trees were few. She saw scrub brush, mesquite, creosote bushes, saguaro cactus, and paloverde. The saguaro was the state flower, if she remembered right. Some of the plants were huge, standing over forty feet high. Almost as ancient as sequoias, she seemed to remember.

The Indians followed a bend in the river, and suddenly they were at the mouth of the canyon. Amanda stared in wonder at the brush-covered wickiups spread in the shelter of the high canyon walls. It was a peaceful scene. Dogs slept in the sun. A large herd of horses grazed on bunch grass in the distance. She saw several boys shooting arrows at a target; a couple of boys were wrestling while a handful of others looked on. She saw young girls playing with dolls made of corn husks and deerskin; others were making animals and houses out of mud. Primitive Play-doh, she thought with a grin. She saw a group of children swimming in the river, while women with babies sat on the bank, keeping watch. Men sat in small groups, working on weapons, talking, gambling. Women throughout the camp were cooking, sewing, nursing their young, scraping hides. The men were clad in little more than breechclouts and moccasins; they wore a band of cloth around their heads to keep their hair out of their faces. The women wore fringed dresses of deerskin that fell past their knees. Their moccasins seemed less durable than those worn by the men, and reached only a little above the ankle. The children wore hardly anything at all.

Elk Runner and Two Horses stopped in front of a hut that was circular in shape and covered with brush. Smoke curled from a hole in the middle of the roof. A deerhide covered the doorway, which was low.

Elk Runner spoke to Trey, and then the two Apaches moved on.

Amanda glanced around, aware that many of the Indians had stopped what they were doing and were now watching them, their dark eyes alight with curiosity.

"What's going on?" Amanda asked.

Moving slowly, Trey dismounted. "This is my grandmother's wickiup."

"Oh." She looked at the dwelling again. It wasn't very large, perhaps twelve feet by eight. "Are they expecting you?"

"I don't know," Trey replied. "Grandfather always seemed to know when I was . . ."

He paused as a man stepped out of the wickiup. He was of medium height, broad-shouldered and virile looking in spite of the gray in his hair and the deep-cut lines in his face.

"Long Walker," he said. "Welcome home."

"Thank you. Grandfather. This is Amanda. Amanda, this is my grandfather, Walker on the Wind."

The old Apache looked up at Amanda through knowing dark eyes. "You are welcome in my lodge," he said.

"Thank you," she replied. Conscious of the old man's scrutiny, she dismounted and stood beside Trey.

"So," the old man said, turning his gaze back to Trey. "Relámpago has brought you safely home."

Trey nodded. "Just as you promised."

Walker on the Wind called to a teenage boy and instructed him to look after the horses, then turned toward Trey. "Come," he said. "Let us eat."

The old man ducked back inside his lodge. Trey followed him, and after a moment's hesitation, Amanda followed Trey.

It was dim inside. A small fire pit was located in the middle of the wickiup. An old woman with long gray braids sat beside the fire. A smile lit her face when she saw Trey.

"Long Walker," she said.

Walker on the Wind helped the old woman to her feet. She laid a gnarled hand on Trey's cheek, her gaze moving lovingly over his face.

"You are hurt," she remarked, noting the way he kept his arm curved around his middle.

Trey nodded. "I think I broke a rib, maybe two." He glanced at Amanda over the older woman's head. "This is my grandmother, Yellow Calf Woman. Grandmother, this is Amanda."

Yellow Calf Woman nodded. "Aman–da. Welcome to my lodge."

"Thank you."

"You, sit," Yellow Calf Woman said to Trey.

Trey did as he was told, then held his hand out to Amanda. "Sit with me."

She did as he asked, watching as his grandmother helped him out of his shirt and then removed the strips of cloth wound around his middle.

Yellow Calf Woman ran her hands over his back, speaking to him in rapid Apache.

"What did she say?" Amanda asked.

"She wanted to know who shot me," Trey answered. "She also said my ribs aren't broken, just badly bruised."

"Well, that's good."

Trey grunted softly, then clasped her hand in his while Yellow Calf Woman ran her fingers lightly over his middle, spread a sweet-smelling ointment over his side, then wrapped a strip of rawhide tightly around his rib cage.

"Geez, Grandmother," he muttered in English, "leave me some room to breathe."

When Yellow Calf Woman had finished tending Trey's injuries, she offered Trey and Amanda each a bowl of thick stew and a spoon made of horn.

Amanda looked at the contents of the bowl, then looked at Trey.

"It's all right," he said. "It's venison."

They ate in silence. Amanda kept her gaze on the bowl in her hand, aware that she was very much out of place in this setting. More than anything, she wanted to be back in her own time, in her own house. In her own bathtub. She couldn't recall ever being quite so grimy, so in need of bathing. She wasn't sure, but she was afraid she smelled bad.

Yellow Calf Woman sat down beside the fire again; Walker on the Wind sat across from his wife. He pulled a pipe from a buckskin bag, filled the bowl with tobacco, lit it with a coal from the fire, and then lifted the pipe to the four directions.

She couldn't help wondering if the smoke was meant to mask her body odor. Perhaps later, when she was alone with Trey, she would ask if there was someplace where she could take a bath and wash her clothes.

When they finished eating, Yellow Calf Woman collected the dishes and took them outside. A small spotted puppy emerged from the shadows in the back of the lodge and followed her out the door.

Trey let out a long weary sigh. Every movement sent slivers of pain lancing through his left side.

Walker on the Wind leaned forward. "You need rest, my son. Yellow Calf Woman has prepared a lodge for the two of you."

A cold shiver tiptoed down Amanda's spine at the old man's words.

"*Ashoge, Shinale*," Trey replied.

Walker on the Wind smiled. "You will find your lodge behind this one. Go, rest. We will talk later."

With a nod, Trey climbed slowly to his feet.

Amanda stood and followed Trey outside. She blinked against the light of the sun, stood a moment basking in its warmth, unable to shake the feeling that she was caught up in the Twilight Zone.

"Are you coming?" Trey called.

"Yes." She hurried after him. He was, after all, the only familiar thing in this strange new world.

The wickiup that had been prepared for them was almost exactly like the one that belonged to his grandparents.

Amanda stood inside the doorway, her arms folded over her chest, while Trey lowered himself down on a pile of soft-looking furs.

"How did he know?" she asked. "How did your grandfather know you were coming here? That *we* were coming here?"

"He's a *diyini*," Trey replied. "A holy man. He often has visions that foretell the future."

"Your grandfather mentioned that Relámpago had brought you safely home. Did he work some kind of Indian magic to bring us here?"

Trey closed his eyes. "I don't know. But he always said 'Pago had magic powers to take me away from danger."

She remembered her dream of a white horse and a warrior who resembled Trey. "How old is Relámpago?"

257

He shrugged. "He was full-grown when I was a little boy. He doesn't seem to age very fast, though. He could always outrun any horse in the tribe."

She turned her thoughts to a more pressing concern. "How long are we going to stay here?"

"I don't know."

"Well, what *do* you know?"

"I know that I hurt all over."

She let out a sigh. "Of course you do. I'm sorry."

"Well, don't lose any sleep over it," he muttered wearily. "It's not your fault."

While she considered a reply, he fell asleep.

With a sigh, Amanda went to the door, lifted the flap and peered outside.

Dusk had come to the canyon, though the afternoon sun still burnished the high cliffs. Cook fires blazed in front of the wickiups; mouth-watering odors drifted on the lazy campfire smoke. Mothers called to their children, warriors brought their favorite horses in from the herd and picketed them close to their lodges. Dogs fought over scraps of meat. Three old men sat together, sharing a pipe, oblivious to the activity around them.

Standing there, watching the Apaches get ready for the night, she felt an overwhelming wave of loneliness. She would never belong here. Never. The wickiup suddenly seemed too small, and she stepped outside. No one paid her any attention as she walked away from the camp toward a clump of trees along a narrow, winding stream. She walked along the edge of the water, following it away from the camp. The Indian horse herd grazed nearby. The horses lifted their heads as she drew near, ears twitching, nostrils flaring as they took in her strange scent. Relámpago was the only white horse in the herd, and easy to spot.

She smiled as the big stallion trotted toward her. He rubbed his forehead against her chest, begging to have his ears scratched.

"Guess I'm not totally alone," she murmured. "Not as long as you're here."

The stallion made a soft snuffling sound in reply.

She stood there for several minutes, her gaze moving over the floor of the canyon and up the sides while she scratched the stallion's ears. Surely there were sentries posted, but if so, she couldn't see any. Then again, there was only one way in and one way out. If any sentries were posted, they were most likely at the mouth of the canyon.

She ran her hand along the stallion's neck. If she rode out of the canyon while Trey was sleeping, would anyone try to stop her? She wasn't a prisoner, after all.

She thought about it a few more minutes. It was a risk, riding out alone, but a risk she was willing to take, since Trey had made it clear he wouldn't take her back to her own time. And she had to get back! She just had to, before it was too late. Before Trey became more important to her than he already was. Before it became impossible to leave him. She swallowed hard. She was already falling in love with him. She had to go while she could, before he broke her heart.

Stepping up on a rock, she climbed onto the stallion's back, grabbed a handful of mane, and drummed her heels against the stallion's flanks. The horse moved out smartly, guided by the pressure of her knees.

She took the long way around the camp, skirting the

far edge. It was dusk as she drew nearer to the canyon entrance. So far, so good. A few children had seen her pass by. They had stared at her curiously but done nothing to stop her.

It was almost fully dark, and her heart was pounding wildly by the time she reached the canyon entrance. And still no one had made a move to stop her.

She was heady with relief when, for no apparent reason, the stallion came to an abrupt halt. Amanda looked around, searching for whatever it was that had brought Relámpago to a stop, but there was nothing to see.

"Come on, boy." She clucked to the horse. "Come on, let's go."

With a shake of his head, the stallion backed up.

"No!" Amanda drummed her heels into the horse's flanks. She was so close! "Come on," she coaxed. "Let's go." She smacked the horse on the rump with the flat of her hand. "Come on! Take me home!"

The stallion's ears went flat as it slowly rose up on its hind legs. With a startled cry, Amanda slid over the horse's hindquarters and landed on her backside, hard. For a moment, she just sat there, too stunned to move, and then she became aware of a sharp pain in the region of her tailbone.

Glaring at Relámpago, she gained her feet.

"Forget it!" she said when the stallion rubbed his forehead against her arm. "Scratch your own ears."

Trey was still asleep when she limped her way back into the lodge. Relámpago trailed at her heels like an overgrown puppy. She wasn't sure, but she thought the stallion was having a good laugh at her expense.

"Go on," she said, making a shooing motion with her hands. "Go on, you traitor, get out of here."

With a snort and a shake of his head, the stallion trotted back to the herd.

Amanda scowled after him, then ducked into the lodge. "Ungrateful beast," she muttered.

"I hope you're not talking about me," Trey muttered sleepily.

"What? Oh, no." She closed the door flap.

"Well, what ungrateful beast are you talking about?"

"That horse of yours! I tried to . . . oh, never mind."

He started to sit up and thought better of it. "What about my horse?"

She sucked in a deep breath, debating whether to tell him what she had done. Or tried to do.

"I asked you a question." He was fully awake now.

"Oh, all right. If you must know, I tried to leave the canyon, but that horse of yours refused to leave."

Trey lifted one brow. "What do you mean?"

She crossed the floor and sat down on a blanket. "I mean, he wouldn't leave. He went right up to the entrance, and then he just stopped and refused to go any further. You've certainly trained him well."

"I had nothing to do with it."

"So it was Relámpago's idea?" she asked, somewhat sarcastically.

"I don't know. 'Pago is a medicine horse. You have any questions, I reckon you'll have to ask my grandfather."

"How long are we going to stay here?"

"Until I'm ready to leave."

"Oh, you are the most impossible man I've ever known."

His hand captured hers, his thumb making lazy circles over the back of her hand. "And you are the most beautiful woman I've ever known."

"Stop that." She tried to jerk her hand away, but he refused to let her go.

"Why?"

Her gaze slid away from his. It wasn't fair, the maddening effect he had on her senses. His thumb continued to make circles on the back of her hand, his touch sending shivers of sensual delight down her spine. She must have been crazy to even think of leaving when everything she wanted was right here.

"Amanda?"

"What?" She met his gaze reluctantly.

He gave a little tug on her hand. "Come here."

"Why?"

"Come here."

She let him pull her closer, didn't resist as his mouth captured hers. A flutter of excitement unfurled in her belly. Heat flowed through her veins as his tongue explored her lower lip.

Moaning softly, she stretched out beside him. Needing to be closer, she pressed against him, her body molding to his, her hand sliding up and down his chest, reveling in the warmth of his skin, the way his body felt next to her own.

He slid his arm around her, a groan that was half pleasure and half pain rising in his throat.

"I'm sorry." She started to draw back, but his arm tightened around her.

262

"Don't go," he said, his voice thick.

"But I'm hurting you."

"Not as much as your leaving will hurt."

His words sent waves of pleasure rolling through her. "Well," she said, nibbling on his lower lip, "I can stand it if you can."

He grinned at her, then captured her lips with his once more. Ignoring the pain, he turned on his side and drew her up against him, felt the heat of her breasts against his chest. She fit him perfectly, he thought, soft and pliant, all woman from head to heel. He ran his hand down her shoulder, skimmed over the swell of her breast, dipped at the curve of her waist, slid over her hip, down her thigh and up again.

She moaned with pleasure, fanning the embers of his desire. "We'd better stop."

"Yeah." She was right. He was in no condition to carry this through to the end, but, damn, he wanted her. Wanted her like he had never wanted anything, any woman, in his whole life.

"Can I get you anything?" she asked.

"Some water."

"All right." She lingered a moment, hating to leave the warmth of his arms; then, with a sigh of resignation, she sat up and reached for the waterskin.

The next few days passed slowly. Peacefully. Trey spent most of his time sleeping, or sitting in the sun while his body healed itself. Yellow Calf Woman brought them food morning and evening; Walker on the Wind stopped by at least once each day to see how Trey was doing.

Amanda was sitting outside a week later when a sudden commotion caught her attention. Rising, she peered inside the wickiup. Trey was asleep. Closing the door flap so no one would disturb him, she followed several other women toward the cause of the commotion.

Five mounted warriors sat their horses in the midst of the crowd. Amanda glanced at them, wondering what all the excitement was about. And then she saw him. The bounty hunter, Langley. He was lying on the ground, his hands tied behind his back. There was a rope around his neck. Judging from his torn clothing and the scrapes on his skin, she guessed he had been dragged for some distance.

The Apaches pointed at him, their voices filled with derision. A couple of young boys pelted him with rocks. An elderly woman struck him across the back with her walking stick.

Langley suffered their abuse in silence, his face impassive, his eyes shuttered and cold. Until he looked up and saw her staring at him. Recognition flickered in his eyes.

She watched as he was dragged away and bound to a post, and then, feeling sick to her stomach, she hurried back to Trey's lodge. She had read books, seen movies. She knew what Indians did to captives. They burned them alive, or covered them with honey and let the ants eat them.

Trey was awake when she entered the wickiup. He frowned when he saw the look on her face. "What is it, sweetheart? You look like you're going to be sick."

"He's here . . . they've captured him . . ."

"Who's here?"

"That bounty hunter."

"Langley?"

She nodded, her arms crossed over her stomach, her face pale. "What will they do with him?"

He knew then what was bothering her, why she looked so stricken. The cruelty of the Apache was well known. Pity was a trait unknown to the warriors of his people. Fighting was in their blood. They had fought with other tribes for generations. They had suffered much at the hands of the Spanish and then the other whites. Little wonder they had learned to repay treachery with treachery, cruelty with cruelty. Loyal to their own, they considered all others to be their enemy. Wrongs against their own were quickly avenged.

"Trey?"

Gaining his feet, he closed the distance between them and took her into his arms. "I don't know."

"You don't know? Or you don't want to tell me?"

"I reckon they'll kill him."

"They can't!" She clutched his arms. "You know they can't. What about Rob? If they kill Langley—"

"Yeah, we wouldn't want anything to keep old Rob from being born, now, would we?"

She gazed up at him, her eyes filled with silent condemnation.

Trey swore a short, pithy oath. "I'll see what I can do."

He found Langley curled in a tight ball in an effort to protect his face and belly from the rocks and sticks being thrown at him by a handful of boys.

Trey chased the kids away, then squatted on his heels beside the bounty hunter. "You lookin' for me?"

Langley sat up slowly, his eyes narrowed. "Long Walker." He spat the name through clenched teeth.

"I should think you'd be glad to see me," Trey remarked. "After all, I'm the only friend you've got here."

Langley glared at him.

Trey ran a hand over his jaw, enjoying the other man's discomfort.

"What are they gonna do to me?"

Trey shrugged. "What do you think?"

"I reckon you'll be right in there with 'em."

"I have to admit, I'd sleep a lot easier knowing you wouldn't be coming after me anymore."

"If I don't get you, some other lawman will."

"Hollinger killed my old man. Whatever happens to him is no more than he's got coming."

"The law doesn't see it that way."

"The law? What do you care about the law? You're nothing but a leech, living on blood money."

"And you're nothing but a dirty—"

"I wouldn't say anything else if I were you," Trey interjected, his voice hard. "Might make me change my mind about getting you out of here."

"Why would you help me?"

"That's none of your business. But if I can get you out of this, I want your word that you won't come after me again."

Langley stared at him.

"Well? Do we have a deal?"

"Yeah," Langley replied sullenly. "We've got a deal."

Chapter Twenty-one

Amanda was waiting for him when he returned to the wickiup, her expression worried. "Where have you been?"

"Talking to Langley."

"Is he all right?"

"For the time being."

"What will happen to him?"

"It's up to whoever captured him, I reckon."

"Trey!"

"We'll just have to wait and play it by ear, see what happens next."

"When will we know?"

He glanced toward the doorway of the wickiup. Drumming could be heard from outside. "I'd say anytime now. Come on."

A festive mood hung over the camp. Langley was bound to a post, his hands secured over his head. Several young warriors paraded back and forth in front of him, taunting him, while a handful of women poked him with sticks, drawing blood with every hit.

Langley endured their abuse stoically, his eyes blazing defiance.

"Stay here," Trey said. He didn't wait for a reply, but left her standing on the edge of the crowd.

The warriors fell back as Trey approached. They murmured among themselves as he withdrew his knife from the sheath on his belt, their murmurs of approval turning to protest as he cut Langley free.

Elk Runner strode forward, his dark eyes angry. "What are you doing? The white man is mine."

"I claim him," Trey replied, "by right of blood."

"What do you mean?"

"We are blood brothers." It was the truth, and a lie, Trey mused. He had shed Langley's blood; Langley had shed his. "I will give you a horse in exchange for his life."

Elk Runner considered Trey's offer. Then, apparently deciding a horse was worth more than the captured *pinda-lick-o-ye*, he nodded his agreement. Gesturing for the other warriors to follow him, Elk Runner left the area. The rest of the crowd drifted after him.

"Come on," Trey said gruffly. "Let's get you cleaned up. My people will expect me to take care of you now."

"I don't like this any better than you do," Langley retorted.

"I guess it's a good thing you won't be staying long, then, isn't it?"

It was left to Amanda to tend Langley's wounds. Besides the one in his shoulder inflicted by Trey, he had numerous cuts, bruises, and abrasions from head to foot. She couldn't help staring at him as she worked. His resemblance to Rob, or, more correctly, Rob's resemblance to him, was remarkable. If she hadn't known better, she would have thought they were the same man.

Langley frowned under her scrutiny. "Something wrong?"

"No. It's just that you look like someone I know."

"Is that right?"

She nodded. "An old boyfriend of mine."

"Well, if you don't mind my saying so, he was a fool to let you go."

She smiled at the compliment as she treated the last of his injuries. "There, that does it."

"Obliged, ma'am."

"You're welcome. Would you like something to eat?"

"Yes, ma'am, I surely would." He glanced over at Trey, who was sitting near the fire pit. "I don't reckon that buck will give me back my horse or my weapons."

"I reckon you're right," Trey answered.

"How am I supposed to get back to civilization?"

"That's not my problem, is it?"

Amanda shook her head. For a couple of grown men, they sounded like two schoolboys.

Langley shrugged. "Reckon I'll just stay here, being your blood brother and all. I hope that won't inconvenience you too much, ma'am."

"I know when I'm licked," Trey muttered sourly. "I'll get you a horse."

*   *   *

It was Walker on the Wind who provided a horse for Langley the following day, as well as a shirt to replace the one that had been ruined when he was captured. Amanda fixed him some food for the trail.

"I'm obliged to ya for what you've done," Langley said to Trey.

"I'm counting on you to keep your word," Trey replied.

Langley nodded. Taking up the reins to his horse, he pulled himself onto the animal's back. "How am I supposed to make it out of here without a gun?"

"My people won't bother you. They think we're blood brothers."

"Yeah, well, your people aren't the only Injuns running around out here."

Trey loosed a sigh of exasperation. "You're lucky to get out of here with a whole skin. From now on, you're on your own."

"I'm obliged to ya," Langley said. "Ride easy."

"Yeah," Trey replied. "You, too."

The next several days passed peacefully. Amanda stayed close to Trey, watching the activity in the village, picking up a word here and there. *Shima* meant mother, *shinale* meant grandfather, *shiwoye* meant grandmother, *ma'ye* was the word for coyote, *chaa* meant beaver, *shikeshi* meant follow me, *ch'ide* was the word for blanket, *gahee* meant coffee, *nada* was corn.

She grew accustomed to bathing in the stream in the Apache way. She felt nervous and exposed the first time she did it, but Trey's grandmother stood nearby to reassure her. Yellow Calf Woman had offered her a chunk of soap that Trey later told her was made from yucca, but Amanda had her own soap. She handed it to Trey's grandmother, who sniffed it and smiled. From then on, the two of them shared the lavender-scented soap until it was gone.

His grandparents were frequent visitors. Amanda quickly grew fond of them both, especially Walker on the Wind. He was a wonderful storyteller, and she listened avidly as he talked of Trey's childhood days with the Apache—a sure sign that she was falling in love, she thought, since women were always eager to know everything there was to know about the men they loved.

Why did she love him? That was the question uppermost in her mind as they sat outside a week later. She studied him surreptitiously. He was handsome, yes, but there was more to it than that. He made her feel safe, alive, important. Of course, the fact that his kisses made her go weak in the knees probably had something to do with it, too. That, and his smile, and the way he made her forget her own name when he looked at her. He had occupied most of her thoughts by day and her dreams by night since the first day she had seen him. Maybe it was nothing more than a simple case of lust . . .

"Amanda?"

His voice scattered her thoughts, and she looked up to find him watching her. His left eye was still swollen but was no longer black. Instead, it was a rather garish shade of purple tinged with puke green.

"What?"

"Do you feel like going for a walk?" he asked. "I'm almighty sick of just sitting."

"Sure, if you feel up to it."

"Let's go."

They walked away from the camp toward the river. She had lost track of the days, but she'd been gone long enough that Rob would be missing her by now, wondering why she hadn't returned his calls. Earl Hennessy would be wondering why she hadn't come to work, why she hadn't called in. Her parents would be wondering why they hadn't heard from her. But there was nothing she could do about any of that now. Or about those horrible men who had come looking for Rob. Had they found him? Was he okay? She didn't want anything to happen to Rob, even though she wasn't sure how she felt about him anymore. She felt bad about leaving Earl Hennessy in the lurch, but that was really the least of her worries. As for her parents, there was no way to assure them that she was all right. Even if she could find a phone, assuming they had been invented, she was pretty sure she couldn't call home. She grinned at the very idea, thinking that a call from 1869 to 2001 would really be long distance.

She drew in a deep breath, held it, then let it out in a long sigh. In some ways, being in the past wasn't as bad as she had feared it would be; in other ways, it was worse. The one constant was Trey. You had to hand it to Western men, she thought with a wry grin. They were made of strong stuff. At least Trey was. Considering all he had been through in the last couple of weeks, he seemed to have remarkable powers of recovery.

"You're awfully quiet," Trey remarked.

"I'm sorry. Are you feeling all right? Do you need to rest?"

"I'm fine. It's a pretty place, though. Let's sit awhile."

"Okay."

Amanda sat down on the grass, and he sat beside her. It was quiet here, away from the camp. Peaceful. He stared at the river, watching the water swirl and eddy around the rocks. There had been precious little peace in his life. And now he had a price on his head. Langley might be out of the picture, but there were plenty of other bounty hunters who'd be on the lookout for him. He cursed Hollinger, cursed himself for not killing the man when he'd had the opportunity. Why hadn't he pulled the trigger? He'd probably never get another chance, not now. But he'd never been a cold-blooded killer. Much as the man deserved killing, it looked like someone else would have to do it.

"Trey?"

He glanced over at Amanda to find her watching him, a look of concern in her eyes. She had beautiful eyes. They were a deep dark green, open and honest. Eyes a man could trust. Eyes a man could get lost in.

"Are you all right?"

He nodded. "I'm fine." He reached for her without conscious thought, reached for her because she was warm and soft, because her eyes were filled with concern, because, heaven help him, he needed her in a way he'd never needed another living soul.

She leaned into him, unresisting, her lips parting as

his mouth slanted over hers. He felt a twinge in his side as he drew her up against him, but letting her go would have hurt more.

He kissed her deeply, drank from her lips like a man dying of thirst. And she was kissing him in return, holding nothing back. They stretched out on the grass, bodies pressed intimately together. He was lost in her nearness, mesmerized by her touch. She moaned with pleasure as he caressed her, her quick response adding fuel to the flame that burned between them.

Her mouth was warm and softly yielding, sweeter than anything he had ever known. He tasted desire on her lips, a fiery yearning that matched his own. He kissed her until they were both breathless, and then, reluctantly, he drew away. As much as he wanted her, as much as he needed her, anything more between them would have to wait until his ribs healed up.

She looked at him, her green eyes cloudy with desire, her fingers kneading his biceps. "Trey . . ."

"Sorry, sweetheart," he said, his voice low and husky.

"It's okay." Sitting up, she took a deep breath, ran a hand through her hair. It was just as well that they'd stopped. As tempting as he was, she didn't belong here, couldn't stay here. Letting him make love to her would be a huge mistake. She wanted to go home, and she wanted to take her whole heart with her, although she was afraid that was already impossible.

He sat up, quietly cussing the pain in his side.

"It is pretty here," Amanda remarked after a while.

"Yeah."

"What was your mother like?"

"She was a gentle woman, soft-spoken, patient. She drew people to her without even trying. I got jealous sometimes of the attention she gave to the other kids in the village. They swarmed around her. She would have liked more children. She got pregnant when I was five or six, but she lost the baby." He shrugged. "She never got pregnant again."

"How did she meet your father?"

"I'm not sure. She never talked about it. From the little I overheard when I was growing up, I gathered they met at a summer rendezvous. I think she must have run off with him."

"Did you ever ask your father?"

"No." He turned to face her, his gaze meeting hers. "What do you think of my people?"

"I like them, especially your grandfather. I wish I could talk to the other women."

"Do you know any Spanish? Most of my people can speak it, some fluently."

"I understand a little. That seems odd, their speaking Spanish. I always thought the Apaches and the Mexicans hated each other."

"They do," he said curtly. "That's why we've learned their language. The Mexicans pay a hefty bounty for Apache scalps. It was to our advantage to learn the language of our enemies."

"They pay for scalps? That's awful!"

"One hundred dollars for the scalp of warrior, fifty for a woman or child."

"How do they know if the scalp belonged to a man or a woman?"

"They don't."

She stared at him, her horror clearly reflected in her eyes.

"Back in the old days, white scalpers got two hundred dollars for every scalp they brought in, and two hundred and fifty for a live warrior. Of course, it was safer to bring in a scalp than a warrior. The bounty hunters sometimes passed off Mexican scalps as Indian."

"That's awful. I always thought it was the Indians who took scalps."

Trey shook his head. "My people do not take scalps. Apaches avoid the dead. They do not take souvenirs. We bury our dead as soon as possible, and the names of the dead are never spoken again, lest their spirits be called back to earth. When someone dies, his wickiup is burned, as is everything he owned. Those who burn his belongings also burn the clothing they were wearing at the time, and then they purify themselves in sagebrush smoke." Trey looked at her and grunted softly. "I suppose our customs seem strange to you."

"Well, a little. It must be difficult for you, living in both worlds."

He picked up a rock and tossed it into the river. "Sometimes."

"You called the Apaches 'your' people. Do you consider yourself more Apache than white? I mean, aren't you as much one as the other?"

"No. To the whites, if you have a drop of Indian blood, you're Indian. The Apache have accepted me as one of their own because I'm Apache here." He put his hand over his heart. "The whites have never accepted me. To them, I'm a half-breed. And that's the nicest thing they've ever called me."

"I'm sorry, Trey."

"No need to be. I've lived my life pretty much the way I wanted. My only regret is that I didn't kill that bas . . . that I didn't kill Hollinger when I had the chance."

"Why didn't you?"

He shrugged. "I wanted to, but he was kneeling on the floor, crying like a baby, and I couldn't pull the trigger."

"I'm glad."

He snorted softly. "So was he, I reckon."

"Trey, what are you going to do with the rest of your life?"

"I was plannin' to settle down in a little valley I found," he replied ruefully. "And raise horses."

"And now?"

"Now I don't know. The money I was countin' on to buy the land with is sittin' in your house." He laughed softly. "Ironically, the land I was going to buy isn't far from your place."

"Really?"

"Really."

"Let's try to go back, Trey, please? You can still raise horses. We could raise them. Together."

"You proposin' to me, Miss Amanda?"

"Sounds like it."

"What about good old Rob?"

She looked at him, a faint smile hovering over her lips. "Who?"

Trey laughed out loud. "Shucks, ma'am, I don't even know your last name."

Chapter Twenty-two

She wasn't laughing.

Trey cleared his throat. "Amanda . . ."

She turned her face away. "It's all right. It was a stupid idea. Forget I ever mentioned it." She started to rise. "We should go."

Trey grabbed her arm, wincing as the movement pulled on his bruised ribs. "Dammit! Wait a minute."

"Just let me go." She jerked her arm from his grasp and started walking. Abruptly she changed direction, her steps gaining speed until she was running away from the camp, toward the stand of timber that grew along the back wall of the canyon.

It felt good to run again. She tried to push everything from her mind, to concentrate on the sheer joy of her feet pounding against the ground, but it was impossible. She had humiliated herself. Tears stung her eyes and were quickly blown away. How could she have been so stupid? She didn't want to marry Trey Long Walker. The man was an outlaw. Sooner or later he would be caught and most likely hanged, and then where would she be? Stuck in the past, alone.

She veered to the right. The horse herd grazed in the distance. Trey's spirit horse might refuse to take her out of the canyon, but there was nothing magical about her gelding. She had to get out of here, had to get away from Trey before she made a fool of herself again. If she couldn't get back to her own time, she could at least live in a city. Trey had said Tucson was only a couple of days away. Surely she could make it that far without anyone's help. She was a seasoned rider now, and the gelding was a good, reliable horse. There would be some kind of work she could do in Tucson, even if it was waiting tables or washing dishes. She wasn't afraid of hard work; she would do whatever it took to earn enough money to buy a train ticket back East, to New York or Boston or Philadelphia. Anywhere, as long as it was away from the wild frontier.

She slowed to a walk, not wanting to spook the horse herd. Brushing the tears from her eyes, she searched for her gelding.

Relámpago trotted up to her. Snuffling softly, he rubbed his forehead against her chest, begging to have his ears scratched.

"Go away, you traitor," she muttered. But she couldn't resist scratching the stud's ears while she looked for her gelding.

"Ah, there you are." She started walking toward her horse, with Relámpago trailing at her heels like a puppy, when it occurred to her that she had neither rope nor bridle. Of course she hadn't had a bridle for Relámpago either, but with the stallion she hadn't felt like she needed one.

With a sigh of exasperation, she turned toward the village, came to an abrupt halt when she saw Trey walking toward her.

Relámpago gave her a push with his nose, and when she refused to move, he nudged her again, pushing her toward Trey.

"Just what I need," Amanda muttered crossly, "a matchmaking stallion."

Relámpago nudged her again, but she refused to move. Let Trey come to her.

She couldn't help feeling a surge of pity as she watched him walk toward her. She knew he was hurting. Well, so was she!

She lifted her chin. And waited.

Trey took a deep breath as he slowly closed the distance between them. He hadn't meant to hurt her feelings, but he had been shocked by her unexpected mention of marriage. Certain she had been joshing him, he had replied in kind. Only she hadn't laughed.

"Amanda—"

"Go away."

"Let's talk this out."

"There's nothing to talk about. I'm leaving."

He lifted one brow. "Oh? Where do you think you're going?"

"Tucson."

He scrubbed his hands over his face. Tucson! The woman didn't have the sense God gave a goose.

"Listen to me," he said, speaking slowly. "Tucson is no place for a woman—"

"Are you telling me there aren't any women there?"

"Of course not, but you're not like those women."

"Oh? What kind of women would those be?"

"Dammit, Amanda, you know what I mean. I'm not letting you go to Tucson alone. The town's full of—"

"Outlaws?" she supplied sweetly.

He curled his hands into tight fists to keep from strangling her.

"If you'll excuse me . . ." She took a step forward, intending to sweep by him, gasped when his hand closed on her arm.

"You're not going anywhere." His eyes burned into her own. "Understand?"

"You can't keep me here against my will!"

"Wanna bet?"

Fueled by a sudden overwhelming anger, she drew back her arm and punched him in the stomach. The corded muscles there hurt her fist, which made her furious, and she hit him again.

He grunted with pain but didn't let go of her arm. "Go ahead, hit me if it makes you feel better," he said grimly. "I've taken harder licks . . . some of them just recently."

Amanda felt the color drain from her face as she remembered what he had been through at the hands of the miners.

Amanda stared at him, her eyes wide with horror as she watched the color drain from his face. "Oh, Trey, I'm sorry!"

He gazed at her, affection mixed with aggravation,

281

and stroked his ribs gingerly. "You pack a pretty good wallop for a city girl," he said.

"I'm sorry," she said again. "Honest."

"You"—he took a deep breath, and the corners of his lips twitched down, then up—"are a lot of trouble."

"Does it hurt very bad?"

"Me brave Apache warrior, used to hardship," he grunted, mimicking the way the Lone Ranger's companion had talked. "Yeah, it hurts a little."

"You don't need to make fun of me. I said I was sorry, and I am."

He nodded. "You have every right to be angry, but I can't let you go. You know that, don't you?"

"Why not?"

"What do you want me to say?" His grip on her arm loosened. "That I need you?" His hand slid down her arm. "That I love you?" His thumb moved back and forth across the inside of her wrist, sending shivers of delight up her arm. "That I can't live without you?"

"Yes," she whispered. "Oh, yes. That's exactly what I want you to say."

He wrapped his arms around her and drew her close. "Will you marry me, Amanda? In the Apache way?"

She met his dark gaze directly, her heart beating double-time. "I'll marry you in any way you want."

"It won't be binding anywhere but here, you know."

"I know."

"I'll speak to my grandfather. As shaman, he'll be the one to marry us."

She nodded, pleased and excited. She had grown

fond of the old man, with his warm smile and gruff manner.

"I think we'd better wait a week or so," he said.

"A week!" she exclaimed. In one way, a week seemed far too short for such a step. But in another way . . . "Do we have to wait a whole week?"

He seemed surprised by her question, surprised but pleased.

"We can get married tomorrow," Trey said. He pressed a hand to his rib cage. "But I'm afraid the honeymoon might have to wait a few days, if you know what I mean."

"Whatever you want is fine with me." Rising on her tiptoes, she kissed him. "And my last name is Burkett."

Returning to the lodge, they told Trey's grandparents of their decision to be married right away. But Yellow Calf Woman shook her head. They would need to wait at least a week, she said. There were things that must be done, and she would need time to fashion a dress for Amanda to be married in, she said. After looking Trey up and down, she declared he would also need new clothing and moccasins, and extended the date another week.

As anxious as Trey and Amanda were, they both decided it would be best to wait. Amanda was touched by Yellow Calf Woman's generosity in offering to make her a dress.

Living in the same lodge made it difficult to keep their hands off each other. A look, the slightest touch, and the attraction between them flared to life. Amanda hadn't done this much necking in high school, she mused, or enjoyed it so thoroughly. Trey tempted her touch at every turn. It was impossible to be near him and not run her hand over his arm, his shoulder, let her fingertips trail down his back, slide down his chest.

Here among his own people, he shunned the clothes of civilization. Clad in a brief buckskin clout and moccasins folded over at the knee, his long hair hanging past his shoulders, he looked wild and completely untamed. She dreamed of him at night, erotic dreams that shocked her upon waking, and made her yearn for the day when he would be hers, when the dreams would become reality. The two-week wait seemed to stretch on forever into the dim future, fanning her yearning for the moment she would be totally his and he would be totally hers.

To pass the time and give her mind something else to think of, she made an effort to learn the language, to understand the Apache customs, to accept with a smile whatever food was offered her. The Apache diet consisted largely of meat, roots, mescal, berries, and mesquite beans. The mescal plant was plentiful in the desert. The women gathered it and roasted the pulp in pits. It was easily stored and carried. Mesquite beans and acorns were pounded into meal and made into cakes. The fruit of the giant cactus was also harvested. Amanda thought it tasted a little like figs.

The women made lovely baskets. There were two kinds, those used to carry burdens and those used for water.

She loved the children, with their luminous black eyes and sweet smiles.

Chase the Lightning

The Apache were a superstitious people. They believed that the devil was in the whirlwind, and that anyone caught in one would die. It seemed an odd belief to her, but certainly no stranger than believing that spilling salt would bring bad luck.

She learned there were many bands of Apache Indians. There were two bands of Mescalero and two bands of Jicarilla. The Chiricahua tribe was made up of three bands; the Western Apaches consisted of four groups. Trey's band was Chiricahua. She had heard of them, of course. Who hadn't heard of Cochise and Geronimo? When she asked about them, she was told that Cochise's band was located further to the southwest, and that Geronimo was most likely in Mexico.

Trey was pleased by Amanda's interest in his people. Though their customs were strange to her, she did her best to accept and understand them. She was polite to his grandparents, gracious to those she met. The children were curious about her red hair, seeking every opportunity to touch it, then crying, "Hot, hot," as if the bright strands burned their fingers.

How had he lived without her? He took pleasure in her laughter, the sound of her voice, the way she touched him, the way she smiled when he touched her. And they found numerous excuses to touch, he mused, especially at night, alone in their wickiup. They spent hours touching, kissing, exploring, the knowledge that they would soon consummate their love giving them the willpower to wait.

And now it was the night before the wedding.

Trey slid out from under the furs and stepped out of the lodge. The village was asleep. He stood there a

285

moment, and then, feeling restless, walked through the camp toward the horse herd. A spotted dog growled softly as Trey passed by.

A few horses lifted their heads as he approached the edge of the herd. Relámpago stood out from the others, his white coat a ghostly shimmer in the fading moonlight.

Trey smiled as the stallion approached. "Hey, 'Pago."

Relámpago whinnied softly, then rubbed his forehead up and down Trey's arm.

"What do you think?" Trey asked, scratching the stud's ears. "Am I making a mistake? Is it wrong of me to keep her here?"

The stallion shook his head.

"She doesn't belong here. You know that, don't you?"

Ears twitching, Relámpago snorted and pawed the ground.

"I tried to take her back," Trey said. "Nothing happened. Maybe she can't get back. Or maybe it's just not time . . ." He looked at the stallion. "Is that it? The timing's not right?" He shook his head. "Why do I have the feeling you know exactly what I'm saying?"

The stallion tossed his head, then turned and trotted back to the herd, sidling up to a pretty little buckskin mare.

"Looks like everybody's pairing up," Trey mused aloud.

If Amanda had been an Apache woman, he would have gone in the night and left horses tied in front of her wickiup. If she accepted his suit, she would care for the horses; if she left them unfed, it meant her answer was no. An Apache maiden was allowed four days to make her decision. Most women waited one day before caring for the horses, as it was not considered good form to feed them immediately. If she allowed the animals to go without food and water more than two days, she was considered overly vain and proud. If a suitor was accepted, there followed a wedding feast that lasted for three days. The prospective bride and groom were not allowed to speak to each other during those three days, but on the third night they would steal away to spend a week or so together in a wickiup hidden away from the rest of the village.

But Amanda was not an Apache girl. She had no family here, and he had no horses to offer her.

Suddenly anxious to see her, to hold her, he hurried back to his lodge and crawled under the furs.

Amanda turned on to her side, snuggling up against him.

"Where'd you go?" she asked sleepily.

"Just out for a walk."

"Your feet are cold."

"Sorry." He dropped a kiss on the top of her head, his senses filling with her scent, her nearness.

Tomorrow. Tomorrow she would be his.

It was her wedding day. Amanda ran her hand over the dress Yellow Calf Woman had made for her. Tanned to a soft creamy whiteness, it was quite beautiful, from the beaded yoke to the long fringe dangling from the sleeves and the hem. Tiny silver bells were fastened to the fringes at the hem. Her hair fell loose down her back and shoulders, save for two narrow braids on each side of her face. She wore a pair of new moccasins.

She ran her hands over the soft deerskin, wished fleetingly for a mirror so she could see how she looked.

Yellow Calf Woman stood back, her gaze moving over, and then she smiled. "Pretty, you look."

"Thank you."

"He is good man. Strong. Brave."

"Yes, he is."

Yellow Calf Woman's dark eyes sparkled. "Handsome."

"Oh, yes," Amanda agreed. "He is that!"

A soft drumming came from outside.

"It is time," Yellow Calf Woman said.

Amanda nodded, suddenly too nervous to speak.

She followed Yellow Calf Woman out of the wickiup, through a throng of smiling faces. Feeling a sudden itching between her shoulder blades, she glanced back to see a woman staring at her with obvious dislike.

Amanda frowned, wondering who the woman was, but then, from the corner of her eye she saw Trey waiting for her. Walker on the Wind stood beside him. The old man wore a buckskin shirt painted with symbols representing hail, rain, and lightning. Several members of the tribe stood behind the two men, but Amanda had eyes only for Trey. Clad in an elkskin shirt that was heavily fringed along the sleeves, a wolfskin clout, and fringed leggings, he looked every inch an Apache warrior. His moccasins were beaded in black and yellow. He wore an eagle feather tied in his hair.

She had always dreamed of being married in a church, of wearing a long white satin dress and a veil of handmade lace, of having her father give her away. How could she have been so foolish? Being married here, in this peaceful canyon, with the sky for a roof, was more beautiful than any church. And a doeskin dress, made by Yellow Calf Woman's loving hands, was far better than any satin gown. She would have liked to have her parents present, but that wasn't possible. And it didn't really matter, because the one person in all the world who mattered most was standing there, his dark eyes filled with love and admiration.

A hush fell over the crowd as Walker on the Wind took her hand and placed it in Trey's.

"This day, let it be known that my grandson, Long Walker, takes a wife. For us, the act of marriage takes place here, in the heart. It is not words that will bind you together, but the love you have, one for the other. From this day forward, there will be two people but one heart. Sorrow will be cut in half, joy will be doubled, because you now have someone to share it with. You will warm each other in winter, and share the laughter of summer days."

Walker on the Wind took their joined hands in his. "Go now to the place Yellow Calf Woman has prepared for you. Let your hearts grow close." He smiled at Trey, and then Amanda. "May *Usen* bless you with many strong sons and beautiful daughters."

"*Ashoge*, Grandfather," Trey said quietly.

The crowd parted and a warrior appeared, leading Relámpago and a dainty little buckskin mare. It was customary to have a feast for the bride and groom, but Trey had decided against it. He knew only a few people in the village, and rather than have Yellow Calf Woman spend hours preparing food to be shared with people he didn't know, he had asked that Walker on the Wind give a horse to a poor family instead. Besides, feasts had been known to go on all night and he was anxious to be alone with his bride.

Trey lifted Amanda onto the mare's back, then swung aboard Relámpago and headed toward the mouth of the canyon.

"Where are we going?" Amanda asked.

"Yellow Calf Woman built a honeymoon lodge for us a short distance from here." He smiled at her. "It was one of the reasons she wanted us to postpone the wedding. We'll stay there for a week or so."

Alone for a week. It sounded like heaven. "But . . . what about food?"

"Yellow Calf Woman will bring it to us each day, as well as wood for a fire. There'll be nothing for us to do but"—his dark eyes moved over her, igniting frissons of desire wherever his gaze touched—"get to know each other."

She shivered with anticipation, surmised he was as anxious as she when he urged Relámpago into a lope.

Their honeymoon lodge was located along the river, hidden within a thick stand of timber. Silver bells had been fastened to the branches of nearby trees; they tinkled merrily in the faint breeze that blew over the water.

After reining the stallion to a halt, Trey dismounted and helped Amanda from the back of the buckskin.

He tethered the buckskin to a tree, then removed the bridle from the stallion, leaving Relámpago free to graze. Swinging Amanda up into his arms, he carried her into the lodge. He held her a moment and then let her slide, ever so slowly, sensuously, down the length of his body until she was standing in front of him, her green eyes glowing, her lips curved in a smile that was both shy and provocative.

She ran her hands over his shirtfront. "So, Mr. Long Walker," she purred. "What do you want to do now?"

He gazed down at her, his eyes smoldering. "I'm sure I can think of something."

"I'm counting on it."

His hands moved slowly up her arms to release the ties that fastened her dress at the shoulders. The garment slid over her skin with a soft whisper to pool at her feet.

"Beautiful." His gaze moved over her, then lifted to her face. "Beyond beautiful."

Smiling, she tugged his shirt over his head and tossed it aside. "Beautiful," she said.

He looked down at his bare chest, then looked back at her, one brow arched. "Beautiful?"

She ran her hands over his chest. "I love the color of your skin, the feel of it." Leaning forward, she licked the pulse beating in his throat. "The taste of you."

Her hands dropped to his waist, and then she frowned. "How do I get you out of this?"

With a roguish grin, he removed his clout and leggings. Bending, he took off her moccasins and then his own. Kneeling there, he looked up at her, his eyes hot with desire.

"Trey . . ."

He rose slowly, took her by the hand, and led her to a bed made of soft furs. He dropped to his knees and drew her down beside him.

"I'll try to make you happy."

She ran her hand through his hair, over his shoulder, down his arm. "I am happy."

"Amanda." Her name was a sigh on his lips as he wrapped her in his arms and kissed her, gently at first, and then with growing intensity.

She clung to him, reveling in the feel of his heated skin against her own, loving the way her body fit against his, the low growl that rose in his throat as he fell back on the furs, pulling her down on top of him. There was no doubt that he wanted her. She was glad now that there had been no one else, glad that she had waited for this man. Like a prince in a fairy tale, he kissed her, awakening all her senses. She had never felt so alive, so aware. Every nerve, every cell, every fiber of her being yearned toward him. She had been made for this man, she thought, and he had been made for her. The fact that not even time could keep them apart only proved they were destined to be together.

Holding her close, Trey rolled over, tucking her neatly beneath him, adoring her with his eyes, his lips. She was the home he had never had, the love he had never thought to find, the future he had thought denied him.

She tasted of sunlight and musk, of sage and sweet desire. Her skin was smooth and unblemished, her hair like silk in his hands, her lips like warm honey.

Soft moans of pure feminine pleasure rose in her throat as he caressed her, arousing her until she writhed beneath him.

He knew a moment of surprise when he realized she was a maiden. It humbled him, left him feeling as though he had been given a gift beyond price.

And then there was no more time for thought, there was only the wonder and the mystery that was Amanda, the touch of her, the taste of her. Her heat enfolded him. Her scent surrounded him. She was life and breath, and he knew that from this moment forward he would be lost without her.

She cried out his name as pleasure burst within her, shimmering, ethereal, and all-encompassing. A moment later he followed her over the edge, tumbling down, down, until they lay together in each other's arms, sated, replete, bodies entwined, hearts forever bound.

Chapter Twenty-three

Amanda snuggled closer to Trey, more content than she had ever been in her whole life. The warm furs, the warmer man, the sweet afterglow of their love-making, all combined to fill her with a deep sense of peace, of being where she was meant to be.

She looked at Trey's profile. Strong. Rugged. More handsome than mere words could tell. He was all the excitement she had never known, everything she had ever wanted. He was strong yet tender, with a wry sense of humor and a deep, sexy laugh that always made her smile. She loved looking at him, touching him. Loved being in his arms, possessed by him, loved making love to him. Happiness bubbled up inside her, sparkling like champagne. How had she ever lived without him? She loved the sound of his voice, loved the way her name sounded on his lips. Loved the sound of his name.

"Trey."

"Hmm?"

"Nothing. I just wanted to say your name."

He turned to face her, the backs of his fingers skimming over her cheek. "You didn't tell me you'd never been with a man before."

She lifted one shoulder and let it fall. "The subject never came up."

He kissed her tenderly, unable to tell her how much that meant to him.

"I guess you've been with a lot of women?" she remarked, and then bit down on her lower lip. She hadn't meant to ask. Whatever he had done before, whomever he had done it with, it was all in the past.

"One or two." His gaze moved over her face. "But when I look at you, I can't remember any of them. I was always looking for you. I know that now."

"Oh Trey . . ." His words made her insides melt like chocolate left too long in the sun.

"Come on." Rising, he took her by the hand and drew her to her feet.

"Where are we going?" she exclaimed, glancing down at her nudity.

He gave a gentle tug on her hand. "For a swim."

She followed him out of the lodge, her arms crossing over her breasts as they stepped outside.

Trey grinned at her. "Who are you hiding from? There's no one to see you but me."

"Well, I'm not used to running around naked, at least not outside."

He drew her into his arms, his hands sliding up and

down her back. "Get used to it," he said with a roguish grin. "I plan to keep you this way often."

She couldn't help smiling. "Do you?"

"You bet." He held her at arm's length, his gaze hot. "I don't think you'll need to get dressed at all while we're here."

She laughed at that, shrieked as he suddenly lifted her into his arms and carried her into the river.

"No! Trey, don't!" She kicked her legs in protest as water splashed over her. "It's cold!" She wrapped her arms around his neck, but to no avail. He went under the water, carrying her with him. She came up sputtering and laughing, Trey's warm body a vivid contrast to the cold water.

He laughed with her, and then his lips claimed hers in a long, lingering kiss that chased the chill from her flesh, rousing her desire once more. It seemed impossible that she could want him again so soon, but want him she did, desperately.

And he wanted her. Carrying her out of the water, he laid her on a patch of grass.

Amanda glanced around. "Here?" she asked, her voice husky with yearning.

"Here." He lowered himself over her, his body a welcome weight. Her hands skimmed over his back and shoulders, down his arms, her hips lifting to receive him, her arms drawing him closer. His hands caressed her. His tongue laved her breasts, then slid up her neck, sending shivers of delight down her spine. And then he was kissing her, and she marveled again at the power of something so simple as a kiss. She writhed beneath him, her nails lightly raking his back as he moved deep within her, carrying her up, up, through rainbow heights and over the edge of pleasure into ecstasy.

She drifted slowly back to reality, the smile on her face turning to soft laughter.

Trey frowned down at her. "What's so funny?"

"Nothing." She couldn't stop smiling. "I'm just so . . . so happy! And I love you so much." She threw her arms out to her sides, then hugged him tightly. "Tell me. Tell me you love me."

Leaning on his elbows, he gazed down at her. "I love you," he replied fervently. "More than you can imagine. More than I ever thought possible."

"Oh, Trey . . ." she murmured, and cupping his face between her hands, she drew his head down and kissed him.

And that one kiss rekindled the blaze between them.

It was late afternoon when they returned to the wickiup. They ate the meal Yellow Calf Woman had prepared for them, and then Trey suggested a walk. When she started to get dressed, Trey stayed her hand, and now they walked hand in hand along the riverbank, admiring the beauty around them. They walked for perhaps an hour, saying little, content to be together, to pause from time to time to embrace and share a kiss.

It was like being in a dream, she thought, or a fairy tale. The land around them seemed like the Garden of Eden, untouched by evil, hidden from the rest of the world. Trey was her Adam, the first man she had ever truly loved, the first man to awaken the passion within her. And she was Eve, fascinated by the world in which she found herself, and by the man who walked beside her. She smiled inwardly as a verse from Genesis flitted through her mind. "And they were both naked, the man and his wife, and were not ashamed."

They came to a curve in the river and turned back, toward their lodge.

"I feel dreadfully wicked," Amanda remarked, shivering. "Do you go naked much?"

"No. Are you cold?"

"A little."

"Come on, I'll race you back. It'll warm you up."

"Yeah, right. Like I have a chance of winning."

"I'll give you a head start."

She grinned up at him, her green eyes sparkling. "You're on!" she said, and took off running.

She ran fleet and graceful as a doe. The late afternoon sun cast golden highlights in her hair, made her skin glow.

He watched her appreciatively, giving her a good lead, and then gave chase. It felt good to run, to feel the earth beneath his bare feet, the wind in his face. His heart began to pound to the thrill of the chase, the anticipation of catching her, holding her.

She continued to run long after he expected her to slow down. He began to run faster, taking pride in her strength and her stamina.

Gradually, he closed the distance between them. She glanced over her shoulder as he drew close, shrieked when his arm snaked around her waist. They fell to the grass in a tangle of arms and legs. Trey pinned her to the ground, his breath fanning her face, the heat of his body mingling with her own. Desire stirred between them, stilling their laughter.

"Trey, I never thought it would be like this. Never thought I could feel like this."

"Me, either, sweetheart." He cupped her cheek in his hand. "You're gonna wear me out."

"Are you complaining, mister?"

"What do you think?"

"I think I'll die if you don't kiss me."

She didn't have to ask him twice. Lowering his head, he claimed her lips and entrenched himself a little deeper in her heart.

Later, back at the wickiup, they sat outside on a buffalo robe and watched the sun set. Amanda rested her head against Trey's shoulder. It had been a wonderful day, she thought, filled with love and laughter.

"Still happy?" Trey asked.

"Oh, yes."

He squeezed her hand, wondering how long she would be content to live here, among his people, how long it would be before she began to miss her own home, her own time, all those near magical appliances she used so easily. Life was not easy among the People. They had none of the modern conveniences she was accustomed to having. To tell the truth, there were things in her time that he missed, like hot running water and electric lights. He had not seen much television, but he had enjoyed what he had watched and would like to have seen more. Riding in her car had been exciting, the speed unlike anything he had ever known. He would have liked a chance to learn how to drive it himself, to be in control of that much power. And the grocery store. So much food in one place. Food that was ready to be eaten. Ready-made bread. Meat in tidy little packages. No hunting, no skinning, no curing, just pick it off a shelf and cook it. And if you didn't want to cook, well, you could buy pre-made dinners that only had to be warmed up. If he hadn't seen it, he never would have believed such things were possible.

He drew Amanda into his arms and held her close, suddenly afraid that whatever magic had brought them together would end.

It was a week she would never forget. Days of sweet loving, of falling deeper in love with the man she had married. She learned about his childhood, his years of living with the Apache. She told him of trips to her grandmother's farm, of the time she had tried to ride an old milk cow and fallen in a mud puddle, of going trick or treating on Halloween.

They took long walks, swam in the river, watched the sun set, went horseback riding. It was a week of being pampered as Yellow Calf Woman brought them food and wood each day, careful to do it when they were away from the lodge so that for seven days they saw no one else.

All too soon, it was time to return to the canyon.

Amanda couldn't help feeling a twinge of regret as they dismantled the wickiup.

"Can we come back here sometime?" she asked, and realized that for the past week she'd given no thought to returning to her own time. "Maybe on our anniversary?"

Trey looked at her, and she knew what he was thinking, knew he was wondering if she would still be there in a year's time.

"Sure," he said quietly.

Silence stretched between them as they packed their few belongings.

"Trey?"

"Yeah?"

"What's wrong?"

He shook his head. "Nothing, sweetheart."

"I don't want to leave you. Ever. You know that, don't you?"

"Even if it means staying here?"

"Even if it means staying here."

"Amanda!" He drew her into his arms and held her tight. "I don't want to lose you."

"You won't."

He buried his face in the wealth of her hair, one hand stroking her back. "Every day when I wake up, I'm afraid you'll be gone. Every time you're out of my sight—"

"Oh, Trey, I don't think you have anything to worry about. We tried to go back and nothing happened. I think maybe I was born in the wrong time, and this is Fate's way of putting things right."

He drew back a little and grinned at her. "Is that what you think?"

"Well, it's as good an explanation as any."

"Maybe you're right. Come on, let's go."

Walker on the Wind was sitting outside his lodge when his grandson and the white woman returned. He stood up, narrowing his eyes thoughtfully as he glanced from one to the other. He watched as Long Walker lifted his bride from her horse. And then he smiled. *Enju.* It was good between them.

He nodded at them both, his heart light as he watched the young couple duck into their lodge.

"So," Yellow Calf Woman said, emerging from their wickiup. "They have returned."

"Yes."

Yellow Calf Woman moved beside him, her gnarled hand resting on his arm. "Do you remember our honeymoon, old man?"

He looked down at her, a twinkle in his eyes. "I am not so old that I have forgotten those days," he replied. "Nor have I forgotten how beautiful you were the day I took you as my wife."

"It was the best of days," she recalled with a quiet smile. "All the women envied me as we rode away from the village."

Walker on the Wind placed his hand over hers. "We have shared many good years, old woman. I hope our grandson will be as fortunate."

"What have you seen?" Yellow Calf Woman asked sharply. "You were gone long yesterday, and silent when you came home."

Walker on the Wind lowered himself slowly to the ground, his expression pensive. He had gone to his secret cave early in the morning. Clad in his ceremonial shirt, a pair of eagle feathers tied into his hair, he had sprinkled hoddentin and white sage into the fire.

He had purified himself in the smoke, then stared into the flames. He had repeated the ritual several times. Always it was the same.

"I am not yet certain what the vision meant."

"It troubles you?"

"Only because I do not yet understand what it means." His gaze strayed to the stallion. "I saw Relámpago ride into a dark mist. He was carrying Long Walker and the white woman when he disappeared into the mist. When he returned, Long Walker and the woman were gone."

Yellow Calf Woman's eyes grew wide. "You don't think . . . ?"

"I do not know," he said, his voice troubled. "I do not know."

Chapter Twenty-four

Amanda sat in the sun in front of her wickiup, concentrating on sewing the top to the sole of the moccasin she was trying to make for Trey. Sewing had never been her strong suit, and her fingers were sore from pushing the needle in and out of the thick rawhide. A little light mending was about all she had ever done. If something was in need of repair, she either took it to a seamstress or tossed it out. One thing she had certainly never expected to do was make moccasins. Yellow Calf Woman had shown her how to punch holes in the buckskin with a fine-pointed awl; she used sinew for thread.

She had learned that Apache moccasins turned up at the toe to protect the wearer's foot from being pierced by cactus thorns; the long legging was to keep the sand out and to protect against snake bites. She had also learned that winter moccasins were often made of buffalo or bear hides, and sewn with the fur inside for added warmth.

She had learned a lot in the last few weeks. She was growing more adept at cooking over an open fire; she participated when the women tanned hides, which was a long, rather disgusting task in Amanda's opinion. She was able to understand more and more of the language. The women had accepted her and now made her feel welcome among them, smiling at her when she met them at the river to draw water, or when she was gathering wood for the fire. Well, all except one woman. Her name was Red Shawl, and she looked at Amanda as if she hated her. And maybe she did, Amanda thought. After all, she was a white woman, the enemy. Fortunately, she didn't see Red Shawl very often.

Amanda put the moccasin aside, turning this way and that to stretch her back and shoulders. Trey had left the canyon to go hunting with a half dozen other men. It was the first time since their marriage that they had been apart for more than a few minutes, and she missed him. Was he missing her? And what would she do if he came back with a deer or something? She hadn't learned how to skin game yet, and she wasn't sure she wanted to learn. She had watched Yellow Calf Woman skin a deer and then soften the hide. It was a long, drawn-out process. First the hide was soaked in water, then it was rubbed with lye made of ashes to loosen the hair, then the hair was scraped from the hide. When the hide was clean, it was washed and wrung out, then stretched out on a wooden frame to dry. The next part involved rubbing a paste made of deer brains into the hide. When this was done, the hide was removed from the frame and soaked, twisted, wrung out, and then soaked, twisted and wrung out again and again until it was soft and pliable. Next, the skin was smoked. This was done with great care until the hide was the desired color, either yellow, tan, or brown.

It was much easier to make rawhide. A green hide was soaked in water; the fleshy parts, fat, and hair were removed; the hide was scraped until it was the desired thickness, and then the skin was stretched on a frame and left to dry. Rawhide was used for the soles of moccasins, and for making quivers and parfleches.

It was late afternoon when she finished sewing both moccasins. Rising, she placed them inside the door of the wickiup, thinking how surprised Trey would be when she gave them to him. She was pretty sure they would fit, since Yellow Calf Woman had given her the pattern. The only other thing she had ever made was an apron in homemaking class in high school, and that had been a disaster. At least the moccasins looked like mocassins!

She glanced toward the canyon entrance, wondering how long Trey would be gone. She couldn't believe how much she missed him. He was never far from her thoughts. She walked through the camp toward the river, nodding at the women she passed, smiling at a group of little boys who were shooting toy arrows at a rabbit skin.

Leaving the camp behind, she found a quiet place in a bend of the river where she could bathe. The water was cool but not yet cold. After glancing around to make sure she was alone, she stripped off her dress and moccasins and stepped into the water.

Submerged, she gazed up at the darkening sky and wondered what was happening back home. If time was moving along there at the same pace as here, her absence would have long since been reported, and whatever search had been mounted would have been unsuccessful. By now, her parents might well have given her up for dead and be in mourning. It was not a pleasant thing to contemplate. She wished for the thousandth time there was some way to get in touch with them and let them know she was all right.

Her mail would be piling up, her bills overdue. No doubt the gas and electricity and water would eventually be shut off for lack of payment. She was pretty sure Rob or her mom would look after the house, or what was left of it if those ruffians hadn't trashed it. She had a vague notion that you had to be missing for seven years before you were declared legally dead. Uncle Joe's inheritance would be piling up interest, and the various financial institutions would look after it automatically until someone stepped in. She had named her mother beneficiary.

She blew out a long sigh. There was no sense worrying about any of it. There was nothing she could do from here. And for now, she was happy to be here.

She was wading toward shore when there was a faint rustling in the underbrush along the bank. She went suddenly still. Her heart seemed to stop, then leap into her throat when she heard it again. There was something sinister about the sound. She told herself it was just a squirrel or a rabbit, a bird perhaps, but she didn't believe it for a minute. Hardly daring to breathe, she crossed her arms over her breasts and darted a glance at her clothes, wondering if she should get out of the water, grab her things, and make a run for it. Of course, she was going to feel awfully silly if it was just an animal of some kind. Unless it was a bear . . .

That thought spurred her forward. Forgetting about her clothes, she plunged back into the water and scrambled toward the far shore, her heart pounding like a drum.

She screamed when a hand closed around her ankle. Panicked, she began to struggle against her unseen assailant.

"Amanda! Amanda, it's me!"

"Trey!" She turned in his arms and punched him on the shoulder, as hard as she could. "What's the matter with you? You scared me to death!"

"I just wanted to surprise you."

"Well, you did!" she said, and sagged against him, her knees weak with relief. "I thought you were a bear."

"What are you doing down here alone?"

"Bathing. What does it look like?"

"Next time, ask Yellow Calf Woman to come with you. You shouldn't leave camp by yourself."

"Why not?"

"What if I had been a bear?"

"There aren't any bears in the canyon," she said. Why hadn't she thought of that earlier?

He wrapped his arms around her. "I just don't want anything to happen to you."

She smiled up at him, touched by his concern, by the love she read in his eyes.

He slapped her lightly on the rump. "Come on, we've got work to do."

"Work?" She leaned forward and pressed a kiss to his cheek, then licked a drop of water from his neck. "Now?"

"Now. I've got a deer that needs skinning."

She looked at him, pouting. "You'd rather skin a smelly old deer than spend time with me?"

He grinned at her. "We'll be together. You need to learn how to skin game."

She made a face at him, then thrust her hips against his in a slow, suggestive grind. "That's not the kind of together I had in mind."

"Sweetheart . . ."

She looked up at him. "Yes, love?" she asked innocently.

With a wry smile, he lifted her into his arms. "The deer can wait," he said, and carried her out of the water.

Amanda shook her head, her expression bleak. "I don't think I can do this."

"Of course you can, sweetheart."

"Well, I don't think I want to."

"Come on, Amanda, it's not that bad."

"Then you do it."

Trey sat back on his haunches and grinned at her. "It can't be any worse than digging a bullet out of my back."

"Wanna bet? If I'd had to skin you to keep you alive, you'd be dead now."

He laughed out loud. "You're something, you know that?"

"Trey, can't you skin the deer?" she asked sweetly.

"I killed it. You skin it."

"But—"

"Skinning is women's work."

"Really? And I suppose it was a man who decided it was women's work?" From what she had observed in the past few weeks, it seemed everything but hunting and gambling was women's work. Women did the cooking, the sewing, the washing, the mending. They gathered the wood and the water. They looked after the children. They tanned hides, made baskets, gathered whatever roots and fruits were in season.

"And what is men's work?" she challenged. "You sit around and smoke and gamble and occasionally go hunting."

Trey shook his head. "I didn't realize how stubborn you were."

"I'm not stubborn."

"Faint-hearted?"

She lifted her chin defiantly. "I am not!"

He guessed he couldn't blame her lack of enthusiasm. She had never been hunting, had probably never been hungry for more than an hour or two at most in her whole life. In her time, meat came in neat little packages, all the dirty work done by someone else.

"All right," he said, "I'll skin it and butcher it. But I draw the line at cookin'."

She hugged him tight, her eyes shining with happiness. "Thank you!"

He knew he'd be in for some ribbing from the warriors before he was through. He'd just started butchering when a couple of men he knew passed by and stopped to watch.

"Long Walker does this work as if born to it," one of them remarked.

Trey ignored them and proceeded with his work. The next time he looked up, there were half a dozen men lounging nearby, amusement in their eyes. A game of chance was interrupted as the players came to see the novelty. He was drawing quite a crowd. Gritting his teeth, he kept working.

Then the lounging warriors parted silently, and Amanda stood there. "What's going on?" she asked, glancing at the men gathered around.

"It seems I'm the entertainment for the day."

"What do you mean?"

He waved a hand in the direction of the warriors. "I mean, I'm doing your job, and they find it damned amusing."

"Oh." A tide of red washed into her cheeks. "I'm sorry, Trey."

"Come here and sit beside me."

She did as he asked without question. He spoke to the crowd in Apache, and then proceeded to explain to her what he was doing. She felt her stomach churn, and it took all her willpower to make herself watch him lay out each piece of butchered venison on the skin side of the hide as he sectioned the meat. His hands were slick and red with blood. It was a messy task, one she wasn't sure she would ever be able to manage.

Gradually, the crowd grew bored and restless and drifted away.

"I'm sorry," Amanda said. "I didn't mean to embarrass you."

"It's all right." He looked at her, grinning roguishly. "I'm sure I'll be able to think of a way for you to make it up to me." His tone softened, grew warm and husky. "Later. Tonight."

Unbelievably, a month went by. Looking at her reflection in a quiet pool, Amanda hardly recognized herself. Her face, neck, and arms were a golden brown; she wore her hair in braids to keep it out of her face. She could skin a rabbit and quarter a deer without getting sick to her stomach, though they were tasks she would never enjoy. She was growing more fluent in the language, more understanding of Apache ways. They were a proud people, honest and loyal to their own, merciless to their enemies.

Sometimes at night she sat with Trey, listening to Walker on the Wind tell stories of the old days, of brave warriors and warrior women, of battles won and lost. She was particularly impressed with the story of the warrior woman Rides Two Paths.

Rides Two Paths had been known as Flower in the Rain when she was a child. She had started life like any other Apache girl, but as she reached the age when boys began to go with their fathers and grandfathers, learning to hunt and track, she asked her father, Tall Elk, for a bow and arrows. Her father, who

312

had no sons, was pleased, but her mother was not. In spite of his wife's objections, Tall Elk did as Flower in the Rain asked. He taught her to hunt and to track, and when she proved capable, he allowed her to go hunting with him and several other warriors. It was while they were hunting that a band of Comanche attacked them. During the battle, her father's horse was killed and her father was wounded. It was then that Flower in the Rain showed her warrior heart by riding back to rescue her father. Seeing her brave deed, the other Apaches renewed the fight, killing all the Comanches who had attacked them. When Flower in the Rain's father recovered, he sang of his daughter's bravery. He gave her an eagle feather to wear in her hair, and a new name. From that time forward, she was known as Rides Two Paths, and was allowed to ride the warpath with the men. Her fame as a fighter grew, and upon her death she became a legend among her people.

It was a brave tale, one that stirred Amanda, made her feel inadequate, and yet, when she was caught up in some chore that seemed impossible, she thought about Rides Two Paths. Thinking about the Apache woman's courage made whatever task Amanda was facing seem easy in comparison.

She had assumed that the canyon was the Apaches' permanent home, but a few days later, Trey told her they were moving. With winter coming, there wasn't graze enough for the horses, or food enough for the people, and they were headed for their winter stronghold.

The women packed up the contents of their lodges,

prepared food for the journey, and gathered their children together. The men rounded up the horses, and they were ready to go.

Amanda felt a strange sense of loss as she followed Trey out of the canyon. She had been married there, discovered the true meaning of intimacy and love there. In a way, she had grown up there. And now they were leaving. She glanced back as they cleared the entrance, knowing somehow that she would never see it again.

There was a holiday air among the People as they traveled toward their winter stronghold. The young men rode up and down the line, showing off their horsemanship, which Amanda found quite spectacular. The young women watched it all while pretending to be uninterested. Young mothers nursed their children on horseback. The warriors rode at the head of the column and at the back, keeping watch. The horse herd brought up the rear of the caravan, guarded by teenage boys and a handful of seasoned warriors.

Amanda glanced at the women riding nearby. Save for the color of her hair, she looked like any other Apache woman. It gave her a keen sense of satisfaction to know she fit in with the Indians more every day, that they regarded her as a friend. She had been so afraid they would shun her because she was white, the enemy, but, for the most part, they had made her feel welcome. All except Red Shawl. Amanda usually had been able to avoid the woman in camp, but now on the march, she saw her glaring at her from a distance.

When Trey rode up a short time later, she asked him about the woman. "What's Red Shawl's problem?"

"Problem?" He frowned. "I didn't know she had a problem. What is it?"

"Not exactly a problem," she said, realizing he had taken her literally. "I mean, I don't think she likes me. I don't know why. I've never done anything to her. Why doesn't she like me?"

He hesitated. "Perhaps she's jealous."

"Jealous? Why?"

"We're old . . . friends."

"Yeah?"

"Yeah. When we were growing up, she hinted that she'd like to be my woman."

"Oh?"

"Yeah, but I was too young at the time. She's about five years older than I am. I wasn't interested in women then. I wasn't interested in anything but avenging my father's death. She got upset when she found out I was leaving the tribe."

"Well, I think she's still upset. Did she ever get married?"

Trey shrugged. "I don't know. Want me to ask her?"

"What do you think?"

"Just trying to help," he replied, stifling a grin.

"Uh-huh."

"You're not jealous of her, are you?"

"Of course not."

But she was, and they both knew it.

It was a long day. Amanda was bone weary by the time the People stopped for the night. When Trey came to

take her horse, she sank down on the ground, too tired
to think of anything but sleep.

And sleep she did. When she woke, it was fully dark
and the camp was set up for the night. Most of the
women and children were asleep. Most of the men,
too, save a few who were talking quietly a short distance away, and those whose duty it was to stand the
first watch.

Blinking the sleep from her eyes, Amanda sat up,
looking around for Trey, but he was nowhere in sight.
He had covered her with a blanket and left a small fire
burning to warm her. She smiled at his thoughtfulness.
Where was he?

Needing some privacy, she wrapped the blanket
around her shoulders and walked a little ways off from
the fire, out of sight of the rest of the camp. She paused
where the underbrush began to thicken, wondering if
it was safe to walk any further in the dark. While she
was trying to decide, she heard Trey's voice coming
from deeper in the brush, speaking rapid Apache. She
peered into the darkness, looking for an opening in
the thick undergrowth that might lead toward him, but
before she could move, she heard a softer voice answering his. A woman's voice. She hesitated, feeling
as though her insides had turned to ice.

Trey spoke again. She couldn't make out individual
words. If only they would speak louder and slower!

The woman's reply carried an intimacy that was rec-
ognizable in any language. Amanda's heart began to
pound in her ears as Trey spoke again, somewhat
more sharply.

The woman's reply was louder, too, the intimacy

replaced by anger. Amanda heard a twig snap, and shrank back into the shadows.

Trey and Red Shawl moved into a patch of moonlight, walking close together. Too close together. Red Shawl spoke again, her voice low. Trey shook his head. Amanda stood stock-still and tried to be invisible. They passed within yards of her. Red Shawl spoke again, her voice harsh, and then turned away from Trey. Trey put his hand on her shoulder in what appeared to be a gesture of appeasement and said something in a soothing voice. Amanda stared at him, shocked by the sight of him touching another woman. He said something else, and Red Shawl shrugged his hand off angrily. He turned and strode back toward camp.

Trey was sitting on their bedroll when she returned. "Where've you been?" he asked.

She gestured toward the trees. "I needed some privacy. Where have you been?"

"Talking to an old friend."

"Oh?" She stared at him, one hand clutching the blanket, her heart pounding loudly in her ears.

He nodded, and she felt the sting of tears in her eyes.

Trey clenched his hands, his gaze sliding away from hers, and then he stood up.

Amanda looked up at him, afraid to speak, afraid to move for fear she might shatter into a million pieces.

He closed the distance between them, his hands folding over her shoulders. "I was talking to Red Shawl."

His admission left her feeling physically weak.

"What did she want?"

"She told me she knew how difficult it must be for me to have a wife who was not Apache, who didn't understand our ways. She hinted rather strongly that she wouldn't mind being my second wife."

"Oh, really?" Amanda exclaimed. "And what did you tell her?"

"Calm down, sweetheart. I told her you were woman enough for me."

"Calm down! Calm down! I am calm."

"Yeah," he said, laughing softly as he drew her up against him. "I can see that."

"Second wife! The day you take a second wife is the day they'll be handing you your head on a platter!"

"I'm glad you're not jealous."

She glared at him, and then felt the sick wave of jealousy rush out of her. She couldn't stay mad at him, not when he was looking at her like that. "Well," she admitted, "maybe just a little. Okay, a lot!"

He held her tightly. "Come on, sweetheart, let's go to bed."

The next day, the news that Trey and Red Shawl had met alone in the woods was suddenly, mysteriously being whispered among the women throughout the camp. Not that it was really much of a mystery, Amanda thought. She hadn't said anything. She knew Trey hadn't said anything, and she was pretty sure no one else had been in the woods the night before. That only left Red Shawl. Second wife indeed!

"Over my dead body," Amanda muttered under her breath as she rolled their bedding. "I'd as soon invite a rattlesnake into our lodge."

"You say something?"

She looked up to find Trey regarding her, one brow raised inquisitively. "No, nothing."

He grunted softly. "You ready to go?"

"Whenever you are."

It was another long day of travel. Amanda couldn't take her eyes from Trey. Clad in clout and moccasins and mounted on the flashy white stallion, his long black hair trailing down his back, Trey left a never-to-be-forgotten image indelibly printed on her mind.

They stopped every couple of hours to rest the horses and again at midday for something to eat. Women took advantage of the time to nurse their infants, or let their toddlers run out some of their boundless energy. Amanda used the time to stretch her legs, or steal a kiss from Trey when no one was looking.

It was late afternoon when they stopped for the night alongside a shallow stream. It was a pretty spot, quiet, peaceful. While Trey took the horses down to the water to drink, Amanda spread their blankets on the ground and then went in search of wood for a fire.

She walked along the edge of the stream winding in and out of the scrub brush and trees, pausing now and then to pick up a stick here and there. The camp was out of sight when she felt a sudden prickle along the back of her neck, a sense of someone watching her. Glancing over her shoulder, she looked back the way she had come, but there was no one in sight.

"Probably just your imagination," she muttered, and continued on her way.

But the feeling persisted. She told herself she was

just being silly, but the sense of being watched wouldn't go away, and a few minutes later she turned around and headed back to camp, her footsteps quickening.

She was almost running when she came upon the snake. Coiled in a patch of sunlight, it hissed at her, its tail rattling a warning. She came to an abrupt halt, sweat popping out on her brow, fear like a dead weight in the pit of her stomach. What was she supposed to do? Run? Back up? Stay put? She couldn't seem to draw her gaze from the snake's triangular-shaped head, or the forked tongue continually darting in and out of its mouth.

She glanced around. There was nowhere to go but back. The stream was to her left, a thick stand of spiny brush to her right.

"Amanda. Amanda!"

She looked up, relief washing through her when she saw Trey standing a few yards beyond the snake.

"Stay there," he said quietly. "Don't move."

She nodded, watching in horror as he picked up a long stick and walked closer to the snake. In one smooth gesture, he slipped the branch under the snake and flipped it into the water.

With a sob, Amanda dropped the wood she had been carrying and hurled herself into Trey's arms.

"Hey, it's all right."

She nodded, unable to stop the shivers that coursed through her body. "I kn-know. But I was so . . . so . . . scared."

"Of course you were." His hand stroked her hair, her back. "Come on, let's go back to camp."

"All . . . all right."

Gathering the wood she had dropped, Trey tucked it under his arm. "You did the right thing," he said, taking her hand. "If you see another snake, just don't move. Unusual, for them to be out this late in the day."

When they got back to camp, Trey insisted she sit down. He built a fire, made a pot of coffee, and poured her a cup. Coffee was one of the few things that was familiar in this alien world and she sipped it slowly, grateful for the warmth seeping through her.

Around them, the Apaches settled down for the night. Warriors tethered their favorite horses nearby. Mothers fed their children and tucked them into bed. Teenage boys went to guard the horse herd; seasoned warriors went to keep watch over the camp. A baby's cry was quickly silenced.

Later, after dinner, several adults and children gathered around Walker on the Wind. Amanda sat between Trey and Yellow Calf Woman. It was a lovely night. The moon was full and yellow. A buttermilk moon, her grandmother used to call it. Millions of stars twinkled like silver fireflies against an indigo sky. She rested her head on Trey's shoulder as Walker on the Wind began to speak.

"When the People emerged from the underworld, they traveled south for four days," Walker on the Wind began. "They had only two kinds of seeds for food. The seeds were ground between two flat stones.

"Near the place where they made their camp on the fourth night, one tipi stood apart from the others. When those who lived in the tipi were gone, a raven came and left a bow and a quiver of arrows on the lodge pole. When the children who lived in the lodge came out, they looked inside the quiver and found some meat. They ate it, and grew very fat.

"When the mother returned to the lodge, she saw the grease on the hands of her children. They told her what had happened. The woman quickly told the story to her husband. The members of the tribe marveled at the food that had made the children so fat in such a short time.

"When Raven learned that his meat had been stolen, he flew to his home in the mountains to the east. A bat followed Raven. He went back and told the People where the raven lived. That night, the chief of the People called a council meeting. He chose several brave warriors to go after Raven in hopes of getting more of Raven's meat.

"The warriors reached the camp of the ravens four days later. When they could not find the meat, they decided to spy on the ravens. That night, the *diyini* changed an Apache boy into a puppy. They left him behind to spy on the ravens.

"Next morning, a young raven found the puppy in the abandoned camp of the People. He asked if he could keep the puppy under his blanket. Later, the puppy peeked out and saw one of the ravens remove a flat stone from the fireplace and disappear inside. A short time later, the raven returned leading a buffalo, which was killed and eaten by the ravens."

Amanda glanced around. Though she was certain the Indians had heard the story many times before, both the children and the adults listened in wide-eyed wonder as Walker on the Wind went on with the tale.

"The puppy spied on the ravens for four days. When he was certain where the ravens obtained their food, he resumed his own shape. On the fifth morning, holding a white feather in one hand and a black one in the other, he went through the hole in the fireplace.

"In the underworld, he saw four buffalo. He put the white feather into the mouth of the one nearest to him and told it to follow him. But the first buffalo told him to give the feather to the last buffalo. The boy did as he was told, but the last buffalo told him to give the feather back to the first one.

" 'You are now king of all the animals,' " the boy said to the buffalo.

"When the boy returned to the world above, all the animals that were on the earth followed after him. The noise of their passage to the world above woke one of the ravens, who quickly closed the opening. When he saw that all the animals followed the Apache boy, he said, 'When you kill any of these animals, save the eyes for me.'

"The boy followed the trail of the People for four days before he overtook them. A short time later, they all returned to the camp of the People. When they arrived, the chief killed the first buffalo. The Apache boy remembered the raven and saved the eyes.

"There was an old woman who was annoyed with one of the deer because it ate part of her lodge covering. Grabbing a branch from the fire, the old woman hit the deer on the nose and the ash left a white mark that can still be seen on the descendants of that deer.

" 'From this day on, you will avoid mankind,' she

declared. 'Your nose will warn you when man is close.'

"That was the end of the harmony that had existed between the People and the animals. Day by day, the animals drifted further and further away from the Apache. The People prayed for their return. From then on, it was mostly at night that the deer could be seen, but not too close, because they remembered the old woman's warning.

"The People soon developed their skill in using the bow and arrow so they could hunt the deer, and especially the buffalo, for the meat they loved so much."

After murmuring their thanks to Walker on the Wind for the story, the Indians drifted away to their own fires. Trey and Amanda bid Walker on the Wind and Yellow Calf Woman good night and went to bed.

Bone weary after a day in the saddle and her fright over the snake, Amanda snuggled close to Trey, grateful for his nearness, his warmth. Whatever else might be wrong, being in his arms was where she belonged.

Chapter Twenty-five

During the next week, Amanda was plagued by mishaps. One evening she left a pot of stew cooking while she went to draw water from the river, and when she got back, the pot was on the ground, the stew soaking into the earth. One morning the wood she had collected the night before was soaking wet and wouldn't burn, forcing her to scrounge for more tinder. The moccasins she had made for Trey disappeared.

"I think someone's doing it on purpose," she said to Trey that night. "I'll give you three guesses who it is, and the first two don't count."

"Who?"

"That woman, Red Shawl, that's who."

"Red Shawl! Why would she steal a pair of my moccasins?"

" 'Cause she's jealous, that's why. It wouldn't surprise me if she put that snake in my path, too."

He smiled at that. "Red Shawl's no medicine woman, Amanda."

"No," she said, "but I think I have a name for her."

"What?"

"I'll give you one guess," she said, "and it rhymes with witch!"

His laughter infuriated her still more.

During the next two days, Trey did his best to convince Amanda that the mishaps she had told him about were just that. After all, there was no reason for Red Shawl to be jealous. There had never really been anything between them. But once the seed was planted, his suspicion grew. Aware now, he noticed that wherever he went, Red Shawl was usually nearby. Several times he had caught her watching him. It was true that she had let him know, rather brazenly, that she was willing to be the second wife in his lodge, but he had put the thought out of his mind almost as soon as the offer was made. He didn't need a second wife; didn't want one.

Now he watched Amanda prepare the evening meal. She had learned much in the short time they had been with the People. She could build a fire that cooked evenly. She rode for long hours without complaint. She could set up a campsite as well as any of the other women. The children clamored around her, charmed by her ready smile, captivated by the color of her hair. She treated his grandparents with respect, did her best to conform to the customs of his people. And she was, without doubt, the most beautiful, desirable woman he had ever known.

She looked up from the pot she was stirring, smiled when she saw him watching her.

"Are you hungry?" She picked up the spoon and licked it. "Dinner's almost ready."

"Starved." He wasn't talking about food, and they both knew it.

They were a day's ride from the winter camp when the attack came. Trey had taken the horses down to the stream. Amanda was rolling her blankets into a neat roll when she heard a shout, followed by a gunshot.

There was a moment of silence, and then pandemonium as riders clad in dusty Army blue poured into the encampment, rifles blazing.

Amanda scrambled to her feet. Heart pounding, she looked around for Trey, but he was nowhere in sight. She saw women and children running toward the river, saw young men grab their weapons and ride out to meet the enemy, while older warriors stayed back, providing covering fire for the women and children.

She was trying to decide what to do, where to go, when she heard a whooshing sound behind her. Before she could turn, pain exploded through the back of her head, and then everything went black.

At the sound of the first gunshot, Trey had swung onto the stallion's back, his only thought for Amanda. A trooper rode into his path, bringing his rifle up to aim at Trey.

Trey reacted instinctively. He drew his Colt from the gun belt he wore over his clout and fired in one smooth motion. The trooper went backwards out of his saddle, and Trey bent low over Relámpago's neck and plunged into the thick of the battle.

The fighting raged all around him. The air was filled with dust and the stink of gun smoke, the sound of rifle fire, the war cries of the Apache, the shouts of the soldiers. Urging the stallion on, Trey thumbed the hammer of his Colt repeatedly, reloading from his gun belt as he fought his way to where he had left Amanda. She was nowhere in sight.

The battle was violent and bloody and quickly over. The Apache fought hard, but when the fight turned against them, they scattered like ashes in a whirlwind, taking what they could carry and leaving the rest behind.

Trey took a last look around and then rode for cover, his only consolation the fact that he hadn't seen Amanda's body lying with the others.

By late afternoon, the soldiers were gone. Heavy-hearted, Trey rode back to the camp. It was a grim scene. Wickiups had been knocked down; a few were in flames. He saw men and women moving through the rubble, gathering what blankets and foodstuffs hadn't been destroyed or carried off by the soldiers. Others drifted into the camp as the day wore on. The dead were quickly buried.

Trey found Walker on the Wind tending to a bullet wound in Yellow Calf Woman's shoulder. Dismounting, he propped a rifle he'd picked up during the battle against the side of his grandmother's lodge, which was miraculously untouched. The lodge he'd shared with Amanda was scorched on one side.

After making sure his Colt was fully loaded, he knelt

beside his grandparents. "Have you seen Amanda?"

Walker on the Wind shook his head.

"I saw Red Shawl hurrying toward her soon after the battle started," Yellow Calf Woman said.

"Are you sure?"

His grandmother nodded. "I only saw them for a moment, and then . . ." She gestured at her arm. "One of the bluecoats shot me."

"Where is Red Shawl now?"

Walker on the Wind pointed to a group of people standing a short distance away. "She was with her mother, over there."

"Thanks." Trey looked at his grandmother. "You gonna be all right?"

"Do not worry about me. I killed the *yudastcin* who did this."

Trey grinned, amused by the fire in her eyes. "I need to talk to Red Shawl. I'll be back to help you gather your stuff up later."

"Aman-da is unhurt," Walker on the Wind said as Trey stood up.

Trey stared down at his grandfather. "You're sure?"

Walker on the Wind placed his hand over his heart. "I feel it in here."

Trey nodded. If there was one thing he had faith in, it was his grandfather's intuition.

Looking around, Trey saw Red Shawl standing with her mother and sister. She looked up at him and smiled. He nodded at the other two women, then motioned for Red Shawl to follow him.

"Have you seen Amanda?" he asked when they were away from the others. "Do you know where she is?"

Red Shawl looked up at him. "How would I know? Perhaps she was killed."

She sounded far too pleased about that possibility for Trey's peace of mind.

"Did you see her before the attack?"

"I do not remember." She placed her hand on his arm. "You will need a new woman in your lodge now."

He knew in that moment that Red Shawl had been behind the string of mishaps that had bedeviled Amanda, just as Amanda had suspected.

"Know this," he said, lifting her hand from his arm. "You will never be my woman. And if you value your life, you had better pray that no harm comes to Amanda."

"Long Walker—"

"I know you're responsible for her disappearance," Trey said, his voice cold. His hand gripped her forearm. "Where is she?"

"You are hurting me."

"Where is she?"

"I do not know. You are hurting me!"

"I ought to break your arm."

"Long Walker, let her go."

Trey glanced over his shoulder to see his grandfather walking toward him, accompanied by a young boy.

"Let her go," Walker on the Wind repeated. "Young Bear has information you will want to hear."

Trey released his hold on Red Shaw's arm. "Get out of here."

Rubbing her bruised flesh, Red Shawl hurried away.

"Speak, Young Bear," Walker on the Wind said. "Tell my grandson what you told me."

"I saw Red Shawl hit your woman over the head and drag her away from camp during the battle. Red Shawl left her there." Young Bear pointed to a large rock some distance away. "Two soldiers found your woman and took her away."

"Was she alive?"

Young Bear nodded.

"*Ashoge*, Young Bear."

The boy nodded, his chest slightly puffed out with pride as he walked away.

Trey stood there a moment, then ducked into his lodge. He quickly changed into his shirt and trousers, which the looters had left behind. Everything else of value, including Amanda's dress, had been stolen. Going back outside, he picked up the rifle he had left propped against his grandmother's lodge.

"You are going after her," Walker on the Wind said. It was not a question.

"Yes."

"Alone?"

Trey nodded. He was in a hurry to be on his way. He didn't have time to wait for the Apache to mourn their dead, or for a war party to be assembled.

Walker on the Wind grunted softly. "Sometimes one is better than many." He paused, his head cocked to one side as though listening to a voice only he could hear. "I had a dream last night. You were riding with us, but then your path turned from ours and I saw you riding in a different direction. Your woman was with you, taking you to a faraway place. This morning, the spirits told me it was time for you to give up your quest for vengeance, that a new life awaits you."

"A new life?"

Walker on the Wind placed his hand on his grandson's shoulder. "We will not see each other again in this life, *ciye*. Remember who you are, and where you came from."

"I will, *Shinale*."

"Shortly before you returned to us, I saw you in a strange place," Walker on the Wind remarked, his brow furrowed. "The woman, Aman-da, was with you. You were in a large wickiup, surrounded by the clothing of the white man."

"You saw that?"

Walker on the Wind nodded. "There were many hats there. And on one wall, the head of a white buffalo."

Trey shivered in spite of himself. He had known for years that Walker on the Wind communed with the spirits, but he'd had no idea that his grandfather could see into the future, as well. "What else did you see?"

Walker on the Wind shook his head slowly, his brow furrowed. "I saw you with the woman. You were sitting down, and you were going very fast. I do not know what you were riding. It was like nothing I have ever seen. . . ."

Trey grinned. "It's called a car, *Shinale*. And it was very fast indeed. I wish I had it now."

"Go quickly," Walker on the Wind said. "I shall pray to *Usen* on your behalf."

"*Ashoge, Shinale*." Trey handed the rifle to his grandfather. "This is for you."

Walker on the Wind nodded his thanks as he tucked

the rifle in the crook of his arm. "You will not need it where you are going." He made a small gesture with his chin toward Trey's gun belt. "Your short gun serves you well."

Trey hugged his grandparents, then swung onto Relámpago's back. A last look at all he was leaving behind, and then he was gone, riding hard toward the east.

Amanda woke with the worst headache she'd ever had. Where was she? Raising herself up on one elbow, she glanced around. She was on a cot, in a tent of some kind. There was a folding table and a chair across from the cot; a lantern on the table.

She sat up, groaning softly. What was she doing here? And why did her head hurt so much? She lifted a hand to the back of her head, winced as her fingertips encountered a lump the size of a golf ball. How had *that* happened? And why couldn't she remember?

From outside came the shout of men's voices, the blare of a bugle, the clank of a harness, the whinny of a horse. It sounded like every Western movie she had ever seen.

The fabric was canvas, not buffalo hide. The sun beat down on it, making the interior hot.

Where was she?

Trey . . .

She stood so quickly, it made her dizzy. Pain lanced through the top of her head. She bit her lip to keep from crying out, walked unsteadily to the entrance of the tent, and peered outside.

She was in the midst of a cavalry encampment. She

333

blinked, closed her eyes, and looked again, half expecting to see John Wayne come striding down the line of tents. There were soldiers everywhere, engaged in various tasks. Some were cleaning their weapons, some were watering the horses tethered to a picket line a short distance away, some were sitting in the shade, drinking coffee.

A tall, slender man wearing the bars of a lieutenant on his shoulders was talking to a trio of soldiers. He had a strong profile, blond hair, and a sweeping, cavalry-style mustache.

There was no sign of Trey or his people.

She backed away from the tent flap as a rather portly man in a rumpled blue uniform strode toward her. His bars made him a captain. An Army doctor, she assumed, noting the black satchel he carried.

"Ah," he said, entering the tent. "You're awake."

"Yes."

"How are you feeling?"

"Where am I?"

"In the back end of beyond, by the looks of it," he replied good-naturedly. "I'm Captain Rathburn. You've had a rather nasty blow to your head."

She nodded. Not a good idea. The tent seemed to spin out of focus.

"There, there," the doctor said, grasping her arm to steady her. "Here, I think you'd better sit down."

She didn't argue. She sat on the cot while he pulled a stethoscope from his bag and listened to her heart, checked her pupils, examined the lump on the back of her head.

He tucked the stethoscope back into his bag. "Do you know your name?"

"Amanda Burkett."

"Where do you live?"

"Canyon Creek, Arizona."

"Do you know who the president is?"

"George W. Bush."

The doctor frowned. "Who?"

She realized her mistake then, but couldn't recall who had been the president in 1869.

The doctor patted her knee in a fatherly gesture. "It's only temporary, dear, I'm sure. That was quite a blow you got. Give your memory time. Do you remember how you got here?"

"No. Why can't I remember?"

"It's not unusual, when one receives a blow like that, to forget what happened immediately before and after. It might come back to you, it might not."

"How long have I been here?"

"A few hours."

She started to rise. "I've got to go—"

Rathburn put his hand on her shoulder, holding her down. "We'll be moving out first thing in the morning. I think you should rest until then."

"No. I've got to go back—"

"Now, now," Rathburn said soothingly. "You're free now." His gaze moved over her, taking in her Apache dress and braids. "How long were you a prisoner?"

"What?"

"It doesn't matter. We'll take you back to the fort and get in touch with your people. Do they live very far away?"

"Far?" She thought of her parents, 132 years in the future, and started to laugh. She sounded a little hysterical, but she couldn't help it. "Doctor, you have no idea just how far away they are."

Trey left the stallion at the bottom of a ridge. On hands and knees, he climbed to the top and peered over the rim down into the Army encampment. Below, he could see soldiers going about their business. A large tent was set up in the middle of the rows of smaller tents belonging to the soldiers; the Stars and Stripes flew above it; below the flag, the red and white troop guidon fluttered in the breeze. There were sentries posted at regular intervals. Those men not on duty were at mess.

There was no sign of Amanda.

He stayed there, watching, as the sun sank behind the distant mountains.

The soldiers made ready for the night.

The lieutenant bedded down on a cot outside the large tent.

Trey grunted softly. That was right strange. Could it be that Amanda was in the shavetail's tent? If she was here, it was the only place she could be.

Settling in, he waited.

Amanda turned over on her stomach and tried to sleep, but sleep wouldn't come. The doctor had looked in on her several times. Each time, he had asked her name and if she knew where she was. A trooper had brought her dinner, leaving her to wonder how the Army survived. The bacon, beans, hardtack, and black coffee were hardly a gourmet feast.

With a sigh, she rolled onto her side. Where was Trey? Had he survived the attack? What about Walker on the Wind and Yellow Calf Woman? She wished she could remember what had happened, how she had come to be here, but her mind was a blank. She remembered watching the women and children run for cover and nothing after that until she woke here.

Trey . . . he had to be alive. She'd know if he wasn't. Somehow, she would know. Tears stung her eyes. What if she was just fooling herself? What if he was dead? How would she live without him? She knew that women in love said that all the time: *I can't live without him.* But in her case, it could be literally true. She was smart, computer-savvy, able to get around in the city on her own, but sadly ill equipped to survive in the Old West.

She blinked back her tears. He wasn't dead; she refused to consider the possibility.

Closing her eyes, she listened to the sounds of the night. The wind scratched against the tent. She heard the stamp of a horse's hoof, a sentry calling that all was well. . . .

With the patience instilled in him by Walker on the Wind, Trey watched and waited until the camp was bedded down before he made his way back to his horse. The stallion whinnied softly as he approached.

"Quiet, 'Pago." He patted the stallion's neck, then took up the reins and swung into the saddle.

It took three-quarters of an hour, moving slowly and quietly, to come up behind the lieutenant's tent. Dismounting, he ground-reined the stallion. Pulling the knife from his belt, he inserted the razor-sharp tip into the canvas, then stroked downward gently and quietly, opening a shoulder-high gash. Silent as a shadow, he slipped through.

Amanda was asleep on a narrow cot.

Padding silently across the floor, he put his hand over her mouth, then shook her gently.

She woke with a start, her eyes wide, then threw her arms around his neck.

He hugged her close for a long moment, then moved away from the cot, motioning for her to follow him.

Amanda did so without question, her heart pounding with happiness at seeing him again.

Relámpago was waiting outside. Trey lifted her onto the stallion's back, then swung up behind her and walked the stallion away from the camp.

She leaned back against Trey, her heart overflowing with gratitude that he was alive.

They hadn't gone far when a shout roused the camp.

Muttering an oath, Trey slammed his heels into the stallion's flanks, and Relámpago took off at a dead run, streaking across the land like the lightning he'd been named for.

There was a flurry of gunshots, the pounding of hooves behind them, the loud report of a rifle, the flare of a muzzle flash as one of the sentries tried to head them off.

Trey's arm tightened around her waist as they raced away into the night. She knew she should be afraid, but, strangely, she wasn't. The stallion ran effortlessly, easily outdistancing the weary cavalry mounts behind them. The sounds of pursuit grew faint, then faded away. Still Relámpago ran, his long legs eating up the miles.

Trey finally slowed the stallion to a canter, then a rocking-chair trot.

Her head resting against Trey's shoulder, Amanda lost track of time. Her eyelids grew heavy and she closed her eyes, drifting in and out of sleep until she felt the stallion come to a halt.

"Where are we?" she asked sleepily.

"About halfway to Tucson." Trey slid over the stallion's rump and lifted her from the horse's back. "We'll stop here for the night."

"All right." She leaned into him, twined her arms around his neck, reveling in his nearness. "I was afraid," she said; "so afraid you'd been killed."

"Are you all right?"

"I am now."

He drew her closer, his hand sliding up her back, tunneling into her hair.

"Ouch!" A wave of nausea pulsed through her.

"What's wrong?"

"My head. Feel the size of that lump?" She winced as his fingers gently probed the bump.

"Damn Red Shawl," he muttered. "I should have taken a stick to her."

"Red Shawl? What does she have to do with anything?"

"She's the one who hit you. Young Bear saw her."

"Oh! I told you she was out to get me!"

He folded her into his arms again. "I should have listened to you. I will, next time."

"See that you do." She closed her eyes as the pain throbbed through her head. "Tucson?" she said after a moment. "You said Tucson." She opened her eyes and looked up at him. "Are we going there? Why are we going there? Aren't we going back to your people?"

"No."

"Why not?"

"My grandfather said my life was to be somewhere else. With you."

"Do you want to leave the Apache? I thought you were happy there."

"I was, but . . ."

"But what?"

He shrugged. "When Walker on the Wind said my path led in a different direction, I knew he was right." He ran his knuckles over her cheek. "Come on, let's get some sleep."

Tucson. She had seen the town depicted in numerous Westerns, but the real thing was a lot rougher and cruder than what she'd seen on television. And she'd never watched TV with a headache the size of the one she had when they arrived in town.

"We're not going to stay here, are we?" she asked dubiously.

"Just long enough to get you a change of clothes, a bath, and a good night's sleep."

She couldn't decide which of the three sounded best. "Maybe some Tylenol, too?" she asked.

"What?"

She closed her eyes. Had aspirin even been invented yet? She wasn't sure. "Headache medicine," she said.

He grunted softly. "We'll find something."

"And a real meal, in a restaurant?" she asked. "Fixed by a real cook?"

He laughed softly. "That, too. I found a couple of dollars in my jeans."

They left Relámpago at the livery barn at the end of town and walked down the street toward Naismith's Dry Goods Store.

Amanda was acutely aware of the curious glances sent their way as they walked along. She sighed inwardly. First her tank top and Nikes had made her the object of curious eyes; now her deerskin dress and moccasins were doing the same thing. Though Trey had on his jeans and shirt, he still wore his Apache moccasins.

It didn't take much imagination to know what people were thinking, and none of it was good. A big man with limp brown hair and close-set gray eyes stepped into their path, his expression belligerent. She could feel the tension radiating from Trey. His hand, rock-steady, hovered over the butt of his gun as he met the man's gaze. After a tense moment, the man moved aside and they continued on down the street.

She felt safer inside the dry goods store. Trey remained at her side while she picked out a dress, as well as a red flannel petticoat for warmth, a chemise, stockings and garters, and a pair of half-boots. And then they went to the men's department, where he picked up a blue wool shirt, a pair of black trousers, socks, and boots. She watched him choose a hat, re-membering the day in Canyon Creek when she had bought him a new Stetson. The hat he picked now was a dark chocolate brown. She smiled as she watched him settle it on his head. What was there about a man in a hat?

The clerk allowed as how they had a selection of patent headache remedies, and led them to a shelf where she picked out a couple, hoping one of them would work, though after looking at some of the other "cures" offered, she was doubtful. "Dr. John Ray-mond's Worm Destroyer," "Dr. Phineas T. Paul's Prickly Ash Bitters," "Dr. Jay Arthur's Female Remedy and Blood Purifier," "Dr. Hood's Nerve Tonic." The promises made on the packages had never made any sort of acquaintance with truth in advertising. She glanced at the two headache powders she had chosen. The contents probably wouldn't poison her. She hoped. At the moment, she didn't care, if her head would just stop pounding.

Trey paid for their purchases and tucked the parcels under his arm. Leaving the mercantile, they headed down the street toward the hotel.

The man behind the front desk looked them over with a jaundiced eye. Amanda thought he was going to refuse to rent them a room. His glance shuttled back and forth, but when he met Trey's eyes, he blinked and then focused on the crown of Trey's new hat.

"Welcome to the Savoy," he muttered. He handed Trey a key and directed them up the stairs to Room 12.

Trey nodded his thanks and led the way up the stairs

and down the narrow corridor to their room. He opened the door, and she followed him inside.

You had to hand it to Hollywood, she thought as she glanced around. The room looked just like the set of a B Western. The familiar cabbage rose wallpaper, an iron bedstead, a rocking chair in the corner, a chest of drawers with a porcelain ewer on top, a single window that looked out over the main street.

"Well, it's not much," Trey said. He dropped their packages on the bed, unbuckled his gun belt, and slung it over the back of the rocker.

Amanda sat on the bed and immediately sank down into the mattress. She looked up at Trey and grinned. "Get me out of here," she said, holding out her hand.

Trey took her hand in his and pulled her to her feet and into his arms. She melted against him, her face lifting for his kiss, her headache forgotten.

His gaze moved over her for a moment, and then he claimed her lips with his. Desire unfurled within her, its heat spreading through her like liquid sunshine, settling deep in the core of her being. She sighed with pleasure as his hands slid up and down her rib cage, then cupped her breasts.

"How are you feeling?" he asked. "I don't suppose . . ."

For answer, she nibbled on his lower lip, sucked it gently, feeling pure feminine satisfaction flood through her, blotting out the ache from her injury, as his desire rose against her.

"You're sure?"

She plucked his hat from his head and tossed it on the chair. "I'm sure," she whispered.

He walked backward, drawing her with him. Locked in each other's arms, they fell in slow motion onto the bed and sank into the mattress. Her greedy hands ran over his shoulders, splayed across his chest, roamed up and down his arms. She loved touching him, loved the feel of his heated skin against her own. The fact that she had feared she might never seen him again inflamed her ardor even more. The pounding of her heart overpowered the throbbing in her head as she pressed kisses to his brow, his cheeks, his nose. His lips. She kissed him hungrily. Heat flowed through her. Her heart swelled with love until she thought it might burst.

"I'll never let you go away from me again," she whispered.

"Amanda . . ."

Trey gazed up at her. How beautiful she was, with her cheeks flushed and her eyes glowing with passion. He kissed her deeply, wishing he had words enough to tell her how much she meant to him, how utterly lost he had felt when she was missing, but all he could do was whisper that he loved her over and over again. He wanted her, needed her with an urgency that could no longer be denied. Wanted all of her, heart and soul, mind and body.

Somehow, they managed to get out of their clothes until there was nothing between them but raw, aching desire. His hands moved over her, big callused hands that brought her nothing but pleasure. Hands that worshiped her.

Rolling over, Trey tucked her gently beneath him. Eyes aglow with passion, he claimed her lips with his as their bodies fused together, heat to heat and heart to heart, until he couldn't tell where he ended and she began, until, in the end, they were truly one body, one flesh. . . .

Chapter Twenty-six

They napped, snuggled together in each other's arms, and then made love again, slower this time. Trey. He was every wish come true, every fantasy she'd ever had made flesh. She dozed, her head on his shoulder, and knew she wanted nothing more of life than to be with Trey, to bear his children and grow old beside him.

When she woke, she realized she wanted two other things, badly. A bath, and something to eat.

When she mentioned it to Trey, he agreed to go downstairs and see about getting some hot water sent up.

Rising, he washed up using the cold water in the bowl on the bureau, then went downstairs to talk to the clerk.

A short time later, Amanda slipped into her tunic and padded barefoot down to the room at the end of

346

the hall where a young boy was pouring the last bucket of hot water into the tub. He looked at her sideways, murmured something unintelligible, and left the room just as Trey came in.

She luxuriated in the tub under Trey's amused glance, smiled when he took the soap from her hand and washed her back. And her front. And all the places in between. The water was growing cool when she stepped out.

He peeled off his shirt while she toweled dry.

"What are you doing?" she asked.

"I'm gonna take a bath."

She glanced at the tub. "But the water's dirty."

"It's clean enough for me. Besides, if we wait for more hot water, we'll never get out of here to eat."

A short time later, dressed in their new clothes, they left the hotel and headed for the nearest restaurant. Amanda felt much better. Earlier, she had taken one of the headache powders they'd bought, though she couldn't swear that was what had made her headache go away. It could just as easily have been the nap, or the hot bath, or just being with Trey again. In his arms again. Warmth engulfed her when she recalled how fiercely they had made love.

Now, waiting for the waitress to come and take their order, she smoothed her hand over her new dress. Not for the first time, she felt as if she had stepped into a Western movie. The restaurant was a large rectangular building. Square tables were placed at intervals around the room, covered with red-and-white checked cloths. Matching curtains hung at the windows. There was sawdust on the floor.

She glanced at the people at the other tables. Men in shirts and vests, canvas pants, cowboy boots; women clad in long-sleeved dresses and bonnets.

Trey ordered steak; Amanda ordered fried chicken.

"How's your head?" he asked.

"Much better." She touched the lump; it had gone down quite a bit. "Why?" she asked. "Why did those soldiers attack us?"

"They don't need a reason, but I reckon there was a raid somewhere. Maybe by another band of Apaches, maybe Comanches, maybe Kiowas." He shook his head, his expression hard. "It doesn't matter. To the Army, one Indian is the same as another. They won't be happy until they've wiped us all out, or confined us on reservations where they can keep an eye on us."

"That's awful." Her eyes widened. Why hadn't it occurred to her before? Many of the historical characters she had read about or seen depicted in movies and on television were alive now. Frank and Jesse James. Custer and Crazy Horse. Geronimo and Cochise. She thought of the movie *Broken Arrow*. She had seen it several times on the classic movie station, and it had become one of her favorite old movies. Jeff Chandler had been a surprisingly effective Cochise, and Jimmy Stewart had been perfect as Tom Jeffords, the man who had traveled alone to the Chiricahua hideout and made peace with the Apaches.

"Do you know Cochise, and Geronimo?"

"I've met them. Why?"

"I just wondered. They haven't been forgotten, you know. In my time, they're still making movies about their lives. I'm not sure how accurate the history is, but . . ."

"The whites are a strange people. First they try to wipe my people out, and then they tell stories about them."

Amanda sat back as the waitress approached and served their dinner. Chicken and potatoes and corn on the cob. Fresh bread and butter. And coffee. She picked up her cup, inhaled deeply before she took a sip.

They ate in silence for a few minutes. Amanda savored every bite. The chicken was tender, succulent; the potatoes were swimming in gravy. Apache fare had been filling, but nothing like this.

When the waitress came by to offer dessert, Amanda ordered a slice of chocolate cake and another cup of coffee. She looked at Trey. "Aren't you going to have anything?"

"No."

She looked thoughtful a moment. "Why don't you have a piece of apple pie?"

"Why?"

"Well, I'd like some pie, too.

"Then have some."

"Well, I want cake, too. So if you had pie, we could share our desserts." She smiled at him. "What do you think?"

With a shake of his head, Trey ordered a piece of pie.

Later they walked arm in arm down the street. "I'm stuffed," Amanda remarked.

"I'm not surprised," Trey said, grinning. "I didn't know a little bit of a thing like you could pack away so much grub."

"Well, you were supposed to eat half the cake and half the pie, you know. That was the whole idea of ordering both."

"You were enjoying them too much."

"Well, they were mighty good." Or maybe it was just being with Trey that made everything seem brighter, sweeter, better.

Trey paused when they reached the hotel. "Why don't you go on up to the room."

"Where are you going?"

He jerked a thumb in the direction of the saloon across the street. "It's time to make a little money."

"Oh." She ran her fingertips up and down his arm. "Will you be gone very long?"

"Not with you here waiting for me."

The look in his eyes sent a shiver of anticipation down her spine.

"All right," she said. "But be careful."

He winked at her. "Don't worry, sweetheart. I'm always careful." He kissed her, hard and quick, gave her an affectionate swat on her behind as she turned to open the hotel door.

She glanced at him over her shoulder. "Hey, watch it, cowboy."

"Oh, I'm watching it," he said with a roguish grin. "I'll be back soon."

"I'll be waiting."

"I'm counting on it."

* * *

The saloon was in full swing. The gambling tables were crowded, the bar girls were swishing back and forth from the bar to the tables, smiling and serving drinks. They were pretty girls, if you didn't mind the heavy rouge on their cheeks and the world-weary lines around their eyes. A piano player sat in the corner pounding out a rendition of "My Old Kentucky Home" while three couples danced. The air was thick with smoke.

Trey found a place at a table in the back and sank into an empty chair. The game was five-card draw, the stakes were high, and he was feeling lucky.

An hour later, he was more than four hundred dollars ahead.

He was thinking about calling it a night when Wolf Langley slid into the chair across from him. Trey's eyes narrowed as he met the bounty hunter's gaze.

"Evenin'," Langley said.

Trey grunted. "I didn't expect to see you here."

Sensing the underlying tension between the two men, the three other men at the table went suddenly still.

Langley raised his hands in a gesture of surrender. "I didn't come in here looking for any trouble. Just looking for a friendly card game. Hell, I didn't even know you were in town."

At Trey's nod, the other cardplayers relaxed.

"Everybody in?" the dealer asked, and when the pot was right, he dealt a new hand.

Trey played for another hour, winning more than he lost. It was nearing eleven when he left the table.

Leaving the saloon, he started across the street, his

thoughts on Amanda. He felt a rush of desire when he thought of her waiting for him in the hotel. She was likely in bed, her hair spread like wildfire on the pillow.

He had just reached the boardwalk in front of the hotel when something warned him. He wasn't sure what it was—a shadow, a footstep, or just that sixth sense that had saved his hide more than once. Dropping into a crouch, he spun around, reaching for his gun, as a bullet whined through the space he had just occupied and buried itself in the boardwalk. A muzzle flash across the street was followed by another booming report and the thwack of a slug hitting the wall behind him.

He fired at the dim silhouette the muzzle flash had illumined and heard a man grunt in pain, then the sound of a body hitting the ground.

He started to straighten up when another shot rang out down the street. A cry of pain echoed through the night, coming from above him, and he sensed rather than saw something falling from the roof of the hotel. A man's body slammed hard onto the street, raising a cloud of dust.

Trey leveled his gun in the direction from which the last shot had come, the shadows near the saloon he had just vacated.

A voice called, "Don't shoot!"

Langley! Trey walked toward the bounty hunter cautiously, his gun ready. "What the hell's going on?"

Langley replaced the spent cartridges and holstered his gun. "Looks like those two were after the reward on your head."

"You saved my life," Trey remarked, unable to keep the surprise out of his tone.

"Only seemed right, since you saved mine."

"Yeah." Trey eased the hammer down on his Colt. "So where does that leave us?"

"Don't worry. I said I wouldn't come after you again, and I won't. But if you're smart, you'll hightail it out of here. This is Tucson, not some one-horse town. The marshal will be on his way. And he's bound to recognize you, too."

"You're probably right, dammit." Trey slid his Colt into his holster. "Obliged for your help. I never would have seen the one on the roof in time."

"Yeah, well, I may regret it later," Langley said with a wry grin. "You'd better get going."

"On my way." Turning, Trey almost plowed into Amanda, who was running across the street toward him.

"Are you all right?" Her worried gaze moved over his face, her hands running restlessly over his arms and chest.

"I'm fine. Come on, we're getting out of here, now." She didn't argue.

Twenty minutes later, they were ready to go, riding double on Relámpago because Trey didn't want to take the time to buy another horse. He noticed that a crowd had gathered in front of the hotel. A man holding a lantern was kneeling beside one of the bodies. Trey heard someone say, "Here comes the marshal," and the crowd parted.

Trey swore softly. "Time to make tracks," he said grimly, and reined the horse around, heading away from the hotel at a walk so as not to attract attention.

Once out of sight of the hotel, he urged the stallion into a lope.

Amanda clung to Trey, her arms tight around his waist, her cheek resting against his back. One thing about life in the Old West, she mused, it was never dull.

"Where are we going?" she asked as they left the town behind.

"There's a piece of land I've had my eye on," he replied. "I was planning to settle there after I'd squared things with Hollinger. I think now's a good time to light out in that direction. No one knows me there."

"Oh, I remember. You mentioned it once before, didn't you? You were going to use the money from the bank robbery . . ." Her voice trailed off. The money he had stolen was sitting in the back of her bedroom closet, in a house that she probably would never see again.

"Something wrong?"

"What? Oh, no."

"Come on, sweetheart, what's bothering you?"

"Nothing, really. I guess I was just feeling a little homesick."

He placed his hand over hers and gave it a squeeze. "We'll build a new home. Together."

She nodded, her heart swelling with love as she imagined them building a house, raising a family. A boy and a girl, she thought, with Trey's dark hair and eyes. She slid her hand over her stomach. She could be pregnant even now. The idea thrilled her even as it gave her pause. Having a baby in a modern hospital with a doctor and drugs and emergency help if needed was one thing; having it out here in the wilds was something else entirely. Sanitary conditions were poor, hospitals few and far between. Childbirth would be risky, at best.

She was still considering the implications of being pregnant when they stopped for the night.

They had done it often enough so that it took no time at all to make camp.

"No fire tonight," Trey said when she started looking for wood.

"Why not? Oh. Of course." A fire could be seen for miles out here where the land was flat and there were no trees to diffuse the smoke.

They settled down on the blanket with Trey's arms around her. She shivered, and he drew her closer, his lips moving over her face, along her throat, the curve of her shoulder. And then he kissed her and she shivered again, right down to her toes, but not from the cold.

It was nearing midnight two nights later when they reached Canyon Creek. Amanda stared at the town. Late as it was, the saloons were still open. Yellow lamplight spilled out onto the street. Someone was playing a lively song on a piano that was sadly out of tune.

"Seems we've come full circle," she murmured, and even though home was over a hundred years in the future, she felt a sense of homecoming as they rode down the dusty street. This might be as close to home as she ever got.

As always, Trey's first thought was for Relámpago.

He left the stallion at the livery barn after instructing the owner to be sure the stud got a good rubdown and a quart of oats.

"It's too late to go to the land office tonight," Trey said as they walked toward the hotel. "I'll go first thing in the morning."

"What if they've sold the property to someone else?"

It was a possibility he refused to consider.

"How far is your property from here?"

"A shade over forty miles."

She nodded. Her house was about fifty miles from town. She wondered who was living in her house, and how long it would take to get there on horseback. They would be almost neighbors. She might even meet them. It would be interesting to see how the place had looked when it was new.

Thinking of home made her ask, "Is there a house on this land of yours?"

"Yeah, but it's not much. Just an old adobe shack." He took her hand in his and gave it a squeeze. "We'll build a new one together."

Later that night, lying in bed in each other's arms, they made plans for the future. They'd build a barn and corrals first, Trey said, since they could live in the shack for a while. They'd have to find some brood-mares, just a few to start with, mares with good bloodlines.

"How big a house will we build?" Amanda asked.

"Nothing too big to start with," Trey replied. "We can always add on later."

"I want a big window in front," Amanda said. "And

one in the kitchen, so I can look out and watch you work."

"And a big bedroom," he said, grinning, "with a big bed."

"And a bathroom, inside the house."

Trey grunted. "Well, a tub, anyway. And a big wood stove to heat the water. I doubt if we'll be able to find a blue tub."

"The color won't matter," she said wistfully. She put her hand over her stomach. "And a smaller bedroom, just in case."

He stared at her.

"Well, it could happen, you know," she said, feeling suddenly defensive. "You want children, don't you?"

He dragged his hand over his jaw. "Sure, it's just that I never . . ." He shook his head, his gaze darting to her stomach. "Are you expecting?"

"I don't know." She made a face at him. "It's possible, you know." More than possible, she thought, as often as they had made love lately. And now that she thought of it, she realized she hadn't had her period since she'd been here. She felt a flutter of apprehensive excitement. "Very possible."

Trey stared at her. The timing couldn't be worse, he thought bleakly. He was on the run. There was no telling what the future held, or how long Amanda would be here. He'd never given any thought to having kids before, had never known he wanted one, until now. His child. His and Amanda's.

"Trey? You're not mad, are you?"

"No, sweetheart, I'm not mad." He laid his hand over

hers. "It's just that the whole idea of being a father is new to me."

"You want kids, don't you?"

He nodded as he drew her into his arms and nuzzled her neck. "A pretty little girl with red hair, just like you."

They went to the land office first thing in the morning, even before breakfast. The property that Trey wanted was still available, being held by the local bank. They visited the bank next, and Amanda sat back and watched while Trey and the bank officer haggled over price and terms. Trey's poker winnings made a sizable down payment, and the bank officer said the papers making him the owner of 150 acres of land would be ready for signing by the time they finished breakfast.

Their next stop was the restaurant, where they ordered ham and eggs.

"Not as good as yours," Trey remarked, though she noticed he ate enough for a small army.

Next, they went to the general store and loaded up on supplies. Amanda bought dish towels and a zinc washtub, an apron, soap, flour, sugar, salt, pepper, baking soda, yeast, coffee, and a coffee grinder. She picked up a variety of tinned fruit, a hunk of cheese, dried apples, several boxes of matches, a kerosene lamp, a flour sifter, an iron, which weighed a ton, a Dutch oven, and numerous other household items.

She found a couple of shirts and a sheepskin jacket for Trey, two cotton dresses, underwear, and a coat and bonnet for herself. She picked out blankets and pillows for their bed. Trey added a shovel, a wheelbarrow, an ax, a rake, a hammer and nails, a rifle and several boxes of ammunition, a curry comb and a couple of brushes, and a rasp.

They looked through a mail order catalog and picked out a high-backed sofa, a kitchen table and two chairs, a brass bed, and a stove. Lastly, they bought a rooster and a half dozen red hens.

It was really going to happen, she thought. The two of them were going to set up housekeeping in an adobe shack and build a horse ranch. She sure hoped Trey knew what he was doing, because she didn't have a clue!

They had to rent a wagon and horses from the livery to haul their supplies in. Trey tied Relámpago to the back of the wagon, gave Amanda a boost onto the high-sprung seat. Hopping up beside her, he took up the reins and they were on their way.

It was, indeed, a shack. A fair-sized one, though, with a living room, a kitchen that faced the east, and a bedroom barely big enough to turn around in. The windows were covered with burlap; the door was made of oak and had a sturdy crossbar on the inside. The floors were dirt. There was a large fireplace for heating and cooking.

Trey squeezed her hand. "Remember, it's only temporary."

Nodding, she forced a smile.

Only temporary became her mantra.

Living in the adobe shack was no worse than living with the Apache, but here she had no other women to laugh with while she looked for wood or hauled water from the stream or washed their clothes, no one to talk to while she cleaned the game Trey brought home. She missed Yellow Calf Woman and Walker on the Wind.

But she didn't complain. Couldn't complain, not when Trey worked so hard. He spent long hours laying out the foundation for the barn, plowing the ground behind the shack so she could plant vegetables, cutting trees for poles to build a corral for Relámpago and for the mares he hoped to buy the following spring.

So much work, and none of it easy.

At first, she didn't think she'd ever get the hang of cooking in a Dutch oven. Time and again, the food came out cooked on the bottom but not on the top, or burned on one side but raw on the other.

Washing clothes was perhaps the worst chore of all. She grew to hate the big old washtub. A fire had to be kept going under the tub to keep the water hot, the clothes had to be rubbed back and forth over a scrub board to remove the dirt, then rinsed and hung to dry. Oh, Lord, how she missed her washer and dryer, her dishwasher, the microwave. Not to mention the grocery store, where bread came in lovely packages and meat was already aged and butchered. She missed hot bubble baths and running water. And toilet paper. Relieving herself in a chamber pot, or in the privy that Trey built out back, was perhaps the worst part of living in the past.

She missed indoor heat and plumbing, her refrigerator, television. Right now, even old *I Love Lucy* reruns sounded good.

Sometimes she was overwhelmed with homesickness. Whenever that happened, whenever she thought she couldn't go on for another minute, she would go find Trey. In his arms, whatever trivial thing was bothering her melted away. She never tired of looking at him, watching him work. Tall and lean, he moved with an assurance that she found oddly comforting. There was nothing to be afraid of so long as he was here, nothing they couldn't do, together. He never seemed to get discouraged. He knew what had to be done, and he did it.

He was easy to live with, never critical of her efforts, however bad they might be, willing to let her make her own mistakes but always ready and willing to help her if she asked for it.

And no matter how difficult the days might be, the nights were always wonderful. Sometimes they sat under the stars and imagined how things would be when the house was finished and the corral was filled with prime horseflesh. Sometimes they went skinny-dipping in the stream, then curled up in front of the fire with a blanket over their shoulders and thought about names for the baby.

The baby. She was certain she was pregnant now. She had all the symptoms her married girlfriends had complained of. She was weepy and irritable, her breasts were tender, her ankles were swollen.

Trey was the soul of patience, always understanding, ever tender, able to laugh her out of her moods. She woke up in his arms in the morning, fell asleep in his arms at night.

By the time she was four months pregnant, her moodiness seemed to have passed, she was full of energy, and she was certain that being pregnant was the most wonderful thing in the world.

Now, standing in the doorway waiting for Trey to come to supper, she was filled with a sense of contentment. The corral was finished. The barn was almost up. Their furniture had arrived and they had a table to eat on, a bed to sleep in, and a stove to cook on. She had made curtains for the windows, a tablecloth for the table. She had planted flowers in front of the shack, a vegetable garden in the back, made a winding path lined with rocks that led from the house to the stream. Chickens scratched in the dirt, digging up worms for their chicks.

She blew out a sigh as she placed a hand over her burgeoning belly. She couldn't wait to see her child, hold it in her arms. Trey's child. A son, with his dark hair and eyes.

She smiled as she watched Trey walk toward her, felt her heart beat a little faster as he drew near. His face and chest were sheened with sweat, his hands were dirty, but she didn't care. She threw herself in his arms and kissed him.

"Hey, sweetheart."

"Hey yourself. I missed you."

He grinned down at her. Whether he was gone an hour or all day, she always met him with a hug and a smile, always told him she missed him. He couldn't imagine his life without her, didn't know what he'd ever done to deserve her.

He placed his hand over her belly. She had always been beautiful, but never more so than now, when she was carrying his child. "How's my son?"

"Sleeping, I think. Dinner's ready. Are you hungry?"

He nodded. "Just let me get cleaned up."

He washed up in the tub alongside the shack while she went in to set the table. There had been times, when she was first learning how to cook Western-style, when it had been all he could do to choke down his dinner, but she'd become a darn fine cook in the last couple of months. She had even learned to make a melt-in-your-mouth apple pie.

He dried off, then took a minute to look out over the land. His land. It had taken a lot of hard work, but it had been worth it. The corral was sturdy. As soon as the barn was finished, he'd start looking for some broodmares. And then they'd get to work on a new house.

Whistling softly, he walked around the shack to the front door and stepped inside, thinking himself the luckiest man in the world.

They had worked hard the last few months, and Trey decided it was time for a trip to town. Amanda didn't argue. She was ready for a change of scene, especially when it meant spending the night in town, bathing in a real tub in hot water she didn't have to heat on the stove. Shopping. Eating a meal she hadn't had to prepare. Seeing other people, even people she didn't know. Besides, there were a few things she wanted to buy for the house. She also needed some flannel so she could start sewing things for the baby, and muslin for diapers.

She put on her bonnet, tied the strings beneath her chin, tucked her shopping list into her skirt pocket.

Trey was waiting for her outside. He lifted her onto Relámpago's back and handed her the reins before swinging effortlessly onto the back of a leggy bay. The mare was the first he'd bought. She had long, clean lines and a gentle disposition, but she was still a little wild and he didn't trust her to carry Amanda.

"Ready?" he asked.

"Ready."

It was a beautiful morning for a ride, warm and clear. The saguaro and the paloverde were in bloom; wildflowers made bright splashes of color between gray-green clumps of sage and spiny cactus. They passed a slow-moving tortoise. An eagle soared effortlessly overhead, making lazy circles before plummeting to earth to snatch some unsuspecting creature in its talons. Trey's mount shied to one side as a rabbit sprang across her path. He spoke softly to the mare and she quickly settled back down, soothed by the sound of his voice and the gentle touch of his hand on her neck.

He had a way with females, Amanda thought with a grin. Human or equine.

It was after dark when they arrived in town. After leaving the horses at the livery, they got a room at the hotel. After washing up, they went to get something to eat.

It was wonderful to sit at a table she hadn't set, to eat a full-course meal she hadn't had to prepare, to know she wouldn't have to heat a pan of water and wash and dry the dishes when they were through.

Feeling spoiled and happy, she sat back in her chair and smiled at Trey, thinking, not for the first time, that he was easily the most handsome man she had ever known.

"What are you thinking about?" she asked, noting his sober expression. "Is something wrong?"

"You're gonna have a baby."

"Yes, I know."

"We ought to get married."

"We are married."

"I mean here, in town. I don't want anyone calling my son a bastard because his parents weren't properly married."

There was an edge in his voice, a tinge of bitterness that made her wonder whether his father had married his mother. "All right, if you think we should."

"I'll see about it tomorrow, first thing."

"That means another honeymoon," she said, smiling at him in hopes of lightening his mood. "Although I don't think we can top the last one, do you?"

He grinned at her, his eyes suddenly hot. "I'll do my best."

"I know you will," she said, laughing softly. "I'm counting on it."

True to his word, Trey arranged for them to be married the following afternoon. But first they had business to attend to. Trey took the horses to the blacksmith shop for new shoes; Amanda went to the mercantile, where she picked up several bars of soap, a sack of Matoma Rice, a few cans of salmon, and a dozen lemons and tomatoes, as well as a variety of tinned meat and vegetables.

While she was waiting for the clerk to add up her

purchases, her gaze fell on a dress. It was just a simple frock with a square collar and full skirt. The material was cotton, white with tiny blue flowers. Best of all, it was big enough to accommodate her increased size. She handed it to the clerk, telling him she would take the dress with her and pick up the rest of her order later.

She returned to the hotel, surprised that Trey wasn't already there.

Taking off her old dress, she stepped into the new one, then brushed out her hair.

A moment later, Trey arrived. He'd been to the barbershop. His hair, still long, had been freshly trimmed. He'd had a shave, too.

"New dress," he remarked, shutting the door.

She twirled around. "Like it?"

"You look pretty as a filly in a patch of clover."

"You look mighty nice yourself." She ran her fingertips over his jaw. "And you smell good, too."

He grinned at her. "I told the barber to give me the best he had 'cause I was marrying the prettiest girl in the territory."

She blushed with pleasure.

"Ready?" he asked, offering her his arm.

"Ready."

She hadn't expected to feel so nervous, but standing in front of the preacher in the little white church at the end of the street, she felt like a real bride, getting married for the first time.

He introduced himself as the Reverend William Applegate.

The preacher's wife, a tiny little woman with curly

brown hair and gray eyes, stood in as Amanda's maid of honor. The preacher's teenage son, a tall, gangly boy with carrot-red hair and freckles, stood beside Trey, looking bored.

Amanda looked up into Trey's eyes, warmed by the love she saw there as she said the words that made her his wife. There was no doubt in her mind that she had been made for this man and no other, knew that if she had married Rob or any other man, she would never have been completely happy. She would have spent her whole life yearning for the other half of her soul, searching for a way to fill the emptiness in her heart, an emptiness that only Trey's love could fill.

She was surprised when Trey slipped a wide gold band over her finger. When had he found the time to buy one?

The preacher pronounced them man and wife.

Amanda gazed into Trey's eyes, all else forgotten as he took her in his arms. "I love you," he murmured. "Now and forever. Only you."

"And I love you," she repeated. "Now and forever. Only you."

Lowering his head, he claimed her lips, sealing his love with a kiss.

Chapter Twenty-seven

The sound of the preacher loudly clearing his throat brought Amanda back to reality. She knew she was blushing when Trey released her.

The preacher's wife signed the marriage certificate as witness, then kissed Amanda and hugged Trey.

"Such a lovely couple. I hope you'll be as happy as me and the Reverend have been," she said, beaming at them.

The preacher harrumphed, and Trey grinned.

They went to dinner in the town's finest restaurant after leaving the church. Strange as it seemed, Amanda was so nervous she could hardly eat. There was no accounting for the way she felt, all shivery and excited. After all, she had been sleeping with Trey for months now, but there was no denying that tonight was special. The Apache ceremony had been lovely, but for some reason, this was different. Perhaps it was because they had been married in a church. Maybe it was the piece of paper in Trey's pocket that proclaimed to all the world that they were man and wife. Or maybe it was just the intense expression in Trey's deep brown eyes when he looked at her, a purely masculine look of desire and possession that spoke to everything feminine within her.

She was trembling with anticipation when they left the restaurant, their footsteps quickening as they neared the hotel. At the foot of the stairs, Trey swung her into his arms and carried her up to their room.

She opened the door and he carried her inside, kicked the door shut with his heel. Still holding her in his arms, he kissed her deeply, his tongue sliding sensuously over her lower lip, causing the tinder of her desire to burst into full flame. She clung to him as he carried her to the bed, placed her on the soft mattress, and followed her down, his body covering hers, his hands as eager as hers as they undressed each other.

She ran her hands over his back and shoulders, up and down his arms, over his thighs, loving the way he responded to her touch, the way his muscles rippled beneath her hands, the heat of his skin, the brush of his hair over her breasts. She was ready for him in moments, ready and eager and wanting . . . wanting . . . wanting.

She sighed with pleasure as their bodies came together, moving slowly, rhythmically, to the music only their hearts could hear, moving ever faster as the melody soared, carrying them up, up, toward the last sparkling note. . . .

* * *

"Mrs. Long Walker. Mrs. Trey Long Walker. Mrs. Amanda Long Walker." She wrote across his chest with her forefinger, smiling as she tried out every variation of her new name that she could think of.

It was such a lovely chest, bronze and well muscled, she couldn't resist pausing from time to time to admire it, or kiss the man who watched her, his eyes alight with amusement.

"Mrs. T. Long Walker," she continued, writing across his chest with a flourish. "Mrs. A. Long Walker. Mrs. Amanda Nicole Burkett Long Walker."

"You forgot one." His hand cupped the back of her head and drew her down for a kiss. "Mr. and Mrs. Long Walker." His hand slid down her neck, over her shoulder, to cup her breast.

"Hmm, that's the best one of all," she replied dreamily. "Mr. and Mrs. Long Walker. Has a lovely ring to it, doesn't it?"

"Yeah. We're all nice and legal now," he remarked. "No matter what happens, you'll always be mine."

His words sent a cold shiver down her spine. Easing up on one elbow, she stared down at him. "Why did you say that?"

"No reason."

"Trey! Why did you say that? You think something's going to happen, don't you? Something bad. Trey—"

"Calm down, sweetheart."

"What do you think's going to happen?"

He drew her back down beside him, his arm tightening around her shoulders. "I didn't mean to upset you."

"But?"

"I can't forget that you don't belong here, that I could wake up some morning and you'd be gone, and—"

She put her hand over his mouth. "Don't say that!" She had been so happy here with him, she had put the possibility of being zapped back to her own time out of her mind, but the reality of it hit her now, and hit her hard. What if she had the baby, and then, somehow, she was sent back to the future, alone?

The unwelcome thought haunted her for the rest of the night and on the long ride back home the following morning. And then she forced herself to think rationally. It could happen, but would it? She had tried to go back home before and nothing had happened. It didn't make sense that she would suddenly be zapped back to her own time without rhyme or reason.

She smiled as they rounded a bend in the trail and their house came into view. It was a cozy little place, with the rock-lined path leading up to the front door and the flowers blooming on either side. Hens scratched in the dirt, digging up plump grubs for their chicks; the rooster sat on the top rail of the corral like a sultan surveying his harem. Next year at this time, they would have a real house with two bedrooms and wood floors and glass in the windows. And a baby.

She glanced over at Trey. "Next time we go to town, we need to buy a cow."

"I was thinking about that," he said. "Maybe we'll get a couple of sheep, too, and a pig."

She nodded, thinking what fun it would be to have a yard full of animals, and then she frowned. The animals wouldn't be pets. They'd be for food. The thought gave her pause. She wasn't sure she could feed an animal every day, watch it grow, and then eat it. She remembered how horrified she had been when she was a little girl and found out that the pork chops her grandmother served her for dinner had come from the cute little pig she had watched grow up on the farm.

Trey reined his horse to a halt. Leaning forward, he folded his arms over the pommel. "We need to build a smokehouse," he mused, "and maybe a springhouse, over there."

Dismounting, he lifted Amanda from Relámpago's back. "You okay?"

"I'm fine." She arched her back and stretched her shoulders. "Just a little tired."

"Here." He turned her around and began to massage her back, his big hands gentle, soothing.

She closed her eyes, her head lolling forward. "That feels wonderful."

He massaged her shoulders, then, turning her to face him, he kissed the tip of her nose.

"Go on inside and sit down," he said with a wink. "Put your feet up. I'll bring the supplies in after I put the horses away."

She smiled up at him, thinking how sweet he was. "Thanks, love."

She watched him head for the barn, admiring his long-legged stride, then hurried toward the house, eager to take Trey's advice.

She paused, her hand on the latch, at the sound of hoofbeats coming fast. Glancing over her shoulder, she saw three men riding toward the house. She didn't recognize any of them.

"Amanda!" Trey was running toward her, leading the horses. Grabbing her around the waist, he lifted her onto Relámpago's back and thrust the reins into her hand. "Get the hell out of here! Now!"

Gut-wrenching fear swept through her. "What's wrong?"

"Bounty hunters," he replied, and slapped the stallion on the rump.

Relámpago sprang forward. Clinging to the saddle horn, Amanda looked over her shoulder, her heart pounding wildly.

She saw Trey swing onto the back of the mare. He slammed his heels into the bay's flanks, drew his gun, turned and fired at the men pursuing him as the mare broke into a gallop.

Answering gunfire came in a series of sporadic pops; lost in the vast outdoors, the sound was not nearly as loud as in the movies. But this was the real thing. Trey fired again, and one of the bounty hunters tumbled over the back of his horse.

Amanda gave the stallion his head and Relámpago lined out in a dead run, the mare close on his heels. Amanda shrieked as a bullet whizzed by her cheek, so close she could feel the heat of it.

She looked back at Trey, her eyes widening in horror as a bullet struck the mare in the neck. The bay stumbled and went down. Trey rolled free and scrambled to his knees, his gun leveled at the two men riding toward him.

Relámpago raced toward a distant hill, his long legs

eating up the ground. She pulled back on the reins, but the stallion didn't respond. Taking the bit in his teeth, he surged forward.

She tugged on the reins again, harder this time. Trey was in trouble. She couldn't leave him. She looked back again. Trey fired, and one of the riders slumped forward in the saddle. The second rider slowed his horse, sighted down the barrel of his rifle, and squeezed the trigger.

Time seemed to crawl to a stop.

The gunshot echoed and re-echoed in her mind. She whispered, "No, oh no," as the world around her seemed to grow fuzzy around the edges. Long fingers of swirling gray mist rose up around her, blinding her to everything else. A familiar soft buzzing noise rang in her ears.

And then she knew no more.

She was home. She looked behind her, hoping to see Trey, but there was no sign of him.

She stared at the house in disbelief. Her house.

"No, it can't be. It can't end like this!"

She reined Relámpago around and rode toward the place where past and present had come together the last time. Nothing happened. Again and again, she tried to find the corridor that led into the past, but to no avail.

Hours passed. The sun was beginning to set when she gave up and returned to the house.

Dismounting, she led Relámpago into the corral. She unfastened the girth, removed the saddle and dropped it over the top rail of the corral, spread the blanket beside it. The stallion nudged her as she removed the bridle and draped it over the saddle horn. She scratched the stallion between the ears for a few minutes; then, with a final pat, she left the corral.

She was home. Slowly, her feet feeling like lead, she climbed the stairs. The front door was closed and locked. She kept an extra key buried in the dirt beside the porch. Retrieving it, she opened the door and stepped inside. After living in an Apache wickiup and an adobe shack, the house seemed enormous. She moved slowly, woodenly, from room to room, turning on the lights, the TV, running her hands over the back of the sofa, the tabletops, the mantel. Everything was coated with a fine layer of dust. She saw a residue of black powder on various surfaces here and there. Where had that come from?

In the kitchen, she ran her hand over the faucet, turned on the tap, and marveled when the water gushed forth and began to turn warm. The water and electricity still were connected!

How long had she been away? Had time here passed at the same rate as it had in the past? If she'd been gone more than a month or so in this time, wouldn't the utility companies have shut off the gas and electricity?

Turning on the cold water, she filled a teapot, put it on the stove, and turned on the flame. So easy, so quick. No need to hunt for wood or coax a reluctant fire to life.

She opened the fridge. It was empty, save for a big dish of baking soda on the top shelf to absorb odors. Someone had been here to clean it out.

Leaving the water to heat, she went upstairs to her bedroom. Had it always been this big? The whole adobe shack would have fit inside her bedroom. She opened her closet and looked at her clothes, ran her hand over the coverlet on her bed, gasped when she caught a glimpse of her reflection in the mirror. How different she looked! It wasn't just her old-fashioned dress or the fact that her skin was now a deep golden brown, or that her hair was longer. She looked . . . older. Grown up. Sad. She placed her hands over her belly. Pregnant.

The whistle of the teakettle took her back downstairs. She made a cup of tea, sipped it while she stared out the window. She felt numb inside, all her senses dulled. She was home, but there was no joy in it.

She put her empty cup in the dishwasher, then walked down the hallway to the guest room. There were more of those black smudges here and there; some kind of dust storm? she wondered. She stood in the doorway, staring at the bed where he had slept as memories engulfed her: Trey thinking she was in danger from a man on a TV show; trying on jeans in town; rescuing her from the snake; holding her in his arms, whispering he would love her forever . . .

Sobbing his name, she threw herself on the bed and cried out her grief. She wondered if he had been killed by the bounty hunters. But whether he was dead or alive in the past, he was lost to her now, and she feared she would never see him again.

Chapter Twenty-eight

Trey gained his feet, the acrid odor of gun smoke filling his nostrils as he stared at the three men he had killed.

He punched the spent cartridges from his Colt, reloaded, then went to check on the mare. She was lying on her side. Blood pumped from the wound in her neck, and even as he watched, she made one last effort to rise, and then lay still.

He regretted the death of the beautiful mare more than the three men.

Where was Amanda?

He peered into the distance. Relámpago had done his job once more, carrying her away from danger. At least she was safe. Holstering his Colt, he considered the three bodies. The least he could do was bury them before she returned.

Only one of the gunmen's mounts had stayed close by, its reins trailing. He caught up the reins of the gray gelding, speaking to it quietly, adjusted the stirrups for his long legs, then loosened the rope coiled on the horn and dallied a loop over the hindquarters of the dead mare.

He dragged the carcass a mile out into the desert to spare Amanda the sight of what the desert scavengers would do to it. Then he rode back to the house, got a spade, and found a spot far from the house to bury the bodies.

He cursed J. S. Hollinger as he worked. He'd just been kidding himself. As long as there was a bounty on his head, he'd never be able to settle down, never be able to make a home for Amanda and the baby.

Pausing, he wiped the sweat from his brow. Where the devil was she? How far had 'Pago run?

He used the rope to drag the three bodies to the crude gravesite, filled it in, and covered it with rocks to discourage coyotes. Then he tracked down the other two horses. They hadn't run far.

He stripped the rigging from the other two horses and turned them out in the corral. Taking up the reins of the gray, he swung into the saddle and went in search of Amanda.

He had no trouble following the stallion's tracks. The trail was clear and easy to read until it simply disappeared. He sat there for a long time, staring at the place where the stallion's tracks ended. He had put her on Relámpago knowing the horse would carry her to safety. He hadn't figured on the stallion carrying her back to her own time.

Knowing it was useless, he urged his mount forward. No mist rose up to meet him. The world didn't spin out of focus, there was no buzzing in his ears, and he knew that even if he rode forever, he would never find her.

Amanda woke feeling disoriented. Where was she? She reached for Trey, but he wasn't there, and then it all came back to her. She was home again.

Rising, she went into the living room. How long had she been gone? Did the days pass the same in the past as in the present? The blinking light of her answering machine caught her eye. She had twenty-seven messages.

Sitting on the arm of the sofa, she hit Play.

The first one was from Rob. "Mandy, if you're home, please call me."

After several more from Rob, there was a message from her mother. "Amanda, sweetheart, please call us. We're so worried."

Most of the remaining messages were also from Rob and her mother. There were half a dozen from her father, three from Earl Hennessy, the first wondering why she hadn't shown up for work, the second asking if she was coming to work, the third saying they had found someone else. There was a message from her dentist's office informing her she had missed her annual checkup; three were wrong numbers. The last two were from telephone solicitors.

How long had she been gone? She realized she didn't remember the exact date of that shootout in the front yard. . . .

The shootout. There had been no traces of it when she rode in.

She turned on the TV and turned to the all-news channel. The sheer familiarity of the images on the screen brought tears to her eyes. The announcers rattled on about one disaster after another—nothing new there—but the date displayed on the screen told her that she had been gone several months. Months!

Just like in the past.

With a sigh, she picked up the phone and called her mother, wondering how she would explain what had happened, wondering who on earth would believe it. She considered making something up, but she'd never been a good liar, especially where her mother was concerned. Florence Burkett could spot a lie in a heartbeat. As Amanda had expected, her mother was dubious. Finally, weary of trying to convince her, Amanda said good-bye and hung up thinking that, in this case, she should have tried a lie first.

Her next call was to her father. She was relieved when he wasn't home. Next she called Earl Hennessy. She apologized for her absence, told him something unexpected had come up and she was sorry for not calling him sooner. She assured him she understood why he had given the job to someone else. And then, taking a deep breath, she made the call she dreaded most.

Rob picked up the phone on the second ring. "Hello?"

"Hi, Rob, it's me."

"Amanda! Where are you? Are you all right? I've been going crazy here, wondering where you were."

"I'm home, I'm fine—"

380

"Don't move! I'll be right there," he said, and hung up the phone.

Amanda stared at the receiver in her hand. She really wasn't ready to talk about this with anyone face to face, but when she hit Redial, she got his answering machine.

With a sigh, she put the receiver down.

He was there in record time. Watching him hurry up the stairs, she figured he must have run every red light and broken every speed law to get to her so fast.

He burst into the house and swept her into his arms. "Amanda! I've been worried sick. Are you all right? Where the hell have you been? Why didn't you call?"

He hugged her so tight she could scarcely breathe. "Rob—"

"Oh, sorry." He loosened his hold, but didn't let her go. "Amanda." He gazed down at her, and then he kissed her.

When she didn't respond, his arms fell away and he took a step backward, his eyes narrowed. "What is it? What's wrong? I know we didn't part on the best of terms when I was here last, but . . . you're not still upset about that, are you? No," he said, answering his own question. "You've never been one to stay mad. It's Long Walker, isn't it? Is that where you've been? With him?"

She nodded. "Yes, but not the way you think." She blew out a sigh. "You might as well sit down."

He looked at her a moment, then dropped into the nearest chair.

Amanda sat on the sofa, wondering where to begin. "I know you have a lot of questions—"

"Damn right." He frowned. "What are you doing in that getup?"

She glanced down at her dress. Her wedding dress. She'd had so much on her mind, she hadn't thought to change. Or maybe she just hadn't wanted to change.

"Well?" Rob asked impatiently.

"I don't suppose you believe in time travel."

He lifted one brow. "Time travel?"

She nodded. "Trey came here from the past."

"Uh-huh."

"It's true. Relámpago brought him."

"Who?"

"The stallion, remember?"

"Sure. Whatever happened to the horse?"

"He's outside . . . isn't he?"

Rob shook his head. "Go on. The horse brought him here. From the past."

"Yes. You remember his gun? The one you thought was a well-preserved original? It was original—and almost new. Like this dress."

"He brought a dress with him?"

"No. Somehow Trey came here from the past. We went riding one day, and when we got back here, Bolander's brothers and a cousin were waiting for us. They were looking for you. Trey shot one—"

"Cletus. He's dead." Rob swore softly. "County investigators matched his blood to some found in the yard here. But there wasn't enough evidence to make a case against the others, not officially. I went after the other two. They told me some cock-and-bull story about chasing a couple of riders on a horse that disappeared. At first, I thought maybe they'd kidnapped you, killed you, but Nate and Arnie both swore they'd never touched you. They even took lie detector tests. The cops were all over this place."

He gestured at a smear of black powder by a light switch. "Fingerprinting, the whole nine yards. They finally decided that if you'd left, you'd left of your own free will. So where were you all this time?"

"Relámpago carried us into the past."

Rob stared at her, disbelief etched on his features.

"It's true! I don't expect you to believe it. I don't expect anyone to believe it. But it's true."

"I don't know whether I believe you or not," he said, "but those cartridge boxes he left behind didn't come from this century. And neither did those bank notes. The sheriff's office says they're worth a fortune today. Collectibles." His mouth twisted. "So where's the cowboy?"

"Back in his own time."

Rob shook his head. "Incredible. So you've been to the past, and now you're back. Where does that leave us?"

"The sheriff's office took his money?" she asked, ignoring his question.

"It was his?"

"Trey had it when he got here. In his saddlebags. He . . . he'd robbed a bank."

"Nice guy. But he could be delusional, you know." He ran a hand through his hair. "Hell, maybe you are, too. The money doesn't prove anything."

She stared at him. Trey would have believed her, she thought, no matter what. "All right," she said.

"Don't believe me, I don't care. But where do you think all that old money came from?"

"I don't know." Rising, he began to pace the floor.

She stood there watching him, wondering how she could make him believe, wondering what difference it made. Nothing mattered now that Trey was gone, nothing but the child beneath her heart.

Rob came to an abrupt halt. "You didn't answer me before. Where does all this leave us?" He reached into his pocket, then held out his hand. "Wherever you went, you left this behind. I guess that's my answer."

She stared at the diamond ring in his palm, remembering the day she had taken it off, the day she had known she could never marry him. "Rob . . . I'm pregnant."

His hand snapped shut around the ring, tightened into a white-knuckled fist. "I guess I don't have to ask who the father is. I know for damn sure it isn't me."

"I'm sorry, Rob. I don't know what to say. I didn't mean to fall in love with him, it just happened. We . . . got married."

"Yeah. Well, I hate to tell you this, but your cowboy bank robber is long dead. Over a hundred years dead, if what you say is true."

The words stabbed her to the heart. Tears welled in her eyes, slid down her cheeks. She made no move to wipe them away.

He shook his head, his eyes as cold as blue ice. "I hope you'll be happy with your decision. Good-bye, Amanda."

Tears ran down her cheeks as she watched him walk out of her house, and out of her life. But the tears weren't for Rob. They were for herself, and the child that Trey would never see.

Rob's big truck had barely cleared the driveway before she rushed to the corral, hoping against hope he had been wrong. But Relámpago was gone, and with him her only hope of returning to the past, and Trey.

She looked outside first thing every morning, hoping to see the stallion in the corral, and every morning her hope that he would return to her grew fainter.

She moved through the next few days like a sleepwalker, her thoughts more in the past than the present as she relived every day, every minute, she had spent with Trey, from the first day she had seen him slumped over Relámpago's neck to the last time, when he had been fighting for his life.

She found out that her father had been paying the utilities. Over his protests, she wrote out a check and mailed it to him. Needing to keep busy, she methodically cleaned the house, obliterating the dust of disuse and the last traces of fingerprint powder. She washed all the silverware, and every dish, glass, pot, and pan in the kitchen. She washed the windows, the curtains in the kitchen and the bathrooms.

Every night, she fell into bed exhausted, only to lie awake, thinking of Trey, wondering, always wondering, what his fate had been. She prayed he had lived a good, long life, that he had found a place where he could live in peace. As much as it hurt to think of him with another woman, she hoped he had found someone to love, someone to love him as much as she had.

As for herself, she knew she would never love again.

Her only solace, her only reason for living, was the child.

Trey Long Walker's child, growing in love beneath her heart.

Chapter Twenty-nine

The baby's kicking woke Amanda from a sound sleep. She placed her hand over her belly, smiling sleepily as a tiny foot moved under her palm. It had to be a boy, she thought, a boy with Trey's dark eyes and black hair. A boy with Trey's roguish grin. She would have to go to the doctor soon, make arrangements for a hospital, buy a crib. Notify her parents . . . she would wait for that. Her father hadn't been any more impressed with her story than her mother. He had even suggested she consider professional help. He had offered to come and stay with her until she regained her senses, but she had turned him down, causing a strain between them. Her mother had also offered to come and stay for a few days, but Amanda had asked her to wait a few weeks. Her mother had been hurt, but not angry. Amanda was sorry for that, but she needed some time alone, time to adjust. Time to grieve.

Rising, she took a shower and dressed. Grabbing her keys, she left the house. The Jag, covered with a layer of dust, was where she had left it. Putting the top down, she backed out of the garage.

It was a lovely day for a drive. The sky was a bright blue, the air warm and clear. She drove toward Canyon Creek, then veered off on a dirt road, hoping she was going the right way.

When the surrounding countryside started to look vaguely familiar, she pulled off the road and began to walk.

Trey was beside her every step of the way.

There wasn't much left of the shack save for two walls and part of the roof. The barn was still standing, warped and weathered by time. The corral was gone.

"Trey." She whispered his name. "Trey, Trey, what happened to you?"

Had he been killed by those bounty hunters? Or had Relámpago returned in time to carry him to safety?

"Stupid horse," she muttered. "Where are you when I need you?"

Trey. Had he survived the fight? Fallen in love again? Married someone else? Or spent the rest of his life on the run?

As much as she wanted him to have lived a long and happy life, the thought of him being with another woman was like a dagger in her heart.

She ran her fingers over her wedding ring, remembering the words he had spoken on their wedding day. Closing her eyes, she heard his voice in the back of her mind: *I love you. Now and forever. Only you.*

"I love you," she whispered. "Now and forever. Only you . . ."

The barest hint of a breeze stirred, ruffling the leaves of a nearby paloverde, moving through her hair like a lover's caress.

She heard a faint sound, like distant thunder, or the pounding hoofbeats of a horse. She glanced around. The sky was still clear. There was no one else in sight.

The breeze picked up, creating a dust devil near the front of the adobe's remains. It reminded her of her time with the Apaches, of their belief that evil spirits lived in the whirlwind.

From the west, gauzy fingers of pale gray mist rose from the ground, blurring her vision, obscuring the sun.

The hoofbeats grew louder. She could feel the vibration beneath her feet.

She whispered his name, not daring to believe even as hope sang in her heart. "Trey."

She saw him through the mist, riding hard, knew he was being pursued. She saw a vague image of half a dozen men riding behind him. There was a flash of fire, the sharp bark of a rifle.

She cried out as he jerked in the saddle, screamed in pain and denial as he fell forward across Relámpago's withers, and then the stallion was racing toward her out of the swirling gray mist.

Relámpago slowed to a walk, halted with a toss of his head.

Trey looked up. She heard him whisper her name as their gazes met, and then he toppled sideways from the saddle to lie still at her feet.

She stood there for a moment, unable to move, afraid to move. What if he was . . . she couldn't form the word in her mind.

On legs that felt like lead, she moved toward him. "Trey . . ." She knelt at his side, her gaze running over him, her stomach clenching in horror when she saw the blood dripping down the side of his head. "No. Oh, no . . ."

Relámpago whinnied softly. Coming up behind her, he gave her a shove. With a startled cry, she fell forward across Trey's chest, her eyes widening, her heart soaring when he grunted.

Scrambling to her hands and knees, she looked down into his eyes.

"You're alive!" she exclaimed. "Oh, Trey!" She reached for him, her hands moving over chest and shoulders, feeling solid flesh. "You're here! You're really here." She drew back, her brow furrowed. "Your head . . . all that blood."

He lifted one hand to his temple. "Bullet grazed me. Gonna have a hell of a headache, I reckon. Nothing but trouble since you've been gone," he muttered.

"Oh, Trey . . ."

"I've been on the run since you disappeared." He grunted softly, his lips twitching in a wry grin. "Only good news I had was hearing that old man Hollinger got gunned down in a holdup."

"Well, I'm still glad you didn't kill him," she said absently. With a hand that trembled, she removed his kerchief and wiped away the blood, revealing a shallow furrow along his hairline.

"We've got to stop meeting like this." She held up

her hand. "How many fingers do you see?"

"Three." His gaze moved over her. "Stop worrying about me. Are you all right?" He placed his hand over her belly. "How's my son?"

"We're both fine. Now that you're here."

He slipped his arm around her waist and drew her down until she was resting on his chest. "I missed you."

"I missed you." Cupping his face in her hands, she kissed him exuberantly. "Come on, cowboy. Let's go home."

Epilogue

Five years later

Amanda stood on the front porch, contentment washing through her as she watched Trey put a young chestnut filly through its paces. Her oldest son, Trey, Jr., nicknamed TJ, sat on the top rail of the corral; her two-year-old, Louis, leaned on the bottom rail. Both boys were the spitting image of their father.

She glanced around the yard. There were four corrals now, where before there had been only one. A dozen hens scratched in the dirt near the barn. Two sheep, a nanny goat, a half dozen cattle, and a shaggy-haired buffalo grazed in the pasture. Under the porch, a cat nursed four newborn kittens. TJ's dog was digging in the flowerbed again. Even as she shook her head in exasperation, she knew she wouldn't change a thing.

The last five years had been the best, the happiest, the most fulfilling of her whole life. She had a wonderful husband, two healthy sons, and another baby on the way, a girl this time, the doctor said.

She had been truly blessed. Together, they had built the ranch Trey had always dreamed of. There were a dozen mares in the barn, all in foal. Horses sired by one of the Long Walker studs were in constant demand. Their top stallion was the get of Relámpago out of a gray Arab mare. To her dismay, Relámpago had disappeared shortly after the colt was born, never to be seen again.

But Trey had taken the stallion's disappearance philosophically.

"I'm not in trouble anymore," he had said, "and not likely to be, here with you and the kids. But somewhere out there . . . sometime . . . someplace . . . somebody is in big trouble. And 'Pago will take care of that for them. Just like he did for us."

In the corral, Trey turned the filly loose. Slipping through the bars, he plucked TJ off the top rail and set him on his right shoulder, then scooped Louis up and settled him on his left. And then her men were coming toward her, the two boys arguing over who would be the first to ride the filly.

She smiled into three pairs of dark eyes as Trey strode toward her.

"We're mighty hungry," Trey said with a grin. "Is lunch ready?"

"Ready and waiting. Boys, go in and wash up."

"Cowboys don't wash," TJ said.

"Better do as she says, boys," Trey said, swinging his

393

sons down from his shoulders. "She's the boss."

With a grimace, TJ took Louis by the hand and dragged him into the house.

Trey put his arm around her and drew her into his arms. "Hi, sweetheart."

"Hi, cowboy."

She gazed up into his eyes, warmed by the love she saw there.

She had never been one to believe in dreams and happy-ever-after, but all that had changed the day a handsome stranger on a big white stallion rode into her life and made all her dreams come true.

Dear Readers:

This book was way too much fun to write. As mentioned in my dedication, William Burkett gave me the original idea (hence my heroine's last name). I loved the idea of a ghost horse, and time travel has always been a favorite of mine. You can visit Bill's website at www.geocities.com/wrburkett.

I must tell you that Relámpago was originally a buckskin; however, the cover artist, Pino Daeni, had an idea for the cover and he wanted me to use a white horse. Well, how could I say no? I love Pino's work. He's given me some of the most beautiful covers in the world. You can visit his website at www.pinoart.com.

I hope you enjoyed reading Trey and Amanda's story half as much as I enjoyed writing it.

I'd love to hear from you. You can write me at PO Box 1703, Whittier, CA 90609-1703 or online at DarkWritr@aol.com.

Madeline

APACHE RUNAWAY
MADELINE BAKER

Ruthless and cunning, Ryder Fallon is a half-breed who can deal cards and death in the same breath. Yet when the Indians take him prisoner, he is in danger of being sent to the devil—until a green-eyed beauty named Jenny saves his life and opens his heart.

___4464-1 $5.99 US/$6.99 CAN

Chase the Wind

MADELINE BAKER

Elizabeth Johnson is a woman who knows her own mind. And an arranged marriage with a fancy lawyer from the East is definitely not for her. Defying her parents, she sets her sights on the handsome young sheriff of Twin Rivers. But when Dusty's virile half-brother rides into town, Beth takes one look into the stormy black eyes of the Apache warrior and understands that this time she must follow her heart and not her head. Before she knows quite how it's happened, Beth is fleeing into the desert with Chase the Wind, fighting off a lynch mob—and finding ecstasy beneath starry skies. By the time she returns home, Beth has pledged herself heart and soul to Chase. But with her father forbidding him to call, and her erstwhile fiancée due to arrive from the East, she wonders just how long it will take before they can all live happily ever after. . . .

____52401-5 $5.99 US/$6.99 CAN

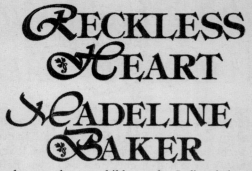

RECKLESS HEART
MADELINE BAKER

They play together as children—the Indian lad and little Hannah Kincaid. Then Shadow and his people go away, and when he returns, it is as a handsome young Cheyenne brave. Hannah, now a beautiful young woman, has never forgotten her childhood friend—but the man who sweeps her into his powerful arms is no longer a child. He awakens in her a wild, erotic passion she has never known. But war is about to erupt in the Dakota Territory, a war that will pit the settlers against the Indians. Both Hannah and Shadow know that the time is coming when they will have to choose between happiness and hatred, between passion and duty, in a conflict that will test to the limit the steadfastness of their love. . . .

___4527-3 $5.99 US/$6.99 CAN

Dorchester Publishing Co., Inc.
P.O. Box 6640
Wayne, PA 19087-8640

Please add $1.75 for shipping and handling for the first book and $.50 for each book thereafter. NY, NYC, and PA residents, please add appropriate sales tax. No cash, stamps, or C.O.D.s. All orders shipped within 6 weeks via postal service book rate. Canadian orders require $2.00 extra postage and must be paid in U.S. dollars through a U.S. banking facility.

Name_____
Address_____
City_____State_____Zip_____
I have enclosed $_____ in payment for the checked book(s).
Payment <u>must</u> accompany all orders. ❏ Please send a free catalog.
CHECK OUT OUR WEBSITE! www.dorchesterpub.com

Spirit's Song

MADELINE BAKER

She is a runaway wife, with a hefty reward posted for her return. And he is the best darn tracker in the territory. For the half-breed bounty hunter, it is an easy choice. His was a hard life, with little to show for it except his horse, his Colt, and his scars. The pampered, brown-eyed beauty will go back to her rich husband in San Francisco, and he will be ten thousand dollars richer. But somewhere along the trail out of the Black Hills everything changes. Now, he will give his life to protect her, to hold her forever in his embrace. Now the moonlight poetry of their loving reflects the fiery vision of the Sun Dance: She must be his spirit's song.

___4476-5 $5.99 US/$6.99 CAN

Dorchester Publishing Co., Inc.
P.O. Box 6640
Wayne, PA 19087-8640

Please add $1.75 for shipping and handling for the first book and $.50 for each book thereafter. NY, NYC, and PA residents, please add appropriate sales tax. No cash, stamps, or C.O.D.s. All orders shipped within 6 weeks via postal service book rate. Canadian orders require $2.00 extra postage and must be paid in U.S. dollars through a U.S. banking facility.

Name_____
Address_____
City_____ State_____ Zip_____
I have enclosed $_____ in payment for the checked book(s).
Payment <u>must</u> accompany all orders. ❑ Please send a free catalog.
CHECK OUT OUR WEBSITE! www.dorchesterpub.com